# DAVID HAIR

# The Exile

## THE RETURN OF RAVANA
### Book III

Jo Fletcher
BOOKS

A version of this novel was first published as *Souls in Exile* in India in 2011 by Penguin India
First published in Great Britain in 2018 by

Jo Fletcher Books
an imprint of
Quercus Editions Ltd
Carmelite House
50 Victoria Embankment
London EC4Y 0DZ

An Hachette UK company

A CIP catalogue record for this book is available
from the British Library

PB ISBN 978 0 85705 362 6
EBOOK ISBN 978 1 78429 082 5

10 9 8 7 6 5 4 3 2 1

Typeset by Jouve (UK), Milton Keynes
Printed and bound in Great Britain by Clays Ltd, St Ives plc

*This book is dedicated to:*
*Mike and Heather, my agents, mentors and wonderful friends.*
*It's a privilege and a pleasure to know you, and I'm looking forward*
*to the next time we can all get together.*

# Contents

Chapter One – Into Exile     1

Chapter Two – Behind the Mask     19

Chapter Three – Surpanakha?     27

Chapter Four – In Another Life     39

Chapter Five – The New Safe House     47

Chapter Six – Ullal: A Beautiful Sunset     61

Chapter Seven – Ullal: Onslaught     69

Chapter Eight – Ullal: Arrows in the Night     83

Chapter Nine – New Memories     95

Chapter Ten – Welcome to Lanka     101

Chapter Eleven – Boyfriend     109

Chapter Twelve – Headlines     119

Chapter Thirteen – The Burning Ghats     123

Chapter Fourteen – Another Séance     135

Chapter Fifteen – Jhansi: Mrs Mutlow     145

Chapter Sixteen – Jhansi: The Edge of Rebellion     153

Chapter Seventeen – Jhansi: Dreams and Deceptions     169

Chapter Eighteen – Jhansi: Flight of the Banished     187

Chapter Nineteen – Was It Worth It?     211

Chapter Twenty – Hunter                                    217
Chapter Twenty-One – Last Will and Testament              221
Chapter Twenty-Two – Coincidence?                         227
Chapter Twenty-Three – Rendezvous                         237
Chapter Twenty-Four – Hit the City                        241
Chapter Twenty-Five – Under Hypnosis                      245
Chapter Twenty-Six – Empty Lake                           255
Chapter Twenty-Seven – The Anguish of Choice              269
Chapter Twenty-Eight – Rakshasa                           273
Chapter Twenty-Nine – The One and Only                    283
Chapter Thirty – Come With Me to Hell                     295
Chapter Thirty-One – Sleight of Hand                      299
Chapter Thirty-Two – Waking the Beast                     309
Chapter Thirty-Three – From Shrine to Temple              317
Chapter Thirty-Four – Maricha                             323
Chapter Thirty-Five – Memories in Ancient Stone           337
Chapter Thirty-Six – Pitiless Queen                       343
Chapter Thirty-Seven – Waking the Old Things              349
Chapter Thirty-Eight – A Well at Panchavati               355
Chapter Thirty-Nine – Late                                361
Epilogue                                                  365

Glossary                                                  371
Author's Note                                             375
A Brief Introduction to the Ramayana                      377
Acknowledgements                                          387

# CHAPTER ONE

# INTO EXILE

*Mumbai, 14 November 2010*

Within three hundred yards, Vikram knew he was in trouble. The frigid air streaming over his hands was agonising, threatening to rip him from the arrow he clung to. His fingers were turning numb; brittle sticks that could snap any instant. The lights of Mumbai raced beneath him as he soared past tower blocks and over tangled power lines. While he was still going up this wasn't too much of a problem, but the arrow's trajectory meant he'd soon be coming down. Air whipped past his open mouth as he fought for balance, thinking: *There are good reasons why hanging on to a two-and-a-half-foot-long arrow hasn't caught on as a mode of travel.*

He clung on for another half a minute through sheer desperation as the arc of his shot began to level and then to fall. By now he was out of Bandra and soaring towards the Point, although there was no time to enjoy the view. Everything blurred past: streaming constellations of streetlights and apartment windows. *Don't look out of your window right now, people of Mumbai – you won't believe what you see!*

He'd lost all feeling in his fingers, but his mind refused to let them untwine from the arrow. The ground was far below and he was travelling faster than one hundred miles an hour. He was mentally and physically spent, but to fall would be to die.

He had a brief second to wonder if Amanjit and Rasita were faring any better. And was Deepika going to be all right? Had he done the right thing in leaving her? Could Tilak – or whatever he was called in this life – protect her? *Have I failed them all, yet again?* Then the power lines and all the other things he could barely make out in the darkness were flying into his face, driving all other thoughts from his mind. He wrenched at the arrow, making it duck left and right, as if this were some insane live-action video game. He barely evaded a monkey walking across the phone wires and it screeched furiously at him. He whisked past oblivious couples chatting on their balconies, and met the eye of one old man who stared in disbelief, then glared at the whisky bottle in his hand.

A building rose ahead of him and he guided the arrow's flight towards the tower block as his velocity slowed, aiming at a certain window and desperately hoping he'd counted the floors correctly. The arrow slammed into the window frame and he hit the wall beside it feet-first, cushioning his impact enough that he merely crashed into the detritus that had accumulated in the unused window box, rather than knocking himself out or breaking anything. The breath was punched from his lungs, leaving him gasping as he flexed his frozen fingers back to feeling and tried to work out if he could get up.

*I* hate *travelling like this* . . .

He wondered again how Amanjit and Rasita were faring. He'd aimed their arrow roughly towards the glowing tangle of light that was Bandra Railway Station, a shorter flight from Bakli's mansion – but could they both hang on even that long, especially with Rasita so weak? Her face swam before him and he recalled the final words she'd said to him: '*I remember everything* . . .'

He knew what she meant: that devastating, terrifying rush of past-life memories which he himself had experienced so many times. It must have been worse for her, taking in the past-life memories of the dying Sunita Ashoka at the same time as her own. He longed to speak to her, to learn where she had been in all his lives. *She's my Sita. I have to see her* . . .

Suddenly the curtains were pulled aside, washing him in harsh light, and he dimly heard his roommate Jai, with whom he shared this dormitory, swearing in disbelief as he wrenched open the half-rusted doors that opened on to the window box. 'Vik? Vik! What the f—? Man, they're saying on the television that you've— Uh . . . how did you get here?' Jai clutched the sides of his own head. 'WHAT'S GOING ON?'

Vikram tried a reassuring smile as he sat up. 'It's all lies, Jai. But they're pinning it on me.'

'It's all over the TV, every channel, bhai!'

Vikram flexed his fingers. The return of feeling to his hands was not very welcome, as they were really hurting.

He extended his right hand to Jai. 'Can you help me up, Jai? Please?'

Jai's doubts were clear: if something was on television, it *must* be true, even if that meant his roommate was really a killer, despite all the times they'd spent together at the movies, working on homework, cooking for each other, living as friends. For several seconds neither moved, until Jai reached down and pulled him to his feet. 'Your hands are freezing, Vik!' Then he saw the arrow jutting from the window frame. 'What's that? And how'd you get up here?'

'I flew,' Vikram replied, winking, as if it were a joke. At the far end of the hallway, the lounge door was closed, but he could hear the babble of voices. 'You've got guests again?'

'Yeah, maybe a dozen – you're lucky I was the only one who heard you out here. It's Dipti and her friends, and Nikhil from across the hall and his mates – the usual crew. We've all been watching the show – it's chaos, bhai! That Uma was pretending to be Sunita, and . . .' His voice trailed off as he looked at Vikram helplessly. 'They're all saying you killed Sunita Ashoka.' His face was a picture of stunned disbelief.

'It's not true. But I've got to grab a few things and go. You never saw me, right?'

Jai stared at him as what he was saying truly began to sink in. 'You're *running away*? This really is happening? The police will come, won't they?'

'Yeah, but I'll be long gone.' Vikram offered Jai his hand and said formally, 'I *swear* I'm innocent, Jai – but I can't prove it yet, and I can't risk going into custody. But I *didn't* kill Sunita.'

Slowly, Jai took his hand, making the decision to trust in friendship. 'Sure, okay. What should I tell the cops?'

'Tell them you never saw me – that I must have crept in unseen. They'll be confused about enough things already; this'll just add to that. Don't let them bully you.' He pulled away, trying to smile reassuringly. 'Go back to your friends, Jai. Keep them out of the hall for a few minutes, will you? And thank you for trusting me.'

Jai backed away, his face torn. Then he took a deep breath and disappeared into the lounge. The cacophony and TV-glare washed briefly over Vikram, then the door closed.

He fought a wash of giddiness. *Come on. You've got a few minutes, that's all.*

He went into his room, closed the door and chanced putting on the light. He'd been keeping his backpack half-packed since this started, anticipating that he might have to run. He laid his bow and quiver beside it, then began shoving in clothes – not too many; he was used to living light, in other lives if not so much in this one. Then he delved under the mattress and pulled out the most precious thing he owned: the leather pouch containing the ancient journal of Aram Dhoop, Court Poet of Mandore. He pushed some photos in beside it – Amanjit and Deepika, his father Dinesh and his stepmother Kiran, Rasita and Bishin, one of Ras alone, and another of Jai and other university friends partying together. He tucked the pouch in the top of the pack, added a notepad, some pens and his iPod and strapped it closed. He found his leather gauntlets and his thickest jacket and pulled them on, then took one last glance around the room, at the life he was leaving behind. All his lecture notes, textbooks, timetables – his dreams of a career.

*Will I ever get the chance to pick this life up again?*

He had to will himself to turn away. The sounds of the lounge beckoned him, the noisy camaraderie evident despite the shock of what they were watching. He heard Jai's voice above the others. 'He's innocent, I know he is. It's all lies.' He smiled gratefully. *Thank you, my friend.* Then he turned to the window box, pulled out his arrow and nocked it again.

Business had been terrible that night. All of India was watching *that* game show and no one had come into Rohit Singh's little mobile phone shop for over an hour. The shop, on a little side street behind the grey stone buildings of the university, usually did well – no one went through mobile phones like students did. But tonight, he'd not had a single customer.

He was about to admit defeat and close up when a young man appeared at the counter. He was wearing a winter coat and gloves and a woollen beanie; he looked vaguely familiar. Rohit eyed him tiredly. 'Namaste. Just closing, bhai. What do you want?'

The young man leaned over the chewing gum and chocolate bars piled high on the counter. His eyes had a strange lustre, like swaying lights in the temple on festival days . . . *oddly fascinating* . . .

. . . Vikram held the old man's gaze carefully. *It's okay, Rohit, everything is fine. Just give me what I want.*

The old shopkeeper's face slowly emptied. 'Yes, whatever you want . . .'

'Great! Okay, Rohit, I need three new pre-paid phones. I've got the cash.' He'd just emptied his account at an ATM a block away, holding his breath while he punched in the numbers lest it had already been frozen. 'Give me the forms to complete, quickly now.' He rushed to fill in the papers with random invented names and details – nothing smart-arsed, just simple, ordinary, everyday names with no connection to each other. Then he fixed Rohit with a stare. 'You've seen the identification details, Rohit, but you forgot to take copies. You will forget that I ever came here. Okay?'

The old shopkeeper filed the papers vacantly.

'Thank you, Rohit. May the gods bless you and your family.'

The old man smiled gratefully as Vikram left the little shop and vanished down the alley . . .

. . . and Rohit jerked back into alertness. *Huh? Was there a customer? Did I just speak to someone?*

He peered out of the shop, but there was no one close by, just the dark, empty street. The only people in sight were those clustered around the few shops that had television sets in their windows. No doubt they were fixated on that silly Bollywood bridal show. Mind you, that Sunita, she was lovely, no doubt about it . . .

*Mumbai, 19 November 2010*

Deepika Choudhary sat in her hospital bed, propped up by pillows, listening to her heart-stone pounding against her chest. Her left shoulder was heavily bandaged and throbbing, despite the anaesthetic. She hadn't expected the cobra bite to be so damn painful. Poison was one thing – her body, the antivenin and the heart-stone were fighting that – but the actual *bites* hurt too. It felt like the fangs had scraped her shoulder blade, they had gone so deep, and the puncture marks were surrounded by huge purplish-yellow bruises.

*But I'm still alive. How cool is that?*

She glanced across at the policeman dozing in the chair beside the bed. *Tilak – no, Tanvir. Weird. He's the man Vikram told us about, the one who died helping us in Mandore in a past life. How do I even* know *that? This is so bloody strange . . .*

'Hey,' she murmured, 'you awake?'

Tanvir opened his eyes and turned towards her. His round face, pocked by old acne and currently stubbled, was made for smiling; his grin at the sound of her voice lit up his eyes. His head was wrapped in a bandana and his right shoulder, where he'd taken two bullet wounds, was bandaged and in a sling. Except for toilet breaks, he hadn't left her side in two days. As far as Dee was concerned, he was all that was keeping the world at bay, the only thing keeping her safe.

'Sure,' he said groggily. 'How are you?'

'I'm okay. What day is it – Tuesday, right?'

'Nearly midnight.'

'I think I'm well enough to leave,' she told him ambitiously. 'Can we?'

'Not until we've been signed out by the head doctor and my boss,' he told her. 'Let's see tomorrow morning, yeah? We'll need clearance from both hospital and police if we're going to move you.'

'What if that man comes . . . what did you say his name was? Majid Khan?'

Tanvir shook his head. 'He's been stood down because he fired his weapon – it's mandatory. Meantime, I've laid an allegation of corruption against him, to keep him from coming down here. I've called in the Chief of Narcotics for Maharashtra. He'll be here soon.'

Deepika frowned. 'Won't that get you into trouble?'

Tanvir half-smiled. 'You bet.'

'You don't even know me,' she whispered. 'Why help me?'

He looked at her squarely. 'Damned if I know myself. But that guy with the bow? He told me to. That's good enough. He must have the gods with him, from the things I saw him do . . .' He shook his head wonderingly. 'And anyway, I was about ready to blow the whistle on Majid myself. We'd been biding our time, waiting to see who else we could net with him. Narcotics will be happy as long as we nab enough bodies to justify the operation.'

'Can you give them what they want?'

'Hopefully. Bakli's dead and we're crawling all over his pad, going over his files and computers. And I've got names and dates, all the deals Majid did for Bakli – we reckon we can blow his operation wide open.'

'Great. Thanks for helping me too. It's really . . . uh . . . noble.'

Tanvir grinned. 'That's me: I'm chivalry itself.'

A portly grey-haired doctor pushed his way in and closed the door. He stifled a yawn, looking like he'd been awake for days. 'Deepika Choudhary, Tanvir Allam? I am Doctor

Mohan, the senior registrar here. I worked on your case when you were brought in, Miss Choudhary.'

'I don't remember,' Deepika responded warily.

'I would be surprised if you did. You were slipping in and out of consciousness. Frankly, I thought we'd lose you.' His face took on an uneasy expression. 'I still don't fully understand how you pulled through.'

Deepika put on a cheery face for him. 'I'm very resilient, Doctor. I'm famous for it.'

'No doubt you are! Miss Choudhary, one bite from a king cobra injects between four and six hundred milligrams of venom: to put that into context, that's enough to kill *twenty men*. You were bitten *three* times, and got no medical aid for more than fifteen minutes. Miss Choudhary, you should be dead. I have never seen such a thing in my life.' Dr Mohan's voice held all the wonder of a child. 'We were treating you, but your heart was slowing – one of the nurses found a gemstone inside your left bra cup. She swears it was pulsing to the rhythm of your heart, except that *it* never faltered, though yours did, time and again. She believes it pulled you back into time with it. I have seen things that ordinary men would call miracles, Miss Choudhary, and most of the time I know it's just the workings of medical science, which can look miraculous to the uninitiated. But in your case, I have no rational explanation.'

'Perhaps it really was a miracle, Doctor.' Deepika thought back to those frantic few minutes: the snake bites, and those weird moments when it felt like someone had died, when light had exploded around her, not once, but twice in succession . . . And then there was the gemstone . . . Had Vikram given it to her? Her memories were dim.

Dr Mohan pursed his lips. 'I'm not a religious man, Miss Choudhary. I prefer my miracles to be clinically explainable and repeatable.'

She shrugged her shoulders, unable to think of anything useful to say. 'Does this mean I can go?'

'Go? No—! You need rest – I need to examine you again . . .' Almost under his breath he added, 'There must be some explanation. And my fellow doctors also need to examine—'

'I'm not a lab rat, Doctor,' she interrupted, letting a little anger show. 'I am a human being, and I have a life.'

'Miss Choudhary, your case is unique. You—'

'I want to go, Doctor. *Now.*' She glared up at him. 'I am also famed for my temper,' she added.

Dr Mohan swallowed. 'But the procedures—'

'DOCTOR, I WANT TO GO NOW!'

He fled, and Tanvir sat back, chuckling, but Deepika was far from happy. *That rage* . . .

She looked at Tanvir and said seriously, 'Sometimes in the last few days, I've felt so angry it frightens me. It's like a volcano, and I don't know if I'm the lava or the capstone. I don't know whether I am the fury, or that which holds the fury in.'

He looked at her, his eyes troubled, and slowly shook his head. 'We all get angry, Deepika—' he started, but she held up a hand to stop him.

'Not like this.' She sat back and tried to calm herself.

\*

Chief Superintendent Sunil Gupta, the Narcotics Bureau chief, was quite a different matter to the timid doctor. A call had come through to say he was on his way, and Tanvir insisted they wait for him. He was tall and lean but powerful across the shoulders, with close-cropped steel-grey hair and a face like an axe-head. He left his two guards outside, but filled the room, towering above them both as he paced.

'What the hell is going on, Detective Allam?' he demanded, his voice suggesting he'd either graduated from Oxford or was descended from a Maharajah's line; both were possible.

'Sir?' Tanvir replied, feigning confusion.

The chief rounded impatiently on Tanvir. 'I've got Majid Khan on "sick leave" until we square this: he's claiming he's singlehandedly blown open the Bakli family, and been witness to this young man, this Vikram Khandavani, murdering one of the most prominent actresses in Bollywood. And Khan went straight to the press, so now the public think he's a damned hero.' He jabbed a finger at Tanvir. 'But *you*: you say *Bakli* shot Sunita Ashoka, you say Majid Khan was feeding girls to Bakli and skimming drug hauls for him too, not to mention directing police resources to deal with Bakli's rivals.'

'You put me into his team specifically to watch him, sir,' Tanvir replied.

The chief paused, then said brusquely, 'True enough. But the stories I'm hearing just don't add up: half the gangsters we've rounded up are claiming Bakli fell down the stairwell: that's sixty fucking feet, Allam – *and then got up again!* One says he saw him *fly*. Two officers say they saw these fugitives — Vikram Khandavani, Amanjit Singh and Rasita Kaur — fly as well? It's a mess, Allam, a bloody mess, and I won't have it! So tell me: *what happened?*'

'You've read my preliminary report?' Tanvir asked meekly.

'Yes, I bloody well have, and I . . . well, good God, Allam, what am I supposed to believe?'

Deepika put up a hand like a schoolgirl trying to interject in class. 'Could you stop shouting, please?'

The chief whirled. 'And as for you — who *are* you? What in God's name were you doing there? How did you survive three cobra bites? What's your connection to the fugitives? And don't try and tell me there isn't one, damn it!' He thrust a finger at Deepika as if he wished he could plunge it into her brain and pull the answers out.

Deepika sat up, staring at the quivering finger. 'I'm the innocent victim here and I don't think I want to talk to you if you're going to come in here and yell at me like that. Unless you're going to charge me with something, you can go and find someone else to yell at.' She glared at him defiantly.

'Girl, if I want to charge you with something just so I can drag your pampered butt down to the station, I will!' The police chief leaned over her. *'So tell me what happened!*'

She refused to be cowed. 'Ask nicely. And say sorry.'

The chief's face turned purple and Tanvir winced. 'Um, sir . . . what she means is——'

Deepika spoke over him. 'What I mean, *sir*, is that I am just recovering from a near-fatal incident in which *I was the victim*, let me remind you once again, and I doubt that I am medically

capable of talking to you, especially under stressful conditions. Perhaps I'll just ring for a nurse – in fact, I feel quite
unwell . . .' She reached towards the buzzer beside her bed,
pausing her finger above it and meeting his eyes. 'Well? We
talk on my terms, or not at all.'

The chief scowled, then visibly counted to ten. 'Wait – all
right – *sorry!* Damn it, I apologise.'

She sat back and smiled. 'There. Who says sorry is the
hardest word? Now, how can I help you, Mister . . . I don't
think I got your name . . . ?'

'Gupta. *Chief Superintendent* Gupta. Head of Narcotics,'
he said through gritted teeth. He pulled over a chair and sat.
'Is your name Deepika Choudhary? University student of
Safdarjung Enclave, Delhi? I believe the Delhi police are
investigating your alleged abduction from Delhi. How did
you come to be at Shiv Bakli's two nights ago?'

'I don't know,' Deepika replied, although she remembered it all quite clearly. 'I was struck on the back of the
head and when I awoke, I was in that house.' She couldn't
stop the nightmare memories of that night washing over
her, and shuddered as she admitted, 'They dressed me in
some *disgusting* clothes – and they put a snake around my
neck. That pervert told them to.'

'By "pervert" you mean Shiv Bakli?'

'Yes, him, whoever he is.'

He studied her. 'We've been joining the dots, Deepika.
You are engaged to a Sikh, one Amanjit Singh Bajaj, yes?
Whose mother, Kiran Kaur Bajaj, recently married one
Dinesh Khandavani. Highly trained police officers at Bakli's
house claim to have seen three people somehow "fly away"

from the roof of the house: Vikram Khandavani, a student, a game-show contestant and *son of Dinesh Khandavani* and two unidentified persons: a *Sikh* male and a young woman. And surprise, surprise, we also have an open missing persons case for one Rasita Kaur Bajaj: daughter of Kiran, sister of Amanjit, your fiancé.' He looked up at Deepika. 'Can you confirm that these three persons – Vikram, Amanjit and Rasita – are the three people who fled the scene?'

*I can't really deny it when they already know.* 'Yes.'

Gupta leaned forward and said intently, 'Deepika, how did they do it?'

'I don't know.' *You wouldn't believe me if I told you.*

'Where did they go?'

'I don't know.' *That's true, anyway.*

'Who killed Sunita Ashoka?'

'I didn't see.' *But I know . . .*

'What were you doing there?'

'I told you: I was *kidnapped*. That horrible man – Bakli – was going to—' She started shaking suddenly as the reality of what she'd escaped hit her again. She took a deep breath to calm herself, then went on, 'He said he was going to *rape* me.' She glared at the superintendent. 'I'm *glad* he's dead!'

'Do you know Inspector Majid Khan?'

'No – who is he?'

'Your family's maid was found dead at Bakli's mansion. Why was your maid helping Bakli?'

'I don't know.' *You wouldn't believe me, not unless you believe in ghosts . . .*

Superintendent Gupta hissed in frustration. 'You *do*

know! Damn it, girl, I'm trying to help you – I'm trying to *protect* you. Give me something to work with—'

She looked him in the eye and said, 'Then keep this Majid Khan away from me – and stop chasing Vikram and Amanjit and Ras. They're innocent. I'm tired now,' she added, truthfully.

Chief Superintendent Gupta rolled his eyes heavenward and glared at Tanvir as he stood. 'Officer Allam, you are stood down. I'll assign protection for Miss Choudhary. Go home. Get some sleep.'

Tanvir also stood, but he was shaking his head. 'I'm staying right here, sir.'

He looked exasperated. 'Why? You've only just met this girl . . . haven't you?'

'I met her for the first time at the Bakli house on Saturday, sir. But I've promised to protect her.'

'Promised *whom*?'

'Myself.' Tanvir stood a little straighter, and Deepika remembered Tanvir standing on the roof of Bakli's mansion, swearing to Vikram that he would keep her safe. He clearly was a man of his word.

'I'll send back-up,' the chief offered.

'No others, sir, please. I'd only have to watch them too.'

'What exactly are you implying, Allam?'

Tanvir met his chief's stare firmly, his expression unyielding. The chief superintendent didn't look away until his mobile rang. 'Hello, Gupta . . . Yes . . . What—? He's—? How many? Damn – well, keep me informed.'

As he hung up, Deepika could see that he was trying to compose himself.

'Sir?' Tanvir asked tentatively.

The superintendent collapsed into a chair as if his legs had drained of strength. He stared blankly at the wall. 'It's Majid Khan . . .' His voice trailed away, his face aghast, any trace of composure gone. 'Oh my God . . .'

# CHAPTER TWO

# BEHIND THE MASK

*Mumbai, 19 November 2010*

Ravindra was wearing a mask – not of papier-mâché or wood, but a mask of flesh and skin, made of affability and calm. The mask had a name: *Majid Khan*. But behind the detective's face, Ravindra seethed, struggling to leash his fury. Endless interviews and reports were tying up his time while Aram Dhoop and Madan Shastri and his queens, Padma and Darya, slipped further from his grasp.

He'd been stood down for discharging his firearm a dozen times into Shiv Bakli's back – although, ironically, that had been none of Ravindra's doing; he'd actually been wearing Shiv Bakli's body at the time. But when Majid Khan had panicked and shot his boss, Ravindra had had no choice but to leave his former host and take over Khan's body, leading to this *ridiculous* delay. *He*, Ravindra-Raj, deathless sorcerer and once King of Mandore, was locked in an interview room deep within Mumbai's police headquarters in the Bandra district. *How ironic.*

It had given him time to think, though – and he'd started to remember things he'd not recalled for many centuries. He knew now that there was a rakshasa, one of the demon-folk, who had watched over him in eighth-century Mandore. It was this rakshasa who had revealed that he, Ravindra Atrappatta, Raja of Mandore, was the reborn demon king Ravana. The rakshasa had shown him how to unlock his magical potential by sacrificing seven particular women to the flames. For Ravindra to come into his full power, his specially selected queens had to die wearing the heart-shaped gemstones the rakshasa had made – and he'd come so close . . . But that *wretched* court poet, the weakling Aram Dhoop, and his own warleader Madan Shastri, had betrayed him, contriving to steal two of the gemstones and one of the queens, making the ritual go disastrously wrong. Ever since then, Ravindra had led a tormented existence: condemned to live as a ghost, inhabiting human bodies only when he could remember how. During those lives, he'd dedicated himself to killing the reborn poet and the soldier and hunting the heartstones, convinced that somehow that would restore him and complete the ritual. But his failures at Mandore had somehow damaged his mind, so that even his own soul could not fully recall all that he was. Skills he had once known would elude him, then surprise him by reappearing briefly. It was, quite literally, maddening: he knew he wasn't sane – which was both liberating and terrifying.

In this life, though, the rakshasa had finally found him again, and in the few weeks since it had revealed itself, it had begun to remind Ravindra of all he was – of all he *could* be: Ravana, King of Demons.

But the rakshasa was dead, slain by that traitor Madan Shastri – reborn in this life as Amanjit Singh. He'd said there were others of his kind, though. *So where are they?*

Ravindra looked down, suddenly realising that his finger-tips were bloody, stinging like acid burns where he had gouged furrows in the desk. He sucked them thoughtfully, brooding.

Then the door to the interview room opened. Ravindra rifled through Majid Khan's memories, but couldn't place the men who entered. Both wore Internal Investigations ID. They immediately launched into a 'good cop/bad cop' routine, though neither looked the part.

'Detective Khan,' smiled Good Cop, an older man with a face like a gravestone. 'I trust you are refreshed. More chai?'

Ravindra shook his head. *I could snap you in half with a gesture . . .*

The one he'd dubbed Bad Cop, plump and balding in a sweaty shirt, growled impatiently, 'Let's go over your story again, then. These are the questions I want answering, *right now*. How did you come to be at Shiv Bakli's house? *How* did you come to shoot him in the back – *in the back!* – eleven times, Inspector Khan? *Eleven* times. Did you actually *see* Vikram Khandavani shoot Sunita Ashoka? And what is the link between Sunita and Bakli?'

Ravindra looked about him nonchalantly. It was almost midnight and other 'Interminable Investigations' cops had been questioning him for two days. They obviously thought he must be close to exhaustion; in fact, the only thing that was exhausted was his patience. There was no CCTV or tape running, so clearly they wanted this to be off the

record. Well and good: so did he. He extended his senses
further: the station was far from empty, but most of the
officers were out and the cells were less than half full. It was
the time of the cleaners and vending-machine fillers, and
stressed-out officers trying to clear their paperwork.

*I could slaughter them all.* He played with the thought until
the fat man interrupted him.

'Inspector Khan?' He leaned forward impatiently, clicking his fingers to get his attention back.

Ravindra sighed, flexing his hands. 'I've already told your
colleagues: it was a legitimate undercover sting. I had gained
Bakli's trust – he thought he had me turned. I've documented it all. I was providing security that night – he told
me he'd hired some whores for a private party.'

'Did you know the girls?'

'I'll tell you *again*: I met Rasita Kaur during a drug-
trafficking investigation. She claimed she wasn't a hooker,
but let's face it, she was with a known felon and she was
clearly working the truck stops, just a common two-bit
prostitute. She asked me for connections: she told me she
wanted to set up here in Mumbai, so I supplied her to Bakli.
I did such things occasionally as part of my cover, to maintain my credibility: anyone who goes undercover has to do
such things from time to time.' He kept his tone reasonable:
*we're all men of the world here.* 'She went voluntarily. The other
girl, this Deepika? I didn't know her and I never saw her
until after the attack, when she was already bitten by the
snake. But she's probably just another hooker.'

'Is Detective Tanvir Allam aware of your undercover
role?' asked Good Cop.

'No, he's ignorant. He just thought I was a bent cop.' *And I'm going to gut him for delaying me with these damned allegations.* 'He had no idea of my true purpose.' *And, of course, he's Tilak: another of those who betrayed me in Mandore. That's reason enough for me to slaughter the swine.*

'How did Sunita Ashoka come to be shot by an arrow? It looks the same as those found beside Bakli,' the fat cop asked. 'Who shot Bakli's men in the gardens? And who the hell uses a bow and arrow anyway?'

'Game-show competitors, apparently,' Ravindra sneered, exasperation seeping into his voice. 'I will repeat this *one last time*: I was on the roof when Bakli's helicopter was blown up – I think by a rocket-launcher. I was thrown to a lower-level roof garden below – I was lucky, I landed in a recently dug flowerbed, so I had a relatively soft landing. I was stunned for a time, but when I came to I was able to descend to ground level. I directed Allam to the rear of the building before I went inside and ascended the stairs – I didn't see anyone "flying", so I cannot corroborate that story, but Bakli's men are drug-users and illiterates, so I wouldn't credit their accounts.' He chuckled dismissively. 'I went up to the top of the spiral stairs, where I saw Sunita Ashoka with an arrow in her chest. I saw Vikram Khandavani holding a bow – then Bakli struck him from behind with the butt of a gun, Khandavani dropped the bow and Bakli went to shoot him. I tried to stop him: I fired when he went to shoot and I must have thumbed the gun to automatic in the confusion.' He pretended to falter, saying regretfully, 'When I found that I had killed him I was stunned, and that was when Khandavani and his accomplices

fled past me to the roof. When I realised, I directed the
arriving police to arrest them, but they resisted. They must
have had some kind of rope-and-pulley system rigged up.
Men can't fly, after all,' he concluded with heavy irony.

'Why would Vikram Khandavani bring Sunita Ashoka
there?'

'Kidnapping and ransom? Maybe he was in collusion with
Bakli. Use your imagination – oh hang on, that's a bit of a
stretch for you boys, isn't it?' *Damn this! Where are Aram
Dhoop and his cronies now? Where have they gone? I had them! And
damn you, Majid Khan: without your intervention, I would have
been victorious.* He rolled his eyes at the irony of cursing his
own host body.

'What's so funny, Inspector?' asked Bad Cop sharply.

'It's hard to explain. Are we done?'

'We've not even started. None of this adds up, Inspector.
*None of it*. So we're here until this story makes sense, even if
it takes all night.'

'I have rights——' *One last time, I told you. I warned you . . .*

Bad Cop curled his lips. 'Do you? Well, Inspector, I'm
here to tell you that you can shove your "rights" up your
arse, you stinking bent bastard. You're here all night and
every night until we break you.'

Ravindra sat back, hooding his eyes. He smiled as he
made a small gesture and the pencil in the fat cop's pocket
gently wafted through the air towards him. The two men
rose, staring, as he caught it and spun it on his fingers. 'You
really should be more polite,' he told them mildly, still
twirling the pencil – until it was aimed towards the fat cop's
chest, when he muttered an ancient spell. The pencil blazed

brilliant orange and flew at the officer's chest. With a searing *pop* it punched through cloth and flesh straight into the man's heart as he stared open-mouthed at his oncoming death. Then he staggered and fell on his back as Good Cop gaped.

He met Ravindra's amused gaze, then went for his gun, not realising that it was also too late for him: it'd been too late from the moment he'd entered the room.

Ravindra gestured again and his victim watched helplessly as his own hand turned towards him, pointing the gun at himself. He tried to say something, to beg, his eyes conveying his pleading horror, but Ravindra winked cruelly and shook his head.

The gun roared. Blood and tissue spattered on the walls, the floor and the desk as Good Cop collapsed.

Ravindra picked up the gun thoughtfully. His senses, still attuned outwards, detected nothing: the room was admirably soundproofed.

'Personally, I think we're about done here,' Ravindra remarked to the corpses, and without another glance, he walked from the room and from the station. Only a couple of cleaners glimpsed him, but they paid him no attention: he was just another overpaid officer.

It was almost an hour before the alarm was raised, and by then, he'd gone further than they could conceive.

# CHAPTER THREE

# SURPANAKHA?

*Varanasi, Uttar Pradesh, December 2010*

The most wanted man in India walked down the muddy steps of Meer Ghat and immersed himself in the murky waters of the Ganges, holiest of rivers, shuddering at the chill wash of the current. It was early winter and the river was growing colder by the day. Morning mists clung to the surface. Leaf-boats containing marigolds and floating votive candles swirled past him, many still alight, their tiny tongues of flame winding northwards past the western bank of the river, beneath the grimy old palaces and hotels that lined the western shore. The eastern shore, by contrast, was barren of life other than a few tents and a couple of cooking fires dimly visible through the haze, a weird contrast to the decrepit splendour of the buildings crammed together on the city side.

Vikram Khandavani came up gasping. They said washing here purified your soul, but purifying and cleaning were clearly entirely different things. The water was anything but pure; it felt oily, like used bathwater. All about him thousands of Hindus — and a few tentative tourists — were also immersing themselves as the sun kissed the town: holy Varanasi, where strangers swarmed in every day to seek enlightenment or absolution, or merely to gawk and marvel. Filthy, sacred, incredible Varanasi. Where better to hide?

He ducked under again, rinsing soap from his skin, then rose. He was wearing only a soaked pair of boxers. All about him old, young, fat, skinny, balding, grey, reverent or merely dutiful men were doing the same. Twenty yards away a group of women were bathing, but they were modestly wrapped in brilliantly coloured saris. Somehow they were managing to wash everywhere while showing no flesh; he'd never understood how they managed. A young woman looked back at him and smiled shyly; for an instant, with her wet clothes clinging to her slim form, she could have been Rasita. His throat tightened and he submerged himself again — but no amount of washing could take away the memories.

He'd been hanging around in Varanasi for three weeks now. It was almost Christmas, and the hotels were decking themselves out with tinsel and lights, trying to attract Western tourists — and they were pushing their rates up in anticipation. But he'd found a tiny hotel in the alleys behind the ghats where they didn't ask questions and you got exactly what you paid for: a cheap little room that stank of mould and bleach and the wafting stench of the communal toilets next door. He knew what his old friends in England would think if they could see him now. His few possessions were beneath the bed, concealed by cunning little spells from the prying eyes of the untrustworthy cleaning staff. There were many better places to stay, but he was on the run, so privacy and anonymity were priceless. The larger places were too busy, their registration too well run; they'd be too closely monitored by government officials.

He'd programmed the number of one of the mobiles he'd bought in Mumbai into the others and posted them to Professor Choudhary in Delhi, but no one had called him yet. He caught flashes of television news and saw headlines in newspapers pulled from the rubbish, and they were still screaming the same questions: *Where is Vikram? Why did he kill Sunni?* The latest theory was that a kidnapping and extortion plot had been planned between him and Shiv Bakli once he 'realised' that he wouldn't win *Swayamvara Live!*. The Bollywood actor, his chief rival Praveet Khoolman, was in the papers and on the television all the time now, cursing 'that murdering queer Vikram' and insisting Sunita had always intended to choose him as her husband – which therefore entitled him to Sunita's fortune. Occasionally there were quotes from policemen, but nothing more from Majid Khan; everyone had gone oddly silent on the inspector. There was nothing about Deepika, now she was out of hospital and hidden in some secret location, and nothing concrete about Amanjit or Rasita either. It was both reassuring and worrying.

He climbed out of the river, towelling himself off amidst the other men. He'd not shaved since fleeing Mumbai, nor cut his hair, and he barely recognised himself any more. *The Hindustan Times* had recently published a helpful little article for Vikram-spotters that showed a dozen different looks he might have adopted as a disguise, using a Photoshopped picture taken during the televising of *Swayamvara Live!* He look didn't like any of them.

Nobody paid him any notice here, where everyone was a pilgrim. He pulled on a drab kurta, slipped his feet into his sandals and walked up the steps, past a woman rolling cow dung into balls; she'd slap them against a wall to flatten them, then leave them to dry in the sun. By dusk the dried patties would be ready to sell as fuel for the increasing number of fires that would burn through winter nights. Her business partner – a gelded Brahman bull – lugubriously chewed the cud beside her, and she was talking to him happily. A trio of tall Westerners in orange kurtas, all man-buns and beards, dropouts from the rat race, sauntered past. A plump black man in traditional African garb was photographing the bathers and the half-ruined palaces, still partially shrouded in mist, above the southern ghats. Smoke rose from the funerary ghats to the north, where the dead were brought from all over India to be cremated. The shoreline teemed with humanity.

Vikram climbed the steps following painted signs and arrows for a German Bakery. The only thing German about it was its name; it was one of those Indian things. Germans were supposed to be good at baking, so bakeries claimed to be German. It was like English Wine Shops, which sold no wine and nothing English, only local beer and whisky. This particular bakery did fresh eggs on toast, though, and strong spicy chai with good fresh milk. He was so tired of UHT. He wound through the narrow alleys, stepping carefully over the muddy puddles and cowpats and past rotting heaps of rubbish, dodging pedestrians and the odd imperiously roaring motorbike. The bakery was busy with tourists from all over the world; most were speaking English, but he recognised the cadences of French, Spanish and a bemused-looking German couple puzzling over the steaming pile of food on their plate, presumably trying to reconcile it with how dishes of the same name looked in their homeland.

The bakery was taller than it was wide and spread over several floors: a hodgepodge of stairs and cubbyholes, nooks and crannies. He finally found a seat near a tiny concrete bunker that had a low table and flat cushions inside where a group of Americans, three burly young men and a curvy blonde girl, were loudly teasing each other. He sat on the small stool opposite and ordered eggs and chai from a passing waiter. Trying to ignore the tourists' racket, he pulled out his notebook, studying the names and dates joined up by a spiderweb of lines as he tried to link ideas and suspicions, people and memories. *There must be a way to escape this endless cycle of life-death-rebirth where Ravindra keeps killing us all . . . there must be!*

But apart from killing Ravindra themselves – and he had no idea how to do that – he couldn't think of anything. He didn't even know where Ravindra was any more; not even a compass-arrow could find him. *Clearly, for him, victory involves capturing Deepika and Rasita alive, and their heart-stones too. Deepika has hers, but Rasita's has been missing since 1192. So at least he's no closer to victory than I am . . .*

But there were other things troubling him. Almost everything that was happening appeared to be recalling the *Ramayana*. He, Amanjit, Ras and Ravindra all had their parallel personae in the epic, but Deepika didn't, not that he could see – so who was she in Rama and Sita's story? Urmila, the wife who slept for fourteen years while Lakshmana was away? That wasn't likely; sleeping through the action wasn't Deepika at all. Or was she just caught up in this accidentally, some kind of a cosmic mishap caused when a court poet named Aram Dhoop saved Queen Darya from the sati pyre in Mandore a thousand years ago?

Thinking of the *Ramayana* raised another issue. If their lives really were following the epic, then they were about to enter some of the darkest chapters. He flipped to the page where he'd jotted down the things that happened after Rama won Sita in the swayamvara.

*Jealous queen manipulates king in favour of own son; has Rama exiled.*

*Rama and Sita + Lakshmana go into exile together.*

*King dies of sorrow.*

*She-demon Surpanakha tries to seduce Rama, then Lakshmana; she fails and is disfigured by Lakshmana.*

*Surpanakha tells Ravana about trio; demon Maricha lures away men.*

*Ravana kidnaps Sita.*

He stared at the list morosely. It wasn't hard to comprehend the jealous queen aspect – his father had a very hostile ex-wife, and their son, his half-brother, was in her custody. Vikram's own mother was dead and Dinesh was newly wed to Kiran, Amanjit and Rasita's mother.

*So my ex-stepmother Tanita might kick up trouble again? No surprises there . . .*

But he couldn't stop staring at the line: *The king dies of sorrow.* That was the one that haunted him. *Dad has been so happy since he met Kiran. I can't let this curse touch him. Please, all you gods, forbear!*

As for exile . . . Hadn't that already happened when he'd won his 'Sita'? Only to have Sunita become Ras – and now he and Amanjit and Ras were on the run.

He struggled against a sudden wave of hopelessness, shutting out the increasingly loud Americans in the niche opposite. *In every life since Mandore, Ravindra has seen me die. When I think about it, many of those lives have had faint echoes of the* Ramayana, *but never so obvious as in this one. It's as if all this is scripted.*

*What if——?*

A balled-up tissue hit him in the face and he blinked in stunned surprise.

'Ha! That's got his goddamn attention,' guffawed a burly American across the aisle. He leaned towards Vikram, his red face a mix of irritation and relish at throwing his weight around. 'I said – *you deaf dork!* – that we want another round of coffee – *capisce*? Speakee English?'

Vikram stared into the puffy face as several lives spent learning meditative calming techniques warred with the urge to jam his fist down this cretin's throat. Meditative calm won. *Just.*

'I'm not a waiter,' he responded in English, then went back to his notes.

'Told ya,' drawled one of the others, a young black man in basketball gear. 'You're the dork, Frankie.'

'All Indians are waiters,' the first man – Frankie, presumably – snickered. 'It's genetic.' He reached across and thrust a ten-rupee note at Vikram. 'Hey, buddy, go get us a round of coffees. That's your tip. Baksheesh, y'know? Comprende?'

Vikram stared at the youth's pudgy hand. 'I said, I am not a waiter. And I'm also not your "buddy". Someone will come past shortly.' He looked down at his notes again. *Interrupt me again, and I'll . . .*

'Hell, here's another twenty: just get us the round, okay? God, I hate this shitty country.'

*Give me patience!* Vikram was about to do something he'd probably regret when a boy in a dirty apron came past. Quick as a snake, Vikram snatched the notes from the American's hand and thrust the money at the boy. 'Another round of coffees for this table,' he said in Hindi. 'The thirty is their tip for you.'

The boy looked at him in surprise, flashed a tiny grin and scampered away. Frankie glared at Vikram, who looked back mildly. His black friend in the corner guffawed. 'He gotcha, Frankie.'

Frankie rose, his fists balled, but the blonde girl pulled him back down, telling him, 'Don't be such a jerk, Frankie. He's not a waiter, he told us that. Sorry!' she called over to Vikram.

Vikram acknowledged her with a terse nod, then blocked them out again. He picked up the pen and underlined a word. *Surpanakha.*

In the *Ramayana*, Surpanakha was the catalyst. Some accounts described her as a right old hag, some as a real beauty, so no hints there. She began the final war, first through her attempted seductions, then by her goading of Ravana. She was the archetypal she-demon, the manipulative female instigator of chaos and evil. *If this pattern holds true, she's going to come after me . . .*

His imagination conjured a temptress with beguiling eyes swaying towards him, her body provocatively posed, her diaphanous veils hinting at the voluptuous pleasures beneath. It wasn't even tempting. *In this life I finally have my Sita!* Visions of Ras washed Surpanakha from his imagination. *What hold could some imaginary seductress have over me, when I'll soon be with Ras, who is Padma, the woman I should have loved in Mandore so long ago. It's a* destined *love: no Surpanakha she-devil is going to come between us.*

At last the Americans finished swilling their coffee and clambered away down the stairs, still bickering. Frankie glared as he lumbered past, his piggish eyes hostile, but all he did was flick a rude finger at Vikram before leaving. The sudden quiet was glorious.

He was contemplating ordering more chai when a woman said, 'Namaste.' Her Hindi was oddly accented, a little hesitant. Vikram looked up in surprise to see the blonde American girl. Her cheeks were pink and her sweaty hair plastered to her skull; she must have just struggled back up the stairs from the ground floor. She was pretty, though, if you liked buxom girls. He realised that she was embarrassed. 'I'm so sorry Frankie was so rude to you. I wanna apologise on his behalf.'

'Did he pay you to say sorry for him?' Vikram asked waspishly, and the girl coloured. He was a little surprised she could speak any Hindi at all. 'But thanks, anyway. Apology accepted.'

She waggled her head, just like an Indian would, and said, 'He has his good points.' She sounded a little wistful, as if saying so would make it true.

'You speak Hindi well,' he complimented her, a peace offering. 'But use English if that's easier.'

'Thank you!' she said, switching gratefully. She had a lilting American accent. 'I was born and raised here – my Dad ran a company in Mumbai – and what Hindi I got was from my ayah. I love this country and I just had to come back here once I finished college – I feel bonded to it, y'know? I've got three months before the money runs out; maybe I'll just stay on, earn some more . . . anyway, you've got real good English.'

'Thanks.' He didn't bother to explain the years he'd lived in England. She had a nice smile. 'Is Frankie your husband?'

'God, no,' she snorted. 'He's just my boyfriend – well, sorta. We met up at Rishikesh and we've just been, like, cruising the tourist sites, y'know?'

*What does she see in him? He's such an arse, and she's really quite nice . . .*

He smiled politely, and then raised his notebook to signal that he had things to do. He met her eye to say goodbye – and then it hit him.

*She's Kamla reborn!* The unwanted wife of his fourth life, in the twelfth century, whom he'd come to appreciate for her intelligence and humour, and his wife or lover in at least three other lives. He'd spent more time with Kamla in all his lives than any other woman and had learned to love her. His heart began to pound with a hollow bass thump.

*Kamla . . . and she's never been as pretty in her other lives.*

Something must have shown in his gaze because she stared back. 'What's your name?' she asked.

'Vikas,' he replied, his current alias.

'Vickers!' she chirruped. 'Nice name – kinda English, you know? You local, Vickers?'

He let the name thing go. 'No, just hanging around. Trying to find myself.' Americans were always trying to find themselves. Then a thought struck him: *Between Ras and you, Surpanakha isn't going to stand a chance . . .*

She smiled warmly. 'Yeah, ain't we all.'

'And you are . . . ?'

She stuck out a hand. 'I'm Sue. Sue Parker.'

'Sue Parker?' He burst into uncontrolled laughter. *Sue Parker? Surpanakha? Surely God's sense of humour isn't that bad?*

She looked at him like he was insane, withdrawing her hand, and he realised he was being incredibly rude.

'I'm sorry,' he said, 'it's hard to explain – I'm really sorry.'

'I don't get the joke,' she said, looking hurt.

'I'm doing a thesis on a character from the *Ramayana*,' he improvised. 'Surpanakha – she's Ravana's sister.' He watched her intently, but she didn't react to either name. 'I was thinking about her while I was having breakfast, and then you said your name. Sue Parker – Surpanakha. It just struck me as funny, that's all – I'm sorry; I wasn't laughing at you, I promise.'

Confusion gave way to a grin. 'Shucks, don't worry. I get

it now. And it is kinda funny.' She stuck out her hand again and this time he shook it properly. 'Nice to meet you, Vickers – and good luck with your thesis.' She beamed at him before turning and going back down the stairs.

He stared after her, wondering about the tricks of the cosmos.

# CHAPTER FOUR

# IN ANOTHER LIFE

*Chandni Chowk, Old Delhi, December 2010*

'Sikhs don't cut their hair. They don't shave. They wear turbans and carry knives. They go to gurdwaras, not temples.' With each point Amanjit held up a finger. 'Therefore, I'm going to do the opposite in every case. You should too, Ras.'

Rasita stared at her brother as if he'd been replaced with an alien life form. 'You're joking, aren't you?' She peered up at his shaven skull. 'There's *no way* I'm going to cut my hair.'

He primped slightly in front of the tiny mirror, staring at a total stranger: bald, with a pale skull, a smooth chin and jaw. It wasn't him at all. *Too late now, it's done*. He scratched his naked scalp, which felt weird to the touch, like reptile skin, and belatedly wondered what Dee would think.

He turned and looked at Ras. 'Then what are you going to do, hide inside all day?'

'No, much simpler. I bought a burkha.'

'*A burkha? A Muslim* burkha?' He looked at her, outraged. 'But—'

'Why not? They're totally anonymous. I met Deepika's father at Connaught Place today – he had a package for us. Anyway, all *I've* done is bought a cover-all – *you've* violated most of our religious principles and managed to still look like a dork.'

Amanjit grimaced; he wouldn't concede the point although he always lost these arguments. Ras might be sick half the time, but she was sharp as a pin.

Thanks to Professor Choudhary, the two of them had spent the last month hiding out in a property in Old Delhi. The place was ancient and smelled musty, but it was furnished and had two bedrooms; enough for their needs. Once the professor had convinced the family that the four teens were innocent, hiding Ras and Amanjit had become a family project, and they were doing it with relish.

'Indians love a conspiracy,' the professor had chuckled on his last visit.

Amanjit hated sitting around idle, but Rasita was inured to having nothing to do from years of illness, wasting away in hospital or doctors' waiting rooms, and she endured stoically. And anyway, she had a lot on her mind: she had been almost overcome in the deluge when Sunita Ashoka had poured her soul into Ras' mind. She couldn't process it at the time, locking it all away to worry about later – but now she had nothing to do but think. She envisioned her mind as a warehouse where she was rummaging around carefully, one fact at a time – although she was discovering that memories could leak out too, at the oddest of moments.

What made it even harder was the realisation that she'd never really lived a full life before. In all her past lives, she'd not made it past the age of fourteen. *Ever*. Had it not been for modern medical science, she wouldn't have lived any longer in this life either.

And now she knew why: when Padma had been immolated on the pyre in Mandore in 987, her soul had been ensorcelled by the heart-stone given to her by her husband, Ravindra-Raj. She'd disobeyed his command never to take it off, instead slipping it to her brother, Madan Shastri, without any idea what that simple act of rebellion would mean. Ravindra had drugged her and burned her alive, forcing her to commit sati – but dying without the heart-stone had ripped her soul apart; her very essence had fractured into three, one part so weak it could no longer take on flesh. That hungry ghost still lurked somewhere, but the other two damaged part-souls had been capable of rebirth as humans: the insane Gauran, who had repeatedly met Aram/Vikram; and the sickly Rasita, who never lived to grow up.

Until this life.

'Ras?' Amanjit was frowning, the expression odd on his newly egg-like skull. 'You zoned out again.'

'I was just remembering something new.'

'Don't tell me; I don't want to know.' He was still finding the whole 'past lives' thing profoundly unnerving. 'What was in the professor's parcel?'

Ras grinned. 'Mobile phones from Vikram – and he's programmed a number into each. They're pre-pays, already topped up with loads of cash—'

'—so we can call him? At last! Where are they? Have you tested them yet?'

Ras pointed to a drawer, shaking her head. 'I . . . I was kind of nervous.'

'Nervous? But it's only Vikram, and——' At her glare, he paused. 'Oh, yeah.'

'*Exactly*. What does one say to the man who is apparently one's cosmically destined love? Discussing the weather and the soaps feels a little . . . well, inadequate. You're best friends, but *I* don't know him: we've barely met. Oh, and the last time I saw him he was competing to marry someone else – who is now also me, of course.' She sighed. 'It's complicated.'

'You're telling me!'

'If you think about it, I've barely spoken to Vikram properly; we've had maybe a dozen conversations. Sunita talked to him more than I did. Mind you, at least she liked him, which I guess is reassuring. What's weird is that I *really* thought I was in love with him when I ran away from home, even though I didn't know him. That all feels incredibly childish now – and such a long time ago! So, big brother: what do I do?'

'Beats me. Emotional dramas aren't my thing,' Amanjit admitted. 'You should call Dee; she loves that sort of shit.' He went to the drawer, pulled out the two phones and tossed one over. 'Although we don't know where Dee is either,' he added gruffly. Being apart from her was visibly wearing him down. 'Are you sure these phones will be safe?'

'Yeah – oh, there's a letter. You might want to read it first.'

He grabbed the envelope and pulled out a piece of paper. When he glanced over it, he recognised Vik's writing.

*Hi guys. The phones are in made-up names and fully charged.*
*My new number is programmed in, but I've read that security*
*agencies can use word-recognition software to home in on*
*calls, so we need some ground rules:*

1. *No personal names — we call each other by our Mandore*
   *names.*
2. *No place names.*
3. *No reference to the main protagonists.*
4. *No calls longer than three minutes.*
5. *Use only sparingly.*

*We'll rendezvous at you-know-where in March. I look*
*forward to hearing from you.*
*Love to all,*
*V*

Amanjit whistled. 'The cops can really do all that?'

'They probably can in Hollywood movies and TV shows.
Who knows, here in India? We've got a space programme
and thirty-five per cent illiteracy, so I guess anything is possible. No harm in having a few precautions, I guess.'

'I guess.' Amanjit called up Vikram's number – Ras might
be reluctant, but he was dying to talk to Vik. He doubled
over laughing at the burst of music that greeted his call: a
popular song from *Om Shanti Om*, one of Bollywood's top-
grossing movies – a story of doomed lovers who resolve
their problems in their next lives. He was still laughing
when Vikram answered.

'Hello, is that Shastri?'

'Vik! Oops, I mean, Aram.' He tried the strange name on his tongue. It felt odd, yet right too. 'I was just laughing at your choice of music, bhai.'

'"All hot girls, put your hands in the air and sing Om Shanti Om",' Vikram sang. 'Yeah, it felt appropriate. How're you doing?'

'I'm good – but that arrow ride was insane! You might've mentioned how to steer . . . I only figured out how I could change its flight-path half a second before we smacked into a twenty-storey apartment. We nearly died—'

'Yeah, sorry. There wasn't time to brief you but I figured you'd work it out.'

'You're a cowboy, Aram.'

'Rich coming from you, Shastri. Is Ra— I mean, Padma . . . Is she okay?'

Amanjit looked at Ras, who was straining to hear. 'Yeah, she's okay. She's got a lot to deal with, but she's handling it. She misses you, though. We both do.'

'Same, bhai,' Vikram replied softly. 'Have you been in touch with Darya?'

'No – I don't know where she is. Even the Prof doesn't know, and she's his daughter. But Ras talked to Uma and she's pulling some strings.'

'Okay. Did Padma remember the details of the rendezvous?'

'Yeah . . . "Laketown" in March. We'll be there, bhai. We just wish it was sooner.'

'Yeah, me too, but we have to let the dust settle. Two months and we'll be old news. And it'll give us time to get used to things . . . like Padma and her memories.'

'I hear you, bhai. I understand.'

'It's good to hear your voice,' Vikram said after a pause.

'You too!' Amanjit fought back the belly-load of questions that were trying to fight their way out – *Where are you? What are you doing? Do you know what this is doing to my sister? What's the plan?* – and in the end all he asked was, 'Are those three minutes up?'

Vikram's voice was reluctant. 'Yeah.'

'Padma sends her love, bhai. She sends all her love.'

'I hear you, bhai. I send mine too. Shastri, Padma, I love you both. Bye, just for now.'

In the corner, Ras whispered, 'I love you too, Aram.' A tear was running down her cheek.

'Goodbye for now, bhai,' Amanjit whispered, feeling his own eyes well up. He thumbed the phone off and sank to the floor. It was a full minute before he felt able to look up.

Ras met his look with a taut grin. 'Thank you, bhaiya. You're a good person.'

'Yeah, I'm amazing.' Amanjit replied, as if it were a confession that had been dragged out of him.

'Egghead.'

'Muslim wannabe.'

'Betrayer of the Faith.'

They poked out their tongues at each other and remembered how to laugh.

# CHAPTER FIVE

## THE NEW SAFE HOUSE

*Mumbai, late December 2010*

Deepika ran from the apartment foyer to the black-windowed car in the driveway and slid in, Tanvir a heartbeat behind her. After so long in safe houses, she dreaded the boundless sky like an agoraphobic. But the cabin fever was beginning to get to her too, after weeks of scurrying from one hidden place to another as the police sought to protect her.

*I'm still alive, so we must be winning. I wonder by how much . . .*

The only constant was Tanvir Allam. He felt more familiar to her now than any other person in her life except her parents. His wide face, smiling or frowning, relaxed or watchful, was as much a part of her as her father's, her mother's, even Amanjit's. His red bandana was like her own personal national flag. She was dangerously close to falling in love with him. Her life had become so frightening, so surreal and detached from normality, that she wanted to cling to him, the only pillar holding up the plummeting sky.

She also knew that if he were a man of less integrity, he could have easily come to her room and she wouldn't have refused him. Only memories of Amanjit sustained her: his laughter; his smiling face; his grim determination; the way he moved. They were anchor chains, lifelines – but she was still scared to touch Tanvir, to hug him, even casually.

He was just as tormented; she knew that from the way he sometimes looked at her, and from the things he didn't say. He was older than her, no innocent; he knew what could be, which made his restraint more admirable than hers. All she could do was pray for a way out of this labyrinth.

The car purred through yet more nameless streets in yet another nameless district somewhere in vast and mighty Mumbai. The police kept moving them: into rich areas or poor; filthy hovels or marble-floored apartments . . . *but why?* Deepika wondered. *Are we still being hunted?* The police were certainly acting like they were.

There were few secrets left between them: she'd finally decided she owed it to Tanvir to tell him everything she knew about Vikram and Amanjit and their past lives. She'd thought he might scoff, but instead he'd told her that in that instant when Majid had shot at him, he'd seen something alien and demonic in the man's eyes, and that had made him *believe*. They were both sure Majid was possessed by Ravindra; and that he was out there somewhere, searching for them.

'Where are we?' she asked Tanvir, beside her in the back seat, carefully out of reach.

He peered out the window. 'Nariman Point.'

The name of one of Mumbai's wealthy business districts evoked palatial central-city apartments and luxury cars. 'Perhaps the plumbing will work, then,' she commented, remembering the last place they'd been stashed.

Tanvir snorted. 'Hot water would be nice too.'

She wondered what kept him going. Rational reasons for him helping her were as shallow as a puddle, yet his loyalty ran deep. It was scary to be so dependent upon something she could barely understand. 'Maybe we'll even get a TV and a DVD player. I really want to watch a movie tonight. Something funny and silly.'

Tanvir rolled his eyes. 'Not another romcom chicky-flicky thing, please!'

'You like them too,' she accused. 'I've seen you, pretending not to watch and then humming the songs for days after.'

'At least I don't practise the dance moves in the mirror.'

'You don't? That's *abnormal*.'

They grinned at each other, then both looked away awkwardly.

*Oh, Amanjit, where are you . . . ?*

The car pulled into an apartment car park and the black-suited guards escorted them to the bank of lifts. She was surprised when one pushed the button for the top suite; this was a departure. All the other places they'd stayed had been unremarkable: security through obscurity. But this . . .

*Are we betrayed?* The thought made her freeze for moment. She studied the guards more closely. Were they more nervous than normal? Were they avoiding eye contact? Tanvir had picked up on her mood; she saw his hand now hovered near his concealed gun. The lift door opened onto a marble lobby and a facing wall filled with shelves of tasteful gold and bone artefacts set between large tubs of artistically arranged flowers.

No one shot them.

'The lounge is that way,' the first guard indicated, stepping away.

Tanvir looked at Deepika, then led the way to the lounge. Behind them, the guards dumped their bags on the lobby floor, then retreated into the lift, vanishing behind the closing doors.

*Normally they check every room before leaving.* She felt her breath shortening and a tingling weakness in her knees: fear.

She suddenly realised there was a man standing beside the window, but her tension didn't ease when she recognised the angular frame of Chief Superintendent Gupta. He looked at her with unwelcoming eyes. They still disliked each other, though she had no concrete reason not to trust him.

'Miss Choudhary. Detective Allam,' Gupta said. 'Welcome.'

'What's this place, sir?' Tanvir asked. 'Is it secure? Why haven't the men stayed?'

'It has already been swept: it's clean. It's a new facility, especially for you.'

'Especially for us?'

Gupta scowled. 'Yes. It appears you have a benefactor. We have checked . . . *her* . . . out and we believe this is genuine, not to mention a definite improvement on what we can offer in terms of facility and security.'

This sounded worse, not better. *A benefactor?* Deepika thought. *Who?*

There was a low cough from behind them and Tanvir whirled, his gun out and cocked.

The newcomer put a hand to – *her?* – mouth. 'Oh, my – how dramatic!'

She was wearing a western-style business suit, smart jacket and knee-length skirt in sombre greys and blacks, but gold glittered at her ears and nose and throat, a diamond and sapphire necklace sitting below a large Adam's apple. Long black hair cascaded over the left shoulder. The pudgy face was heavily made-up. She was transgender – a hijra.

Deepika had seen her before, on television, standing beside Sunita Ashoka. '*Uma?*'

'Oh, it's lovely to be recognised,' the hijra purred. 'I do love being a celebrity.' She hurried forward and kissed the frozen Deepika on both cheeks before she could react, then the bemused Tanvir, ignoring the macho policeman's visible flinching. 'Welcome! Welcome to your new home.'

The superintendent exhaled impatiently and explained, 'Miss . . . *erm* . . . Uma has come forward with an offer of protection. She has far more than we could provide. This house has closed-circuit digital security, bulletproof glass, one-way windows and a panic room. The ownership records are so convoluted that even a forensic detective would struggle to unravel them, meaning you can't be traced here. You are not obliged to accept this offer, but I strongly suggest that you do.'

Deepika stared. *So you can wash your hands of us . . . Are we costing too much to protect, Chief Superintendent?*

She looked at Uma. 'Why?'

'For Sunita.' Uma's voice was warm and she was

composure itself. She stepped close to Deepika and touched her arm. Her hands were the only ungraceful thing about her, carefully manicured, but still big and masculine. 'Sunita would want it.'

Deepika thought that through. By contesting for Sunita's hand, Vikram had been the cause of the actress' death. Why would someone so devoted to Sunita want to help anyone related to Vikram? That didn't make sense. 'Why—?'

Uma leaned in and whispered, 'Sunita is alive. She asked me to take you in.'

Deepika's heart thumped. 'But—'

'You'll see. She's going to call tonight.'

*The poor woman . . . She's gone mad!*

But still . . . the offer was generous, and probably better than anything else they might hope for. Deepika didn't feel entirely happy about this new arrangement, but she was certainly intrigued. Having battled ghosts and undead sorcerers recently, she was ready to believe that anything could happen.

Once she and Tanvir gave their assent, Chief Superintendent Gupta left them his number and departed with almost unseemly haste.

Uma pressed wine upon them, but Deepika awaited Tanvir's verdict before tasting it herself. Their new hostess appeared to be entirely genuine, but Dee couldn't quite shake her sense of unease; she'd never met anyone like Uma before. There was no doubt the apartment itself was magnificent, though: decorated in sumptuous purple and gold, marble floors covered with intricately woven silk carpets from Kashmir and Anatolia. Tanvir pointed out the cameras discreetly hidden in the corners of the room and thought-fully tapped the glass windows facing west, where the lights of the city flowed towards the darkness of the sea.

After what felt like hours of awkward half-conversations, the phone rang.

Uma looked at Deepika and smiled, then picked up the receiver. 'Hello,' she said, then a look of sublime joy stole over her. 'Sunita! Yes, yes, Sunni, she's right here.'

Deepika took the receiver with trepidation, looking at Tanvir as she answered, 'H – hello?'

She heard someone swallow, as if choked by sudden tears. 'Dee? I mean, *Darya*? Is that you?'

'*Darya?* Oh, right . . . but Ras – um, Padma? Uma said . . .' Her voice trailed off as she struggled to frame her question.

Fortunately, Rasita understood. 'Uma told you the truth. It's hard to explain, but "R" and "S" . . . well, we're kind of the *same person* now. Trust me, it's okay.'

Deepika's mind was reeling. 'You're the same person?'

'When Su— When she died, her spirit entered mine—'

'Ras, that's awful—'

'No, no, it's not: it's *right*, and it's *good*. Believe me, it's *very* good. We were two halves of a whole and now we're one.' Deepika was struggling to take the words in, but Ras went on cheerily, 'Listen, Shastri is here too – we're *both* fine.'

Deepika's hands were shaking. She hunched over the phone, trying not to cry. Finally she found her voice. 'Where are you?'

'I can't tell you; it's too dangerous. But we're fine, and we'll all be together soon. Aram is fine too – he's not with us, but he's okay.'

Then the voice she'd been longing to hear growled, 'Give me the phone! Darya? *Dee?* Don't cry! If you do, I will, and then my little sister will never let me forget it . . .'

She wiped her eyes. 'I'm sorry.'

'Don't be! I wish I was there to wipe your tears away.'

'Yeah, well, you'd need a mop.' Her eyes were streaming; Uma and Tanvir were just a blur, like faces behind a window streaked with rain. 'Are you okay?'

'Sort of. I miss you. Always.' His voice was husky. 'I love you.'

'I love you too.'

Ras butted in again. 'Yeah, yeah, whatever. Hey, that's as much time as we can use on a call. Dee— Darya, this is urgent. I'm going to email you some really important stuff. Things I've, you know . . . *remembered*. About past lives – about you and me.'

'About me?'

'Yes, you! Listen, I've remembered so much, and a lot of it's about you . . . It's hyper-important stuff, right? Too much to talk about here. Aman— Shastri's got a laptop and I've got a nice anonymous Hotmail ID. Write this down . . .' She read out an email address, then said, 'You need to create your own ID on Hotmail or Yahoo or something, and email it to me. Then we can talk properly.'

Deepika was scribbling down the address. 'Okay, got it.'

Amanjit's voice came back on. 'Okay, last few seconds. This whole three-minute time restriction is probably nonsense, but we can't take the risk that Aram may be right. I wish I was there with you. I can't wait to see you again.'

'Me too, darling. Me too.'

They both started to talk at once, then laughed nervously. 'Gotta go,' Amanjit whispered. 'Bye for now.'

'For now,' she echoed.

Then he was gone, but she closed her eyes and it was as if she could feel his arms around her, warm, snug and safe. When she finally looked around again, Uma was sniffing and dabbing at her own eyes with a tissue. Tanvir was gazing out the window, a sad, wistful smile on his face.

Once she'd calmed down, she logged into Hotmail, created a new account and then emailed the address Ras had given her. A response came back a little later, as she was staring out over the city with music playing faintly in the background. Just a one-line email, but with a zipped attachment which she read with growing curiosity and wonder.

Hey D, <u>so</u> good to hear your voice. I zipped this to confuse any software scanning for keywords – don't know if it helps but V has made us all paranoid. You got that we're to use Mandore names only, right? So V is Aram, I'm Padma, A is Shastri and you're Darya. Your hunky bodyguard (U told me!) is Tilak, right?

I've had <u>loads</u> of time to think and remember things – it's such a weird sensation, scary and wonderful all at once, like I'm a living history book. I've remembered lives where you and I knew each other, and one is REALLY IMPORTANT – the thing is, YOU HAVE TO REMEMBER IT TOO. VITAL.

Luckily, you've got two people with you who were also involved. So, here's what I want you to try – and yes, this is going to sound <u>weird</u>, but Aram showed me how in the 1800s (how freaky is that?!).

You must sit in a circle with the two people with you. Get
U to chant the following: Uday – Karnataka – Anupa – U
(her own name).

Get T to chant: Tilak – Karnataka – Pradeep – T (his own
name).

You must chant: Darya – Karnataka – Abbakka – D (your
own name).

Sounds weird, I know, but please, TRY IT. Be serious, and
have belief – SOMETHING WILL HAPPEN! It is really, really
important, I promise.

Let me know what you find out!

Love to you all

Padma & Shastri

Deepika read the note over again, then, with some trepidation, she showed it to the others. Tanvir looked at her
sceptically, but didn't voice his clear doubts. He'd retreated
into himself and she couldn't blame him. But Uma was fascinated, and they sat up late into the night making plans.

The next morning, filled with enthusiasm, Uma went shopping, returning with vivid yellow and red traditional southern
clothing for the three of them, and the ingredients for a special coconut fish dish. 'Karnataka is in South India,' she
explained, 'so perhaps having authentic food will help. Oh—
I've just had a thought: what about jewellery? And candles:
we need scented ones . . . It's just like the movies!'

Deepika tried to calm her down. 'I think the state of mind
is more important than the trappings, from what Ras says.'

'She's Sunita, dear – Ras too, of course, but also my

Sunni. I know how she thinks. So, when shall we try? I can't wait!'

Deepika looked at Tanvir, who was pacing beside the window. 'Tanvir?'

The policeman shrugged noncommittally. There was a distance reasserting itself between them, which felt awkward, even painful – but it was necessary. Just hearing Amanjit and Rasita's voices had rekindled hope in her . . . but she wished he would smile again.

'Let's do it tonight,' she said brightly, trying to quash her nerves.

'Do you think sixty-four candles is enough? I was thinking, eight times eight, because eight is auspicious, so eight eights would be even more so, and—'

'That's plenty, Uma. It's fine,' Deepika exclaimed, laying a calming hand on her forearm. Uma had been babbling nervously for the last hour.

They turned off all the lights, leaving the multitude of candles surrounding them in a flickering circle, and made themselves comfortable on cushions set around a brazier – Uma's idea of how a séance should work. Tanvir had put on his South Indian lungi without a word, and Uma and Deepika were arrayed in vivid nine-yard-long saris (not the northern-style seven yards) and heavily veiled. It would have been easy to treat this as a costume party, forgetting the seriousness of what they were trying to do, but Deepika suspected that if they treated this trivially then nothing would happen.

What she *expected* would happen, she had no idea.

'Did you like the fish?' Uma demanded. 'It's an authentic southern recipe.'

'It was great,' Deepika reassured her, but in truth, she actually felt a little woozy since eating – and she'd not even touched her wine yet.

'And the clothes! I think you look splendid, Tanvir. Have you ever worn——? No, I guess not. But——'

'Uma,' Deepika said flatly, '*shush*. Now, are you ready, Tanvir?'

He looked her in the eyes for the first time that day. 'I don't know,' he admitted. He glanced at the brazier, where a dozen heady incense sticks were burning. 'Do you really think something will happen?'

'Yes.' *I have to think so.*

'Very well then.' Tanvir was clearly reliving that night which had changed everything for him, when he saw Amanjit, Rasita and Vikram fly from Shiv Bakli's rooftop, suspended from arrows. If *that* was possible, what else might be? 'Let's give it a try.'

'It'll work,' Uma put in. 'If my Sunni can die and then come back, then nothing is impossible.'

They inhaled the incense, which Uma had found in a market she knew from darker days. 'These are party sticks,' she told them afterwards, 'laced with opium and ganja. Oh, and those mushrooms in the curry? They weren't all regular field mushrooms.'

Deepika's hand flew to her mouth. 'Uma——!'

'I figured we might need a little extra *chemistry*. Don't worry, I know the dosages. I've done this kind of thing before, you know.' She laughed and added, 'Drugs, that is, not séances.'

'No wonder we could never get on top of the drug traffic in this city,' Tanvir muttered. He looked dazed and his words had started to slur.

Deepika, worried she might pass out before they started, said urgently, 'Let's do it. Come on!' She reached out and placed her left hand in Uma's and her right in Tanvir's. Both were hot and sweaty. 'Ready?' She felt the room begin to spin slowly about her. 'Then on my count: one . . . two . . . three . . . *Darya. Karnataka. Abbakka. Deepika . . . Darya. Karnataka. Abbakka. Deepika . . .*'

At first they were all self-conscious, but the dizzy disorientation from all the things they had inhaled and ingested began to remove any sense of embarrassment. The smoke from the brazier was thick and heady and Deepika's throat was dry, but her mouth was full of words. She threw her mind into memories of a holiday in Karnataka: palmy beaches, warm turquoise seas, people laughing, ambling through slow unchanging lives, the seasons' rhythms like the slow beat of a drum; the echo of songs, a counterpoint harmony to her own chant.

'*Darya . . . Karnataka . . . Abbakka . . . Deepika . . .*'

She found herself floating away, no longer aware of her companions. Her skin was streaming with perspiration, her hair floating free, swaying like seaweed in unseen currents, shifting this way and that in time to the drums and song . . .

She saw a woman walking gracefully along a beach at sunset: a plump woman, but light on her feet, with a face that was both hard as the rocks on the shore and gentle as the waves caressing the sand. Her mouth was slightly open, her eyes searching, her head cocked to hear voices. She turned towards Deepika, not seeing her, yet somehow aware. Could she hear their chant? Was she swaying to the unheard music? Her eyes had crow's feet and her temples were grey, and glittering gold chains ran from a nose-ring to earrings festooned with rubies.

Deepika reached for her and felt herself float towards the woman, spiralling and turning as she fell into the woman's head . . . and cast about the darkness . . . *remembering* – a *moment* . . .

. . . when she walked along the beach and had the *strangest* passing fancy . . .

# CHAPTER SIX

# ULLAL: A BEAUTIFUL SUNSET

*Ullal, Karnataka, 1568*

. . . the strangest fancy, that she heard voices from the sea mingling with the gentle murmur of the waves sliding over the sands, calling her through the hiss of the receding water.

Abbakka Chauta, Rani of Ullal, had been walking along the shore, watching the sun set over the water. To the north her harbour town home of Ullal slowly faded into shadow. To the south was the Goa coast, rocky headlands and pristine sandy coves backing on to the lushly wooded interior. A light breeze stroked her skin and set her silks fluttering.

She liked to walk the shore alone – although for a queen, 'alone' was a relative term; thirty yards behind her marched her guards, a dozen maids and about sixty servants bearing parasols, cushions, extra shawls, sherbet, fruit bowls – whatever a rani might suddenly decide she needed. She often thought she heard music in the waters, but never so vividly as just now. Just for a moment the walls of the world felt strangely flimsy, as if eyes had met hers across time . . .

The sensation passed as the voices of her daughters pulled her back from some strange brink. For an instant she almost fainted, but then the girls were running towards her, holding up conch shells into which they were hooting gaily.

'Mother – listen,' called Anupa, her eldest, a big-boned girl always determined to be first. She tipped her head back and emptied her lungs into the conch, making it moan horribly. 'I'm loudest, say I was—'

'Me, *me*,' shrilled graceful little Tashi, who could barely make any noise at all, despite puffing until her cheeks turned scarlet. They worried about her, she was so frail, but Anupa was very protective. They all were.

'Of course you're louder, Anupa; Tashi is barely half your age and very small for her years.'

'I'll always be louder than Tashi,' Anupa proclaimed. 'I'm the noisiest girl in the world.' It was very likely: Anupa was bigger than all the boys her age. She liked to dress up as a warrior and join in the boys' mock battles with a wooden sword that seldom left her side. Her father said she was more son than daughter, and usually added some sneering comment about how much she took after her mother.

'I don't doubt that at all, darling. Now run along, I need to talk to Senapati Pradeep.'

The two girls looked crestfallen, but bobbed their heads dutifully. 'A good soldier always obeys his queen,' Anupa told Tashi, leading her away. The younger maids fussed about the princesses, their fluting voices like chattering birds. Abbakka Rani watched them fondly as a heavily built soldier joined her, his blunt face sober.

'Rani, I apologise, but we must speak.'

She inclined her head and her eyes flickered up and down his muscular form. 'Senapati Pradeep.' She allowed him the tiniest of smiles, in token of all the more intimate things they shared. 'A beautiful sunset.'

His lips twitched. 'I know my queen, and she isn't thinking about beautiful sunsets. If she is gazing at a fire, then she is musing upon gunpowder and cannon. If she is looking at a hill, she is picturing how to fortify it. If she sets her eyes upon a horse, she is wondering about cavalry. And if she is gazing out to sea, she is thinking about Portuguese warships.'

'You know me too well, Pradeep.'

'It's been fifteen years, Rani.'

'Fifteen years? Since a frightened young captain was asked to attend upon the queen late one night?'

'Since a young soldier learned that an older woman could teach him a great deal.' He stared out to sea, not really seeing the glorious dusk sky; he might tease her, but his mind worked the same as hers. 'About the Portuguese fleet—'

'My Pradeep: so focused on the practical. It is why I trust you so.' *And also why I cannot love you as you wish.* 'They have moved out to sea?'

He pulled a face, as he always did when she second-guessed him. 'The Portuguese coastal fleet are at sea nearby, somewhere over the horizon – we don't know where they are.' He lowered his voice. 'Rumour has it that they may be coming here.'

'Why should they? We have a treaty with the Portuguese, and alliances with all the neighbouring kingdoms. They'd be starting more than they can handle. Our trade is profitable to them, so why would they disrupt it? It isn't in their interests.'

'So your husband thought, Rani, but it is just a dozen years ago that they almost razed Mangalore. Now he's their puppet – he pretends alliance to us, but he can't be trusted, and nor can his masters.'

'I don't trust *any* of them, Pradeep, you know that. I assume you've already strengthened our watch.'

'Of course, Rani.' He stared out into the red sunset as if expecting to see sails on the horizon. 'It will be a full moon tonight, Abbakka, bright enough to sail by. And the men are nervous of the Portuguese: they're frightened of their god and their guns.'

'I've been thinking those guns,' she replied. 'We've seen them in battle, all flash and thunder. The massed volley is impressive, no doubt, but their rate of fire is poor and they're inaccurate. A trained archer can fire six shafts in the time it takes them to fire once.'

Pradeep didn't blink at this most unqueenly conversation. 'You hit upon the answer right there, Rani: "trained". Archery demands a lifelong devotion and constant practise. A gun does not. *Anyone* can aim and fire one. Our men are frightened by the noise they make in battle, Rani, and they're frightened by the men using them. They're taller than us, and stronger, alien in every way. Our soldiers whisper about their god, their "Yayzus Kristus", saying he is a war-god who is Creator, Protector and Destroyer in one. Their god drinks blood to gain invulnerability, so before battle, the Portuguese priests serve blood to the soldiers, to make *them* invincible.'

'That's nonsense, Pradeep—'

'You know so, Rani: you are an educated woman. But I

am telling you, this is what your people say, the lowly people whose men fill your armies. To them it's all real.'

Abbakka took this in with mounting anxiety. Such stories could leave her men half-defeated before battle was even joined – and battle would come soon; that was certain. She'd been watching the pale-skinned foreigners' power and influence grow along the coast all her life. She'd seen their curious mix of piety and treachery, their assumption of inherent superiority which they used to justify any betrayal or atrocity. She'd seen them struggle ashore in stinking rags, thinking themselves above a raja in his silks. The Portuguese, the Dutch and the English: they were all the same.

Abbakka Chauta came from a matrilineal hereditary system; the Raja of Ullal's daughter had been raised as a male prince, and on her father's death, when she was still only sixteen, her uncle Tirumala Raya ensured that she succeeded the Ullal throne. He'd arranged her marriage to Lakshmappa Arasa, the King of Mangalore, whose city lay on the opposite shore of the bay to Ullal. But Lakshmappa turned out to be effete, a weakling, where she was martial and strong; although the marriage was still legally in place, they hated each other and lived apart. He had many lovers and other queens; she could not remarry and still retain power. All she had were her secret nights with Pradeep, who was man enough for her.

'Tonight, after the feast, come to me,' she murmured. Then she turned to the waiting courtiers and clapped her hands, crying, 'Home, my lords and ladies.' She patted her expansive belly. 'I'm hungry.'

\*

Dancers danced, musicians played and the courtiers applauded. Fire-eaters blasted balls of flames about them, leaving an acrid, oily tang in the air. Abbakka's court babbled and jested merrily as they helped themselves to the steaming bowls of curried lentils and coconut-cocooned fish. The rani and her closest confidants ignored the cacophony as they sat cross-legged on the floor about her, eating informally as any field workers.

'Mullah Hassan,' Abbakka said, turning to her chief Muslim advisor, the Zamorin of Calicut's ambassador to her court. 'Tell me more of this strange faith of the Portuguese. Do these Kristus worshippers plague Muslims also?'

The mullah, clad in sumptuous scarlet and elegantly turbaned, groaned. 'They plague us *everywhere*, Rani. Their faith is related to ours; nonetheless, they are our mortal enemies. Their mistake has been to elevate one prophet, Kristus, over all others. There is common ground between the True Faith and this lesser branch, but they are nevertheless heretical and barbaric.'

The skinny Hindu sitting beside Mullah Hassan lifted a finger theatrically. Her cousin Aniket, a poet and scholar, was her Uncle Tirumala's eyes in her court, but he'd also been her tutor in many things when they were younger. Many of the men didn't esteem him, for he was small, with a deformed left foot, but she loved him like a brother.

With a mischievous look, he said, 'I've heard they claim their faith to be older than yours, Mullah.'

'A shallow claim to superiority,' Hassan said dismissively. 'Revelation means more than longevity. The religions of the Romans and Greeks predate these Kristyans, but they have no credence. Truth is greater than antiquity.'

Abbakka was a Jain and favoured religious, racial and even caste tolerance in her kingdom. That had enabled her to pull together a strong band of allies, not just Hindus and Jains, but Arab Moors and Persian settlers. Without these people, they would have been quite unable to resist the Portuguese.

Predictably, Pradeep, a deeply pragmatic man; unable to believe in anything he could not see, touch or wield, changed the subject. 'Rani, I have doubled the watch on the seaward side.'

'Is there any word from Lakshmappa?' she asked. Abbakka's estranged husband still held the northern side of the harbour, for all his capital of Mangalore had often been assailed. They needed his vigilance to give them warning of attack, but he was increasingly unreliable.

'He sent word that the Portuguese warships had sailed northwest and that all is quiet.'

'Then treble the watch, don't just double it,' grinned Aniket. He still looked boyish, though he was in his fifties now, his thinning hair completely grey. 'I wouldn't trust that bastard husband of yours for a second,' he grunted and slurped at his drink – Portuguese wine, purchased before the recent tensions.

Abbakka gazed down at the next table, where lumpish Anupa was giggling with her favourite maid. Tashi was clapping her hands to the music, visibly itching to join the dancers. 'He gave me two good daughters,' she pointed out. 'It wasn't all bad.'

'Lakshmappa thought marrying you gave him your kingdom, not merely alliance with it. The man is a liability, and his nephew Kama is a bigger one. He's been seen in Goa, at the Portuguese headquarters.' Aniket spat into a bowl at his side. 'Kama is Kola reborn, I swear,' he muttered, whatever that meant. Aniket was prone to odd utterances. Once, after too many drinks, he'd inexplicably said, 'I've never lived longer.' He'd always been a bit strange, but she loved him despite that. She'd heard him argue passionately that reincarnation was real, and that their Hindu gods walked the earth, but he too preached tolerance of all faiths – even if only to win allies.

Mullah Hassan inclined his head. 'My spies say the new Portuguese admiral is—'

Whatever the Muslim scholar intended to say was lost in a sudden thunderous rumble from the north, followed by a crash that shook the very ground. A cloud of dust swept through the open windows. The room fell silent, then screaming and the sound of shattering glass tore the air. Abbakka's hand flew to her bosom and her eyes found Pradeep's. For a second her lover looked like a lost child – then Aniket seized his shoulder. His voice was urgent but calm, as if this were routine. 'Secure the perimeter and send scouts to locate their batteries. The rani will take charge here. Send reports directly to the armoury – our command room will be there. *Go*, Senapati, and the gods be with you.'

Pradeep kissed her hand then hurried away, as Abbakka felt eyes turning towards her, frightened faces needing reassurance. *Show no fear*, she reminded herself, *only controlled anger*. She rose unhurriedly. 'Well, my friends, it appears we have unexpected guests. Shall we see to their welcome?'

# CHAPTER SEVEN

## ULLAL: ONSLAUGHT

*Ullal, Karnataka, 1568*

The reports came in throughout the evening: the Portuguese had sailed into the harbour in the long twilight and were bombarding her shore batteries with impunity – but worse than that, they'd landed marines south of the town and more soldiers were moving in from the north, through Lakshmappa's territories. There'd been no warning from her husband and now Ullal was almost surrounded.

Abbakka put on her armour and weapons – Lakshmappa had always been so derisive about her 'dressing-up' – and set up her command position in a tower near the armoury. She and Aniket watched the flashes and the rising smoke from the town that signalled where the invaders were currently skirmishing. Pradeep was out there somewhere; safe, she hoped. Mullah Hassan had gone to the masjid to rally support.

Aniket spoke in her ear. 'Abbakka, I want you to

remember the spell-words I taught you as a girl. If you go into battle, *remember* them.'

'They never did me any good in training, Cousin,' she replied sceptically.

'With you, such things come out only in moments of extreme danger, Abbakka. You have the potential: when your passions rise, use what I told you.'

'Cousin, I'm the queen – if an enemy gets close enough that I must fight, we've probably already lost.' She waved at a messenger running into the courtyard below. 'You – Jayan, isn't it? Report to me.'

The man was ragged and powder-streaked but he swarmed up the stairs, his features wild in the torchlight. 'Rani, they are coming – they are coming here! Senapati Pradeep begs you to seek safety—'

'We don't retreat on hearsay, Jayan. Where's the enemy? What is their strength?'

'They are very many, Rani—'

'Calmly, Jayan. How many? What numbers?'

A sudden rattle of musketry near the palace gates almost drowned out the man's reply. 'The Senapati says there are more than three hundred – they have driven a wedge into the town. Half our men are trapped on the north side, Rani, so he is retreating into the forest. He begs you to do the same.'

Abbakka turned to Aniket. 'Cousin?'

'Pradeep knows his business.' Aniket's eyes were quick and lively, his demeanour eager.

'I've already moved my daughters inland, plus some valuables. Should we destroy the provender?'

'We recently took possession of a large shipment of wine, did we not?' Aniket winked at her. 'Ensure it's left untouched, for the entertainment of our conquerors.'

Abbakka caught his meaning immediately; she whirled, and called to her captains, 'Destroy nothing. We'll retreat to the woods. Retreat in appearance of poor order, you understand? They must think us routed – you know the drill. Aniket, go with them – I'll command the rearguard.'

That she, a woman, would lead the most perilous mission, was unquestioned. Aniket gave a small bow. 'I am a slow traveller these days, Cousin. I will catch them up as I can.' He touched her arm. 'Be safe, Darya.' He hobbled away, looking frail.

*Darya?* Abbakka stared after him, but there was too much to do. Aniket did sometimes call her odd names. *The onset of senility, no doubt.* She put it from her mind as she moved to a position above the main gates. A group of her men were coming in – then shots flew among them and they scattered, redoubling their speed. Beneath burning torches a squad of Portuguese clad in steel breastplates and curved helms appeared, knelt in a line with presented guns and awaited the order to fire.

*Discipline: that's something in which they exceed us. But it can be learned.*

Young Captain Haran approached. 'Please withdraw, Rani. They may rush us. This place isn't safe.'

'Don't worry, Captain Haran. When there's real danger, I'll retire. For now, get our men inside. Cover them from the ramparts.' Her mind buzzed with calculations of range, estimates of numbers. *Where is the main body of the enemy? What are their objectives?* Dimly she registered that the enemy had fired: shots were pinging off the stone walls and there was the *zip* of a near miss. She was under fire and had barely noticed.

'Rani, please,' young Haran begged, 'they are massing to attack—'

*These children think they own me.* The boy was right, mind, but she had to ensure the defence was organised . . .

'Haran, you must fire once, then withdraw. Do not come into close contact with them. Controlled withdrawal, Captain. They won't pursue beyond this position, not with all the plunder in here.'

He bowed, then ran to order his men. She couldn't resist watching the enemy gather, then march forward. They launched their attack at walking pace, which surely added to their casualties? *Why not just charge?* But it was menacing, that implacable advance. She frowned, trying to work out how many volleys a coordinated defence could effect.

'Rani—' Another young man extended his hand. 'Please, *come!*'

She grinned at him. 'I just want to see our volley.' She glanced at Haran, striding behind his men on the walls, and signalled.

Haran begun to order the volley. 'Ready, aim . . . *fire!*'

A ragged burst of musketry erupted, muzzles flashing, billowing smoke. She peered through the haze and cursed as she realised how ineffectual her soldiers' fire was – and how close the enemy was. She crouched as a return volley scythed along the walls. One of her men collapsed before her and she stumbled over him. A ragged call echoed outside as the Portuguese charged.

*Now you've done it, you stupid cow: you'll be trapped in here —
and even worse, Lakshmappa will think it hilarious.*

She straightened. 'Second rank, form and fire! First rank,
pull out!' She waved her arm at Haran frantically. 'Get them
out, Captain – pull out, pull out, *now!* Through the courtyard.' She ran through them as the second rank knelt. The
second volley was even more ragged than the first, but this
time she didn't pause to see what effect it might have had.
She shoved men towards the stairs, crying, 'Get down!
We've got to clear the courtyard so that the reserves can
cover us – *move!*'

*You didn't want me to learn about any of this, Lakshmappa . . .
What use would I have been then?*

They hadn't even made the bottom of the steps when the
gates exploded inwards. She flinched, physically shaken, but
her mind was still whirring. *They mined it, the bastards!*

'*MOVE!*' She leaped from the steps directly to the ground,
landing awkwardly, but others followed her. At the far side
of the small courtyard, a bank of her men waited with
loaded guns. Haran was with them, brandishing a sword.

Then the Portuguese swarmed through the shattered
doors.

The waiting squad fired, and this volley was more effective: the first row of enemy soldiers staggered backwards,
clutching at blood blooming from their flesh, twisting and
falling. But more came on, pikemen with long axe-headed
blades. As they fanned out, she realised that she was at the
forefront of their charge.

'Rani—' Three men surged past her while another
grabbed her shoulder. 'Rani, *run!*'

Pikes hacked at her three protectors and one went down, but the other two flailed their curved swords, holding off the enemy blows. Beyond them a Portuguese captain aimed a pistol at her, but one of her guards stepped before her, twisted and fell. She finally remembered her own pistol and when she fired into the press of the enemy a man crumpled, but she couldn't see if it was the enemy captain; he'd vanished. More hands dragged at her, pulling her away, as her two swordsmen danced amongst the pikes, giving ground.

'Rani,' someone shouted in her ear, 'this way—' and dragged her with them.

They were cut off from the main line of retreat, but there was a sortie gate on their side of the courtyard – and others had remembered it too; as they reached it, someone pushed her through the wall of men. One of her officers turned to her and shouted in her face, 'They're moving into our line of retreat, Rani – we need to go inland—' He pointed along the wall, to the right.

'No, we move as planned,' she replied, pointing the other way. 'We're not cut off, and the masjid lies that way – Hassan will have men there.'

'They'll decimate us as we go, Rani—'

'They'll annihilate us if we stay.' *Gods, can't these boys think for themselves?* 'Go!'

They ran, bunching for protection until she made them fan out. 'Their guns are only effective against massed targets, so spread out, use cover.'

'Rani,' a soldier shouted, 'they're coming—' He pointed to the west, where a rank of enemy silhouettes were marching towards them in the smoke and fading light, drums tapping.

'If you're loaded, *fire*,' she called. 'Make them pause – shoot, then run!'

A ragged burst of gunfire issued from no more than ten of her men, and she saw only two of the enemy drop. The drums still rolled.

'Move,' cried a young man who appeared on her left, shielding her from the enemy's fire.

'Bless you, lad, but run!'

They put on a spurt, but she heard the Portuguese commander shout, 'Aim: *um . . . dois . . .*'

'DROP!' she shrieked, throwing herself to the ground, and thank the gods, most of her men followed suit, just in time, for the air above them was singing with whizzing lead that whined and slapped and ricocheted off the wall at their back.

She rose first, slapping the lad beside her and crying, 'Up – up and run—' and they steamed through the shattered twilight. With a roar, the Portuguese shouted and came on, maintaining their ranked formation.

Abbakka felt her heart hammering. She was bathed in sweat and dizzy at the exertion; it was far too hot for this madness. A hoarse shout rang out over the enemy ranks and the Portuguese soldiers broke into a run.

'Rani, they're charging,' the lad shielding her called fearfully, as if she couldn't see them for herself.

Her gaze was fixed on to the end of the wall and the copse that lay beyond. *If they've encircled us completely, we're done. I shouldn't have lingered. Lakshmappa will* die *laughing.* She glanced sideways, calculated the distances and realised there was no way they could avoid being caught.

She stopped. *I'm damned if I'll be cut down from behind.*

'Chautas, form up: face the foe,' she ordered. *I can't run further anyway. I'm too fat and old for this.* 'Form a rank.' About two-thirds obeyed, enough to slow the Portuguese down – for about a heartbeat. The men looked at her with frightened eyes. She wanted to tell them, *Show no fear. It is only death: a brief thing* – but instead, she called, 'Stand firm! The enemy have fired, their guns are empty. This will be hand-to-hand.'

*The first contact will bring the axe-heads down on us, and they will wade right over the top. We'll be lucky to scratch them.*

The faces of the enemy were clear now, gleaming teeth and whites of eyes, ferocity etched on their faces. The dim light reflected on steel helms, and lank hair flew as they closed in. She drew her second pistol and aimed it. *Well, looks like I'm going to end up just like Lakshmappa said I would: a fat corpse.*

Then the ground shook; a rolling thunder from the right as a cloud of horsemen streamed around the corner with Pradeep at their head.

'*ATTACK!*' the senapati bellowed, and before the Portuguese soldiers could re-form, Pradeep's riders had struck their ranks side-on, sabres slashing, the horses kicking out and sending men to the ground with broken limbs and crushed skulls. Their riders staggered at the impacts, but stayed mounted as the foreign soldiers were tossed aside.

But there were only a dozen riders, and the desperate charge gained just a momentary respite . . . worthless, unless they used the time well. '*RUN!*' she roared again, and this time everyone obeyed.

As she pounded over the uneven ground, she sensed breathing behind her, whirled and without bothering to aim, fired — straight into a grizzled Portuguese soldier, blowing him over backwards. She sheathed the smoking gun and drew her sword, but she'd only made the shadow of the trees when the Portuguese regrouped, forming a defensive square against the horsemen, pikes extended at the front while the rank behind reloaded their guns.

The game was up.

Pradeep reared his horse about as she shouted, 'Pull back, pull back!' She drew a deep breath, then screamed, 'Pradeep, get out of here, they're going to fire—'

He'd heard her, she knew that, but he met her eyes and shook his head. He meant to buy her more time to escape. 'Get out of here, Abbi – *get out*,' he shouted, his eyes bidding her farewell.

The sight froze her as nothing else could have, until the young lad who'd stuck to her side tugged at her, begging, 'Rani, come this way—'

'*PRADEEP*,' she bellowed, '*PRADEEP—!*'

The Portuguese volley thundered, the orange spurts of flame rippling along the line of the enemy, and unseen lead tore through them. The youth who'd been her stalwart protector clutched at his chest and spun as smoke washed over them. Her eyes streamed with the sudden sting of the powder. A horse pitched over, screaming hideously, and crashed to the ground before her, thrashing weakly. Its rider was shouting in agony; his leg trapped beneath the body and even amidst the ear-splitting din, she heard the bones break.

It was Pradeep.

'*No,*' she bellowed, but in vain, for the enemy were flooding forward now, barely thirty yards away. And despite everything, her mind continued to race: *Can we counter-charge? Impossible; we're not set for it . . .*

'Run, Rani,' Pradeep begged through gritted teeth, as his horse sagged and went still, its full weight upon him. He too had been hit, in the side, where blood ran from a hole punched in his breastplate. His face was a mask of pain. 'Get out of here, Abbi!' Men pulled at her, dragging her away, as the wall of the enemy loomed. Too many.

'Pradeep . . . I love you . . .'

She tore her eyes from her lover's stricken face as a chill washed over her and the air rippled with menace, discernible even amidst the din of the melee. A Portuguese officer stalked towards her through the fray, and for an instant, all she could see was him. He wore a gaudy plumed hat as if he were on promenade, but in his left hand was a smoking pistol and in his right, a long straight sword.

But it was the feral eyes and the curved ram's horns and tusked mouth that tore something loose in her mind.

She backed away, staggering, as the man — *no, no man: a demon!* — stepped over Pradeep's fallen horse and drove his blade into her lover's chest, his face filled with vindictive glee as he twisted the sword. She heard herself howl as he fixed his eye on her and smiled in surprised glee. '*Queen Darya?*' he mouthed, and somehow the words reached her ears amidst the din, his voice both incredulous and gloating.

Then her own men surrounded her and started a mad counter-charge of desperate savagery — but before she could push through to the front to lead them, someone grabbed her and dragged her away.

Even as she ran, a voice was hooting above the clamour of battle, shouting words she understood despite not knowing the language: '*The Darya – the Darya is here!*'

There was a small stone storeroom beneath a latticed grille under the masjid. Her men shut Abbakka inside, finishing piling debris over the door just moments before the first enemy tramped into the shrine.

Mullah Hassan awaited them. She stood there for a moment, seeing his feet through the latticework, then she realised someone might spot the grille and hold a lit torch to it to peer inside. She found a pile of sacks and huddled beneath them, still able to hear what was said above, although she was in shock at Pradeep's loss, her thoughts swirling through grief and hate.

The mullah spoke Portuguese. Words were exchanged, the invaders brusque and sneering, the mullah cool and placatory. She didn't need to see him to *know* the Portuguese officer in the room above was *him*: the ram-horned demon, presumably with that inhuman visage disguised somehow. Her heart burned with recriminations and rage; at the Portuguese and their gluttony for invasion; at the gods for allowing their enemy to summon demons to their aid, but mostly at her husband, for being too weak or too lax or too treacherous to give her warning.

*Lakshmappa, are you cur or coward or both, you swine?*

'Of course she isn't here,' Hassan replied smoothly. 'Surely you know women may not enter a masjid under any circumstance – not even a queen, and not even in war. A woman's presence would pollute this holy place. The sanctity of the shrine outweighs all other considerations.'

'How barbaric,' the Portuguese officer jeered. 'In Christian lands even an enemy may claim sanctuary in our churches.' He spat, and his spittle struck the latticework and dangled there. 'I don't trust you, Mullah.' He shouted at someone, 'Sergeant, search this place – and if she's here, bring her to me and behead this heathen.'

'I am the Ambassador of his Majesty the Zamorin of Calicut,' Mullah Hassan protested.

'And that should make us trust you? We'll be coming for him next,' the Portuguese snapped.

Abbakka followed the progress of the search with her ears, heard them breaking things, laughing as they went. Once she knew that *he* – the demon in Portuguese guise – was right above her, but she buried herself in silence and sorrow and somehow – *somehow* – they didn't find her.

Finally they gave up and went, leaving her sobbing with grief and shaking in relief.

*Pradeep, I should have married you. Why do we never see what we have until it's too late?*

That was all the weakness she permitted herself though. As she left the masjid, her mind burned with cold fury. She led her escort to the woods, hearing the sound of revelry and the invaders' strange music filling her own palace. Fires burned in the town. At the top of Watchtower Hill she paused to mark the likely pickets and counted the warships in the harbour, but though she took it all in, inside all her resource was consumed with girding herself for battle, seeking the courage to die bravely.

*Pradeep, there will be an accounting. This I swear to you.*

Aniket greeted her gravely. He clearly already knew about Pradeep – he always knew everything. 'Do you feel it, Abbakka?' he asked, as he embraced her. 'Do you feel the anger? That anger is a power, an energy. Call upon it.'

'I don't have time for your fairy stories, Aniket,' she growled. 'I am here to kill, and to die.' She thought of that *thing* walking among the Portuguese and drank deep of the well of hatred inside her. 'I am going to kill the man who slew Pradeep. If he is a man.'

Aniket threw her a startled look. 'What did you see, Abbi?' When she shook her head silently, his expression became knowing. 'I'm with you, Abbakka.' He lifted an ancient bow from where it leaned against a tree trunk. 'This old fellow needs an outing.'

She stared. 'Are you *mad*? This is the age of guns, Aniket – you're not joining my attack anyway, and you are certainly not taking *that* relic anywhere near the enemy.'

'I've still got a few old tricks up my sleeve, Abbi.'

'No: your value is in court,' she retorted. 'You know about law and politics, not battle. Please, put that damned thing away and get some sleep. I can't afford to lose you too.'

She left him and went among the young officers, all looking shocked at their defeat. She grasped the shoulder of one and asked, 'Binat, will you follow where I lead?'

'Of course, Rani,' Binat replied with the cockiness of youth, of one who knows himself to be invulnerable; after all, he had survived the day, had he not? So surely that proved it. 'I am always ready,' he boasted, and the young men about him loudly affirmed their own willingness to do whatever the queen wished.

'Tomorrow we will retake the town,' they shouted lustily. 'We will drive them into the sea——'

'Not tomorrow,' Abbakka said. 'Tonight.'

# CHAPTER EIGHT

## ULLAL: ARROWS IN THE NIGHT

*Ullal, Karnataka, 1568*

In the aftermath of the attack, confusion reigned. There was no way to get messages through to her allies and anyway, there was no time, not for what Abbakka Rani had in mind. She had only the soldiers at hand: two hundred survivors, give or take. Many were lightly wounded, but all were burning to strike back, especially when she told them that the scouts reported revelry in the palace.

Aniket had vanished. She worried briefly, then put it from her mind. *Be safe, Cousin.*

They retraced the route of their flight from the palace until they were all gathered in the treeline. Binat, beside her, was tense, bravado and anxiety warring on his face, and she gave him a reassuring smile as a scout slipped back to her position. Jayan, the messenger who had brought warning of the assault on the palace, flopped to the ground before her, panting. His eyes were amazed. 'Rani, I've seen a sign — the gods fight on our side tonight—' he started.

*But demons fight against us . . . we* need *our gods tonight . . .*

'How so, Jayan?' Any good news that would boost the courage of her men before their suicidal raid was welcome. 'What is it?'

'The enemy sentries, Rani – they're all *dead—*'

Her heart leaped. 'All of them?'

'They've all been slain with arrows, Rani – a single shaft to the heart, every one of them.'

'Lord Rama fights for us,' Binat exclaimed. 'Lord Rama himself!' His words travelled down the lines.

'The gods are with us,' Abbakka agreed, but in her mind she saw a small, club-footed man with an ancient bow, and she recalled his drunken boasts of what he said he could do – boasts she'd never believed. *Perhaps I should have*.

'Rani, we shouldn't waste this chance,' Binat said urgently. 'We should press the attack, before they realise they're vulnerable.'

It was good advice, and exactly what she planned to do. Whispered instructions were passed back through the ranks, then with guns primed and swords loose in scabbards, she led them across the fields towards the shadowy bulk of the palace. As they neared the town she saw a man lying spread-eagled, a long arrow buried in his chest. She examined the shaft, recognising the familiar fletching. Behind her, the men murmured eagerly, but she put a finger to her lips, then waved them forward.

No one challenged them.

They passed the masjid, where more corpses littered the earth. Another Portuguese guard lay nearby, also skewered by an arrow. She pulled his gun from lifeless fingers and went on. The music rising from the palace covered their stealthy movements.

*That's* my *palace, you farang matachods!*

They pulled the dead sentry at the sortie gate out of the way so Binat could open the door. As he pushed it gently inwards, she saw another corpse propped against a wall, his slack face eternally puzzling over the arrow in his heart. *Thank you, Aniket . . .* She checked the purloined musket was primed as her soldiers entered behind her.

Still no one raised the alarm.

They fanned out beneath walls devoid of living sentries and encircled the palace complex, grateful for the racket caused by the unholy music and raucous boasting laughter. The Portuguese leaders were celebrating in *her* court. Pradeep's face floated in the air before her for an instant, to be replaced by the bestial visage of the demon-thing that slew him, and she felt her rage and hatred rise again.

She shaped it into a cry, screaming, '*ATTACK——!*'

She led the way through the doors, her stolen musket blasting a hole in the chest of the first man she saw – just a boy, no, *an enemy soldier* – then she drew her pistols as her men poured past her, others joining them from the other side. The Portuguese leaped for their weapons, but they were too drunk and too slow and the first volley cut them down like a scythe through wheat. Among the bodies she spotted an admiral in all his plumed battle glory – but not so glorious now, with blood splashed vividly across his golden braid and bleached white jacket. Wounded men were writhing among the dead — until the Ullal girls who had been forced to serve the invaders in every way crawled from beneath the tables and began knifing the survivors.

Abbakka watched a musician smash his instrument over the skull of a soldier — then he stared at the broken sitar in horror.

'Surrender!' she shouted, and those of her men who spoke Portuguese took up the call: '*Renda-se!*'

For a heartbeat she thought the enemy would fight on. Guns were aimed, many trained on her. She straightened her back defiantly.

'Look at her,' she heard someone whisper. 'Our fearless queen!'

*Fearless? I can barely keep myself upright.*

But somehow she kept her face calm, and the Portuguese weapons clattered to the marble floor.

Abbakka organised another group of fighting men and pushed on into the town. More and more of her people were joining the assault as word spread, which was making coordination impossible. Local citizens were arming themselves and would come bursting in from alleys and side roads and butcher any Portuguese they found, until the remaining Europeans, bereft of leadership, started falling back to the ships.

Binat strode beside her, his face exultant. War was *easy*. 'They're retreating,' he crowed.

She missed Pradeep's tactical awareness, but forced herself to put him from her mind. She could grieve once her people were safe. 'They're retreating to their warships, where they have their heavy cannon, Binat. If we don't stop them, they will pound us from offshore, out of range of our own guns.' She lurched into a waddling jog, once again wishing she'd made an effort to get her figure back after her pregnancies. 'Pick up the pace,' she ordered.

*Where's Aniket?* she wondered, but there was no sign of her cousin. Then a distant *thump!* sent a shiver through her and cannonballs burst into the docklands before her, smashing through market stalls, wrecking them and the storage huts alongside. The scavengers, people and animals, scattered. But she could see knots of Portuguese on the wharfs, launching longboats.

'Chautas, advance!' she cried, and they struck the wharves in a ragged column. Shots flew about her, but the darkness ruined accuracy. Muzzle-flashes from a cluster of men at the end of the second wharf drew her eye and she pointed. 'There they are—'

She could just make out a huge dark shape, only fifty yards off the shore: a Portuguese man o'war, all towering masts and flapping sails. When she squinted through the darkness, she could see five more, further out, dimly lit by lamps. The moon rode the western skies as dawn approached, illuminating the shapes of the Portuguese rearguard, waiting on the wharf in serried ranks, their guns gleaming dully. Behind them, rowboats were filling fast.

She turned to Binat. 'Send any man who knows anything about gunnery to the shore batteries – *hurry*. They mustn't escape!'

As the young man pranced merrily away, she grabbed the next man, his friend Rishan, pointed her sword at the enemy rearguard and said, 'We must sweep them into the sea.'Then she cried to her men, 'Come, Chautas!'

She walked towards the arrayed muskets, and her men rushed past her, shielding her once again.

'Rani, do not tempt fate,' a familiar voice reprimanded her, and Mullah Hassan appeared at her side. He was holding his holy book, the Koran – and a curved sword.

'I didn't know Muslim holy men were also men of war,' she remarked.

'There are many examples of holy men who fight for Allah,' the mullah replied, falling into step, brandishing his holy book like evidence in a legal dispute. 'And what true man does not defend his homeland from foreign devils?'

*Devils? Has he seen something strange too?* She went to ask, but the Portuguese officer at the end of the quay opened his mouth and bellowed, '*Umo*—'

Rishan raised his sword. 'Present arms—'

'*Dois*—'

Rishan looked at her helplessly as he suddenly realised they were going to shoot second, and unable to think past the consequences.

*Fool boy!* 'FIRE!' Abbakka roared.

A staccato rattle greeted her order, as half the Ullal men reacted and the other half, listening only to Rishan, didn't – but it was enough, for many Portuguese soldiers jerked and cried out, and when Rishan shouted, 'Fire!' a second later, just as the enemy officer did, the Portuguese volley had already been broken and lacked its usual devastating punch. Only a few of her men fell, but the foreigners were left reeling.

'*Chautas,*' the Ullal men shouted, and they poured towards the enemy.

'Charge!' Rishan shouted belatedly, running to catch up with them.

A strong hand grabbed Abbakka's arm and pulled her up, hard. 'Let your men do the butchery, Abbi,' Aniket said firmly.

She strained against his grip for a moment, then relented, knowing he was right. A hundred questions were welling up in her mind, but right now there were more urgent issues. Ahead, her men were already engaged in hand-to-hand savagery, hacking desperately at the enemy. She could hear bodies hitting the water, men crying out to their gods, to their mothers, to each other.

Then the Portuguese voices fell silent as the Ullal men started cheering over the fallen.

Abbakka strode forward again, stepping over corpses, and grabbed Rishan. She pointed at the rowboats riding the swell. 'The rowboats – fire on them, before they are out of range.'

*I'm going to make them too fearful to ever return . . .*

The young nobleman pushed his men into ranks, and in moments muskets were flashing and smoke erupting. She could hear the screams of the enemy as more bodies splashed in the harbour water, while others were left slumped in their seats as their boats drifted.

'Reload – keep firing!' she ordered, as a thunderous *crump!* echoed across the bay: the cannon of her western shore battery had fired. A pair of massive splashes framed one of the nearest warships and she swore. '*Hit* the damned thing,' she shrieked, though the gunners were three hundred yards away and likely deafened by their own blast; they'd not be able to hear a word.

The closest warship, the one standing off the wharf, tacked around until it was side-on to the quay, only sixty yards away. The cannon were already run out and her words died in her throat as she realised her danger. As she opened her mouth to bawl a warning, the moment flashed in her retinas: Rishan's men, milling about on the wharf; Mullah Hassan, praying aloud; Aniket, shouting something into the din . . . and twenty-two enemy cannon, suddenly trained on them all . . .

She saw the demon-man, surely a rakshasa, aboard the ship. He doffed his plumed hat ironically, not bothering to conceal what he was from her. *My Queen*, he whispered into her mind, *I am Prahasta, and you are mine . . .*

Then he signalled with his blade, and every cannon on the starboard flank of the Portuguese warship fired: a massive broadside aimed squarely at the dock. Chain-shot scythed through her men in one devastating blast, each pair of linked cannonballs ripping through the men of Ullal and turning them to bloody pulp. Abbakka staggered as the wharf about her turned into a charnel house, shattered bodies reduced to blackened meat and brittle bones amongst the smouldering wrecked timbers of the dock. She saw Hassan's upper torso twitching, lips still muttering a prayer as he slid into oblivion. Nothing at all was visible of her beloved cousin Aniket, except for his bow and quiver, lying on the still-shaking ground where he'd been standing.

The smoke flowed over her and she choked on it as

molten fury roared through her. Her body was coated in ash and she felt like she was ablaze. She howled in defiance and felt something give inside her, something fundamental that had been holding back her fury: that which kept her human and anchored her sanity. Remembering what Aniket had told her about the power of her anger, she abandoned reason and gave in to the rage. Her voice reverberated with the roar of a tiger, even as a gust of wind cleared the fog of cannon-fire and she realised that she was the only person standing. She could almost believe that they'd deliberately missed her, leaving her alive and alone . . .

*You will rue that* . . . The air about her crackled and she felt as if the crushing eyes of the gods were on her. She wondered what she looked like to the Portuguese gunners – she was clearly visible through their gun-ports; they must be staring, disbelieving. She focused her rage on the demon, the rakshasa, Prahasta, as he blanched. She felt omnipotent. Aniket's bow flew to her hands and words she'd been taught but never learned snarled from her blackened lips: '*Agni, bless this shaft!*'

Without pausing, she shot the arrow, and it flew true.

The shaft punched through the six-inch timbers of the warship as if they were paper and buried itself in a powder keg. For an instant, no one moved.

Prahasta raised his blade . . . the line of marines on board aimed their muskets . . .

Then the ship burst apart from within, the concussion rolling over her in waves as wood and metal and men were torn asunder and tossed above the maelstrom of the waters before cascading into the churning white waters of the bay.

She staggered again at the blow, but drew another arrow and fired at the next closest ship. It too exploded, and her own people cried out in terror as debris rained down and smoke rolled over the waters. The rowboats heaved to and desperate Portuguese started diving into the ocean, trying to swim for safety – but those of her men still standing opened fire, or waded out where the water was shallower to hack down the foreigners as they struggled ashore.

Suddenly water splashed over her face and she gaped. One moment she was burning with fury, with *potency*, an awesome rage, and just as suddenly, it was gone.

Losing it felt like a kind of death.

Aniket was standing before her, his hands dripping wet.

'Why did you do that?' she spluttered.

'You shouldn't go too far down that path, Abbi. It's too hard to come back.'

Part of her wanted to strike him, to regain that power and might again – then she caught sight of the sickening gore surrounding her and began shaking. Now she understood. 'Then I suppose I must thank you.' She could not quite keep the regret from her voice.

Aniket clapped her shoulder. 'It's too much to sustain for long, Abbi. Anyway, we've won.' He pointed at the remaining warships. 'They're sailing away, without most of their men. We've won.'

She remembered Prahasta with a shudder. 'And that *thing* – is it dead?'

He gave her a troubled look. 'For now,' he replied enigmatically.

'What did I do?' she whispered. 'What was that arrow?'

'The agneyastra, and as fine a one as I've seen,' he replied. 'I knew you could do it, given the right circumstances. Your legend will grow, Cousin: the Fearless Queen.' His voice held both pride and regret. 'But I counsel you to avoid that dark power. It is very perilous.'

She thought of all she might achieve, turning her hatred into power like that. 'Can anyone do that? Become so enraged that they can do the impossible?'

'No, Abbi. In all my lives, I have seen it only once. In you.'

*In all his lives . . .*

Suddenly she didn't want to talk about this any more. She wanted to walk away and grieve. She embraced him quickly, then staggered through the cheering crowds, seeking clean water to wash this all away . . .

# CHAPTER NINE

# NEW MEMORIES

*Mumbai, late December 2010*

Deepika jerked awake, her hands flying to her face as cold water splashed over her and she coughed. She was stunned to see no ash, no blood; in her ears she could still hear the echoes from the Portuguese cannon-fire, but here she was surrounded only by the silence of Uma's luxurious apartment in Nariman Point. Her senses reeled in utter confusion, and then Pradeep – no, *Tanvir* – grabbed her and held her firmly until her limbs stopped jerking.

'Deepika,' he was saying, 'Deepika, it's okay. You're back.'

She seized her heart-stone and held it, feeling that tiny pulse within. When she looked at Tanvir, all her new memories of Abbakka and Pradeep washed through her, and for an instant she almost fell into all the habits of that life, of leaning on this solid man to whom she was bound, for all she didn't love him. She was about to raise her face to his, *almost* . . . and for a second she saw a painful kind of hope kindle in his face.

Instead she rolled onto her side and sat up, re-establishing distance. Uma was still lying on her back, emotions and expressions sweeping across her face at bewildering speed. Her lips twitched; a constant stream of words were issuing incomprehensibly from her lips.

*She's speaking Kannada, the tongue of Karnataka*, Deepika realised. *We must all have been.* 'How long . . . ?'

Tanvir indicated the clock on the wall. 'Three hours . . . But only two for me,' he added. 'I fell out after two hours, after—' His voice choked. 'After that thing – a rakshasa? – killed me. This is too strange.' He rubbed his face, visibly putting aside the memory of the death of his past self. 'So I've been keeping an eye on things. But I didn't like the way you were talking and moving just then; I was worried – I thought it best to wake you.'

'Are you all right?'

'Physically I'm fine, now I'm over the shock – but how can we trust *anything* after going through that? How can we trust walls to be solid, or time to pass?' He stared at her. 'How do you stand it?'

'You just do. Tanvir, I'm sorry I put you through that. I don't think Ras knew that in that life, you and I were . . .' She, stopped, gulped and whispered, 'We were lovers. I'm sure she just thought your presence would make it more likely that I could trace those memories. I wish you hadn't had to go through that.'

Tanvir's face was sad, but showed no regret. 'I don't. I've always believed that you shouldn't flinch from something just because it might hurt. I still believe that, even now. You can trust me, Deepika. I will see you safe, and I will see you married to Amanjit, no matter the danger. Maybe I'll even get used to the weirdness along the way?'

She had to fight hard not to hold him close, to kiss that dependable, faithful face.

'So,' he asked, 'did you learn what you needed to?'

She thought back to that moment of transported fury, when all the world had been mutable, that fleeting instant when she had been filled with a rage so enrapturing that creation itself seemed fragile and she had been capable of absolutely *anything*.

'Yes. Yes, I did.' *I just pray it doesn't take so much loss for me to get to reach it again.*

Uma coughed and rolled over, moaning, her hands flying to her throat. She convulsed and then slowly calmed as Tanvir held her. When she looked at them, tears streaming down her face, she spluttered indignantly, 'The bastards cut my throat!' She caught her breath, then shuddered. 'They caught me, and . . .' She huddled over. 'I can't talk about it . . .'

They went to their separate beds frightened and exhausted. Deepika took a long time to fall asleep, and when she did, she dreamed of faces from other times. When she woke it was nearly eleven, and the smell of cooking came seeping under the door. Her stomach rumbled. Ten minutes later she was at the dining room table with her two companions, wolfing down a freshly made omelette.

'I'm going to write a biography of both of my selves – Uma and Anupa,' Uma commented glumly. 'I'm going to call it "Gender Confusion Through Time". Can you believe

it? I have this whole life as this Anupa woman – I'm a prin-
cess, I could choose any man I want . . . and guess what? I'm
a *lesbian*! This silly twit Anupa is surrounded by gorgeous
manly men, and all she – *I* – want to do is fool with the
maids? Pah!'

Tanvir winked at Deepika. 'So you were homosexual in
that life too, Uma . . . that's almost funny.'

'Am I laughing?' Uma whined. 'Being homosexual isn't
funny, big boy. It's just the way I am . . . and all the time, it
seems.' She wolfed down a sausage, then jabbed a fork at
Deepika. 'So, was that horrible experience worth it for you,
girlfriend?'

'Yes, certainly. I think what Ras wanted me to experience
was that moment when I set fire to the Portuguese ships. I
guess she thinks I'll need to know that in this life.'

'If it means you can burn the balls off that Majid Khan
creep, then it was worth it!' Uma glowered. 'Can you do it
again?'

'I think so – but it looks like I have to be in a state of
extreme distress and anger to trigger it.' Deepika looked at
Tanvir. 'I really hope I never have to be in that state again,
not ever.'

Tanvir flinched. 'I hope so too.'

'Amen,' Uma agreed. 'So, what's the plan?'

'I don't know. Until the four of us—'

'There are six of us,' Uma interrupted. 'Tanvir and I are
part of this too; that's very clear.'

'Especially after that dream,' Tanvir agreed. 'We saw a
rakshasa, Deepika: an actual demon . . . and I don't even
believe in such things.' He was still visibly realigning his

worldview. 'How could we not be with you after seeing such things?'

'I need to talk to the others before I can fully let you in on everything,' Deepika warned. 'So, anyway, Uma: what happened next? Tanvir woke me just after we sank those warships.'

Uma pulled a face. 'We lost in the end. The Portuguese come back in force a couple of years later. They killed the Zamorin and imprisoned you to await execution. You and that Aniket – your cousin? – got shot dead trying a suicidal prison-break. I got to be queen for ten years. I even got married—'

'So you did get a guy after all,' Tanvir teased.

'Huh! I – er, Anupa, I mean, didn't enjoy it,' Uma grumbled. 'She never even had a baby. Then they got her too. If I ever meet a guy from Portugal I'm going to chop his—'

'Okay, we get the picture,' Deepika interrupted. 'So I guess we're stuck with each other for a while then. We're not supposed to rendezvous with the others until March.'

They contemplated two months in the apartment together in silence for a while. 'I've got *Scrabble*,' Uma offered glumly. 'And *Monopoly* too. We're going to have *so much* fun.'

'Ras – I mean, Padma?' Deepika whispered down the phone.

'Hi, Darya – are you okay? Did it work?'

'Yeah. If that bastard Majid comes here I'm going to fry his butt.'

Rasita chuckled. 'That's what A—Shastri says too. He's out, sorry. He gets restless without you.'

'Tell him I love him.'

'He knows.'

'Tell him anyway. Tell him all the time.'

'Okay. Too much lovey-dovey!' They giggled together.

'Who were you, in Ullal?' Deepika asked finally.

Ras' voice was sad. 'I was your other daughter, the sickly one. My name was Abbakka, but you all called me Tashi. I died the following year. Aram was Aniket, of course. I don't know what happened to him, but I guess R— I mean, that *bastard* got him in the end. He always does.'

Deepika contemplated this new information in silence. Their relationships kept getting more complicated. Eventually she voiced the question she'd really rung to ask. 'Hey, Padma, what's it like without your heart-stone?'

'I don't know. What's it like to have one?'

'It makes me feel strong. Healthy. Like I can endure anything.'

'Then not having one is the opposite of that. I've never lived long in my own past lives, and from what I now know of Gauran's lives, well, they weren't long either – *that bastard* usually saw to that.'

Deepika swallowed. 'I'd been wondering if I should hide mine, to make things harder for him.'

Ras didn't hesitate. 'No, keep it on you, sister. Keep it with you, always.'

# CHAPTER TEN

# WELCOME TO LANKA

*Mumbai, January 2011*

Ravindra, as Majid Khan, walked out of the police station in Mumbai leaving the mutilated bodies of the Internal Investigations detectives behind him, and then walked out of reality.

It wasn't a conscious decision. The back streets of the midnight city had closed about him, wrapping him in anonymity. The alleys were ageless, the old British Raj façades like mausolea, uncannily lit by garish neon signs. The old and the new pressed up against each other. He was just another lonely, hunched figure scurrying through filthy streets, where only the desperate went. Men slouched against walls as he passed, but none tried to stop him; something about him didn't *smell* right. The smoky air clung to him, following him in eerie swirls that you could almost imagine were women, faithfully dogging his heels. He noticed them with no surprise.

And then the streets *changed* . . .

It was subtle at first, something in the play of light on the stones of the buildings: dirty, decaying walls brightened as if peeling off strips of paint restored them. The people were replaced by others, anachronistically garbed: English red-coats on patrol, men in top hats and women in bustles and dainty hats stepping into horse-drawn carriages, many of them Indian, while the poor now wore rags, not jeans and T-shirts. Even his jaded eyes turned round with wonder.

*Where am I?*

Then it was elephants and handcarts and men like strutting peacocks being borne in palanquins by burly slaves. He felt the nervous fear of his remaining queens – only three now, after the destruction of the two heart-stones back at Bakli's mansion, but their purpose was served. The only heart-stones that mattered now were Darya's and Padma's. The former was in Deepika Choudhary's hands, but Padma's had been lost for centuries.

A palanquin halted before him and the man leading it bowed low. 'Welcome, Lord,' the stranger said. His eyes were those of a deer, big and amber, but there was something feline about his face – and his shadow in the torchlight bore little resemblance to a man, being hunched, with antlers, backward knee joints and folded wings. 'Welcome and thrice-welcome,' said the demon in man-shape. 'Are you ready to come home?'

Even as the being spoke, Ravindra felt the thrill of memories re-opening. Somehow, he *knew* this creature. Behind him, his three remaining queens formed in the mist, barely coloured watery images painted on to the mist. Halika stared at her hands and exhaled with gloating surprise.

Behind her, Jyoti and Aruna sighed in pleasure. Meena and Rakhi had perished for ever at Shiv Bakli's manor, their husk-souls absorbed when their heart-stones disappeared. When one of the ghost queens was destroyed, her soul should have entered the strongest living kindred being present: so Rasita or Deepika, then. He wondered what effect that might be having on those girls.

But those were thoughts to ponder at leisure; for now, he had mysteries enough. Somehow, he was clothed in princely robes. He felt like he was slowly being immersed in deep waters.

The faces of the burly bearers who were lowering the palanquin were animal-like, with vestigial horns, slitted eyes and fur, their shoulders were taut with slabs of muscle. They bowed to the ground, reverence and fear lighting their faces.

'Hail,' they murmured, 'hail!'

In all his long existence, in all of the lives he had worn wrapped in other men's bodies, he'd never seen such a thing – and yet it was strangely familiar. 'Who are you?' he asked. 'What's happening?'

The antlered man bowed. 'My Lord, I will answer all of your questions as we travel. Please, take your seat – we have far to go.'

He got into the palanquin and the three ghost-queens followed. The conveyance was larger inside than out, and his shadowy queens became more solid than they had been in all the centuries since Mandore. They preened, stroking the jewellery that had formed at their throats and wrists, purring with pleasure. 'Will we live again?' Halika murmured in his ear. 'Will we be whole at last?'

He couldn't answer that.

As the antlered man sat opposite him, his presence dropped little memories into his mind. 'You are my Uncle Maricha,' he exclaimed, studying the man with the twisted shadow.

'Yes, Lord, yes. I have waited all these long years – we all have – searching, looking and waiting for you, to take you home.'

'Home? Where's that?'

Maricha smiled. 'Home is Lanka.'

Ravindra couldn't tell how long they journeyed – it might have been days, or weeks, or only hours. The stars and the moon and the sun swirled overhead like the blades of a slowly spinning fan; day and night swapped places in the sky. Food came and he ate. He sipped wine. The dead queens sniffed and stroked the food impotently, sighing with longing, until Maricha brought them a chalice of blood, which they slurped greedily.

Outside, the landscape changed from coastal palms to hinterland farms, to jungle to desert, and back, from hills to open empty plains. Directions changed, the sun at times rising on the right or the left, in front or behind – and it wasn't the normal sun, either, but a golden chariot pulled by eight mighty horses, while eight shining stags pulled a chariot of silver, which was the moon.

Finally, they disembarked at a beach where a barge awaited them, basking in moonlight. More of the beast-men appeared, each bowing low as they stepped onto the sand. He stretched and looked around, seeing an island across the shimmering waters. Maricha knelt before him, offering a crown in one outstretched hand and a sword in the other. He took the crown first; it was heavy, gold-encrusted iron, surmounted with Shiva's Third Eye. He placed it on his head and the beast-men — asuras, he suddenly recalled — murmured hungrily.

'Your sword, my king,' Maricha proffered. '*Chandrahas*, the Moon-blade. Take it, first of all things you will take back.'

He took the naked blade from the kneeling demon and held it aloft in the light of the moon, admiring the pearly sheen of the curved steel, the glittering ice of the edge. He ran his finger along it and drew blood, which he offered to Halika, kneeling beside him. She licked it thirstily, gazing up at him with lustful worship in her eyes. He swirled the blade, making it sing, and no sooner had he found himself wishing he had a sheath, than one appeared at his belt. He slid Chandrahas into it, chuckling softly. The few remaining shreds of his life as Majid Khan — all the drugs and girls and gangsters and broken oaths — faded. He was becoming Ravindra again . . . or *someone else*.

He stepped onto the barge, his three queens trailing behind him, and left his other lives behind.

They floated to an island that flickered between a place of lush green, with paved roads and tall palaces, to a desolate grey wasteland of ruins. There was a multitude awaiting him on shore: more asuras, all of them caught somewhere between human and monster. The males were clad in warrior finery, the women in shimmering, diaphanous gowns. Their grotesque faces were strangely alluring. They led him down boulevards lined with cheering demons: his subjects, welcoming him home. His throne-room was a rich hall draped in bright silks, with murals etched into the marble. It was thronged with people.

He offered his arm to his senior queen, and Halika ascended to the smaller throne set beside and slightly below his. Her sister-queens sat at her knees. Her eyes were glowing as she took it all in.

Maricha knelt before him and the most senior of the asuras closed in: the noble caste known as rakshasa. He found he knew their names – but some he would have expected were missing. 'Where are my sons?' he asked, for once he'd had sons, and they'd been beings like these.

'They're abroad in the world, Lord, seeking you. They will come when you call them, Lord.'

'Then have I somehow succeeded?' he asked, puzzled. 'Am I restored?'

'Not yet,' Maricha answered. 'Aram Dhoop still lives. Madan Shastri still lives. Queen Darya and Queen Padma are still to be sacrificed. But the lives entangled in your own grow closer to those they once lived, as they remember more and more, and as all of your lives began to follow the set path, so we have at last been able to find you. The swayamvara was the clue: we monitored it, and so we found you. We have been watching and waiting for you for so long.'

'Then all those past lives when I have annihilated Aram Dhoop and his coterie . . . Was I wrong to do so?'

'You are king, Lord. To be king is to never be wrong. What you do defines what is right.' Maricha peered up at him, choosing his words. 'In this life, the actions of you and your enemies are more closely mirroring the true history than ever before. That is unlocking doors for all of us, for your enemies and for you. The stakes are higher in this life, Lord. The rewards and the perils are greater.'

'The perils . . . Have Aram Dhoop and his people become a danger to me?'

'They will never be mightier than you, Lord, but they are not without threat. They too learn. I have felt it. We began to realise just who the boy Vikram was during that amusing show. We were preparing to strike when one of our operatives, a member of the Mumbai gang, realised that you were resident in Shiv Bakli – we were overjoyed at finding you after so long.'

'How long?'

Maricha didn't quite meet his eye. 'It was Mandore, Lord. And that rakshasa didn't share that knowledge; we found out much later.'

Ravindra thought for a moment. So there were factions among his servants . . . which meant he could not trust them implicitly. He stored that thought carefully, alongside the other implication: that Mandore hadn't been the beginning of this struggle. But memories of the time before refused to come.

'Then we must strike soon,' he said. 'Find this Vikram and his associates.'

The throng gathered beneath him shifted, murmuring hungrily. Teeth bared and claws unfurled at the thought of violence.

Maricha growled for silence. 'We are seeking them, Lord, but as yet they remain hidden.'

'The *Ramayana* is the key. We must learn from it and use it. But we must not fail, not this time.'

Maricha shuddered. 'The story is telling us,' he answered cryptically.

'Where is my sister?' Ravindra asked, scanning the court. 'Where is Surpanakha?'

'She is shadowing our enemies, Lord. She is our link, and the means to bring them down.'

'Then let us begin.'

A shiver of anticipation rippled through his court and they all crowded closer, promising their allegiance, for ever. 'Yes, Lord, let it all begin!'

# CHAPTER ELEVEN

## BOYFRIEND

*Varanasi, Uttar Pradesh, January 2011*

'Hey, Vickers! How're you doin'?'

Vikram started and peered up at Sue Parker as she puffed up the stairs of the German Bakery and sat down heavily beside him. 'Ah, hi,' he responded lamely, closing his notebook.

'Aw, c'mon, gimme a look. You're always scribbling something, boyfriend.' She tugged at the notebook insistently. 'C'mon—'

'It's private, and I'm not your boyfriend,' he told her, even though she called every male she knew 'boyfriend'. They'd been bumping into each other regularly here and he'd been unable to avoid her banter. He kept the notebook out of her hand. 'I'm working on a poem.'

'Hey, cool! A love poem for your fiancée? Let me look, okay?'

He'd told Sue he was engaged, to try and discourage her attention, but it didn't appear to be working.

By late afternoon, the heat was beginning to fade from the ancient stone ghats; in midwinter the cold of the nights took hours to weaken its grip, only warming into a gentle heat when the sun had burned off the river-mist. Tourists — mostly Indian, but also many Westerners escaping the snows of the European and North American winters — thronged to the place. Vikram kept meaning to leave, just for a change of scene, but somehow he'd not yet gone. He pretended to himself he didn't know why, but of course he did; he just didn't want to think about it. He wrote about it in his notebook, as a substitute for talking about how he felt.

'You wanna come out with us tonight?' Sue asked. 'We're going to this new bar behind Tulsi Ghat.'

'I don't think so.'

'Aw, c'mon Vickers — it'll be fun.'

*No, it won't. It'll be torment.* 'Sue, your boyfriend despises me, your friends think I'm trying to steal you and, let's face it, the bouncers won't let me in anyway.'

'They would if you made an effort to dress better,' she chided. 'I can stand you a new shirt, Vickers — my credit ain't maxed out yet.'

'Thanks, but no,' he said firmly. *The truth is, I'm afraid of dancing with you, Kamla, because I remember earlier dances and Ras is far away and I've never really talked to her, but I know you so well . . .*

Sue was undeterred. 'The guys're all moving on soon, but I'm sticking round. I like it here.' Her eyes added, *You're here.* 'They're all going down south, to the beaches round Goa.'

'It's nice there, even in winter,' Vikram agreed. 'The sea is warm — you can swim all day. Palm trees and cocktails. My dad used to take us there on holiday.'

'Yeah, well, it could be nice.' She laid a hand on his arm. 'You could join us.'

'Leaving aside the fact that *I'm* engaged, aren't *you* forgetting Frankie?'

'He's just someone to get me through the night while I'm on vacation, not some long-term thing,' she replied. 'I won't miss him.' She grinned slyly. 'Anyway, so what if you're engaged? You ain't married yet — and your wife'll appreciate you knowing what you're doing in the sack.'

*Americans! And anyway, I've fifteen previous lives of love's lessons . . . many of them learned from you, Kamla.* He schooled his face into amused neutrality. 'We can learn together, she and I.'

'Yeah, yeah. You Indian guys: you all talk about true love and waiting till you're married, but the number of guys who hit on me in bars — and mind, Vickers, I'm talking as many married ones as single; hell, if I wanted to, I could— Well, anyway, my point is, you're all such hypocrites. You all think Western girls are yours for the asking.'

'All your movies make it look that way,' Vikram countered. 'Don't blame us.'

'You just can't handle women as equals. You want prim little maidens who don't know anything and can't threaten your male-dominated world.'

'That's not true: women are very influential in Indian society. Our Parliament even mandates thirty-three per cent female members, which is more than the US does. You're just—'

'Huh — you're *decades* behind the West, kid. Parliament quotas? *Hah*. Female emancipation, that's what I'm talkin' about: the freedom to be who you wanna be, control over who you hang with, when and where, not just conforming to some male fantasy of domestic goddesses.' She nudged his shoulder. 'You guys don't want competition so you rig it all to suit yourselves.'

'Where do you get your ideas from?' he grumped. 'Women's magazines?'

'No, from all over: newspapers, watching people, even Indian girls I know — you gotta face it, Vickers, Indian women just don't have the same freedoms as in the West. You may not see it, but I'm part of both cultures and I *know*. It's tougher for girls here: you gotta do the marriage-and-children thing, obey the husband, look after the house. And most of the time you can't even choose your own man — and if you do, you run the risk of some psycho father or uncle or brother splashing acid in your face or even knifing you because you've upset their precious pride.' She was getting really angry now. '*Honour* killings? There's no fucking honour in that, boyfriend. Women who try to forge their own lives have to fight *way* harder here — and you don't even see it.' She waggled a finger at him as if it were all his fault.

*In my last life, most women weren't even educated.* He might not like it, but some traditions were best abandoned — even in Britain there'd been the occasional acid attack or murder of an unsuitable partner. But before he could acknowledge her point, Sue had already moved on.

'Anyway, Vickers, I came to invite you on a date, not pick a fight.'

'You go with Frankie. I'll catch it some other time.'

She put on a crestfallen face. 'I knew you'd chicken out. Ah well. Persistence pays off, that's what my dad always says. I'll get you on the dance floor yet, my man, you'll see.' She stood up, her blue eyes already twinkling again. She was irrepressible, her cheery optimism always overriding disappointment. 'See ya round, Vickers!'

He watched her go, admiring the graceful way she moved – *just like Kamla used to* – then angrily pushed those thoughts away. He flipped open his notebook to a page entitled *Surpanakha*, filled with lines of notes from the *Ramayana*. On the next page he'd listed all the facts he had gleaned about Sue Parker: none of them were linked to the *Ramayana*, at least that he could see, and he'd spent days puzzling over it. She appeared to have no malice in her. She upset his equilibrium, but he liked her, enjoyed her company. He knew he was playing with fire, but he needed the human contact.

*I should have talked more to Ras*, he chided himself. *I should have known! That's why I feel so vulnerable to Sue. Here she is, confusing my heart, challenging my love for Rasita. She could lead Ravindra to us if I don't take care. She's dangerous.*

*I should just leave Varanasi. I don't have to be here . . .*

He sighed and turned to another page where he'd written down everything he could glean from the *Ramayana* about the death of King Dasaratha, Rama's father. *That's where I should be: with my father, trying to prevent his death*. But the police were almost certainly watching Dinesh and Kiran and if he were spotted, he could end up killing innocent cops just to escape. He couldn't risk it. All he could do was pray Dinesh would be all right.

He stared at his phone. *I need to hear a friendly voice — one that isn't Sue Parker's.* He stood slowly and headed back to his tiny room for the night.

'Padma?'

'Aram? Hi! I wasn't expecting you to call tonight.' Ras sounded distracted.

'Just wanted to hear a friendly voice.' *No, I needed to hear your voice.*

'Sure. What's happening?'

'Nothing much. Keeping my head down. Missing you all. What about you?'

He heard her bedclothes rustle. 'Remembering. Thinking. You know what it's like.'

He did: past lives kept intruding on thoughts, changing what you were thinking, changing who you were. 'I wish we'd talked more before I went away to Mumbai,' he admitted.

'Yeah, but I was pretty sick — and I wouldn't have understood anyway, not the way I do now. You know, you weren't always good to me — well, to Gauran, and all her other lives.'

'I did try,' he whispered, 'but you know, sometimes she was *impossible* — she'd do all these crazy things. Her mood would change by the minute. She drove me insane too, sometimes.'

Ras was silent a long time. 'I guess. My memories are so confused. To me, at the time, everything I did was rational. Even my oddest behaviour had a reason, however faulty the thinking. But I only raised it because I wanted to say that I forgive you.'

'Forgive me for what?'

She snorted. 'Typical male: doesn't think he's ever wrong! I forgive you for not understanding. For having other wives. For not healing me. For not loving me when I needed you.'

He felt a lump of sorrow clog up his throat.

'I hope you forgive me too.'

'What for?' he managed.

'For not being there – for being unfaithful in some of my lives. For not recognising you in any of the lives we shared, and not believing you when you tried to explain. For getting you killed with my ignorance. I'm sorry, Aram. I'm so very sorry.'

He bit back tears. 'I forgive you too, Padma,' he whispered.

They sat hundreds of miles apart and listened to each other breathe. At last Ras spoke. 'Three minutes is up, Aram. I have to go. But thank you for calling.'

He choked back tears and tried to say that three minutes was only a guess for how long any police agency, if they existed at all, might take to trace the call – it was a made-up time, just something that sounded right from the spy thrillers he used to read back in England.

But the line had already gone dead.

Sue found him in a bar, a few days later. 'Hey, Vickers!' She looked cheery, happy even, and gave him a hug, pecked his cheeks. 'Y'know, I love how everyone does "hello" here with a kiss on both cheeks and a big hug! We're so stand-offish in the West. We need to lighten up.' She looked at his empty beer glass. 'Another?'

He wavered then shrugged. 'Why not?' He'd come in an hour ago, alone and bored, and no one had spoken to him.

Everyone was always caught up in their own groups —
Indians often socialised in packs: family and friends all
mixed, chaperoning and escorting each other. Loners were
exiled, left out in the cold.

'My shout,' he added, waving a hand to a barman. 'Two
more Kingfishers, please.'

'Why, thank you, kind sir.' Sue settled in beside him in
the booth, trapping him against the wall. 'Ain't seen you for
days. Whatcha been up to?'

'Not much.' *Waiting, brooding. Hiding from the police. Hiding
from you. Have I mentioned that I'm a wanted criminal?* 'Just
hanging around, really.' *Mostly I'm just hiding out and praying
my father doesn't die.* His nightly dreams were beginning to
worry him. They were filled with visions of enemies gathering, and sometimes he even saw Ravindra himself, ruling
some ghastly demonic court.

They clinked glasses and he wished for a second he could
sink into her Kamla-arms and forget all his fears.

'So, how's that thesis on Surpanakha going?' she asked,
momentarily chilling him — but there was no cunning in her
eyes, just amiable curiosity. She clearly believed he was a
research student. 'I've been reading it — the *Ramayana*, I
mean. What a crazy story! Reckon there's any fact to it? Like
the legends of Troy?'

That was the *last* thing he wanted to talk about. 'Who
knows?' he said shortly. 'So, how are you?'

'I'm fine. Frankie and the guys are all in Goa. He keeps
texting me to go there.'

'But you're still here.'

'Yeah, well, I was kinda over Frankie anyway. He was just

a fling.' She looked at him. 'I know what you're thinking: "bad girl" – but hey, no harm done, no regrets. It was just a bit of fun.'

Vikram thought about the layers of cynicism that had accrued as a result of all his failed relationships in past lives and wondered about 'no harm done', but he didn't feel like a fight, not when he finally had some company, even if it was Kamla . . . *or Surpanakha*.

'So what are your plans, then?'

'Well, I've got months to go before I have to get back to reality, and a list of cities I really wanna see – I was thinking of working my way across Uttar Pradesh and into south Rajasthan. There are so many cool places: Khajuraho, Orchha, Lucknow, Kannauj – then Udaipur, Pushkar . . .' She poked at him. 'Wanna show me around? Come on – we don't have to share a room. We can be separate, be all chaste and innocent if that makes you happier. I just like hanging with you. It'd be fun!'

*I could do it and Ras needn't even know*. He almost agreed – but he paused and slowly shook his head. *I'm not that strong*, he told himself, *not when this is Kamla, who owns a part of my heart*.

'Sorry,' he said.

She sighed. 'Aw, Vickers, you're one tough nut to crack.'

His mobile chimed: a text from Amanjit. He thumbed it open, read it and felt his heart break in two.

### Brother, call me. It's your father.

*It's happened.*

After he'd spoken to Amanjit and confirmed his worst fears, Sue held him as he cried.

# CHAPTER TWELVE

# HEADLINES

*Chandni Chowk, Old Delhi, January 2011*

Amanjit and Ras felt like they had lost a father too, although they'd barely had a chance to get to know Dinesh Khandavani. The Bajaj family had been under the increasingly vicious rule of their Uncle Charanpreet when Dinesh came into their lives: he'd not only seen off their terrifying uncle with dignity and courage, but won their mother's heart with his quiet, honest charm. He had seen Bishin, Amanjit and Rasita as adults from the start, neither overly familiar with them, nor walking around them on eggshells. He had treated them with respect, and earned it in return. They had begun to love him as their mother did. And now he was gone.

Ras was glad Amanjit and Vikram had risked a long conversation after the warning text — Vikram was understandably stricken, and he couldn't even say goodbye to the father he adored. She wished he was here so she could comfort him. Her dreams all revolved around him now, but there was always something coming between them, keeping them apart.

The newspapers were full of headlines that disgusted them.

VIKRAM'S FATHER IN SUICIDE SHOCK!
COME HOME, VIKRAM, IF YOU LOVED
YOUR FATHER!
FUGITIVE VIKRAM KILLS HIS FATHER!

They were all lies: Dinesh had died of a heart attack, sharp and simple, and the coroner's report would reveal the truth in due course. The will would be read in Mumbai, after the funeral in Varanasi; Dinesh's dying wish was to be cremated there and have his ashes scattered on the sacred river.

'Can't we go to the funeral?' Ras pleaded with Amanjit yet again, but he shook his head firmly.

'You know we can't. It's just too dangerous,' her brother replied, rubbing his shiny shaven skull and scowling. 'Stop asking, Ras – I want to go as much as you do, but it would just be stupid.'

'Mum must be feeling awful – widowed twice? It's not fair. Bishin needs our support – can't we just go home for a quick visit?' she begged. 'We can be secret – the police would never know.'

'No, Rasita.' Amanjit was trying not to let his exasperation show. 'No, that's exactly what they'll expect. If home wasn't bugged and crawling with cops before, it will be now. And Ravindra will expect it too: he'll have watchers – the dead queens, or worse.'

'You don't think Ravindra killed Dinesh, do you?'

'I'm trying not to think so. The coroner says heart attack – we have to believe that.' Then he hung his head and admitted, 'But we don't know what Ravindra is capable of.'

# CHAPTER THIRTEEN

# THE BURNING GHATS

*Varanasi, Uttar Pradesh, February 2011*

*Today they burn my father.*

It had been just a week since Amanjit's text, but it felt like a year. Dawn was not far off; in a few hours, his half-brother Lalit would lead his father's funeral procession to the burning place at Manikarnika Ghat, here in Varanasi.

He'd seen the newspapers and was still seething over the cruel headlines – and he'd also seen the influx of men of a certain look, all well built, casually dressed, snooping about aimlessly: undercover cops, without a doubt, looking for him. He'd been lying low.

He'd told Sue only that his father had died and that he had to go away; he'd been avoiding her since that night, afraid of the barriers he'd burned in the aftermath of that awful news. He'd barely left his room, and every disturbance in the corridors outside had him reaching for his bow.

*I should be there. I should be bearing you, Dad, and setting the flame to your body.* Instead, Lalit would fulfil that duty.

Tanita's son was only fourteen, a shy, scared boy Vikram hardly knew any more. That train of thought led him back to the *Ramayana*, in which Rama's younger brother remained loyal to Rama, despite the treachery of his mother. Which led to uglier thoughts . . . did his former stepmother Tanita have a role in Dinesh's death?

The inquest said no: Fatal Coronary Arrest, apparently. Vikram wasn't sure he believed that, but there was nothing he could do just now. His immediate priority was perhaps foolish, but necessary: somehow he had to find a way to attend his father's funeral.

A few days ago, he'd started collecting ash from burnt-out fires in the darkened alleys. This morning, as the city stirred, he was turning the ash into a paste. He disrobed and knotted an orange cloth around his loins, then pulled his lank hair up into a topknot. He bent over the bucket of grey-black gloop, shuddered, then shook away his distaste and began to coat his body.

His plan was simple: the Manikarnika, the burning ghat, was full of itinerant holy men, sadhus and ash-streaked Doms, the men whose role it was to tend the sacred fires from which all cremations were lit. He would cover himself in ash and mingle, find a vantage point so he could bid farewell to his father, in secret but close. If it was fated that he was spotted, then what would be, would be. As disguises went, it wasn't perfect, but it would have to do.

He daubed the paste over his chest and back, his arms and legs, and especially over his face and through his hair. It dried quickly, scabbing into itchy, flaking pieces. He felt frozen by the predawn chill, but he steeled himself. This had to work.

Picking up the walking stick he had purchased from an eld-
erly man in the market, he turned go. He caught sight of
himself in the cracked mirror on the wall as he opened the
door – and stopped dead, staring.

The ash on his skin had turned a deep blue.

He stood there for a long moment and then bowed his
head in acceptance. He put down the walking stick and
strung his bow instead. Apparently the plan had changed.
This morning, he would be Rama.

In his new guise, he strode through the now-familiar
backstreets of Varanasi, walking as if he belonged but avoiding the main roads in favour of the quieter alleys. The
ordinary people stared, many pulling amused faces, but
others made reverential gestures. He passed at least two
police-watchers – who raised eyebrows and peered, then
let him through. After all, devotees dressed as gods were
not uncommon in this tourist town.

After that, it was easy. He reached the burning ghat, mingling with worshippers and mourners for other funerals.
Some touched him for luck, muttering quick prayers as if he
were the god himself. He climbed to a spot on the roof of
the shrine to Shiva, smiling at the religious irony of that. As
the sun rose, it found him sitting cross-legged above the
main processional, with a clear view of the river, the shrine
and the cremation ground.

Dawn on the Ganges was the usual mêlée of devotees
immersing themselves and paddle-boats taking tourists and
hippies out on the waters to release votive candles on leaf-
boats, a sea of light in the darkness that grew tones and
shades of colour as the sun kissed the skies to blushing pink.

It spread south and east of his vantage point as he gazed out across the river, thinking of his father. They'd spent a lot of time together and there'd been plenty of bad years between marriages and business failures, but he'd never seen Dinesh lose his temper, or his dignity. His sense of humour, his kindness, his generosity, had always set him apart. No wonder Amanjit and Rasita's mum had fallen in love with him, for all he was a small and unremarkable-looking man . . .

*Father, I am many things, with my roots set deep in past lives and tragedies, but the best parts of me come from you. I've never met a better man, and I'll never stop missing you.*

The burning ghats were a well-trodden piece of muddy foreshore where the waters of holy Ganga lapped the edges. A silvery-black stream of ashy mud swirled into the river. Stacks of wood were piled there, ready for the bodies. The other ghats stretched to left and right, hunched beneath the palaces and temples, facing the rising sun.

Vikram studied both the people around him and the rooftops overlooking the ghats: he'd already spotted two snipers setting up their kit a hundred yards or so above him. One saw him watching and gave an ironic wave: the sharpshooter to the archer.

*Do they really think I'm that dangerous?* Then he thought, *To them I'm the man who murdered Sunita Ashoka and was cutting deals with Shiv Bakli. They truly think I'm a murderer . . .*

The ghat was now packed with journalists and camera crews jostling for position amidst the mourners, while security men tried to create a channel for the funeral processions – so much for tradition, which forbade cameras here; apparently that could be ignored when it came to the funeral of the father of one of India's Most Wanted. It felt cruelly disrespectful of the other mourners — his father was one of dozens of cremations today; devotees were brought here from all over India to give back their bodies to the great river and speed their soul's journey onwards. How did those families feel to have this circus going on around them?

A child looked up at Vikram and pointed and in seconds dozens of cameras had turned his way. He must make a good shot: the devotee, clad as his patron deity, high above the cremation. He listened hard for signs that his disguise had been penetrated, but so far, so good.

The sun rose, turning everything golden along the river, gilded by the stream of devotional candles drifting past. He heard the cameramen stir and the journalists' voices rise: his father's funerary procession was coming. There would be no private grief; this cremation was going out live to the nation.

Then the procession appeared through the buildings, the mourners filing down to the burning ghat in a dignified slow trudge. His half-brother Lalit led the procession. He looked older than Vikram remembered: serious, dry-eyed, well-schooled in dignity by his pricklish mother. Then came the body, surrounded by friends of his father. Then his step-mother Tanita appeared, clad in elaborate mourning clothes in an ostentatious show of grief. Vikram wished she would slip in the muddy ash and make a fool of herself; she'd been nothing but trouble to his father. Beside her was Bishin, supporting Kiran. The two wives, current and ex, didn't look at each other. The hostility was palpable.

Behind them, he saw with consternation, was Deepika, being supported by Uma and the bandana-wearing cop he'd last seen on the roof of Shiv Bakli's mansion: Tilak of Mandore, reborn. He sucked in his breath and ducked his head slightly. He hadn't thought they would come, not with the risk of Ravindra's spies being here.

No one looked up at him, although occasionally he caught a camera panning across his face. All through the ceremonial lighting of the torch, held by Lalit, journalists babbled into their microphones, ignoring the resentful looks of the mourners. A great many sightseers had come to see this high-profile cremation. He swallowed a sob as Lalit lit the pyre and the first tongues of fire kissed the wrapped body.

*Farewell Dad. All you gods, take him to your hearts . . .*

Then he heard a known voice – and made the mistake of looking towards the sound. A few yards below him, staring upwards, was Sue Parker. Before he could gesture to her to be quiet, her mouth fell open and her shrill voice rang out.

'*Vickers?* Vickers, is that you——?'

He was moving even as the cameras swivelled and a journalist shrieked, 'Oh my God! It's Vikram – *it's Vikram*——' Someone screamed, as if they expected India's Most Wanted to lob a grenade, and he caught a glimpse of Sue Parker's wide eyes before he was running, leaping from roof to roof, an arrow nocked and ready. As the first sniper swung his gun about, he released and the shaft, empowered by his ancient spell, flared as it streamed away.

Before the gunman could pull the trigger, the arrow-head had whipped into the muzzle; the gun exploded, blasting the barrel apart, and the concussion threw the sniper backwards, his face streaming blood. Vikram landed on the next roof and ran on, away from the river, as the crowd below him erupted fearfully. He twisted as he leaped the next gap, shooting on instinct as three guns chattered from different directions. An arrow took the right shoulder of the first officer, who dropped from sight. Bullets whined and hammered into the stonework behind him, sending splinters spraying. A shrill cry from behind him was followed by a concussion that shattered windows facing the river, and elicited more screams. In the momentary silence that followed he heard someone shouting, 'Stop shooting, we want him alive!'

No one appeared to be listening: to his left he glimpsed another sniper pulling his heavy rifle about. Vikram fired and the arrow became a snake mid-flight – a non-poisonous one, but the gunman wasn't to know that. The man tore the reptile from his throat, yowling in terror, as Vikram struck the next roof, an open-air flat space fouled with rotting leaves and old furniture; he found himself slaloming across the dank detritus. A bullet whined above his head and he crouched behind an old chest, took stock of the landscape, then aimed and launched a musafir-astra. The traveller's arrow hung before him until he had grasped it one-handed, then it set off, pulling him through the air. Legs flailing, he fought to right himself, ignoring the gasps as a dozen people witnessed this miracle. He looked ahead . . .

. . . and realised he was flying straight towards another sniper, positioned in the highest cupola of an old palace.

The gunman had been aiming at the spot further west where he'd last seen his target, but as Vikram whooshed towards him, he twisted, correcting his aim and squeezing the trigger. Tracer-bullets slammed past, the first yards wide, the second mere inches away.

*Next bullet, I'm dead!*

Vikram twisted the arrow's flight slightly, then let go.

Deepika heard the clear cry of surprise – an American voice – and whirled in horror. All eyes flew to a generously proportioned woman with a blonde ponytail, and then up to where she was looking at the slim blue-painted figure on the roof.

*Vikram——?*

As Deepika watched, he rose like a startled gazelle as a frightened clamour began and people screamed, whirling in all directions.

'It's Vik – *do* something,' she shouted to no one in particular. Tanvir blinked at her as Vikram leaped the gap, firing an arrow as he went, and for a second the image of him, his body arched and graceful, etched itself across the vision of every one of the hundreds of mourners and gawpers filling the ghat. People gasped, shouted, screamed – some even cheered – but Deepika saw many well-built, casually dressed men whose hands flew inside jackets as they prepared to give chase.

'*Nooo!*'

The sound erupted from her throat and from her soul, resonant with protective rage, and every camera lens within the perimeter of the ghat shattered, thousands of dollars of equipment turning to shards in an instant. Microphones crumpled as if grabbed by hidden fists and a wind from nowhere smashed a group of plain-clothed police to their knees, while others dived to the ground, suddenly terrified. She scanned the rooftops, but Vikram was already out of sight. She began to chase after him, then realised that would be completely futile. Instead, she fixed her eyes on the American girl, who was still gaping at the rooftop where Vik had been – until she felt Deepika's gaze and turned. The American blanched, and tried to run.

She made it to the alley before Deepika caught up and seized her shoulder and slammed the young woman against a wall. The American shrieked weakly and fell to her knees. Onlookers gasped, but did nothing as the blonde looked up at Deepika in terror, as if she were seeing something far more than just a furious Indian girl. Deepika raised her hand above the girl's face and cried, 'Who are you? *Who are you?*'

'Sue Parker,' the American babbled. 'Don't hurt me—'

*Surpanakha?* Deepika's mind reeled.

Tanvir appeared, Uma behind him, and she realised people were staring at her and backing away, as if they saw something feral in her.

'Get away from me!' she growled at the onlookers, and they were all flung backwards as if by a wind exploding from her mouth. It took a moment or two, then they were scrambling upright and running for their lives, leaving them alone in the alley.

She looked down at the terrified face of the American.

*Surpanakha: Rama's betrayer.*

'You're coming with us,' she snarled.


Vikram plummeted into a pile of red-brown clay pots, which shattered, gashing his shins even as they broke his fall. Blood oozed from a dozen cuts as he fought for purchase, then he was up and scanning the roofs ahead. He could see the sniper in the cupola above: his musafir-astra had caught the gunman's arm and pinned it to the stone wall. The gunman had passed out, probably from the pain and shock, but he'd live. Vikram leaped to the next roof, hurtling past a meditating old woman who didn't even move, then he was on a window box and grabbing some of the clothes hanging from the line above it. He could hear someone downstairs, singing to herself, oblivious as he passed, but he was gone in seconds and jumping up to a flat roof, where three teenage girls stretched out in bikinis screeched in horror at his appearance.

He blew them a kiss and was gone, leaping down into a broken-down courtyard where two cows grazed. He bent over double, gasping for air, as the cows gazed up at him placidly, then looked around to take stock.

He was four doors from his lodgings.

Less than five minutes later, as armed police stormed through the alleys, he was alone in the communal shower, watching the blue turn back to grey ash as he washed it off his flesh. Two minutes after that, as loudspeakers screechingly demanded his surrender, he was checking his ever-ready backpack had all the essentials. One minute before the authorities closed the alleys all along Godaulia Chowk, sealing off the ghats, he was on the roof of his little hotel and aiming a traveller's arrow towards the west. Five minutes before the first helicopter tore across the river, he was already just another face in the crowds in western Varanasi, far beyond the cordon, walking towards the far side of the city and the open fields.

*

Tanvir pulled the American to her feet and frogmarched her past bewildered shopkeepers and onlookers. Between the sirens wailing and the shouting of the people, the noise was deafening, but Tanvir was flashing his badge, shouting, 'Police, police – *make way.*'

They forced their way through the press and hailed the first taxi they could find.

By the time Vikram was washing off his disguise and the police were still struggling to create a cordon, Deepika, Tanvir, Uma and Sue Parker had left the riverside district.

'What do we do with her?' Uma asked from the front seat, her voice filled with uncertainty.

Deepika looked at the young woman beside her. Her rage was gradually subsiding to a simmer, but it could flare again any moment. *This is Surpanakha*, she thought. *This is Ravindra's evil sister.*

Perhaps this was a major breakthrough, an unexpected victory in their secret war with Ravindra. The American didn't look very frightening, though – or even pretty, for that matter, with her pallid skin blotched with tears and fear. But if she was Surpanakha, then she would be more dangerous even than Halika.

'She could be vital,' Deepika told them. 'We need answers from her.'

Tanvir looked at her grimly, already calculating how they could get her safely away.

'You've got to let me go,' the American girl whined. 'You'll be arrested – you'll be—'

'SHUT YOUR MOUTH, DEMON,' Deepika snarled, baring her teeth as her fury rekindled. She had to stop herself from lashing out at this creature who'd tried to get Vikram killed.

The young woman cringed, pulling away from her as if she were a snake, and even Tanvir and Uma looked a little shocked.

'We'll need our own car,' Tanvir said, looking at her worriedly, and glancing at the cab driver. Despite the police badge Tanvir had shown him, the driver was looking increasingly nervous with every cop car that screamed past in the opposite direction, sirens blazing. 'We'll need a car-hire place,' he told the driver.

Deepika stared at the girl. *Is this pathetic creature really a demon? But she's following our conversation . . . what kind of white girl speaks our language?* 'Who are you, bitch?' she spat in Hindi.

'Don't hurt me,' the American begged, responding in the same tongue. 'Please don't hurt me.' Then she looked straight into Deepika's eyes and said, '*Don't hurt me, Trishala.*'

*Trishala?* The name echoed inside Deepika's soul and she felt a vortex open inside her. She jerked her eyes away. 'Don't call me that,' she hissed. 'Shut your damned mouth and keep it shut.'

# CHAPTER FOURTEEN

# ANOTHER SÉANCE

*Kannauj, Uttar Pradesh, February 2011*

The photograph was a little blurry but still unmistakable. The still, from an image transmitted digitally to the breakfast television studios in Mumbai and New Delhi, showed a young man, lean but toned, with longish wavy black hair caught in a topknot, his skin painted powder-blue. A bow and quiver lay in his lap as he stared out from a stone temple roof. The caption read: *The blasphemous face of a killer*.

The headlines of the newspapers warred for attention.

SUNITA'S KILLER MOCKS JUSTICE!
VIKRAM ATTENDS FUNERAL THEN ABSCONDS
INDIA'S MOST WANTED ESCAPES AGAIN!
HUNDREDS OF COPS FAIL TO NAB VIKRAM!

Amanjit put down the top paper and chuckled softly.

'Good for you, bhai. Good for you.' He glanced across at Rasita. 'That's my brother: the cool dude in blue warpaint.'

'Keep your voice down, you idiot.' Ras glanced about the train carriage, but no one was paying them any attention. There was no doubt that Vikram-fever, which had abated a little through the winter, was now back in full flood. The media was full of Vikram profiles, Vikram sightings and Vikram rumours – the papers, TV and radio couldn't get enough. Their own photographs were in heavy circulation again, too – but none of them showed a shaven-headed young man or a girl in a burkha.

'Chill out, Ras,' Amanjit told her. 'Act suspicious and people will get suspicious – act cool, and people just think you're cool.'

'Huh. Then why're you acting like a dork?' she snapped back.

He glanced out of the window as another town appeared across the paddy fields. The PA system crackled to life. 'The next station will be Kannauj. Passengers for Kannauj are asked to disembark on the left-hand side of the train. Please ensure you have all your belongings.'

'Hey, only three hours late,' Amanjit noted. 'By Indian Rail standards that's practically on time.'

'Smile while you can: Dee is going to divorce you when she sees what you've done with your hair.'

Amanjit ran a hand over the thin stubble on his scalp. He'd grown it a little after becoming nervous that Deepika really would hate his clean-shaven disguise. 'It's only until we're cleared, Ras. And anyway, we're not married yet, so she can't divorce me.'

'She can cancel the wedding though, *skinhead*.'

The train puffed and panted past the squatting homeless and the trash heaps banked yards deep against the brick walls that lined the track and finally into Kannauj Station: the rendezvous that Deepika had suggested in her phone call, following the events in Varanasi. They disembarked onto a packed, grimy platform, the heat and stench of sweat and diesel overpowering. Dark faces crowded round, shoving and pressing their way on or off the train with little or no order. Ras clung to Amanjit as he waded towards a space where they could breathe and get organised.

They were settling their backpacks onto their shoulders when a round-faced man in a blue bandana approached them. 'Excuse me, I'm looking for Shastri and Padma,' he said carefully.

'That's us,' Ras told him. 'Are you Tanvir?' She'd barely glimpsed the man who had pulled her and Deepika from the fire and smoke of Shiv Bakli's manor.

'Indeed I am.' The policeman ran a sceptical eye over Amanjit's head. 'I thought Sikhs never shaved,' he commented.

Ras tittered. 'Real ones don't.'

'I'm in disguise,' Amanjit growled.

'So am I,' Tanvir replied, with the hint of a smile. 'I normally wear a *red* bandana.'

The policeman looked Amanjit up and down, measuring him. Though he was not yet twenty, Amanjit was every bit as burly and solid as Tanvir. Lately he'd been growing a little nervous, wondering what had passed between Deepika and her protector these past months. Deepika spoke rather too fondly of him . . .

Ras put her hands on her hips. 'You two look like two mountain goats about to lock horns. Lighten up, guys!'

*Fair enough*. Amanjit slowly put out his hand. 'You have kept my fiancée safe when I couldn't. I'm in your debt for ever.' Tanvir took his hand, and Amanjit drew Tanvir to him and hugged him. 'I mean it. You are my brother.'

'Yay: global peace and love,' Ras drawled. 'Now can we go before someone recognises us?'

Tanvir pointed to the far end of the platform. 'Yes, good idea. I have a car waiting.' He courteously took Rasita's back-pack for her, then led them down the platform, through the thinning passenger crowds and into a car park. 'How did you get past the ID checks on the train?' he asked as they loaded his rental car. 'Professional curiosity, you understand.'

'We borrowed IDs from friends,' Ras explained. 'Where are you staying?'

'We're renting an apartment on the north side. We've got the girl there.'

'And she's really a demon?' Amanjit asked doubtfully.

Tanvir flinched. 'Honestly . . . ? We don't know. She was born in India but to American parents living here. She speaks pretty good Hindi . . . Er . . .' He eyed up Ras, then said, 'She's sweet on Vikram. She claims she didn't intend to give him away at the funeral – she says she had no idea who he was, just recognised him as her friend "Vickers" when she went to the funeral to check out the fuss. She says she blurted out his name without thinking.'

*Sweet on Vikram, eh?* Amanjit could see Ras wasn't at all pleased.

Ras scowled. 'Do you believe her?'

'We don't know,' Tanvir answered. 'I mean, Deepika explained the *Ramayana* thing to me; someone called Sue Parker trying to hit on Vikram while he's in exile – it can't be coincidence, right? Of course, if she *is* just an innocent bystander, then we've kidnapped her and held her against her will for the last four days, which means we'll be lucky not to spend the next decade in jail.'

Amanjit grimaced. 'We're already wanted as accessories to murder, so what the hell?'

'*You* are,' Tanvir corrected. 'I'm not, and I'd like to keep it that way.'

'You new teammates have no commitment.'

They arrived at an unpromising-looking five-storey apartment block in the maze of narrow streets north of the old city. A bird's nest tangle of power and phone cables ran to and from the battered concrete exterior, currently being used as a trapeze by a colony of monkeys. The surly guard took one look at Tanvir and straightened up. He beamed, saluted and waved them through.

'He thinks he's aiding a secret police operation,' Tanvir explained. 'And he's getting plenty of baksheesh for it too. I'm his favourite person right now.'

Deepika and Uma were waiting for them upstairs. Dee's mouth flew open when she saw Amanjit, then she burst into tears and flew to him. For several minutes she clung to him, stroking his cropped scalp and crying.

'Hey, it's not that bad, is it?' he whispered.

'Idiot.' She buried her face in his shoulder. 'Look what you do as soon as I let you out of my sight.'

Uma was staring at Ras. '*Sunni?*'

'Rasita — and Sunni too, Uma,' Ras replied, holding out her arms.

Uma's eyes welled up and she enveloped Rasita, sobbing hysterically.

It was a long time before anyone was ready to talk.

Tanvir unlocked the door and Amanjit peered inside a small stale-smelling room where a plump white girl was lying on her side, facing the window. She turned over, revealing a pale face. When she saw an unfamiliar face, her face lit with hope. 'Who are you? Have you come to get me out?'

Amanjit stared. She didn't look terribly demonic. He shook his head. 'Sorry. I'm Vikram's stepbrother. Who are you?'

'My name's Susan Anne Parker, and I'm an American citizen,' she replied in a quavering voice that dissolved into sobs. 'Why are you keeping me here?' she pleaded. 'You're all insane — I'm not that stupid demon-thing — I'm not your Surpanakha . . . Are you all crazy?'

Tanvir pulled Amanjit outside, shut the door and relocked it. 'She'll go on like that for some time,' he whispered. 'She's terrified of Deepika; she falls apart if she's anywhere near her. I hope we're doing the right thing.'

Amanjit swallowed, feeling sick. 'This is a mess,' he agreed as the American hammered on the door, screaming for help. 'Can the neighbours hear her?'

'The floor below is empty and the outside glass is reinforced. Have you heard from Vikram?'

'His mobile is switched off, so I guess we're on our own

on this one. Ras needs to talk to her. She says she needs to find out why "Sue" – if that's her real name – called Dee "Trishala".'

'Who's Trishala?' Tanvir asked.

'No idea, but I suspect the correct question is "Who *was* Trishala",' Amanjit replied. 'I'm just a soldier – Ras is the one with all the memories. I've no idea what's going on most of the time.'

Tanvir rolled his eyes. 'I'm getting to know the feeling.'

Ras walked up, a grim look on her face. 'Right. I'll see her now.'

'My name is Rasita. May I sit with you?'

Sue Parker looked up from the bed, her head in her hands. Her tear-stained, sullen face looked resigned. 'Ain't got much say, have I? You will anyway.'

Ras sat cautiously. If this really was Surpanakha, then she was alone with a demon and this could go badly wrong. The two boys were outside, listening for the slightest disturbance – although quite what they could do against a demon, she didn't know.

But if Sue wasn't a demon, they'd wronged her, and if that was the case, they deserved whatever punishment came.

*But how does she know about Trishala?*

Ras tried to project calm. 'Please could you look at me?'

The American turned slowly, flinching. 'Are you like her?' she asked, her voice frightened.

'Like who?'

'Your pal Deepika . . .' Her lips quivered. 'When she looks at me there's this *beast* inside her. Her face goes dark and her eyes go golden – it's like she wants to rip me apart. She's possessed—'

*Dee? Possessed? No . . . just angry.* 'Deepika says that you called her "Trishala"?'

'I don't remember that – please, *please* let me go,' she begged. 'I won't tell anyone, I promise – I'll leave the country, honest—'

'Look at me, Sue Parker,' Ras ordered. 'Look me in the eye. I need to recognise you.'

The American edged away from her. 'No – you're like her, I can tell: you're possessed too!'

Ras was worried that they'd made a horrible mistake but still she reached out, put a hand on either side of Sue's head and looked deep into her eyes. As she did so, she reached back into her own store of memories of her lives as Gauran, trying to recognise the soul within this foreigner.

Sue tried to look away but couldn't. Her expression was growing slack – and Gauran recognised her . . .

*Ah . . . she's* Kamla. *Now I understand . . . Oh, Vikram, it's never easy, is it?*

There were other lives too, fleeting moments when their souls had collided, or brushed past each other in the corridors of time. Her Gauran-self had encountered Kamla-reborn several times, but not with Darya-reborn as well, not since the 1100s. So how would Kamla know Trishala . . . ? Then Ras had an inspiration: she brought her Padma-memories to the surface, those brief lives that seldom yielded memories of value . . .

*Oh, by all the gods . . .* Her heart quivered and she clutched her chest, breathing heavily.

Sue Parker was shaking, cowering away and *very* afraid. 'What did you do?' she whispered. 'I saw . . . I felt . . . Who *are* you?'

*It's so complicated, that question — and it's about to get worse. But she has to know.*

'Sue, this is important — *really* important, to Vikram, to all of us. We need your help to prevent something very bad happening.'

'*You need my help?*' Sue repeated incredulously. 'You drag me off the streets and keep me prisoner, and now you want my *help*? You're *fucking* unbelievable — and you can all go to hell!'

Ras could see it from the American's point of view. Her voice filled with sympathy as she admitted, 'We deserve that. I'm sorry, but we're very frightened, and we panicked and overreacted.'

'Damn right you did! Jeez, you people are un-fucking-believable!' Sue stared at her, then looked away. After a moment, she asked, 'For Vikram, you say? So whaddya want?'

Ras bit her lip and thought it through. At last she said, 'A séance. We need you to participate in a kind of séance.'

Sue Parker began to laugh, a hopeless, derisive, despairing sound that once again dissolved into tears. 'You really are insane, aren't you?' she choked out.

Deepika sat cross-legged opposite the American, who was looking across the brazier at her with fear written all over her face. She felt a shiver run up and down her back and exhaled deeply. Seated around them, Tanvir, Amanjit, Uma and Ras looked on with a mix of concern and curiosity.

Ras locked eyes with Sue, holding her frightened gaze, and said, 'Be calm. Don't look away, look at me – only at me – and chant with us the words I gave you, looking only at me.'

Uma's concoction of herbal party drugs and alcohol was taking effect on them all. Sue's pupils were dilated, her skin flushed, her large bosom heaving. Deepika could feel her own body heat rising and her vision was beginning to blur at the edges. Sounds were taking on an incredible resonance: the clatter of her spoon as it dropped from her hand; the rustle of the cockroaches in the ceiling; the gecko on the wall in the next room scuttling into a corner; the foggy sound of all of their breathing.

She whispered her words: *Darya – Jhansi – Trishala – Deepika* . . .

Sue's voice was barely audible. She looked heavily stoned; maybe the drugs were the only thing keeping her calm. '*Kamla – Jhansi – Emily – Sue* . . .' she began.

Their words ran together, swirling. Deepika knew what to expect this time – that strange, out-of-body dislocation, the floating sensations, the feeling that everything was gently fragmenting – but it turned out that *knowing* didn't make it any easier. She clung to her heart-stone for strength.

Someone was crying, someone vulnerable, and she realised it was Sue. Tears were streaming down her face, her shoulders heaving . . .

'*What's happening?*'

# CHAPTER FIFTEEN

# JHANSI: MRS MUTLOW

*Jhansi, Bundelkhand, 18 April 1857*

'*What's happening?*' Trishala gripped the hilt of her sword and jabbed a finger at the sobbing figure in the English dress. 'What's going on here? What are you doing to her?' The woman was crying, and no wonder: here she was in the foul-smelling and filthy public gaol in Jhansi town, with that ghastly gaoler leering at her, tugging at her sleeve as he drooled over her face.

*What's his name? Bakhshish Ali; that's right!*

Bakhshish turned and straightened, his eyes hooded, his face taking on the look of bestial cunning he always assumed around her. His tangled hair and beard shrouded his expression. 'Captain Trishala, I am merely offering comfort to this poor woman whose husband is yet again in my care.' As always, his eyes said much more. She'd seen him watching her before, and something about him nauseated her.

'Comfort? I don't need your so-called comfort, you wretch,' the other woman exploded, speaking English. She pushed him away and turned to Trishala. Her face was a startling mix of dark skin and pale hair. She was big-framed and plump, clad in an English dress, all flounces and frills, but sweat-stained and damp. She was clearly of mixed blood: no doubt the mongrel child of an English soldier. 'My poor Mark is in chains again and they won't let me see him unless I . . .' Her voice trailed off meaningfully, then she spat at the gaoler's feet.

'A misunderstanding, Captain, that is all,' the gaoler responded, his voice full of injured dignity. 'Of course I have not sought to take advantage of this poor woman's situation.'

His eyes remained dangerous, though: still measuring her, seeking weakness. All the men of Jhansi looked at Trishala and her sisters like that, each of them wondering how dangerous these women really were, just because they were taught by the queen herself how to ride and fight.

*Try me and you'll see . . .*

'I'm here to see the clerk, Mark Mutlow, released,' she said coldly.

Bakhshish Ali bowed obsequiously and the woman – presumably Mutlow's wife – gasped in hope.

'At once, Bakhshish Ali,' Trishala added. '*At once—*'

For a moment Trishala thought the gaoler might make an issue of this, but she tapped her sword hilt meaningfully, reminding the man that he was unarmed, and he backed down, glowering as he slunk away to the cells. The woman clutched Trishala's arm. 'Oh thank you, thank you, Captain—'

Trishala's English was good and she replied in the woman's

own tongue. 'It's nothing. Drunk Britishers should never be brought here; they should be returned to barracks. These men know this.' For weeks now, the queen had ordered her officers be vigilant – this despite the rani herself having been evicted from Jhansi Fort and having to live in lesser dwellings in the township – to avoid any flashpoints with the British. Incidents like this could so easily end in violence.

*Truly my rani has the patience of a holy man*, Trishala thought as she eyed Mrs Mutlow curiously; she'd seen her before, but never up close. Half-breeds weren't uncommon; they hung around the camps, living very marginal lives. At least this girl had married, giving her a measure of security. She looked to be Trishala's age, but Trishala recalled seeing her carrying a child around. 'You are Mister Mutlow's wife, yes?'

'Emily Mutlow, ma'am, at your service,' the woman replied, curtseying. She stared frankly at Trishala. 'What a beautiful uniform you have,' she added shyly.

Trishala preened slightly. Her friend Karuna was always saying that she had more than a slice of vanity. *What's wrong with looking fine anyway?* 'I am a captain of the Palaka-Rani, the Queen's Guard. Only women may join,' she added proudly.

'I've seen you all parading through town. You look very splendid, ma'am,' Mrs Mutlow said enviously, her eyes running down Trishala's uniform and ornate steel breastplate and lingering on her curved cavalry sabre in its velvet-lined scabbard.

'If you know how to ride, you could apply to join us,' Trishala said thoughtlessly, then remembered that a half-breed wouldn't be permitted, let alone one married to an Englishman.

'I must take care of my Mark,' Mrs Mutlow replied evenly, as if she recognised the error and forgave it; Trishala found she rather liked her for that. 'My poor husband has a weakness for strong liquor,' she added, as if the liquor were to blame, rather than he who drank it. 'He's not even a proper soldier, just an army clerk. And a poet.'

The rattle of the door presaged the return of the gaoler with two underlings almost as vile-looking. What was it about gaol-keeping that attracted such men? Between them they hauled a diminutive dark-haired white man in a filthy red uniform. He was insensible, reeking of whisky, piss and vomit. 'Here he is, Captain,' Bakhshish Ali said. 'I am thinking you will need our help to get him to barracks.'

*Not if that means tolerating another moment with you.* 'Only so far as the cart outside, Gaolmaster.' Trishala clapped her hands. 'Come!'

They hauled the soldier up the narrow stairs to the furnace-like courtyard near the town square and into the bustle of life. Onlookers pressed close around, peering and laughing. For weeks now there had been rumours of mutiny among the Indian soldiers of the East India Company, although nothing had yet spread to Jhansi. The tension was palpable though, and there was a malicious undercurrent of delight in seeing a British soldier in public disgrace. The local people crowded about, chuckling and callously jostling Emily Mutlow until Trishala intervened.

'Make way,' she snapped, and was gratified to see people back away. 'Make way, in the name of the Rani of Jhansi,' she repeated, and snapped her fingers. Her horse was brought forward and she swung her legs over it easily.

*How wonderful to ride properly, not side-saddle — to be able to stride through a crowd and have it part before me. How glorious to serve my queen, the greatest woman in all Hindustan.*

She watched them haul the drunken soldier onto a bullock cart. Once his wife had clambered awkwardly up beside him she turned her horse and walked it through the crowd, head high, leading the cart towards the massive Jhansi Fort, its towering walls overlooking the town protectively. The fort was built on a solid promontory, aloof from the town, with its close-packed housing and maze of alleys. At its feet were barracks and parade grounds, basking beneath clear blue skies. The land was parched dry as a husk of corn, waiting breathlessly for the monsoon rains to rekindle life and vigour.

Once they were clear of the township and nearing the barracks, curiosity got the better of Trishala and she slowed to ride alongside the cart. Emily Mutlow was cradling her husband's head and now she could see he was a small fellow with a dapper moustache, rather skinny and unkempt. She felt a wave of pity for his wife. *How horrible to be bound to such a pathetic wretch.* 'How long have you been married?' she asked, trying to mask her feelings.

'Two years,' Emily Mutlow answered. 'My father was British, from a place called Sheffield, and my mother was a serving girl in Calcutta when they met and she . . . um . . . well, you know . . . He never married her, and then he died of the gangrene. My mother had family in Bengal, but when the soldiers came, we travelled with them.' Her flat voice spoke of what it must have been like. 'That's how I met Mark – he's looked after me. Without him, I'd be dead already.'

Trishala had seen camp-follower families marching with the soldiers, cooking and cleaning for them, bearing their children, treating their ailments, comforting them at night. They were treated as parasites: lower than the ticks on a dog, the first to be cast aside in times of peril.

'I've never seen a woman soldier,' Emily went on, as if more comfortable talking of other matters.

Trishala's life had been utterly different: the daughter of a noble family of Jhansi, maybe struggling a little, but in truth, not so badly off. She'd been destined for the marriage market until Rani Lakshmibai came to court. The fiercely independent queen had let it be known that athletic young women who liked to run and ride and play at martial pastimes, who wanted to shoot a bow and learn the sword, were welcome at her court, and Trishala's parents, thinking it advantageous to kowtow to the new queen's eccentricities, had let their daughter attend. Trishala had excelled, and when the rani announced she wanted her own guard of women, she'd been among the first accepted.

Her husband the raja had been amused by his new wife's enthusiasms: he would have done anything for his wondrous wife. *Well, almost anything*, Trishala reflected sadly. *Anything except get another child on her after their son died. Anything except live.*

'I was among the first to join the Palaka-Rani,' Trishala told Emily Mutlow. 'Though most people call it the "Durga Dal" now, because we model ourselves on the Goddess

Durga, she who rides the tiger. I can ride and hunt and shoot and use my sword as well as any man,' she boasted.

Emily mopped her husband's brow. 'I know how to use a gun – Mark showed me, in case worst comes to worst.' She gazed down at her drunken husband sadly. 'He's like a candle that's been blown out, but the wick smoulders on for a while.'

*Better for you if his candle is snuffed*, Trishala thought. *How like a man, to wallow in his own problems and forget those whom he drags down with him.*

'When I met Mark, he was kind to me, but already he was sad,' Emily went on confidingly. 'He thinks he's lived many lives before – well, I know a lot of people think that, but he says he can *remember* them. Once he said to me, "I can't even summon the astras any more. This is another wasted life". I don't know what an astra is, but he was very drunk that night. He called me strange names, then he drank a whole jug of whisky and almost died.'

*Astras? The sacred arrows?* Uneasy, Trishala changed the subject. 'Is your mother still alive?'

'I don't know,' Emily said, 'and I don't care. She sold me to Mark for two blankets, a knife and three coins, then headed for the stoops on the arm of a sepoy sergeant. If I see her again, I'll . . . well, I don't know . . .'

'My mother cries every night that I'll never marry,' Trishala told her. 'My father, who would struggle to find a suitable dowry, secretly rejoices.'

'How sad, to never marry,' Emily said.

'No: I'm happy. I never wanted to marry anyway.'

'But to have no children——?'

'*Pah!* – children? Squalling brats who steal your youth and beauty – and for what? I hate them—'Trishala stopped, remembering that this woman was a mother – her child must be with a servant somewhere. She glanced at the prone Mark Mutlow, feeling another wave of contempt for men like him. 'I will *never* marry,' she declared. 'I have seen a fortune-teller and she has told me this: that I am a warrior, from a lineage of queens, and that I will bear no children in this life.' She tossed her head proudly. 'I have all I need in my sisters and my queen.'

Emily Mutlow looked up at her with fervent eyes. 'I wish I was you.'

Trishala smiled down at her. Emily was quite pretty, despite her odd looks and flabby body. Although clearly they couldn't be friends, not with the woman's breeding and status, she could look out for her when her pathetic husband died. 'You may call on me in need,' she told Emily, feeling like a benevolent queen.

They arrived at the barracks and Emily helped the soldiers unload her unconscious husband. Trishala turned her horse and flashed a small salute to the British officer in charge.

*See, I have rescued one of your men. Where is the thanks?*

The man didn't even return her salute, just stared stonily, then turned away.

*To him I'm not a real soldier, either. One day we'll show them all!*

Trishala turned and galloped back to town.

# CHAPTER SIXTEEN

# JHANSI: THE EDGE OF REBELLION

*Jhansi, Bundelkhand, 12 May 1857*

The face of the queen cast all else into shadow: Lakshmibai, Rani of Jhansi, the flawless beauty of all Hindustan. She flashed her glorious eyes and scanned the courtyard, where her woman officers were gathered to dine at the end of another day spent in the shadow of the British. Trishala was among them, gazing up at her ruler with reverence.

Around the courtyard, the old harem windows of the Mughal period watched sightlessly. Crows called from the towers, which were in poor repair. The labyrinthine town palace was large, but old and crumbling. It had its charms, but the fact they were here and not where the rani belonged, within the fortress above the town, made it feel like a prison.

There were twelve chief officers with the queen: they led the Palaka-Rani or Durga Dal, all those women who had been trained at arms. Some of the officers had been the rani's closest friends when she was younger; others, like Trishala, were younger newcomers who had excelled in training. All were daughters of noble families, but, like the queen herself, they weren't the usual sort of court girls. The young rani was fascinated by warfare and had learned the manly skills from an early age, gathering like-minded friends about her. It had begun as a bit of fun, learning to ride astride and shoot, but the game was becoming serious: Lakshmibai was the sole ruler now that her husband and son were both dead and the British were refusing to recognise her adopted son as her legal heir. War was beginning to feel like a very real possibility. Trishala didn't know whether to exult or reel in horror.

The eight junior officers dined at a lower table, including Trishala and her friend Karuna. Sharing the queen's table were her closest friends, Mandar, Juhi, Motibai and Kashi. Trishala longed to be one of that company. She had worked ferociously in the exercise yard to prove herself, and the rani had once told her that she was pleased with her skills. It was her proudest moment so far.

Right now it was Mandar, the queen's cleverest friend, who was holding forth at the high table, and Trishala could sense the tension of a dispute in the air, so she ignored the gossip around her and strained her ears, listening.

'Maharani,' Mandar was arguing, 'when will we assert ourselves with these arrogant Britishers? They have become insufferable! They believe they can push you around because your beloved husband, our glorious king – may the gods keep him – has passed away.'

'Mandar is right,' Kashi added. 'The British East India Company pretend to support you, but it's they who have refused to recognise your adoption of our little prince so they can take greater control of your kingdom.' She spat onto the stone floor of the courtyard – most unladylike, but being unladylike was part of the fun of being in the Palaka-Rani.

The quiet Juhi added her words: 'It was Lord Dalhousie himself who made you leave your rightful place in Jhansi Fort – and he paid a pittance in compensation. I don't always agree with my sister's firebrand ways, but it's time we showed them our mettle.'

'The Doctrine of Lapse, this law of theirs is called,' Lakshmibai replied calmly. 'It is indeed a law they forced on us. But I am in negotiation with Dalhousie. I'll not be rushed into precipitous action.'

'But my Queen, they've cast us out of your *sacred* home—' Mandar looked ready to sweep out her sword then and there. 'You have been most forbearing, even faced with these heinous insults – you have protested, you have used diplomacy when you had every right to use force, and it is true that you have won back some of your ancient rights using their own legalities. Majesty, you are grace personified—'

'Enough flattery, Mandar, please,' the queen said, raising an admonishing finger. 'Get to the point.'

'Then let me be direct, Rani: the vile Britishers are slaughtering our sacred beasts – and not only do they slay cows, but they are using *pig fat* to grease the cartridges of their guns – when they are nothing but fat pigs themselves—' Mandar's voice rose, until she remembered herself abruptly, and bowed her head, trembling visibly. 'Majesty, surely our time has come—?'

'Thank you, Mandar.' Lakshmibai raised her clear voice to

fill the courtyard – by now everyone was silent like Trishala, listening to their betters argue. 'Sisters, I know we all ache for the long-prophesied end of British rule in Hindustan – and Mandar is right; the unrest among the sepoys may present an opportunity for us to show these Britishers – and our own menfolk too – just what we can do.'

'Let us kill the English,' Karuna called fiercely, from the lower table. She was never shy of speaking up before everyone; Trishala would never be so bold herself. 'You know *my* reasons, Rani: my sister and I have never received justice for what was done to us by the Britishers . . .'

Karuna and her fragile little sister Achala had been raped by British officers of the East India Company five years ago, and the perpetrators yet went unpunished. Achala had taken her own life shortly afterwards, and no one would marry Karuna now . . . *Although her murderous disposition might have something to do with that*, Trishala admitted to herself. They were cousins, sharing a family bond, and Karuna now followed Trishala with slavish devotion.

Lakshmibai smiled tolerantly; they all knew Karuna's history, and her zeal. 'We all need refreshment – it was a hard ride this morning. Let us retire to the zenana for chai.'

*And more privacy*, she didn't need to add.

As the twelve officers followed the queen inside, Karuna came to Trishala's side. The two young women could not have been more different: Trishala was accounted second in beauty only to the queen; willowy, with thick, gleaming hair to her waist – and a ferocious temper when roused. Karuna shared the temper, but she was square and solid, and about as communicative as a blockhouse.

The zenana – the women's harem, in past days – was now headquarters for the officers of the Palaka-Rani. Few were married, and many, like Karuna, disdained men altogether. Small rooms piled high with cushions and rugs surrounded the central gathering place where they ate and gamed and chatted.

As the chai-women poured the spicy, heavily sugared chai, the rani told them, 'We have been drilling the girls of the Palaka hard this past year – and let us not forget that our kind English friends are seeing to the training of our menfolk,' she added with an ironic smile, making everyone laugh. 'We even have a few cannon – hidden when the Britishers first came – but we have few trained gunners. The Britishers effectively disarmed Jhansi when they usurped my position three years ago.'

The women murmured their understanding. 'They pulled our teeth, Rani,' grumbled Kashi.

'They did. But we have not been idle. We have procured guns and powder, trading in secret with the southern states – although not enough. I need you to understand this, my sisters: Jhansi is far from ready for war.' She raised a hand to quell their protests. 'Oh, we women are ready, and all of the Durga Dal, but not the men. The sepoys have training, and guns, but they live under English command: not all will mutiny, of that you can be sure. Some will side with the Britishers and others will only follow this or that leader, for their own petty tribal or religious reasons. We lack unity as badly as we lack powder and arms. If we raised the flag of defiance today, men would come – but only in their hundreds. We need thousands, *tens* of thousands.' She looked around them. 'Sisters, last night, two things happened: I received messengers from the north, and when I heard their news, I called a counsel with my advisors.'

'What news, Rani? Is it war?' asked Mandar eagerly.

Lakshmibai drew herself up. 'Two days ago, on the tenth of May, at Meerut, a company of sepoys mutinied against their British officers. Sepoys of the Third Cavalry released prisoners who had refused to use their polluted cartridges and they slew many Britishers. The call has gone out: to revolt against the English. There are five times as many sepoys as English in the armies of the East India Company. They will declare Bahadur Shah Zafar to be Hindustan's Emperor. The mutineers propose to drive the English from all of India.'

Mandar shrieked in joy, a sound echoed on all sides.

'War!' Motibai slammed her fist against her breastplate.

The rani raised her hand, seeking silence. 'Sisters, there is more.' Her voice grew cold and analytical. 'My counsellors gave me their advice, and I agree with it. *Jhansi will not join the rebellion.*'

They stared in sudden silence, the air sucked from their lungs. Karuna clenched and unclenched her fists, her eyes wide with incomprehension, while Mandar groaned in pain.

Trishala felt bewildered, her guts in turmoil. Her every dream involved riding to war and winning the praise of her exalted queen, but she also knew the difference between playing at soldiers and the reality. She'd seen the aftermath of a bandit massacre of a merchant train once and the sight still haunted her. What of the women and children of the Britishers? What of Mrs Mutlow? What of pretty Miss

Brown, who looked after the young children of Major Skene, the political officer whom Lakshmibai had twisted around her little finger. Miss Brown seemed nice – and what of those pale, serious children she'd played with once or twice?

'We're not ready,' the rani went on, her voice dispassionate. 'We are weak, ill-equipped, divided and vulnerable. The Britishers have our stronghold. And this rebellion is already a mess. I would not follow Bahadur Shah Zafar even if he said he was leading me to Paradise! He is eighty years old and a Sufi. He is Mughal – but the Mughal era is *gone*. He is not the one to lead us to freedom.'

'Then what will we do?' Trishala asked, in the echoing silence.

Lakshmibai held up her hand. 'These were the decisions my counsellors and I reached. *One*: we won't openly join the rebellion. We're just not ready. *Two*: we will proceed apace with drilling men from the town in secret. We desperately need men trained to fight. *Three*: we will acquire more weapons, away from the eyes of the Britishers, of course. And *four*: we will display our loyalty to the British, so that they do not suspect that we're readying ourselves to join the rebellion when it suits us.' She looked about the room with a stern eye. 'Am I understood?'

Heads bowed on all sides.

Trishala swallowed, then raised her hand. 'Our people will be confused, my rani. They already wonder why we do not rebel.'

'Our purpose must remain secret,' Lakshmibai replied. 'The people's confusion is necessary for a while. Too many in the know and we will be uncovered. The Britishers have their spies.'

Trishala looked at Karuna, whose face was dark and brooding. 'Soon, Karuna,' she whispered. 'You will have your revenge, I know it.'

As they rose to leave, the rani signalled to Trishala. 'A moment, Trishala, please?'

Karuna squeezed her hand as Trishala suppressed a surge of nerves. Was she to be admonished for speaking her doubts just now? But she hurried to join the queen and her four closest friends, saluting, then waiting in silence.

'So, Trishala, what do you think of this news of mutiny, and our reaction?' the rani asked. 'Your own opinions – speak your mind.' The rani's friends were watching Trishala closely; she could feel the close-knit circle weighing her up.

'I think you are right, my queen. We are not prepared. Not in practical terms.'

'Thank you,' Lakshmibai said. 'It's good that one of our brightest and most energetic young women understands the need for patience.' Her face and voice were approving, making Trishala's heart thud. 'And I hear you've made a friend among the English, in this Mrs Mutlow?'

Trishala blushed, unsure if the queen approved of such a thing. She'd seen Mrs Mutlow a few times since that first encounter – though in truth, she felt more sorry for her than a real liking. 'Oh, not really, Rani – she is a half-breed; she's really just a . . . an informant. I cultivate her for insights into the mood of the English.'

'And what is their mood?'

'They're wary. Some think Major Skene a fool for

trusting you. Captain Dunlop is trying to whip them into better shape and he drives the Indian sepoys in the Company hard.'

'Then he trains our men for us.' The rani allowed a frown to crease her perfect forehead. 'I had thought I had all of their trust, not merely that of Major Skene. Interesting. Well done, Trishala. We must charm them all, the better to strike when the time comes. I will declare a banquet in their honour.'

Trishala blushed at the praise, especially when Motibai said, 'You show promise, sister.'

At a signal from Lakshmibai, a crowd of servants bustled in to dress the rani for the coming evening. A number of silk saris of rainbow colours, each heavily embroidered and encrusted with precious stones, were laid out for inspection and Lakshmibai allowed Trishala to remain with her friends to help choose her attire. They selected a yellow sari, the colour of peace, and then the jewellery was presented.

'What is this one, Rani?' Trishala asked, looking at an ancient silvered necklace with a web of interlocking panels dangling about a dark smoky-looking crystal that was cool to the touch. 'Is it new?'

Lakshmibai picked it up musingly. 'Not new, very old. I've had it for some time, but not worn it often. It came from a Gujarati merchant. I'm not sure I like it, somehow. And the servants say that it's haunted,' she added with a snort.

'It is, Rani,' Kashi asserted. 'The White Lady is seen whenever you wear it.'

The Rani winked at Trishala. 'Then I shall wear it when

the Britishers come for the banquet and maybe a bhoot will gobble them up for us.' She put a hand on Trishala's shoulder. 'We are all warriors, we women of Jhansi. Men have made this world for their own pleasure and it is time for us to wrest it away from them — and we will start by wresting Hindustan from the English, yes?'

'Yes, Rani,' Trishala felt euphoric at such intimacy and drank in the moment.

A hand plucked at Trishala's sleeve in the market and she turned to slap it away until she realised it was a tearstained Emily Mutlow. The baby she was holding on her hip peered at Trishala with huge eyes.

Karuna eyed the half-breed and her child with unconcealed dislike, but Trishala felt only concern. 'Emily? What's the matter?'

'It's Mark! He's . . . oh, Captain Trishala, he's—'

'Just spit it out, woman,' Karuna growled.

Trishala threw her friend a warning look and asked, 'What is it, Emily?'

'He's saying he's going to leave me,' she blurted. 'But I think he means to kill himself.'

'Good riddance,' muttered Karuna.

'Karuna, you carry on. I'll deal with this,' Trishala said firmly. Karuna rolled her eyes and stalked away into the market, while Trishala let Emily lead her towards the barracks where Mark Mutlow worked, in charge of supply records and requisitioning. Emily babbled on about her husband being suicidal but Trishala felt little sympathy at this further sign of his weakness. *She might be better off without him*, she decided.

They arrived at her tiny two-room mud-brick house to find a big-boned Englishman in rough leathers sitting outside. He was handsome, if one looked past the white skin and shaggy sideburns. His face altered when he saw Trishala: he gazed at her as if she were a vision, jumping to his feet and sweeping off his cap.

'My brother-in-law, Joshua Mutlow,' Emily told Trishala.

*You married the wrong brother*, Trishala thought, staring at the muscular form before her. She took in the civilian clothes and the pistol and sword with curiosity, but it was his face that stole her gaze. Confident, frank eyes, and lips made for smiling. 'Captain Trishala, I presume,' he said in a strong, pleasing voice. 'Emily speaks of you constantly. Now I see why.'

'Master Joshua,' Trishala responded, blushing and struggling to remember her manners. The man might be a Britisher, but up close, he had the kind of commanding presence and forthright manner that made her heart race. 'She hasn't spoken of you at all, except in passing,' she said, trying for her usual distant coolness when confronted by a man.

'Overlooked again.' Joshua sighed theatrically, with just the right amount of levity to make her smile, despite herself.

'You are not a soldier?' He looked like the hero in an adventure tale to her.

'I have been. Now I'm something of a soldier of fortune,' he replied, a little apologetically.

'My Mark . . . he's inside,' Emily put in meekly, when Trishala had all but forgotten she was there.

A shadow crossed Joshua's face. 'My brother is prone to these dark moods. The Black Dog, we call it, when a man cannot face the world without a bottle. I came here to try and pull him out of it, but he's worse than I've ever seen him.'

Emily tugged at Trishala's sleeve. 'Could you please see him? He talks of you,' she added.

'Of me?' Trishala looked at the woman in surprise. 'Why's that?'

Emily just shook her head. 'Please?'

Trishala sighed and allowed herself to be led under the low lintel into the pitch-dark room cluttered with household items. It stank of cooking and smoke and unwashed bodies. Emily's Indian ayah wordlessly took the baby while staring in awe at Trishala. Emily led Trishala to an even lower doorway curtained with muslin; the stench of whisky-sweat and fever-ish perspiration clogged the air even before Emily twitched the curtain aside and Trishala had to steel herself to enter.

Mark Mutlow was lying on the low bed, a thin dark blanket covering his hips and legs. His narrow chest was bare and he looked like a famine victim. His face was unshaven and his eyes unfocused.

'Emily . . . I'm . . . thir . . . sty . . .' His head lolled about drunkenly as he felt about on the floor for something – a full bottle, maybe? She could just make out several empty ones on the floor.

Trishala curled her lip. 'Mister Mutlow!'

He started at the strange voice, but he couldn't focus on her. 'Mutlow. Muletto. Mule. Mutt.' He groaned and rubbed at his face, dragging his palms over his unshaven whiskers.

His face was blotched and scratched. 'Why . . . why are the gods doing this to me? *Why?*'

Trishala stared. *Gods? Was this man not a Christian?*

Emily thrust a lit oil-lamp into her hands. 'Please, I beg you, speak to him—'

Trishala took two hesitant steps into the foetid room and the Englishman stared up at her, seeing her properly for the first time. His eyes widened and he moaned, 'No – no, not you – *not now . . .*'

She looked at him in utter confusion.

'No,' he screamed, 'get away from me!' His hands batted the air ineffectually. 'Sanyogita, *get out of here* – I can't protect you, none of us can, not in this life! This one is all to hell – please, Darya, you've got to run – you've got to take Shastri and *run*—' His voice rasped, as if this effort was pushing the limits of his strength, then he curled into a foetal ball and began to sob.

'Mister Mutlow,' she tried, bending over him. 'Let me—'

He uncoiled like a striking snake and grabbed her arm, his eyes burning into her. She almost dropped the oil-lamp in shock when he screamed, 'RUN! YOU HEAR ME! RUN! THE ENEMY IS COMING AND I CAN'T PROTECT YOU! THE ASTRAS HAVE DESERTED ME AND WE'RE ALL DOOMED IN THIS LIFE! RUN, DARYA – *RUN!*'

She snatched her arm from his grasp as if it were burning and staggered backwards into Emily, shocked and horrified. *He's insane – delirious!* And it felt like a contagious delirium, one she had to escape. She thrust the lamp into Emily's hand and reeled outside.

Joshua Mutlow leaped to his feet. 'Captain? Can I help you?'

She glared at him, straightening. 'I'm fine!' She liked this Joshua Mutlow, but she didn't need anyone's aid.

'I heard him shouting,' he said. 'Is Darya your Christian name, Captain Trishala?'

'I'm not a "Christian", Master Mutlow, so I don't have a "Christian name" – and no: Trishala is my given name. I don't know any "Darya", nor a "Sanyogita": he called me both. Your brother is insane.' She gulped down clean air and tried to calm herself. 'Poor Emily.'

'He's been saying strange things ever since he took a bad fever when he was twelve,' Joshua told her. 'He almost died, and he was very changed afterwards: he spoke Urdu, though Lord knows where he could have learned it. He started calling me unknown names too. It was as if he'd seen the future, like Nostradamus, and it had broken him.'

Despite his strange words and alien manner, there was something in Joshua that soothed Trishala, an antidote to Mark Mutlow and his ravings. She found reassurance and recognition in his eyes.

*This is the man I want.*

The thought stunned her with its suddenness and conviction.

'He said something about an enemy,' she stammered, to mask this sudden realisation that was coursing through her, warming her belly and searing her face.

'He's said something of the sort before,' Joshua replied. 'I still don't know what to make of it. But I've never seen him so bad. I don't know what to do.'

They looked at each other silently while some kind of energy speared between them. She felt like a fly in a spider-web made of light and heat and yet somehow she didn't want to escape at all. She wanted to be consumed.

Emily Mutlow came out wiping away tears and oblivi-ously snapped them back to the present need. 'Oh, my poor Mark,' she groaned. 'We have to help him.'

Joshua went to his sister-in-law and hugged her. 'We'll find a way, Emily, you'll see,' he told her. But his eyes never left Trishala's face.

'I'm sorry,' Trishala said. 'I didn't help by coming here.'

'It was my fault,' Emily said. 'I thought he wanted to see you. I'm sorry we put you through it.'

'I'll look after things here, Captain,' Joshua told Trishala, his voice vibrating through her. 'But you'll always be wel-come to call,' he added. '*Any time.*'

It hurt to tear herself away.

Trishala found Karuna in the marketplace, but her friend had no sympathy.

'The clerk is a pathetic little worm,' she spat, 'and his brother is scum. Mercenaries are pigs, everyone knows that. Thieving, raping, murdering scum.'

'He seemed pleasant enough,' Trishala responded, her thoughts faraway. 'He spoke well.'

Karuna eyed her, glowering. '"He spoke well", did he? Idiot! Of course he spoke well to a pretty girl – he wants only one thing! You stay away from that pig, or I'll gut him.' She stomped through the dusty streets, kicking aside any-thing in her way. 'How can you befriend that half-breed creature anyway? She's just another soldier's leaving.'

Trishala glared at Karuna, her temper blazing at the aspersions cast upon Joshua and Emily. 'Yes, just what you would have borne, if you had conceived when those soldiers—' She put her hand to her mouth as Karuna's eyes flew open with hurt, immediately regretting her words. She tried to hug her friend. 'Karu, I'm sorry, I didn't mean that.'

Karuna shoved her away. 'Yes, you did,' she snarled. 'When the rani lets us strike, I'm going to knife that little bint and her menfolk – and pretty little Miss Brown and all of your pink-skinned friends – to show you that on the inside they are made of the same putrid stuff as you and me.'

# CHAPTER SEVENTEEN

# JHANSI: DREAMS AND DECEPTIONS

*Jhansi, Bundelkhand, 3 June 1857*

The tall, balding Englishman with the weak chin raised his cut-crystal glass and proposed yet another expansive toast. 'To our ever-gracious hostess, the Rani of Jhansi, fairest woman in all Hindustan,' Major Alexander Skene proclaimed; the cry was echoed throughout the room and glasses clinked and tilted. Whether the rani herself appreciated the toast was unknown; she was just a silhouette behind a silk screen to the English guests, as befitted a widow. But there were plenty of Jhansi residents hosting the English, who all smiled and bowed in acknowledgement. Trishala surveyed the room, assessing the relative sobriety of their guests.

'We could slit their throats and half of them would die oblivious,' growled Karuna in her ear.

'But Major Dunlop has many soldiers stationed outside and they're not drunk at all,' Trishala replied. She and Karuna had made up their quarrel – they shared a room in the zenana, so harmony was essential. 'Not tonight, Karu.'

The formal reception hall was packed with the nobility of Jhansi, as well as the British officers and their wives. The British looked alien compared to the multi-hued finery of the Indians. The women wore white dresses, ridiculous things with stiff-ribbed bodices, full of hoops and lace. Their pale skins were rosy from wine and the heat of the room. Their men were red-jacketed and red-faced, all booming and haw-haw-hawing away. But Joshua wasn't here: as a mercenary he carried no rank, so he wasn't invited to such a prestigious evening. Trishala ached to see him again, to go somewhere they could really talk, but in a place like Jhansi she couldn't. To be seen with an Englishman would destroy her reputation. But she *longed* for him . . .

For the past two weeks, the rani had been lavishing reassurances upon Major Skene, professing loyalty to the British even as she prepared for trouble. The news from elsewhere was of turmoil, even in places as nearby as Gwalior and Kannauj, but Skene was sending back messages to his masters in Calcutta extolling the loyalty of Rani Lakshmibai – she knew that, because all his messages were dictated to his Indian secretaries, who dutifully related them back to the rani from memory.

'Captain Trishala, please excuse me,' an Englishman murmured in her ear.

She turned, bowing politely. 'Colonel Gordon?'

'Mrs Mutlow commended you to me,' the colonel told her. He had a tough yet jovial face, the signs of a drinking habit on his broken-veined cheeks, but his posture was erect and his eyes alert. Skene might be weak, but men like Gordon and Dunlop most certainly weren't. 'I've ensured our good Doctor Mohamed is tending her husband. Mrs Mutlow has been given a position on my household staff, to meet the shortfall in their income.'

Trishala knew this; Emily spoke well of Gordon, especially that he hadn't tried to exploit her vulnerability. 'Thank you, Colonel. I was concerned for her after her husband's collapse.'

'The natives don't welcome her. It's the least I could do for the poor woman.'

Trishala heard the implicit criticism of her people. 'Feelings are running high among my people,' she said, in an apologetic voice. 'I am sure in normal times they would be more welcoming.'

'I am glad you think so, Captain Trishala. We are a small company here in Jhansi – fewer than seventy English souls. We rely on the friendship of the local community for our wellbeing.'

'Yes, Colonel,' Trishala couldn't help agreeing. 'Yes, you do.'

The colonel raised an ironic brow. 'Is that a warning, young lady?' He smiled good-naturedly, though his eyes were serious. He was no fool.

'Captain, not "young lady",' Trishala admonished, more to change the subject than anything else. She heard a giggle and glanced over to where young Miss Brown was laughing at a witticism from one of the Indian nobles, a distant uncle of Trishala's.

Colonel Gordon followed her eyes. 'A charming young woman, Miss Brown.'

'Very pretty,' Trishala conceded. The Englishwoman had

delicate brown curls, glinting blue eyes and a vivacious manner.

'Makes me wish I were a younger man.' Gordon indicated the screened area where the rani and her closest companions were indistinct shapes, like shadow puppets. 'This custom of receiving guests from behind a screen is . . . irksome. Barriers create mistrust, don't you think, Captain?'

Colonel Gordon was not someone who talked lightly on any subject, Trishala sensed, so she replied carefully, 'The rani is in mourning, and a widow. It isn't seemly for men to view her.'

Gordon gave a very Indian head-wag and snorted, then motioned toward a balcony. 'Will you take some fresh air with me, Captain?'

Trishala hesitated, caught between feeling she might learn something important and her sense of modesty – not to mention the fear of giving something away to this man who, for all his friendliness, was likely to soon become her enemy. But she walked with him out to the dimly lit balcony with its panoramic views of the stars overhead. The castle walls stretched around them, lit by lanterns and dotted with sentries in red jackets.

The colonel lit a cigar. 'You know, I thought I'd seen castles, back in England, but the fortifications here dwarf the keeps of my homeland. They look to me to be the handiwork of giants.'

Trishala, who had never left sight of Jhansi Fort, replied warily, 'Do you English not claim everything to be superior in your homeland?'

'Some say so. Not I.' He puffed smoke and slapped the

stone railing. 'Your land is as alien to mine as to defy comparison – so vast, so dry, so hot, so opulent. So many perils. Have you ever seen a map of the world, Captain Trishala?'

'No.' The largest map she'd seen depicted only the lands about Jhansi.

'The world is a sphere, Captain: did you know that? If you set forth and never stray from your direction, you will eventually reach the place you left, from the opposite direction. The sun traverses that globe in twenty-four hours. And do you know what?' He jabbed the smouldering cigar at her.

Trishala shrugged curiously, wondering what point he was making.

'The sun illuminates only half the globe at any one time. But there is never a point in its cycle that it doesn't illuminate some territory of the British Empire. Indeed, the sun never sets on the British Empire. Can you imagine that? No empire has been greater: not Alexander nor Caesar, not Genghis nor Attila nor Napoleon has ever had as great an empire as Queen Victoria of England.' He took another drag on the cigar. 'Do you know how that has been achieved, Captain?'

Trishala again shook her head, though she could see where this little lecture was going.

'Through sea power, Captain. There's nowhere on this globe that the British Navy cannot reach, and there it can disgorge men and guns. Any rebellion in the Empire is doomed, Captain – especially one as disorganised and hotchpotch as this mess at Meerut. Do you understand, Captain? *The rebellion is doomed.* Your rani *must* understand this, and so must people like you, whose lives would be staked in battle if it came to war. Believe me, Captain, for I know war as a son knows his mother.'

*It* is *a warning then* . . . She inclined her head in thanks, unsure what to say. *The sea is far from here*, she thought, but didn't say so.

Gordon appeared to be satisfied his message had been understood. 'A pleasure talking to you, Captain.' He shook her hand as if she were a fellow male officer then walked back inside.

Trishala looked up at the stars, trying to suppress the unease his words had stirred inside her. When she thought of war, it was mostly dreams of glory, of brave deeds and the acclamation of her queen. But speaking to Colonel Gordon reminded her that war was also maiming and disease and starvation and loss. War was death. *What will it feel like to kill? Can I even do it? Drills and exercises aren't the real thing.* And these Britishers had carried war into every corner of the world.

She stared out over the balcony rail for a long time, until someone touched her arm and she realised with a start that it was Emily Mutlow.

'Emily! What're you doing here?'

The woman looked extremely uncomfortable. 'I'm lost. I was looking for the colonel: his carriage is waiting and his wife sent me to find him. Which way is it to the courtyard?'

'This place can be a bit of a maze – don't worry; I'll show you.'

Trishala led Emily down a level, but was then brought up

short as she rounded a corner into a small garden and found herself before the rani and her closest friends. Lakshmibai turned at the sound of their entrance. 'Trishala, what are you doing here?'

'I'm sorry, rani!' she stammered, dragging Emily into a bow. 'I'm just helping Mrs Mutlow find her way out and this way was faster. I'm sorry—'

Lakshmibai stepped closer and peered curiously at Emily. 'So this is your English friend,' she said. 'Stand tall, both of you.' She examined Emily closely while the Englishwoman gaped as if in the presence of a goddess. 'You had an Indian mother, girl?'

Emily nodded, stricken speechless.

The women about the rani tittered unkindly, but Lakshmibai signed for silence. 'Remember your mother's heritage, girl,' she told Emily. She pointed to the far side of the garden. 'That way, Trishala.'

Trishala bowed again. 'Thank you, Rani.' She grabbed Emily's hand and pulled her along in her wake as they fled the garden.

Colonel Gordon was waiting in the lobby of the palace with Miss Brown. 'Ah, there is our stray nurse. I'm in your debt for finding her, Captain Trishala.' He gestured Emily towards a carriage, then offered Trishala an arm. 'It always looks better if an old fellow like me has a pretty thing like you on his arm,' he joked.

Trishala forced a smile and allowed herself to be walked to the carriageway.

A plump Englishwoman with a ruddy face peered at them and asked, 'Are you flirting, Colonel-sahib?' Her voice was laced with sarcastic humour. Trishala recognised the doctor's wife, Mrs McEgan.

'Heavens no,' Gordon protested. 'This young thing is a warrior – she would have me in pieces were I to overstep even an inch.'

'Then she's my sort of woman,' retorted Mrs McEgan. 'All the ladies of this court are veritable war-hawks, Gordon. Never seen the like before.' She was panting in the heat and sweat had soaked her heavy dress.

'Indeed. I've seen this young beauty beside me galloping hither and thither like a young bravo.'

Trishala shifted uncomfortably, but plucked up the courage to speak. 'The rani says that our body tone improves from the exercise of riding. A woman who succumbs to laziness is diminished in beauty.'

'Then perhaps our wives should join her Majesty's ladies in their riding,' Colonel Gordon chuckled softly, eyeing Mrs McEgan struggling through the too-narrow carriage door and making the whole carriage tilt. He bowed to Trishala. 'Good night, Captain.'

Trishala saw Motibai seeing off a tipsy Major Skene, then paused when the vivacious Miss Brown exclaimed over her jewellery. Trishala didn't like wearing anything but her military attire these days, but the Rani had insisted they dress with all femininity for the night. Even Karuna had been made to don something feminine, though Karu hated the English and could barely be trusted with them socially. Trishala liked Miss Brown, though; the young woman's lively chatter made her smile.

'Is Mrs Mutlow bearing up?' she asked.

'Oh, she's well enough, caring for the children,' Miss Brown replied. 'The major insisted on presenting the little ones to the rani, and as his wife is unwell, he asked me to be his escort tonight. Look, here is our carriage now! Emily and the children will be inside already.' She waved at Trishala in a perky way, then climbed into the carriage. Trishala peered in to see two bleary-eyed children, a boy of perhaps eight and a girl of around five draped over the seats, half asleep. The girl opened her eyes briefly and gave Trishala a drowsy smile. Emily, beside her, waved her thanks, then the door was pulled shut and the carriages lurched noisily away amidst the clatter of hooves.

Trishala found Kashi waiting for her at the far end of the courtyard, who took her into a quiet corner. The palace was drifting towards sleep, but Kashi was wide awake, her eyes shining. 'Trishala, I have a task for you, assigned by Rani Lakshmibai herself. Things are moving. The men are going to act – the Rani cannot dissuade them.'

Trishala stared, her heart thumping. 'You mean——?'

'The sepoys of the local Company are planning to mutiny, so we will have war, ready or not.' Kashi seized Trishala's arm just beneath the shoulder in a hard grip. 'Are you ready to serve the queen?'

'Of course——'

Kashi whispered in her ear, 'The rani must play a dangerous game right now, Trishala. She cannot be seen to aid the rebellion, but she cannot turn her back on her own people either, so we must strengthen our hand. Tomorrow you are to take five empty gun carriages out past the Orchha road to the dell on the north side to retrieve the cannons we buried there. Those guns are big and the paths are cattle-tracks at best, but we need them by midday of the day after tomorrow. Take Karuna and six of the Palaka. A sepoy sergeant called Hassad will be there with fifty men and twelve oxen. You will assume command of the mission, understood? No man will command you. You speak with the voice of the rani.'

Trishala felt a tremor run through her. 'So soon?'

'Our hand is forced: our men will rebel, with or without us. The rani must take a lead or be swept aside. The day after tomorrow, the sepoy cavalry will mutiny, refusing orders, but not attacking. Dunlop will no doubt order them stood down and begin to discipline them. We will protest this, and call all to the masjid for prayer: that is to be the signal. The bungalows will burn while Dunlop and the military officers are taken prisoner and we will regain control of our fort.'

*How calm Kashi is . . . and how scared I am, now that the moment has come.*

'What of the women and children?' Trishala asked, thinking of Emily, and Miss Brown and those ridiculous but harmless dumpling-wives of the Britishers. And of Joshua . . .

'The prisoners will be unharmed, of course,' Kashi replied distantly. 'We cannot afford an outrage that forces the British to retaliate.' She took Trishala's hand. 'Harden your heart, sister. You mustn't see the enemy as human: not in war-time. Battles are won by those with hard hearts who cauterise their emotions. The English regime is evil; it strips our nation of wealth and resource and co-opts our aid against *their* enemies, bleeding our people for their own ends. Their regime must be ended, and to achieve this, innocents and guilty alike will suffer until the Britishers see sense and leave. There's no other way. Do you understand?'

Trishala nodded, thinking about an empire on which the sun never set — and Joshua's face, with smiling eyes and a mouth made for tasting.

'The sepoys will do the fighting,' Kashi went on. 'They need to be blooded. Don't endanger yourself; this is just the first blow.' Then she shocked Trishala by stepping forward and kissing her cheek. 'The queen needs you, Trishala. She needs all of us. So don't get yourself killed.'

Once, at a banquet, Trishala had asked an English officer what being a soldier was like. The Englishman had replied that it was long hours of boredom, interspersed with fleeting moments of terror. 'And the funny thing is, those moments feel like hours too,' he'd added, his eyes far away.

Trishala didn't know about 'fleeting moments of terror' yet, but the hours of boredom she could certainly attest to. The excitement of her secret mission had long dissipated by the time they had recovered the cannon barrels, dressed down the surly sepoys for their flagrant disregard of the rani's female soldiers and her own authority, then wheeled the cannon under sweltering skies back toward the cantonment. Slow, hot and tedious.

Then smoke climbed the skies from the direction of Jhansi and the first cannon boomed like distant thunder. Suddenly she wasn't bored any more. 'It's not yet midday, but they've begun burning the bungalows,' Trishala guessed, and Karuna's nostrils flared at the thought. She looked down at the sepoy sergeant and cried, 'Faster, Sergeant Hassad!'

For once the man didn't grumble. The sepoys came alive with enthusiasm and their pace doubled as they rumbled along the rough path, rattling over the ruts. As they topped the final ridge and heard musket fire, the sepoys cheered, waving their helms and firing guns into the air – but Trishala saw that the British flag still flew in Jhansi Fort, where the rani's flag ought to have been.

'Save your powder,' Karuna snarled at the men, but the sergeant and his men paid her no attention as they whooped happily. Karuna fingered her pistol angrily.

Trishala spotted a rider approaching and went forward to meet him.

'Captain Trishala,' the messenger hollered, 'the Britishers are in Jhansi Fort. The rani has ceded these cannons to the army and I am here to see them deployed before the palace gates by mid-afternoon.' He thrust some papers into her hands. 'Here are the orders!'

Trishala blinked at the papers. *The Rani ceded the guns? Why?*

She looked up in confusion, about to argue, when Kashi galloped up and pulled her aside. 'The sepoys are out of control. The rani has ceded the guns to avoid conflict with them.'

'But . . .'

'Yes, I know – we're caught in the middle, damn them,' Kashi snarled, then waved Karuna over and repeated her news. Karu was furious, but Kashi promised, 'We'll get our chance. These men are all bluster – so far they've failed to retake the fort.'

'How many Britishers are defending it?' Trishala asked.

'Are we going to have to fight our way into our own fortress?'

Kashi scowled. 'They took fright yesterday and moved most of their people inside. The bungalows were burned too soon, by some hot-headed boys who couldn't wait. It was botched, and that gave the Britishers warning. The attempt to seize the fort failed, and now they're holed up in there with plenty of guns and ammunition.'

Trishala spat. Couldn't these men do *anything* right? Why wouldn't they listen to the rani?

The messenger trotted over, grinning bloodthirstily. 'Dunlop and all the Britishers caught at the parade ground are dead, Captain. The bungalows are burned, but many escaped and joined the garrison in the palace. There are some fifty within the palace, but most are women or children. Our commanders have demanded their surrender. Meantime, we need these cannon.'

Karuna was praying, Trishala noticed, no doubt for the chance to kill someone. She herself felt disgusted at the whole thing. 'Then take them,' she snapped. 'We must attend upon the queen. Kashi, Karuna, come with me.' The three women spurred their horses away, leaving the messenger and Hassad spluttering in a cloud of dust.

'We're going to slaughter them all,' Karuna growled, flexing her hands.

Trishala thought of Emily Mutlow, Miss Brown and the Skene children and shivered. Then she thought of Joshua and began to tremble.

*

The narrow defile to the fortress was dotted with rough-clothed corpses – the sepoys had discarded their red uniforms in the first hours of mutiny. Flocks of crows scattered every time muskets volleyed, only to come flying back, squawking hungrily, the instant the racket paused. Whenever the attackers glimpsed a red uniform moving stealthily on the battlements, they fired madly in that direction, for all the defenders were well out of range.

Trishala was among the crowd of Durga Dal officers watching the carnage from the roof of the queen's residence. She peered through a spyglass, counting the corpses: some dozen men were down, victims of the torrid fire the Britishers were maintaining. Gordon was up there, Skene too, and she could see the wives loading and firing guns themselves. Joshua and Mark and Emily Mutlow must be too, she assumed. There couldn't be more than thirty-five adults defending the castle, but unlike the mutinying Indians, their fire was deadly, and now the sepoys were afraid to charge.

'They must have several guns per man,' she commented to Karuna. She glanced at the rani, who was attired in her ceremonial battle-gear, complete with gleaming breastplate and plumed helmet: a true queen at war.

'This is ridiculous – our menfolk are cowards,' Mandar snarled. 'They thought it would be easy and now they see it's not, they want someone else to do the dirty work. They cower and break at the first volley. They have no steel in them!'

'Let us try, Rani,' Juhi begged. 'The Palaka won't let you down—'

Lakshmibai shook her head. 'You are too precious to me, sisters. This is just a skirmish. The English can't have much powder or shot remaining, so it will be over soon. Within a few weeks they will send an army here, and then there will be a real battle. I must preserve you for that greater struggle, sisters.' She glanced down at the earthworks where the sepoys were wrestling the cannons into position. 'Let's see if they can get those cannon set up before dusk.'

Juhi lapsed into sullen silence, glaring at the walls of the palace. Mandar glanced to the west. 'Sunset will be soon, Rani. Perhaps a night attack?'

'I will suggest it. Skene is a weakling: he will capitulate soon.' Lakshmibai indicated a flock of nobles and mullahs and pandits below, as noisy as the crows and about as much use. 'I must join these squabbling men who claim to lead this rabble. They're arguing like washerwomen, so someone must take control.'

Trishala started awake as a serving woman wrapped in a blanket tapped her shoulder and proffered a thimble-sized cup of milky chai. She blinked and gazed about. Amazing how you could fall asleep when men were firing and shouting below, while behind her in the town there appeared to be a massive festival, as if victory were already won.

She sipped the chai gratefully as she tried to determine what was happening. It must be the middle of the night. The dusk attack on the main gate had been as disastrous as the first: the cannon hadn't been properly positioned and none of the sepoys were trained gunners. The mutineering army majors were too busy arguing among themselves – and clearly all the men disliked the rani taking a hand. The result had been an uncoordinated disaster.

*However will we cast out the English if this is the best we can do?*

She'd seen Joshua on the battlement, firing a musket – she'd had a clear shot, but hadn't taken it. He looked wounded already, she rationalised to herself, so it would be a waste of a bullet. Now she couldn't stop herself praying for his survival.

The serving woman touched her shoulder again. 'Trishala,' she said, her voice familiar.

Trishala clutched her chest. 'Emily?' she gasped, suddenly wide awake. 'What are you doing here?' She glanced about, but there was no one near them.

'I had to see you,' Emily whispered urgently. 'There are ways in and out of the fortress, if you know where to look – my ayah showed me.'

'You shouldn't be here – if someone recognises you, they'll tear you apart,' Trishala hissed. 'Please, take this chance and run—'

But Emily laid a finger over her lips and said, 'I can't run, Trishala, not until I've done what I have to do . . .'

'Do what?'

Emily pressed her mouth to Trishala's ear. 'I had a dream about my husband and you and the rani. You know the necklace, the smoky crystal the queen wore at the reception? I saw it when we met her in the gardens . . . In my dream, I saw it dangling in front of my eyes, and then my husband appeared: he told me it was the most important thing in the world, but that an enemy was closing in on us all – but he wasn't just *my* Mark, but many people, all at once – no, don't laugh, *listen*. Somehow I knew that once he and I had true happiness, and we lived in a great fine palace – not this one but another, long, long ago, when there were no Britishers here. There was a great king whom everyone loved and my husband was his friend – and *you* were there, Trishala: you were rani, married to the king, my husband's friend.'

'Did this king have a name?' Trishala asked doubtfully.

'Prithvi,' Emily responded, with a shrug; clearly the name meant nothing to her. 'Prithviraj Chauhan. And Sanyogita, that was your name—'

*Sanyogita! That name again.* Trishala felt as if the ground beneath her was shifting. 'You're talking nonsense,' she heard herself say. *And yet* . . .

But Emily hasn't finished. 'That gem – it belonged to my husband. He gave it to me and made me promise to take it far away so that his Enemy couldn't find it. He kept telling me, over and over, that it was more important than anything else in the world and I had to take it somewhere far away . . . but I don't remember where . . .' Emily looked at Trishala, big eyes welling with tears. 'I have to get the queen's necklace and keep it safe—'

*The haunted gem*, Trishala thought wildly. *The White Lady* . . . Then reality took over. 'You're mad, Emily. You can't steal from the rani—'

'But I have to,' Emily said forcefully, 'I *have* to – please, Trishala, *please*, help me.'

'I should just call the guards,' Trishala flared, hissing into her face. *How dare a half-breed speak of robbing the queen? How dare she imagine I would help her?* 'Go,' she snapped, 'run – get away from this madness.'

'I can't – Trishala, I can't get even sleep any more; the dream won't let me. Please, *help*—'

'Go – I'm warning you—'

Emily pulled away. 'I *will* take it, Trishala. *I must*.' She slipped into the shadows.

'Where are you going?' Trishala called after her.

'Back inside the fort,' Emily replied. 'They need me – they need every hand.'

'It's a death-trap there – you have to leave them—' But Trishala could see that Emily wasn't heeding her. She bit her lip, unable to stop herself asking, 'Is . . . is Joshua well? And your husband?'

'Both live,' came the hesitant whisper from the shadows. 'Joshua sends his regards.'

Then Emily was gone.

Trishala couldn't sleep afterwards, but when she joined the rani the next morning, she couldn't bring herself to mention the incident either – not with the name *Sanyogita* ringing in her mind like a bell.

Lakshmibai Rani wore the ghostly gem about her throat all that day.

# CHAPTER EIGHTEEN

# JHANSI: FLIGHT OF THE BANISHED

*Jhansi, Bundelkhand, 7 June 1857*

Trishala watched the great orange disc of the sun fall through the haze into shadow, yawned and turned back to the defile leading to the gates of the fort. Under the latest truce, a crowd of unarmed Jhansi men were pulling away the fallen: another thirty-three dead and even more wounded. Their cannonade had been incompetent, barely chipping the stone and never hitting the same place twice.

'At least my palace will be intact when I reclaim it,' Lakshmibai had commented sourly.

Trishala had been beside the rani most of the day, acting as her aide while her officers came and went, trying to coordinate the attack on the fort or keeping peace in the town. She relished the chance to be near her queen, but the deathly drama being played out before her made her sick to her stomach.

At the end of another frustrating afternoon of delays

and failures, Lakshmibai laid a hand on her shoulder. 'Come. I must go and meet the latest messengers from Tantia Tope.'

By now all of India was aflame and Tantia Tope, a Brahmin from Nashik, had emerged as one of the Mutiny's leading generals. He was coming to Jhansi to unite forces with the local mutineers.

'What he really wants is to get me under his thumb,' Lakshmibai muttered. 'But we need him.'

They wound through the narrow alleys, struggling against the tide of soldiers and civilians, until someone recognised her and called out blessings upon their queen. As the call was taken up, people knelt in waves, making progress even more difficult.

The queen hissed impatiently and looked around for some way out. 'Let's go through this way and get off the main streets,' she murmured to Trishala, 'or we'll be here all night!'

She turned to the right and led Trishala down a narrow lane, familiar in the daytime but transformed into a place of mystery by the falling light. 'It's a relief to be alone,' the rani admitted. She looked tired, for the first time Trishala could ever remember.

'Rani . . .' Trishala began, about to suggest safe passage for the women trapped in the palace, but the words died in her throat. Even Lakshmibai sucked in her breath in shock at what lay before them.

There was a pale shape at the end of the alley, shrouded in white like a funeral mourner made of mist and gauze. Whispers cut through the sudden silence and a wave of gelid air prickled Trishala's skin. She shivered involuntarily and clutched at the queen's arm protectively. 'The White Lady!' she gasped.

The rani shook her off and stepped forward. 'Who are you?' she demanded, then, 'Come here.'

The pale shape wavered like a reflection in a pool of disturbed water, then flowed into a gap between the buildings. Lakshmibai seized Trishala's hand and they ran towards where the wraith-like figure had vanished. 'That's a dead end,' Trishala panted. 'It leads to a bowri.'

'Then it's trapped,' the rani said, without a trace of fear. 'Come—'

As they turned the corner, Trishala's heart was in her mouth, but the alley was empty. It opened onto torch-lit stairs that led down to the water-tank. The cool, dank air rising from the bowri seemed to bypass the skin and freeze the soul. Something exhaled venomously, but the two lit torches at the head of the steps revealed nothing.

Trishala drew her sword, and said, 'We should go, Rani – it's the White Lady – a bhoot—'

The rani snorted. 'There are no such things as ghosts, Trishala. I'll wager it's some prankster trying to scare us. Let's flush them out.'

Lakshmibai clearly wouldn't be dissuaded, so Trishala stepped in front of her. 'Let me go first, Rani.' Without awaiting approval, she snatched up a torch in her left hand and slowly descended the narrow steps, moving warily past niches and pillars towards the water. Lakshmibai followed six steps behind her, brandishing sword and pistol. The torches guttered at faint breezes and water plinked down unseen. Trishala's eyes swept side to side, vainly seeking any sign of the pale figure.

She reached the final step and peered into the black water. Her reflection stared back up from the still surface. The air was cold and smelled of the green slime on the surface; it radiated fear – or maybe reflected it back from her own heart.

Then she realised that the face in her reflection was wrong. The planes of the cheeks, the shape of the mouth – and the clothing was wrong too: no armour, no weapons . . .

*. . . it's not me . . .*

She went down on one knee, staring. The eyes in the reflection met hers and somehow there was recognition. '*Sanyogita?*' she whispered. But the image in the water shook its head – and then fled, turning and vanishing into the depths . . . or the heights? Trishala looked up at the sloped roof, which was covered in hanging bats – and suddenly they weren't just hanging there but boiling over each other, snarling down at her. Her skin crawled as the rank smell swept over her and she couldn't stop herself squealing as they erupted from above. As she staggered and fell, Lakshmibai gasped too, and fell onto her back, her armour clattering on the stone steps. Trishala cringed as the entire colony of bats swooped upon her, thrashing desperately . . .

. . . at thin air.

The bats swept over her, the wind of their passing washing her with their musky reek as they went streaming up the stairs. Her vision flattened down to a continuous flow of wings and teeth and eyes, lit only by the torch in her hand – and yet not one of the creatures touched her.

'Rani!' she shrieked above the din of wings and the squeaking of the swarm.

'Trishala, be calm – they're not attacking, just flying away . . .' Even the rani sounded thankful.

In a few seconds the bats were gone and Trishala could breathe again – until she saw what the bats had been fleeing. The White Lady stalked over the water towards the two sprawling women as if walking the earth, her hands spread, her nails long and curved. Livid eyes burned beneath a shadowy cowl. Trishala tried to stand, but the bhoot was on her in an instant, swatting her aside with a backhanded blow that struck her throat like a charging horse. She was hurled against the slimy wall and crashed to the ground, unable to breathe, her skin burning as if a block of ice had seared her throat.

A shot reverberated through the chamber and the flash from Lakshmibai's gun turned the bhoot vivid orange for an instant as the ball ripped through the cobwebby form and buried itself in the wall. The ghost-woman snarled and ripped aside Lakshmibai's blade, then reached for the queen's throat.

'NOOOOO!' Trishala heard the word rip from her lips. She lurched upright and threw her blade, which tore through the White Lady's gauzy form. Trishala was still holding the guttering torch as she staggered up the steps.

The thrown sword had no more than a passing effect on the spectral shape, but it did make it turn from the queen, venting a shrill snarl. Trishala read death in the ghostly visage, but pitched forward anyway, desperate to protect her rani. She thrust the torch before her, crying out to the gods for protection – and was shocked to see the White Lady snarl and jerk away from the flames, which gave Trishala time to interpose herself between Lakshmibai and the ghost. She started brandishing the torch like a sword while the rani regained her feet.

'Get away from us!' Trishala shouted, a fury rising inside her that was almost as frightening as the wraith before her. Then the White Lady struck, her clawed hands raking at Trishala's face and throat. She met the first with the torch, but when it went spinning, icy fingernails raked her face, ripping open her right cheek from eye socket to jaw. She howled, and in that moment, as the White Lady flowed past her, she lost control utterly: something primitive and furious inside Trishala exploded, an ocean of rage that came boiling up from her mouth.

Fire washed over the ghost, making it shriek and recoil. Trishala spat something that emerged from her throat as a flame that sizzled through the frozen air and made the ghost's body steam. The White Lady jerked and was instantly ten feet away. '*Come back and die!*' Trishala roared at it.

The ghost gave a wailing cry of rage, turned and plummeted into the water . . . which didn't even ripple as she vanished. Abruptly alone, Trishala reeled, trying to fight down this sudden addictive strength. *I made fire – I spat flames at the ghost and drove it away—*She turned . . .

. . . and saw her beloved queen backing away from her fearfully. That snapped her back into control and her sudden rage vanished, replaced by a fragile clarity. 'Rani – it's all right – it's only me—' They stared at each other as a dizzying weakness swept through Trishala. 'Let's get out of here – she may return if we stay.' But Rani Lakshmibai didn't move. 'Rani?'

'Trishala . . . *or whoever you are* . . . what just happened?'

*Whoever I am?* 'Rani, it's me – just your Trishala . . . I was so afraid – when she reached for your throat, I thought you would die—'

'It wasn't my throat she was reaching for,' the queen replied in a hollow voice. 'It was this.' She clutched the necklace, its smoky stone glinting in the pale light. 'She wanted this.'

Trishala stared at the jewel and Emily's words flooded back to her. 'Yes – of course, that's what it wanted. Rani, you're going to think I'm insane when I tell you this, but—'

'No, *I* am the one who is insane, Trishala. I saw you pour fire from your mouth. I saw you burn away a bhoot before my very eyes. I saw you *change*. Who are you?'

'I am your loyal servant Trishala—' She tried to reach out to her, to reassure her rani, but Lakshmibai stepped quickly away.

'Don't touch me. What are you? What are you doing here?'

Trishala could feel her entire future melting away. 'Rani, I'm just an ordinary girl – please, serving you is all I've ever wanted—'

The queen raised her sword between them. 'You are a rakshasa: I banish you – I abjure you – leave and never return.'

Trishala took half a step towards her and the blade came up, severing Trishala from all she ever loved. 'Go,' Rani Lakshmibai commanded, her voice a blend of dread and fierce courage.

Trishala sagged, tears running down her cheeks as she stared at the queen's sword. *If I take a step closer, she'll kill me.* The salty tears burned her cut cheek, but the blade didn't waver. 'I love you, Rani. I would die for you,' she pleaded.

'*Get out of here, demon,*' the queen ordered again, and Trishala fell to her knees, sobbing, as the rani climbed the steps, leaving her alone in the darkness.

Trishala haunted the streets, cowering beneath her cloak as she paced filthy alleys, passed stinking animal pens and lurked sobbing in doorways, hiding whenever patrols passed. Finally, the rattle and boom of the guns drove her from town, out into the arid farmlands. As the moon dipped westward, she found a tree far from the edge of the town and sat against it, wondering what point there was to breathing any more. She was bereft, every anchor-line of her life cut. Where could she go? How could she exist? Lakshmibai's face hovered above hers, that perfect visage closed and rejecting.

*Exile* . . . It would have been kinder if the queen had run her through.

But as dawn blossomed in the east, she realised there was nothing for her anywhere but here: Jhansi and its queen were her life. She couldn't serve another ruler; apart from anything else, they would treat her as a freak. Everywhere except here in Jhansi, where Lakshmibai ruled, women were for breeding and subservience, and she couldn't accept that.

There was only one person who could make exile endurable. A new life, away from here, would only be bearable if she were to share it with a man who knew the world, someone who would treat her as she wished – no, *deserved* – to be treated. But Joshua Mutlow was currently trapped inside Jhansi Fort.

She walked furtively back into town, wrapped in her cloak to hide her uniform, with a stolen dupatta over her head. The men were attacking the palace once more. They were using elephants to try to break through the gates – but the British fire from within was deadly, and she felt the stirrings of that insane rage inside her again as she saw the Jhansi men fall under the withering accuracy of the defenders. She wept at her people's dithering, half-hearted assaults, torn between the wish to join them and redeem herself before the rani, and thankfulness that their failures were keeping Joshua and his kin alive.

As morning became afternoon she found a vantage point and settled down to plan how to get inside the fort and get Joshua out. How had Emily managed?

But she'd waited too long: with a sudden devastating crash, the cannon finally spoke in unison and smashed the main gates. The British fire slackened and she could hear the townsfolk cheering; she saw the rani herself, near the gates, surrounded by cheering rebel officers. She crept closer, mingling with the onlookers hiding out of the line of fire, watching breathlessly, but no one recognised her beneath the dupatta. Finally the guns fell silent and the royal doctor, Hakeem Saleh Mohamed, entered under a parley flag. He returned soon after, and suddenly all about the rani were cheering exultantly.

The British had surrendered.

Trishala watched the rani lead the most senior men and

women towards a nearby house, her temporary headquarters, which belonged to a cousin's family. Trishala worked her way through the crowds of cheering men firing their guns into the air and hammering excitedly on each other's backs. There was a bloodthirsty heat in their eyes as they chanted, 'Bring out the Britishers!'

The gaoler, Bakhshish Ali, was one of the loudest of the men howling for blood. Frightened of recognition, Trishala ducked her head. There were many new faces in this mob, half-wild deserters who had ridden in the day before, eager for retribution. These 'Irregulars' terrified Trishala: they exuded an indiscriminate savagery, and she was grateful to escape their vicinity.

Stealing into the makeshift headquarters was easy enough; she climbed the back wall onto an upstairs balcony, then crept to an open window. Inside was a babble of voices, until Emir Korani, the commander of the Irregulars, raised his voice, demanding the prisoners be given to him. The hunger for violence in his voice was palpable.

'To let them go now would be an act of treachery to all of the people of India,' he thundered.

There was an explosion of noise, both those in agreement and naysayers, but the rani's voice carried clearly above them. 'The prisoners are mine and I have promised them release. What would it avail us to do otherwise?'

'By what authority can you claim them as *your* prisoners?' Emir Korani bellowed furiously. 'I have brought my men here to kill Britishers, Rani, and kill them we will! Besides, there are those inside whom I have pledged to destroy—'

'Your private vendettas are no concern to me, Emir Korani,' Rani Lakshmibai replied coldly.

But the men shouted against her until the voice of Bakhshish Ali raised above the rest, saying, 'You are no queen of ours if you won't hand them over!'

'Tantia Tope has decreed there will be no prisoners,' Korani stated. 'If the rani doesn't have the stomach for rebellion, then she has no place at this table.'

Trishala could picture her mistress' face at such a statement: beautiful fury. 'How *dare* you?' the queen snapped. 'I am Rani of Jhansi by right and I am a true child of India. This rebellion has begun at my instigation, and will continue in my hands!' Her words were incandescent, but Trishala knew, as all present must have, that this last statement was a lie, and a capitulation. The rani hadn't wanted the rebellion but now that the tiger of war had been unleashed, she had to ride it. 'I have no concern for the English swine,' the rani went on coldly, and Trishala wondered who else could hear the lie in her words, 'but my honour demands that those who surrendered to me are mine to dispose of.'

'Your honour is of little concern to me, Rani,' came the cruel voice of Emir Korani. 'I have personal grievance with men among the prisoners and I will seek justice, with or without your blessing.' The voices of his men rose in support like the snarling of a dog-pack, and Trishala felt frightened for her queen's safety.

The room fell quiet again and Korani spoke again. 'We're waiting, Rani.'

When the rani spoke again, her voice was hollow. 'Then

let the prisoners be taken to the Irregular cavalry at Johtun Bagh Square. Emir Korani will see to their safety.'

The room fell silent. They all knew what that meant. The Irregulars were the least disciplined, most bloodthirsty of the mutineers, corralled from the countryside by Korani and others like him. They were ragged, undisciplined and murderous.

The rani was sending the Britishers to their deaths.

There were several seconds, and then voices rose again, but the rani cut them off. Trishala heard her hands clap, ending the topic of discussion, though her voice had a haunted timbre. 'We have larger issues to worry us. The British will send more soldiers. I want you all at my table in two hours to discuss dispositions. Tantia Tope has promised to join forces with us. We are at war. See to your men, then report back to me in the town palace in two hours for council.'

Trishala pictured the faces of those the rani had condemned: Emily, Miss Brown, Skene and his children, Emily and Mark . . . and above all, Joshua.

*I must get to him somehow . . .*

When all was silent inside, she looked in the window. Lakshmibai was alone, sitting on a stool, her head in her hands and her shoulders shaking. Trishala wavered, then slipped silently through the window into the room. 'Rani?' she whispered.

The rani convulsed, and jerked to her feet. Her face was streaked with tears that she wiped away furiously. 'What do you want?' she demanded fearfully. 'I told you to leave—'

'You've sent the Britishers to die. They're all going to be murdered.'

'You think I don't know what's going to happen to them? I had no choice – if I let them live, I would lose all authority over these men. I'd lose all respect—' She shuddered, then went on, 'They follow me only because they see my strength. If they think me weak, they would set me aside in a heartbeat.'

'But the women . . . *the children* . . .' Trishala longed to go to her, but if she moved, the queen would call for her guard, and her sisters would take her and kill her.

The queen waved her hand angrily. 'I know that. Trishala – or whoever you are – you think like a child. This is a man's world, and all I have done to make our lives as women better will be swept away if I falter. I cannot show weakness, not now – so do not presume to judge me.'

'I believed in you,' Trishala said sadly. 'I wanted you to be perfect, Lakshmibai-ji – indeed, I thought you *were* perfect: the personification of all virtues. But you're only human . . .'

Lakshmibai took a small step towards Trishala, as if forgetting her fear that she was anything but a confused young woman. 'Of course I'm only human – that's all any of us can be. I wanted to protect them, but there was no choice. These are hard times, Trishala – and you're only a child, after all.' She reached her hands behind her neck and took off the crystal necklace. 'Here,' she said, 'take this and go. Perhaps it really is cursed. Give it to the White Lady, or whatever it is you think you must do. Never come back, but live in peace, with your dreams of perfect worlds.'

Trishala took the necklace, and for one painful instant their fingers brushed, sending a shockwave through her. 'I would have died for you, Rani,' she whispered.

'Yes, I know, child. But I don't want you to.'

Trishala took one abrupt step, then another, and wrapped her arms around her beloved queen as if she were a sister. She kissed her cheeks and whispered, 'Be safe, Rani. Don't get all our sisters killed.'

Stepping away from the stricken queen was like having her heart torn in two, but the next step was easier, and then she was moving. Her final sight of her rani was of a regal woman with a torn expression, her eyes streaming fresh tears.

The press in the streets was incredible, sweeping Trishala along. Everyone was going to Johtun Bagh Square, where the Britishers were to be taken. The marketplace at the heart of the itinerants' dwellings was on the south side, outside the town walls, where the dwellings were more tents and hovels than solid houses of mud-brick. As she got closer, darting and pushing through the press, the din of the mob filled the air, baying for vengeance for every wrong they had stored up against the English. Armed men were everywhere, holding back the civilians with crossed spears. She found a precarious perch just as the first of the Irregular cavalry rode past.

Emir Korani was at their head, his bearded face sensuous and arrogant, his eyes piercing. She hid her face behind her dupatta: for no reason she could explain, she felt mortally afraid of being seen by him. Then came Bakhshish Ali, smirking as he walked before a ragged train of Irregulars, all heavily armed, whooping back to the crowd, feeding on their energy.

Behind them came the first of the British. Major Skene walked dazedly, a bandage about his head, his once immaculate uniform smeared with dirt and stained with sweat and black powder. His face had a look of resigned determination she'd never seen on it before. Someone had remarked that he had fought like a tiger during the siege, and now she could credit it. After him came the other survivors, their eyes a mixture of defiance and fear, the wounded men supported by less injured fellows. Gordon was not among them – he'd been shot early on by a sniper. Then came the women: Mrs Skene, staring about her in disbelief, her thin, pale children clinging to her. Fat Mrs McEgan, clutching the hand of her doctor husband, glaring about her furiously. Miss Brown, sobbing helplessly on the arm of a limping corporal. Finally she saw Joshua, cradling Mark Mutlow in his big arms, his head aloft and proud, for all it was wrapped in a bloodied bandage.

A hand clutched Trishala's shoulder and she nearly screamed and fell off her vantage.

'Shhh!' whispered Emily Mutlow, holding her steady.

Trishala turned, aghast. The woman was dressed in a sari, with a wide dupatta that she had pulled over her face. Cheap bangles clattered on her wrists. Her skin was dirtied, her hair dyed with henna. She looked entirely Indian. Trishala swallowed. 'What——?'

Emily touched a finger to her lips, hushing her. 'My ayah hid me among the servants. She's promised to shelter me. Come away – there's nothing we can do here. Please, come with me.'

Trishala gaped at her helplessly, then she heard a child cry out and her eyes were wrenched back to the column of prisoners. Little Ruth Skene was comforting her elder brother, their words lost in the cacophony.

Emily tugged at Trishala frantically. 'Come away!'

Then the noise of the crowd suddenly took on a different quality and their eyes were dragged back to the column and the men about it. Trishala pulled Emily into an embrace, needing to feel the comfort of other arms, but she was shaking uncontrollably. Together, they watched as Bakhshish Ali and his thugs herded the Britishers into a circle. The crowd flowed closer, pushing Trishala and Emily towards the knot of frightened prisoners.

For a split-second Trishala locked eyes with five-year-old Ruth Skene. The little girl raised a forlorn hand, then Trishala lost sight of her. She felt her gorge rise.

'Now, see here,' Major Skene's voice carried loudly, 'we were promised—'

Bakhshish Ali slapped him brutally, making him stagger. 'Promises?' he guffawed. 'Promises are nothing, *pig*. They mean *nothing*.' He drew a huge knife and seized the major's collar. 'My only regret is that this must be so brief,' he drawled.

He slashed the knife across Skene's throat. An arc of blood sprayed. As women and children started screaming, Emily buried her face against Trishala's chest.

The cavalrymen and Bakhshish Ali's thugs closed in like wolves. Doctor McEgan was butchered first, then his wife was cut open as she clung to his body. Miss Brown fell to her knees before a sepoy, begging, and the man reached out a hand to her – then as she looked up at him pleadingly, he plunged his sabre into her breast, grinning maniacally. Trishala heard Joshua roaring in fury, but the noise of the killers and the dying soon blended as one. She turned away, swaying and sickened, fighting the urge to explode in fury.

Emily dragged her through the crowd.

She glanced backwards to see Bakhshish Ali, atop someone's shoulders, brandishing a bloodied spear. For an instant, she seemed to see the gaoler as some fiendish thing, all misshaped horns and teeth. His head turned and his eyes locked on hers. His mouth moved and he raised a blade, shouting and pointing at her.

She pulled Emily into a run and they pelted through the alleys.

She went straight for the stables and speedily saddled two horses, hanging four of the saddlebags left ready-provisioned over the beasts, together with as many extra water-bags as they could carry, her mind thrashing hopelessly. Joshua was dead, and the world was turning to blood. Fiends from legend walked the chaos. Where could she run – and how was she to get Emily and this damned necklace out of here?

She helped Emily onto one horse, then led the horses to the stable doors . . . where a shadow fell across their path.

'I thought you'd come here,' Karuna said.

Trishala's blood froze in her veins, but she found her tongue. 'Karuna, *please*, let us pass.'

'Where are you going, sister?' Karuna asked, her voice betraying nothing. Trishala could see a pistol in her hands. Her face was hidden, silhouetted against the light outside so that her expression was unreadable. But her cheeks were wet with perspiration, or tears, or both. 'Where are you taking this half-breed rundi?' She cocked her pistol. 'All the Britishers must go to Johtun Bagh Square.'

'They're all dead, Karu: every man and woman and child. Isn't that enough for you?'

'I must do my duty,' Karuna replied, her voice cracking. 'Why are you throwing your life away, Trishi?' she asked, but her pistol remained levelled at Emily. 'Why are you ruining everything?'

Trishala stepped in front of Karuna, quailing inwardly to suddenly be staring down the barrel of the pistol, but lifting her chin. 'Step aside, Karu. There's been enough blood.'

*She's going to kill us both.*

'You're like a sister to me, Trishi,' Karuna sobbed. 'But why did the rani banish you? Have you betrayed us? Are you a traitor?'

'I'm no traitor. The rani ordered me to leave over a . . . personal matter. Please, let us go, Karu, if you still have a heart.'

'If I *still* have a heart?' Karuna echoed. 'You think I enjoyed that savagery? Soldiers are one thing, but they butchered the women and children too . . . Those *men* . . .'

Karuna made the word 'men' seem the most hideous word possible.

'It's what they'll do to me and Emily, Karu,' Trishala told her, straining her ears and hearing a distinct clamour and the drumming of hooves. 'They're coming! Please, sister, let us go, before it's too late—'

Behind her back she gripped her own pistol and put a thumb on the hammer. Her heart was pounding fit to burst her ribs, and her hands were shaking. *Dear Gods, don't force me to choose . . .*

'The half-breed isn't capable of flight,' Karu observed, eying Emily coldly. 'You have no chance. Don't throw your life away for her.'

'I have no choice.' Trishala could hear those horse hooves pounding closer and didn't know if there was time for one last appeal, but she had to try. 'Cousin, who will rejoice if two more women die today? Only Bakhshish Ali and his ilk. Let us go – *or come with us* . . . I need you, *sister*.'

*Sister*: the word that could always open up Karuna's tortured heart. Trishala knew that in her cousin's eyes, she was everything poor dead Achala could never be: that bond had always been unbreakable . . . until now.

Would it still hold?

Karuna lowered her pistol as tears streamed from her eyes. 'Sister,' she echoed. Then she set her jaw, her mind now changed and decisiveness returning. 'We have to hurry – those men are coming.'

Without another word, she dragged another horse from a stall and not waiting to saddle it, leaped onto it bareback. Together they galloped from the stables, seeking the nearest road out of the town.

They rode all evening, galloping between knobby outcroppings and rough wadis, plunging through thinly wooded dells and along dried-up watercourses, walking the horses every hour in a vain effort to keep the beasts from exhaustion. As the light failed, they found shelter in a tumbledown old farmhouse, away from the road. They made camp, gulping down their food cold, massaging aching muscles.

'No fire,' Trishala ordered.

'I'm not a child, Trishi,' Karuna muttered, swallowing more water. Her eyes strayed back to the northwest, towards Jhansi. There was no sign of pursuit, not yet, at least. 'Is that half-breed smart enough to do what you told her?'

'She isn't stupid, Karu – and her ayah will care for her.' The idea had come in a flash as they were leaving: that escape would be almost impossible with Emily Mutlow slowing them down – she couldn't ride, for one thing. But if they left her in the town with the ayah who'd been helping her while they drew off pursuit, then they would all stand a better chance.

'What was that necklace you gave her?' Karuna asked. 'I'm sure I've seen it before.'

Trishala didn't answer; the less her cousin knew the better. 'Best we sleep a few hours, Karu. The horses are struggling and we're both exhausted. We have a long way to go tomorrow: all the way to Bhopal.'

Karuna opened her mouth then closed it. *Bhopal?* They had no chance of getting there. Any well-organised pursuit would reel them in tomorrow or the day after, of that there was no doubt.

Trishala turned away and pretended to try to sleep rather than confront their plight. The ground was hard and her body felt as if it had been systematically beaten, despite the years she'd spent riding. The cut on her cheek had scabbed over but itched like mad. She had no idea how many miles they'd covered, but her thighs and behind had been pummelled into numbness. She was tormented by guilt that she'd dragged Karuna into this, and worry that Emily had been captured regardless. But if Karu had seen something in the brutal massacre that had softened her, then perhaps in time her heart might be healed, if fate allowed. And to have a companion was good, not least because any witnesses giving news to their pursuers might think she was still travelling with Emily.

Karuna crawled beneath her blanket and clung to her until sleep took them both. Trishala's dreams were full of beast-men hunting her in the darkness, but she managed to rouse herself from the nightmare just as they closed in. Her heart was hammering and her throat dry, but Karuna snored gently behind her, warm against her back.

Trishala lay sleepless until the eastern sky began to lighten.

Karuna woke with a stifled cry, as she always did. It was the only time of the day she ever looked vulnerable, her inner nightmares exposed briefly in the waking light. Then her face closed up again and she rolled out from beneath the blanket.

'Which way do we go?' she asked. 'Toward Bhopal still?'

Trishala nodded grimly. She'd not washed in two days and her nostrils were assailed by her own stink of ripe sweat and grime. Karu smelled as bad. They remounted and rode in silence, but by midday they could see a cloud of dust growing behind them, getting closer as the hours passed, no matter how much they sped up. The hunt was closing in. By mid-afternoon she could make out the distinct shapes, even several miles back. Somehow, she knew that Bakhshish Ali led them.

Near dusk, they found a deserted farmhouse. The pursuers were currently hidden by the folds of the land, but they weren't far behind. It was as good a place as any for a last stand.

There was nothing to say. They loaded guns and sharpened blades as the darkness fell, their mouths dry and eyes full. They took turns dozing while the other watched the night. It wasn't until well after midnight that Karu fell asleep.

Only then could Trishala take the horses on muffled hooves and lead them away.

Once she was a hundred yards from the hut, far enough that Karu would never catch her, she raised her pistol and fired it to wake Karu; alone and on foot she'd have a chance to evade the pursuers. She heard her Palaka-sister howl in anguish as she realised, but Trishala didn't turn back. She lit a torch and rode south, leading the enemy away from her sister.

The pursuers closed in just before dawn as the second horse collapsed and died. Trishala wondered if she could kill them if she loosed the unholy rage that seethed inside her, and part of her longed to try, but her only certainty was that she mustn't be taken alive.

As the pursuers closed in, she was shocked there were so many of them, circling warily, holding blazing torches aloft. They truly were demons, not even bothering to mask their true faces in the ruddy light. Like the asuras of the old tales there were snarling faces full of tusks and horns and teeth, bodies coated in fur and scale, strangely jointed limbs and curving claws, thrashing tails. But a horrid intellect shone in every eye: calculation and chilling reason that warred with more bestial urges.

Emir Korani and Bakhshish Ali led them as they closed in.

'Queen Darya,' Bakhshish called mockingly. 'Queen San-yogita.' His breath steamed and the reek of them all, like rotting meat, closed about her. 'Where's the heart-stone? Where's the Mutlow woman?'

Trishala straightened defiantly, raising her pistol.

Bakhshish stalked closer, eyeing her gun and blade. 'I'm going to possess you utterly, woman,' he rasped. 'I will visit such suffering and pleasure upon you that your flesh will cleave to mine eternally. I will take you to our realm and you will be mine, until the return of the king. Do you know my king's name? He is known as "Ravana" in your world — and I am his son. My name is Prahasta.' He reached for her. 'Put down the gun, Trishala, and come to my arms. I will be gentler if you come willingly.'

She steeled herself, raised her gun and took the only shot that mattered.

# CHAPTER NINETEEN

## WAS IT WORTH IT?

*Kannauj, Uttar Pradesh, February 2011*

Deepika opened her eyes, her mouth gaping. The whole room was spinning, her body thrashing for balance – and then Amanjit was holding her, his strong arms, his *safe* arms, anchoring her in the here and now. She clung to him gratefully, trying to shake away that ghastly face, the body, the stench . . . She remembered the name: *Prahasta*. Her very soul recoiled from it. Abruptly, she pushed Amanjit away, the touch of another making her skin crawl. He looked at her, momentarily hurt. Then a groan from Sue Parker took their attention.

The American was sprawled on her back across the floor, writhing unconsciously. For a moment no one moved – then Uma fell to her knees and pinned her down, trying to still her.

Amanjit jumped up and brought tea, and after a few minutes, Deepika felt able to talk.

'Well,' Ras asked, 'what did you see? What happened? Is it important? Was it worth it?'

Deepika recalled that final moment, the explosion of pain as she was thrown out of Trishala's body, and shook her head, saying vehemently, '*Nothing* is worth that, Ras. Don't make me go back, *please*. I can't take any more of these other lives. I honestly don't know how Vikram manages.' She shuddered at the awful memory of those dreadful slashed-open bodies, the men, women and the children butchered in Johtun Bagh – and those final awful moments, alone with the demons. '*Never again.*'

Ras stroked her arm sympathetically, but her face was grim. 'We do what we have to,' she said, reminding Deepika momentarily of Lakshmibai. They both looked at Sue Parker, quivering in Uma's arms. 'So did you find out what happened to the heart-stone?'

Deepika rubbed her face, feeling drained beyond bearing. 'I gave it to Sue – her name was Emily in that life. Then Karuna and I led the chasers away and I never saw Emily again. They caught me a few days later – well, the asuras did. A rakshasa called Prahasta said he was going to take me to their realm for ever and I knew he would have tortured the information about the heart-stone out of me, so I shot myself.' She let Amanjit cradle her, fighting fresh tears as she repeated, '*I shot myself.*'

The words hung in the air for a long time.

'Hush,' Ras whispered finally, 'we all die. Sometimes it's worse than others – I know, believe me.'

Deepika hung her head, remembering Karuna, wondering if her loyal friend, her sister, had got away safely – and whether she had ever forgiven Trishala for her actions. Somehow, she doubted it.

Sue groaned and sat up. 'Was that shit real,' she slurred,
'or just one helluva nightmare?'

Ras looked at her dispassionately. 'Not a dream, but
memories of a past life.'

Sue almost stopped breathing. 'Oh my God! You say that
was *real*? Jesus, help me . . .' She buried her face in her
hands, her whole body shaking wildly.

'Uma, will you help me tend her?' Tanvir asked, his voice
filled with pity. 'Let's settle her in bed, give her time to recover.'
His voice held the memories of his own experience of revisiting
past lives. He gently pulled Sue to her feet and led her away.

Deepika turned to Ras. 'You were the Skene girl, weren't
you? Little Ruth Skene?'

'Yes – I didn't recognise Trishala as being you, of course,
but I remembered you when I thought about my brief life as
Ruth. I'm so sorry for putting you through that again, Dee.
I won't do it again.'

'Don't make promises you can't keep, Ras. We don't
know what else we're going to have to do before this nightmare is over.'

Rasita unlocked the door and slipped inside, holding two
cups of tea. She gave one to the drowsy white woman.
Deepika followed her in, also holding a cup.

*What could my Vikram ever see in you?* Ras thought grumpily.
*You're so fleshy – so foreign – and your voice is grating, and you
know NOTHING . . . So why am I so afraid of you?*

'Drink,' she said, trying not to speak unkindly. They'd put
Sue through hell – and she couldn't be Surpanakha; the
memories of Jhansi surely proved that.

Sue sat up and took the cup as if she were contemplating chucking it in their faces. Finally she asked, 'Who are you people? Why did you do that to me?'

'We needed to know what happened to the rani's heart-stone,' Ras said. 'You took it when you were Emily Mutlow, but it had been missing for more than five hundred years by then, and hasn't been seen since. Trishala didn't escape, but you did. What happened to it? Where did Emily take it?'

'If I tell you, will you let me go?'

They'd all discussed this: Sue clearly wasn't Surpanakha; she was Kamla, Vikram's wife when he'd been Chand Bardai and Mark Mutlow and others. She was no enemy. 'Yes,' Ras promised, 'we'll let you go.'

'Thank God!' Sue sighed with relief, then she explained, 'So, that Indian warrior-woman, Trishala, she and her real scary friend led the pursuit away while I hid in the town with my native ayah. She and her family hid me until they got scared too, but others helped after that. I was in Jhansi for months, but they never gave me up, even when this huge reward was posted for my capture. I reckon they were sickened by what those – those *terrorists* did to the Brits. I got out eventually, after the Brits came storming back and drove off the mutineers. Mark – my husband; he looked a bit like Vickers, didn't he? – he was dead, and so was his brother. The Brit soldiers came and I told 'em about what happened, but I never mentioned Trishala or the necklace to anyone, just as I'd promised. It was years until I got the chance to hide it in the place I'd been told in my dreams.'

'Where was that?'

Sue paused. 'If I was this "Emily" back then, who were you?'

Deepika hesitated, then said, 'I was Trishala.'

Sue looked directly at her, weighing up this final revelation. 'Okay, sure, I can see that in you. So I was supposed to take it to Pushkar,' she said at last, 'but see, I don't know if I even got there . . . you people pulled me out of the vision before I arrived – but I know where it's supposed to be: beneath this island-shrine thing on the lake, under the roots of a tree.' She looked at Ras. 'Please, don't make me do that séance-thing again. I can't. I just – I can't.'

'Hush, now. I think that's all we need to know; Vikram will be able to do the rest. *Thank you*, Sue. You might just have saved us all.' Rasita meant it, but she couldn't help thinking that her thanks were hollow compensation for what they'd put her through.

'Mark Mutlow . . . he *was* Vickers, wasn't he, in another life?' Sue said slowly, her face thoughtful. 'And Chand, the man Emily dreamed of – he was Vikram too? They were both *my* husband in other lives, weren't they?'

'Yes,' Ras admitted.

Sue met her gaze. 'Then Vickers belongs to me, doesn't he? You think he's yours, but he's always been mine.'

# CHAPTER TWENTY

# HUNTER

*Lanka, late February 2011*

Ravindra watched the sun rise, sparkling on the waters and bringing light to the lush woods beyond his walls. The roofs of the palace glittered golden and the white marble glowed.

His days and nights passed as if in a dream. Ferocious asura warriors drilled before him every morning, and daily more and more arrived. His afternoons were filled with councils with powerful demon warriors; they had all been sleeping, they told him, awaiting his return. These rakshasas – those asura lords capable of magic – led the beast-men as shepherds warded their flocks. Spies and messengers came and went, taking orders, bringing back reports. And every evening his demonic court flitted about him, swearing allegiance, plotting and planning. Musicians played, singers praised him and the demon-women swayed before him, their eyes alluring, their half-beast bodies strangely compelling.

'This is Lanka, sire,' Maricha, his uncle and one of the greatest of the rakshasas, told him. His antlered feline head inclined deferentially. 'This is one of those rare places where the power of belief and myth create other dimensions: this is not the "Sri Lanka" of the human world, but the Lanka of legend, sustained and hidden from human sight by our powers. Few know it, fewer can come here. You will understand more when your memories and powers are fully restored.'

*What have I forgotten?* he almost asked, then a chilling thought struck him: *If I ask him, will that reveal the depth of my ignorance? Can I trust him with my weakness?*

He did feel that he had lived here before, though – *millennia* before – and that his life as Ravindra of Mandore had not been his first life after all. Maricha had inferred as much, but wouldn't reveal any more. 'It's better to remember at your own pace, Lord,' was all he would say.

'Then we must fully restore my memories and powers,' he declared.

That night, he redoubled their efforts, sending out asura shapeshifters in bird and bat form to hunt down his enemies. He showed them images of Vikram, Rasita, Amanjit and Deepika, goading them with threats and promises. 'Find them – but don't attack; bring me knowledge only.'

After holding court that night, he banished the hangers-on and sat alone with the baleful presence of his three queens and Maricha, now his chief advisor. 'We don't know where our enemies are, Maricha,' he said, 'but we must find them. It is *imperative*.'

'Master, I understand this. Only the Rama and the Lakshmana can stop you. The Darya and the Sita: they alone can restore you. My king, I am the greatest tracker of our kind. Allow me leave to find them.'

Ravindra eyed up the antlered demon thoughtfully. *In the legend, Maricha lures Rama and Lakshmana, enabling Sita to be taken . . . and dies . . . Can I entrust him with this task?*

'What would you do?' he asked.

'I would go where they were last seen, in Varanasi, and *sniff* things out. I have my ways, Lord.'

'Then do so, Maricha. Find them, and I will reward you well.'

Maricha bowed low. 'I go, Master.' He left by a window in a gust of leathery wings, and was swallowed by the night. Ravindra stared after him, then sighed and went back to the pile of scrolls in his study. The tale they told was bewildering, even to him – although he had evidently written them all himself, three thousand five hundred years ago.

# CHAPTER TWENTY-ONE

# LAST WILL AND TESTAMENT

*Mumbai, late February 2011*

'This is the last will and testament of Dinesh Khandavani,' intoned the attorney, an elegant woman named Tripti, patting her sumptuous grey hair. 'All property to be divided into thirds, with one third going to his wife, Kiran Kaur Bajaj, the second to his eldest son, Vikram, and—'

'My client lodges an objection,' interjected a lawyer in a black Armani suit. He was representing Tanita, Dinesh's previous wife.

The whole room froze and Deepika felt her hackles begin to rise. *Again.*

It was a small gathering: Kiran, Bishin and Deepika, and Tanita and her timid son Lalit with their lawyer, Diltan Modi, who apparently spent most of his life representing Bollywood celebrities.

'Mister Modi, I have not completed reading the will,' the attorney said over her glasses.

'My client objects on two grounds,' Modi continued as if

she hadn't spoken. 'Objection one, that Vikram as a wanted fugitive isn't entitled to inherit until his culpability is ascertained—'

The attorney frowned and interrupted, 'That isn't—'

'Furthermore, my client disputes the legality of the marriage of Khandavani and Bajaj, on the grounds that Khandavani was still legally married to my client.'

Kiran stared open-mouthed at the man. Bishin started to say something, but before either could speak, Deepika's short-fused temper smouldered. 'That's rubbish,' she shouted. 'I've seen the divorce papers myself!'

'Forgeries,' Modi said with an irritating snicker.

'They were legally married!'

'I very much doubt that, darling.' He looked her up and down and added, 'Ever considered acting? I know some people and you'd look great on a casting couch.'

Deepika stared at him as rage boiled up inside her. 'Don't call me *darling*, you—'

'Quiet, please,' said the attorney. 'Mister Modi, this is a reading of the will, not a—'

'Wait,' Modi interrupted. 'My client is taking advantage of the occasion to formally contest the will.' He reached into his briefcase and flicked an envelope across the desk towards Kiran, insultingly off-handed. 'Until this matter is resolved, the disposition of the assets of the deceased cannot be effected, so I'm saving you a load of wasted words.' He smirked at the attorney.

'Can they do this?' Kiran asked helplessly, staring at the envelope.

The attorney took out the papers and examined them while

Deepika studied the people across the desk. Lalit wouldn't meet her eyes, but Tanita looked so smug that she wanted to slap the woman. Modi returned her stare frankly, his eyes on her cleavage, and she bunched her fists. *You smarmy creep* . . .

The attorney sighed heavily. 'This stay of proceedings is in order,' she told Kiran.

'Oh, there's another thing,' Modi added. 'As you are present, Ms Bajaj, it is apposite to raise it. I also have a statement here alleging that you and the deceased wilfully defrauded my client Mister Charanpreet Singh Bajaj, the brother of your late husband. My client alleges that you have, through intimidation and falsification of documents, usurped control of the estate of his brother, your late husband. Mister Charanpreet Singh Bajaj has applied to the courts to restore his control of the Bajaj family financial matters.' He flicked another envelope across the table.

Kiran looked stricken, but before she could say anything, Deepika had stood up and stalked around the table, trying – not very hard – to control the fury welling up inside her. She visualised it like lava pouring up the inside of a volcano. She jabbed her finger at Tanita. 'You retract these lies, or I'll—'

Modi stood casually and blocked her. 'Miss Choudhary, go and—'

*Crack!*

Modi's head rocked back and he staggered away, clutching his cheek. Deepika held her right hand, wincing at the pain of the impact, but didn't pause. She leaned over Tanita as Lalit stared wide-eyed, and said, 'You'd better retract, or I'm going to ram your silver spoon up your—'

Modi straightened, roared and swung a fist. Deepika swayed away from the blow and across came her other hand: *Smack!*

Modi reeled again, staggered, and sat on the floor, stunned. On each of his cheeks, a scarlet handprint blazed.

Deepika turned back to Tanita. 'I know why you're doing this, you sow — and you can tell Ravindra and all his pus-drinking brood that he can't frighten us and he will *never* beat us. You tell him that!'

Tanita blinked in utter confusion.

'Miss Choudhary, please!' begged the attorney.

Deepika glared down at Tanita. Behind her, Kiran was holding back her eldest son while Lalit was gaping open-mouthed — but making no move to aid his mother.

Modi jabbed a finger at her. 'That's assault! I'm going to have you jailed, you—'

'Oh yeah? You're going to tell the courts of India that you're such a little cry-baby that a girl can slap you around?' Deepika shot back. 'Then go blub to them — see if I care!' She raised her hand again. Modi flinched and crawled out of reach.

Tanita stood. 'Well, you've shown your true colours, haven't you?' she sniffed. 'If your gloves are off, so are mine. Withdraw? I think not. See you in court, you *peasants*!' She turned and stalked out.

Modi almost ran out of the door, but Lalit trailed behind. Deepika grabbed his arm. 'How can you do this to your father's memory?'

The skinny boy cringed and begged, 'Please let go.' Deepika realised he was trembling and suddenly felt ashamed at her rage. 'I have to go,' the boy pleaded. He met her eyes briefly, as if desperate to tell her something, then he fled.

She watched him go thoughtfully, wondering what it was he wanted to say. Then she turned back to the others, who were watching her as if she were a wild beast. 'I'm sorry. I guess my temper got the better of me.'

'You'll be lucky if you're not charged,' the attorney told her firmly. She looked at Kiran and her voice softened. 'I'm sorry, Mrs Bajaj, but we can't proceed until these matters are resolved.'

They filed from the office to the elevator, where a pretty young woman in a black business suit was waiting. She gave Deepika an admiring look. 'Can I just say on behalf of the entire legal profession: great right-left combo. You rock, girl!'

Deepika looked at her, feeling like a fool. 'You saw?'

'The blinds weren't closed and I was waiting for some photocopying—' She pointed to the copier sitting outside the office. 'Most of us have been longing to land one on Diltan Modi all our professional lives.' She offered a hand. 'Meenakshi Nandita, Junior Solicitor. If you need a lawyer, give me a call.'

Deepika blinked and took her hand embarrassedly. 'Violence isn't admirable,' she replied. 'I shouldn't have lost it like that.'

'I'm betting it was under extreme provocation,' the young lawyer replied. 'And I'm serious, I'd love to take him down in court – how strong is your case?'

Deepika looked at Bishin and Kiran. 'We can't afford too much in the way of legal fees . . .' Kiran said hesitantly.

'I'll work for nothing but a decent cut of the winnings,' Meenakshi told them. 'I'm serious – I'm young, but I'm good, you know. If you're in the legal right, I'll make sure you win.' She looked at the attorney. 'Can I take this one, Tripti? Is it all right? I've been mocked in court once too often by Diltan Modi – I'd love to help these people.'

Tripti considered, then said, 'We don't give away our services for nothing, Meenakshi, but I'm sure we can make this affordable.'

The young woman grinned her thanks and looked at Deepika. 'So, what do you think? Shall we talk business?'

Deepika looked at Kiran and Bishin, who nodded warily. 'Sure,' she said, 'let's talk.'

# CHAPTER TWENTY-TWO

# COINCIDENCE?

*Udaipur, Rajasthan, 24 February 2011*

What happened to Vikram in the rainstorm was frankly embarrassing, and certainly not the sort of thing that happened to proper superheroes.

He'd been working his way west, mostly by night. The sudden shower caught him out at two in the morning as he crossed a stretch of the Yamuna River just west of Manjhanpur; it shouldn't have been a problem . . . except that he was clinging to a musafir-astra three hundred feet in the air. The rain wet the shaft, his left hand slipped, pulling the arrow into an upwards trajectory, his right-hand grip went as well and as he and the arrow parted company, it went soaring off into the stratosphere, and he found himself plummeting earthwards.

He barely had time to think before he plunged into the river. He came up gasping, thrashing desperately for the shore in suddenly saturated winter clothes. Reaching the bank turned out to be a monumental struggle. By the time he crawled through the muddy flats of the shoreline, he was coated in sludge, cow dung and phosphorescent green algae. He lay there panting, thanking the gods it had happened over water and hoping his astra didn't hit the International Space Station on its way through the solar system.

The result: sopping clothes, soaked — and therefore ruined — fletching on his arrows, wet — so useless — bowstrings, wet money and a ruined mobile. Fortunately, the greased leather pouch protected Aram Dhoop's journal and his own notebook. *Why the hell didn't I think to put my mobile inside it too?* It was a serious loss; of course he could get another, but he hadn't written the others' numbers down, just programmed them in. So there was no way to contact Amanjit and Rasita before he saw them in person in Udaipur.

At least the first of March was only a week away.

*I'm sure Rama never had this problem*, he thought ruefully as he lit a fire and hunched naked beside it, his wet clothes steaming from the heat and his pride severely chastened.

*If Ravindra could see me now, he'd be hysterical . . .*

Vikram took greater care after that, though he still had no choice but to travel at night. He was too nervous to hitch a ride — Vikram-fever was probably still at boiling point after Varanasi — so he had to alternate walking and flying, once he'd cured a new bowstring and made new fletching for his arrows. He slipped into roadside dhabas occasionally for supplies and washed in squalid public toilets. Twice someone tried to mug him — he tried not to hurt them too badly. He slept in abandoned concrete buildings full of detritus and the occasional snake, or in tiny mice-infested shepherd's huts made of stacked straw, barely large enough to huddle in.

Finally he found himself nearing Udaipur. He checked out the fields on the edge of town and picked out a farmhouse. *Not exactly like the quaint old farmhouses of England*, he thought as he surveyed the mansion within the huge walled garden. There were no lights on when he slipped in after dark. He mumbled over a samohana, a sleep arrow that sent the only occupant, a guard, into a dreamless trance without even leaving a wound. He used the night to scrub himself clean. He barely recognised himself: his hair was now past his shoulders and he even had the beginnings of a beard. He liked the long hair; it reminded him of Hrithik in *Jodhaa Akbar*, but he put it into a ponytail, then shaved; the beard might conceal his features, but it itched, and felt alien. He laundered all his clothes, and then slept in a soft bed in a guest room. When he woke, he felt almost human again.

He stole away before dawn, leaving the guard oblivious to the presence of an uninvited house-guest. His blissful snores receded as Vikram followed the road into the city.

Udaipur, built around a lake, had been the seat of the Mewar clan for centuries; as Chand Bardai he'd warred against them in the Middle Ages. Now it was a tourist town. Hotels, mostly converted havelis of the once rich and mighty, clung to the shoreline. The lake itself was dark and muddy, but that didn't prevent thousands from bathing or doing pooja or laundry on the narrow ghats, both private and public, that descended from all sides. It reminded him of Varanasi, except that the water didn't move – it just got dirtier. The early morning streets were teeming with those seeking prayer and ablutions. Temple bells chimed as motor-bikes and cycle-rickshaws fought through the foot traffic. Tourists with cameras clicking mingled with the locals, waiting for that perfect shot.

In the midst of the lake was Jagniwas Island, the lake palace: fabulous, and fabulously expensive, where one could wake up in the heart of the city, yet separated from it: a rock on the lake ensconced in marble and gilt. It had featured in the James Bond movie *Octopussy*.

All Vikram wanted was a small hotel with not too many people around, so he could mesmerise or bribe the guy at the desk into ignoring the fact he had no valid ID. *James Bond would have proper fake IDs*, he reflected ruefully. *He probably wouldn't fall into a river, either.*

It was still too early to check in anywhere, so he picked his way down to Ganghaur Ghat, looking for a coffee to pep him up. He still felt fuzzy, as if the night's sleep had just reminded his body of how much it had been neglected rather than refreshing him. *Give me more of that rest and pampering*, it was demanding. *I liked it.*

He pushed his way into a Café Barista near Tripolia Gate and sat blearily at a small table amidst the tourists and locals, the smell of caffeine punching him in the nose in a delicious kind of way. A waiter brought a menu and he ordered, then sat back and let the tension in his shoulders ebb.

*Goodbye, Dad . . . I'm so sorry I couldn't protect you. All I can do now is avenge you . . .*

He took a newspaper from the stand, and checked the date, because he'd lost track. It was 24 February, just five days before Amanjit and Rasita were due to arrive.

Then he read the headlines and groaned softly at a story on page 5:

## VIKRAM'S FATHER'S WILL CONTESTED

He studied the article, trying to suppress his anger. His memories of his stepmother Tanita were hazy – a supercilious woman with no interest in any child but her own; a wilful, petulant and manipulative woman. And Lalit . . . he'd been such a pampered little thing. Vikram had always resented him.

*Well, it's not like I didn't see this coming.* He pulled out his notebook and turned to the page dealing with the next steps of the *Ramayana*. With a heavy heart he crossed out the line about the king dying and stared at the rest. He underlined the bit about the jealous queen and exile – those lines were clearly still in play. Then he scanned the rest.

*She-demon Surpanakha tries to seduce Rama, then Lakshmana. She fails. Disfigured by Lakshmana.*

*Surpanakha goes to Ravana, tells him about trio.*

*Ravana's servant Maricha lures away the men. Ravana kidnaps Sita.*

With a sigh, he pushed the notebook away, dispirited by what it implied. *Surpanakha*, he thought. *She's what happens next . . .*

As if summoned by the thought, he saw a blonde woman walk past the window of the café and instinctively ducked his head while flicking up the newspaper to cover his face. He held his breath until he judged it safe to look again.

*What the hell is Sue Parker doing here in Udaipur?*

\*

He found a room in a haveli on Lake Palace Road, with a rooftop restaurant with lake views, settled in and barely left it. There could be no doubt now: even if her motives were innocent and she was just a pawn of fate, Sue Parker was *dangerous*. Her presence here couldn't be coincidence.

He had to avoid her at all costs.

On one of his infrequent journeys out, Vikram mesmer- ised a mobile phone dealer and obtained another phone and a new anonymous number, ready for when he met the others again. He ate in his room, frightened to venture out in case he was spotted, but four nights later, the last night before the others were due, he decided it was safe to use the hotel's rooftop restaurant. He ordered a south Indian thali and a beer and waited out the evening, brooding on what the next day would bring.

A feminine shape settled into the chair opposite, soft face glowing in the candlelight.

'Hey, Vickers,' Sue Parker said. 'How's it going?'

They mopped up his beer and swept away the broken glass, the waiter brought him another, and one for her, and finally he could speak. 'Sue, what are you doing here?'

She looked drawn around the face, not quite the cheery girl from Varanasi. She'd clearly seen something that was still haunting her. She reminded him of Kamla when she was older, just before the Second Battle of Tarain: a happy per- son turned sad.

'You probably think I'm stalking you,' she said, 'but I'm not – hell, no, I'm just sightseeing. I never thought I'd see you again. I didn't know you were coming here. And I prom- ise, I never knew that you were that guy the cops are hunting.

If you'd told me, I'd've known to keep my mouth shut when I saw you in all that crazy blue paint up there on that temple.'

*Would you have? I wonder* . . . 'I didn't kill Sunita Ashoka,' he said, keeping his voice low. 'I'm not what the newspapers say.'

'Hell, Vickers, I don't even read the damn papers here! In Varanasi I was just showing around some English folks I'd met – we saw all the fuss and came to check it out. I thought I was going crazy when I saw you up there, all painted blue. And that was your dad? Jeez, I'm so sorry about that. That must be so sad, to not even be able to go to his funeral! They should've had some kinda amnesty. Is there anything I can do, Vickers? Anything at all?'

*Is this a ploy, or is it real innocence? Does it even matter?*

'I'm okay, thanks,' was all he said. *Oh, Kamla, I wish I didn't have to suspect you*. 'You haven't asked how I got away.' *Or said what's frightened you* . . .

'Well, I can't say I ain't kinda curious, kiddo. You leaped off like a grasshopper there. You must be some acrobat.' She looked over her shoulder to make sure no one was in earshot, then whispered, 'Vickers, three of your goddamn family kidnapped me.'

'*What?*'

She filled him in, a crazy story of abduction and séances, then added, 'After they let me go, I just ran – I came to Udaipur 'cause I heard an old pal might be here. Your friends frightened the hell outta me, especially that Deepika. Though in the past life thing, she and I were kinda close . . .'

*Dee? Scary?* 'Sue, what happened in the séance?'

'I'm not sure,' she whispered. She ran fingers through her hair and admitted, 'I'm really struggling, Vickers. I'm a true-blue Christian girl: I believe in Jesus and angels and the Devil and I can't make sense of what I dreamed. It felt so real to me at the time, but not any more – you know how you forget your dreams when you wake up? I can barely remember it now: there was this crazy queen and all these Brit soldiers – but it can't have been real. Stuff like that doesn't happen, Vickers.'

He hadn't meant to touch her, but he could feel her pain and had put his hand over hers before he realised. She twisted the grip until their hands were clasped and leaned forward. 'I met Rasita too: your fiancée . . . except she's not, is she? You're not engaged at all, are you, Vickers?'

'It was easier . . .' he stuttered.

'Easier than what – than just telling me to go away?'

He couldn't lie, or tell the truth. He shook his head, wishing she'd relent.

'Vickers, if all this past-life stuff is true, then tell me this: have we known each other before? Who am I to you? I need to know.'

She was talking as if she already knew the answer and just wanted confirmation – but there were too many other people here and he felt horribly conspicuous, up here on a rooftop, open to the sky above. Was that man in the corner watching them?

'Drink up. Let's get out of here.' He waved for the bill and signed it hurriedly.

She scowled, but drank her beer in one swallow. 'I want some straight answers tonight, Vickers,' she said as she followed him down the narrow stairs and along a balcony. Then she looked around. 'Is this where you're stayin'?'

'Yeah.' He turned back towards her, taking in her scent, warm, with hints of jasmine and shampoo, and her tension. 'But I'll be gone tomorrow.' He was very conscious that they were outside his room.

'It's like *The Fugitive*.' She chuckled nervously. 'Well, if Harrison Ford was this skinny little Indian guy. So, what's really goin' on, Vickers?' She reached out and stroked his forearms nervously. The touch made him shiver. 'Who am I to you?'

'You have been my wife,' he murmured. 'Several times.'

The air left her lungs, but she nodded as if this just confirmed her suspicions. 'How do you know?'

'Because I can remember my past lives. *All* of them.'

She looked at him, stunned. 'Oh my God – that must be awful for you.' She wrapped her arms about him and pulled him to her. 'Oh, Vickers, that must be a form of hell.'

'You can choose to disbelieve me – you can think I'm mad and run,' he told her, knowing he was letting himself be drawn into her familiar comforts, but to be held like this when his whole life was in chaos was a balm. He'd not realised he needed such contact so badly. 'Who knows, I might be insane.'

'No, you're not crazy – I gotta believe you. After what I saw in that séance: I really was Emily Mutlow and you were my husband, Mark . . . and Emily dreamed of an earlier time, too, of Chand and Kamla.' She hugged him tighter. She was quivering, and he could hear longing in her voice. 'You feel so familiar. I can almost taste you.'

He felt his mouth go dry. Her breath brushed his cheeks. *I've got to stop this. I can't do this, not in this life: not when Ras has been restored. Even though she is warm and she is Kamla, and she is here . . .*

# CHAPTER TWENTY-THREE

## RENDEZVOUS

*Udaipur, Rajasthan, 1 March 2011*

'How do we find him?' Ras fussed as they disembarked into the hurly-burly of the station, fighting off porters and auto-rickshaw drivers all shouting above the storm of noise. After releasing Sue Parker, Deepika, Uma and Tanvir had returned to Mumbai, while Ras and her brother went back to their hideaway in Delhi until it was time to go to Udaipur. And that day was finally here. She was burning to see Vikram in the flesh at last.

'He'll find us, didi.' Amanjit yawned. 'I hate overnight trains.'

'Huh. You didn't have that creep across the aisle trying to peer through the curtains at you,' Ras grumbled. 'Did you book a hotel?'

'Nope.'

Ras looked about foggily. 'If I remember, we need to get down to the ghats – that's where all the havelis are. And the cafés,' she added longingly. 'Caffeine!'

They took a taxi to the lake and found a Café Barista, but they hadn't been there even half an hour before Vikram found them. 'Hey, guys. I knew you'd come here first: it's the best coffee on the lake-front.' He took in Amanjit's shaven skull with raised eyebrows, then hugged them both. 'Welcome to Udaipur.'

Ras found her heart pounding and her throat so full she choked her greeting. He looked so mature, in a Bohemian kind of way, a look that could have been pretentious but was instead unaffectedly natural. She loved it . . . and hearing his voice and touch and smelling him . . . She wished she could just cling to him and never let go.

'You look as tired as us,' Amanjit commented. 'Didn't you sleep last night?'

'Not really,' Vikram replied. 'Too much on my mind.' He waved to a waiter, ordered a coffee, then sat down. 'What's happening?'

'Dee is back in Mumbai with Uma and Tanvir,' Amanjit replied. 'They've engaged a lawyer to fight the legal stuff – I suppose you've seen the newspapers? Well, Dee says the lawyer is confident, but it's going to take time. She's waiting for word, but she's got the press on her tail so they need to keep their heads down. Tanvir and Uma will keep her safe.'

Amanjit paused to draw breath and Rasita picked up the tale. 'But the important thing is this: we know where my heart-stone is now!' She gave Vikram an excited version of the story Sue Parker had already told him. 'And it turns out, in the Mutiny—'

'—you should call it the First War of Independence,' Vikram put in. 'To call it "Mutiny" implies it was wrong.'

'Old history, bhai,' Amanjit replied. 'Who the hell cares?'

Ras glared at them both impatiently. 'What's important is that Sue – Emily – whatever – took the heart-stone and fled with it to Pushkar—'

'Yeah, it's in Pushkar,' Amanjit interrupted. 'I wanted to go straight there, but then we figured you should be in on it, and Ras thought it could wait another week. But you know, I'm not so sure – we let Surpanakha go and I reckon that was a mistake.'

'Sue isn't Surpanakha,' Ras said tersely. 'Anyone with *half* a brain can figure that out. If she was, she'd have already known what we found out.'

'Says who? Just because she's a demon doesn't mean she can remember past lives.'

'She's not a demon. She's pathetic. And ignorant. And she's your ex-wife,' she told Vikram, a challenge in her voice. 'So we let her go.'

Vikram didn't want to think about Sue. 'Pushkar. That's not far: half a day's trip to Ajmer, then another half an hour from there.' In truth, he'd already be there if he hadn't promised to meet Ras and Amanjit this morning. 'We could do it now.'

Ras shook her head. 'There's a problem: Sue woke up before she got to Pushkar in the dream, so we don't know if she actually made it; we only know what she intended. She was a wreck when she came to; she couldn't have done it again, even under coercion. Emily lived a hard life in tough times.'

'We have to look, though,' Amanjit insisted. 'It's our only clue.'

'I don't think she made it to Pushkar,' Vikram said. 'I've been there in different lives, looking for the heart-stone. Remember, when Chand gave it to Kamla in the twelfth century his instruction was to take it there and leave it buried in the family shrine. I've gone back several times and it's never been there. I looked in the twelfth, the fourteenth and the seventeenth centuries, very thoroughly.'

'Then you've only ever searched *before* the Mutiny,' Rasita exclaimed. 'It's definitely worth another look.' Then she frowned. 'But I wasn't joking about how badly affected she was by the séance. I honestly don't think she could do another one.'

'I might know another way,' Vikram said reluctantly. 'I know a fair bit about recovering past life memories now – if I could talk to her about it, I might be able to recover the exact memory.'

Amanjit snorted. 'No way – I'm telling you, she was freaked out—'

'She'd do it for me,' Vikram replied. 'Because of who I am. And who she is and was.'

Rasita looked at him unhappily. 'We don't even know where she is.'

Vikram felt himself flush. 'I do. She's here, in Udaipur.'

Rasita gasped. She stood up, her lower lip trembling, and ran from the café.

# CHAPTER TWENTY-FOUR

## HIT THE CITY

*Mumbai, 3 March 2011*

Deepika answered the phone on the first ring, desperate for anything to distract her from the boredom of being locked up for another evening. 'Hi, this is Deepika.'

'Hello Deepika, this is Meenakshi Nandita. How're you all getting on?' The young lawyer's purr made Deepika smile. She was such a Mumbai girl, all style and sophistication.

'We're okay,' she replied. *Well, sort of, if you don't count screaming rows with photographers in a shopping mall and a couple of unwise altercations with Diltan Modi's people.* Everyone was tiptoeing around her at the moment, even Uma and Tanvir. If she'd thought she had a bit of a temper before, it was nothing to the rage constantly simmering inside her now. She'd been trying to identify the moment she'd developed such anger.

*It stems from those moments in Shiv Bakli's house and that burst of light that struck me. Something entered me then.* That something had a name, too: Meena, dead queen of Mandore.

*I swallowed a ghost and her rage is burning me up.*

'We're all tense, but we're surviving,' she admitted to Meenakshi.

'Stay strong, Dee,' the lawyer replied.

They'd been spending a lot of time together. Deepika had the best head for legal work in the family, so she'd been co-opted onto Meenakshi's team – although she was still hiding out with Uma and Tanvir, keeping the location of their apartment a secret. She used a mobile to communicate with her family, who were fretting constantly, but Meenakshi was a real rock. The young lawyer had even taken her out clubbing, under Tanvir's watchful eye. It was a risk, but she'd been desperate to unwind a little and forget the stress, just for an evening or two. It had been fun, nothing had gone wrong and she'd felt much better afterwards, knowing that normality could still be attained.

'I'll be fine,' she told Meenakshi. 'What's up?'

'We've got a breakthrough of sorts: Lalit wants to talk to us, in private, away from his mum. He contacted me this morning – he's hinting that he knows things that could mess up Tanita's case.'

Deepika clenched a fist in triumph. It was just like in the *Ramayana*, where the youngest son supported Rama against the wishes of his mother. 'We should definitely see him.'

'I'll tee it up. I'm so looking forward to spanking Modi in court. It's going to be divine.'

They laughed, and Deepika felt her load lighten. 'Thanks, Meenakshi. You've been great.'

'All part of the service. Hey, Dee, do you want to come out tomorrow night and celebrate? It's payday tomorrow, and I've got some bonus money to spend. TGFF, yeah? I'm dying for a big night. There are some serious star-spotting bars down in Lower Parel and Colaba. I've seen Aamir and Salman there, and I even got to dance with Shahid once. It'll be my treat.'

'Um . . . I'm not sure . . .'

'C'mon – before you're all married and stuck at home. Let's hit the city.'

Deepika glanced at Tanvir, asleep on the sofa, and Uma trundling dirty plates to the sink. Through all this rigmarole they had taken a lot of precautions to ensure that Uma's apartment remained a secret. Not even Meenakshi knew where it was. But she was beginning to *really* hate being stuck here.

There was more than just her life at stake, though. 'I don't think I should.'

Meenakshi sighed, then her voice dropped. 'I do have an ulterior motive. Vikram's little brother has agreed to meet us – but he doesn't want the policeman along.'

Deepika nibbled her lower lip. *Lalit could be their weak link – we could gain something from this.*

'Yeah, okay. Why not?' she whispered. 'What time?'

'Good girl,' Meenakshi approved. 'I'll pick you up at ten, when the oldies are sleepy. Where are you?'

Deepika hesitated. Uma's place was a hike from any public transport and trying to get to the Metro in high heels would be a pain. And Meenakshi was practically family by now. She knew all their secrets. *Well, all those from this life . . .*

But the security arrangements were sound. 'I'll meet you at the usual place. I'll be in your hands, so don't let me down.'

'Hey, if you can't trust your lawyer, who can you trust?' Meenakshi drawled ironically. 'See you tomorrow night – and wear something hot, girl: make Lalit pant, and he'll give us all we want.'

They hung up and Deepika sat back, smiling. *This is a real opportunity. Lalit has a role in this, I'm sure. And I need some fun, to stop myself from exploding.*

The decision made, it was easy to rationalise it as sensible. She looked thoughtfully towards Uma's bedroom. *I wonder if she's got anything that'd fit me?*

# CHAPTER TWENTY-FIVE

## UNDER HYPNOSIS

*Udaipur, Rajasthan, 3 March 2011*

It took Vikram a day to convince Sue that his methods wouldn't be as traumatic as the séance, and the lost hours made them all fret. But finally they were pulling up outside the hotel on Lal Ghat where Amanjit and Rasita were staying. Vikram squeezed Sue's hand in reassurance. 'It's going to be okay,' he told her.

She looked like she wanted to be sick, but nodded. 'I'm only doing this for you, Vickers.'

The rickshaw driver leered at them, making his own guess at why a young mixed-race couple would be pulling up outside a hotel. Vikram scowled as he paid him off, then took Sue's hand and led her inside. He got directions to the room from an equally curious old man behind the desk, who looked as if he had half a mind to deny them entrance. 'Our friends are there,' he told the clerk, fuming inside.

As they reached a landing on the stairs, sheltered from sight, Sue suddenly stopped. 'Vickers,' she said in a low voice, 'I read in a magazine the other day that we make up our minds about people – what we think of them, whether we trust them, if we're attracted, all that shit – inside a few minutes.' She gripped his shoulders. 'You tell me we've known each other for lifetimes. I don't remember any of that, but I *feel* it – in my heart, I do. I know you don't think I'm good enough for you, this big ole loud-mouthed Yankee gal. I know that ain't what you want, not in this life: you want that skinny, spooky Rasita upstairs. I won't embarrass you in front of her, Vickers, but you gotta know that I care about you.' Her voice sounded both resigned and hopeful, desperately wanting him to reciprocate her feelings but knowing he wouldn't. 'And I'll always be yours, if you want me.'

*Poor Kamla*, he thought. *Maybe we can free you from this cycle too?* 'I'm sorry,' was all he could say.

'I want one last kiss. Please.' Her eyes pleaded, and drew him into her enfolding warmth. 'Then you're hers.'

Vikram felt the tension in the room the moment he entered, and he could see it in the way Sue and Rasita stalked around each other before settling into opposite seats.

'There'll be no séance today,' he told them, taking a seat to one side so that they formed a triangle. 'We'll use hypnotism: it's safer, more effective, and you don't get the killer hangover afterwards.'

Amanjit, leaning against the wall watching, rolled his eyes. 'You mean I just spent the afternoon buying drugs from these shady types down Hanuman Ghat for nothing?'

'Hell – and I was counting on getting high,' Sue said,

making a brave stab at being nonchalant. She was spoiling the effect by sweating profusely. 'Jeez, it's hot in here.' It wasn't.

'Can you actually do hypnosis?' Ras asked Vikram. She was coiled up like a spring, eyeing the American with a distrust bordering on hostility.

Vikram wanted to reassure her that she was all he wanted, that all he felt for Sue was pity, and the echo of other lives. But now wasn't the time. 'Yes, I can do it.' He looked at Sue. 'All you need to do is relax.'

She flushed. 'Well, ain't that just the thing, Vickers? I'm so shit-scared after last time that I'm shakin' like a leaf.' She looked at Ras and Amanjit. 'Can they go? They're makin' me real nervous.'

'No,' said Ras flatly.

'We'll be fine,' Vikram said softly. 'Just look at me – only me.'

Sue was so wound-up that it took an hour or more, as afternoon faded into evening, for her to finally slip into a state of waking sleep. Vikram was in almost the same state himself. Amanjit's impatient fidgeting and Ras' burning mistrust receded, but the hardest thing to overcome was Sue's dread of returning to a past time. With patience, tenderness and understanding, she gradually went still, her face slack.

'Emily Mutlow,' he called softly, 'are you there?'

'Yes.' The whispered voice was thicker and deeper than Sue's voice, and no longer heavily American but English. He quivered as he recognised the cadences. 'Mark?' she asked. 'Is that you? I remember—'

He heard Ras swallow.

'Emily, you escaped – you went to Pushkar, after Trishala led the pursuit away.'

'Trishala? Mark, I tried to stop her, but it was what she wanted. She said I'd slow them down – and she was right. But I hated myself for it. She was so brave . . . Please, tell her I prayed for her.'

'She knows, Emily. She knows.' He let the girl's guilt and pain subside, then resumed his gentle questioning. 'Emily, what happened next?'

Sue's eyes flew open, but whatever she was seeing, it wasn't here and now. 'My ayah hid me, she and her family, then others – they were so brave! They could have claimed the reward for revealing me, but they never did. I didn't get away until the British returned, months later. I was dressed in rags; all I had to protect me was a dagger I kept hidden . . . I travelled alone for days until I found some refugees fleeing westwards, away from the fighting. So many people – and everyone so hungry and desperate. I hid with them, as one of them. One man tried to rob me of the stone and I had to kill him – they nearly hanged me . . . but I got away, and I endured.' The suffering was plain on her face.

'Did you reach Pushkar?' Vikram asked. 'What did you do with the heart-stone?'

'The shrine was gone – the one the dream talked about. So I placed it beneath the roots of a tree by a shrine on the island in the lake. I had to steal a boat in the night, but I did it.'

Vikram heard Ras and Amanjit stir exultantly. 'Is it still there, Emily?' he asked.

Her face fell. 'No . . . I went back to check a few years later and it was gone.'

The ground fell away beneath him.

They walked Sue to the bed and Vikram sent her to sleep to recover, then they moved in to the hall so that they wouldn't wake her.

'Damn. I really thought we might have it,' Amanjit groaned. Ras looked just as distraught.

'Me too,' Vikram said, rubbing his eyes tiredly. This was a real blow, one that left them with little hope to cling to. 'I think one of us still has to go there, see what we can learn from the site. Maybe there's some clue left behind?'

'That's a long shot,' said Amanjit. 'For one thing, it's a hundred and fifty years ago – and for another, why would anyone leave a clue in the first place?'

'Yeah, I know, but it's our only lead.'

'Let's think about the big picture,' Ras put in. 'The one thing we're pretty sure we know, after all these past lives, is that Ravindra needs to get Deepika and me and our heart-stones to complete his ritual. So if that's his goal, ours has to be to prevent that, and somehow kill him. So maybe it's best it's never found?'

'But we need it to fully heal you,' Amanjit objected. 'We *must* find it.' He put his hand on his sister's shoulder. 'You can't go on like this, Ras. Despite what happened with Sunita, you're still sick. This has to be resolved.'

'We can't ignore the *Ramayana*, either,' Vikram added. 'Our lives are mirroring it: we know that. We're in exile. Father is dead. The next thing to happen is that Surpanakha gets Ravana – or Ravindra – to kidnap Sita.' He looked at Ras. 'That's you. We must prevent it.'

'It happens *after* Rama rejects Surpanakha,' she said mean-ingfully, eyeing the sleeping Sue. 'Lakshmana does too,' she added, glaring at Amanjit, 'and then he cuts her nose off.'

'No fears there,' Amanjit said. 'Though I'll leave her nose alone unless she causes trouble, if that's okay,' he added with a slight smile.

Rasita glared, then said, 'Then the main thing is not to separate – if we need to get to Pushkar, we should go together.'

Amanjit frowned. 'The heart-stone is secondary to keep-ing you safe, Ras. If Pushkar gets messy, we need you to be well away.'

'Rama and Lakshmana lose Sita because they get lured away,' Ras reminded him. 'Everyone knows that. So if we go to Pushkar, we go together.' She turned to Vikram. 'Tell him, Vik.'

Vikram was trying to clear his thoughts and think things through. 'I don't know, Ras. I think I'm with Amanjit on this one. You're still unwell: if we're attacked, you can't even run. I think I should go alone. I've got the knowledge and the skills to track the stone down, if any of us can.'

'No way!' Amanjit pushed himself away from the wall and stood straight. 'It's got to be me – you've got to stay with Ras. If I'm the Lakshmana to your Rama, I'm more expendable.'

'Don't say that,' Vikram replied. 'None of us are expendable.'

'We should all stay together,' Rasita said again. 'You're idiots if you want to split up: total idiots—' She opened her mouth to continue shouting, then her eyes flew wide and she gave a choking cough. Her hands flew to her chest as she felt a sudden tightening, as if some unseen fist had seized her heart and was squeezing. 'Unghhh . . .' She felt the walls sway. Amanjit's arms flew around her while Vikram ran to her.

They carried her back into the room and lowered her on to the other bed. Her brother loosened her clothing with practised hands, his face white with dread. 'Are you okay, Sis?' he whispered.

'I thought joining with Sunita had fixed this,' Vikram hissed in Amanjit's ear.

'Not totally,' Amanjit whispered. 'She's definitely improved, but the heart problem's still there.'

'Then we *have* to find her heart-stone if we're to fully heal her.'

Despite their whispering, Ras clearly heard every word. Once her pain subsided and her breathing smoothed out, she grabbed Vikram's hand, her face full of frustrated rage. 'It's the damned *Ramayana*, having its way. It *wants* me to be taken, to fulfil whatever stupid game it's playing with our lives. It's going to happen now, isn't it? He's going to come, and take me away.'

'Don't say that,' Amanjit replied. 'We'll stay with you – we'll keep you safe.'

'Yes, we're staying here,' Vikram responded, 'right here, with you. If the heart-stone's stayed hidden this long, it can last another few days. We'll wait until you're better, and then we'll go together.'

But once she'd fallen asleep, he looked at Amanjit worriedly. 'Has this happened since she joined with Sunita?'

'No — but what if she's regressing, bhai? What if she's going backwards? What if we don't *have* days to wait? What if that heart-stone is the only hope we have of keeping her alive?'

'Yeah. I've been thinking the same thing.'

Amanjit jerked a thumb at Sue, lying deeply asleep in the other bed. 'And what do we do with the American? I know you love Ras, not her, but Ras hates having her around. We need to ditch her.'

Vikram sighed. 'I know, and we will, but we have to keep her with us for now. If we let her go Ravindra could well grab her. Then he'll know what we know — and he'll be in Pushkar, waiting for us.'

'Yeah, about that: what's Ravindra up to? Where is he? *Who* is he?'

'I've been thinking about that,' Vikram answered. 'Remember how Majid Khan shot Tanvir on the roof of the mansion? Why would he do that, unless he was either one of Bakli's men — and let's face it, he'd just shot Bakli himself so that's not likely. So maybe Majid is now Ravindra himself?'

Amanjit whistled softly. 'That would fit . . . He was alone with Bakli's body wasn't he? So if Ravindra acted fast — and let's face it, he's had plenty of practise! — he might have jumped into Majid.'

'It all fits. And did you notice that the papers went really quiet about the so-called "hero-cop" Majid Khan? I'm not saying I'm right, but we have to be on our guard: he might not be just a corrupt policeman, but a whole lot worse.'

'I think you're nailed it, bhai.' Amanjit straightened decisively. 'One of us has to go to Pushkar as soon as possible.

There's a morning train – or I could rent a car or a bike. I'll go, you stay and watch the girls. That way, if Ravindra comes here, he's got you to face – and I know you can take him.'

They looked at each other for a long moment, then Vikram nodded his agreement. 'It's not both of us, and we're not being "lured": it's just a reconnaissance. But be careful, bhai.'

'You know me.'

'Yeah – that's why I'm worried.'

'Very funny: don't worry, I'll take care.' Amanjit flexed his sword hand, then grinned. 'Hey, brother, wasn't the time of exile in the *Ramayana* supposed to be one big holiday? Just frolicking in the woods and picking flowers and shit?'

Vikram raised his eyebrows. 'Yeah – but they had to kill a few demons in those woods too.'

# CHAPTER TWENTY-SIX

# EMPTY LAKE

*Udaipur to Pushkar, Rajasthan, 4 March 2011*

*It's good to be driving again*, Amanjit thought as he went bar-relling along State Highway 8 towards Ajmer. Well, not exactly barrelling: by the time Amanjit had used his cousin's ID to rent a car it was after nine and the roads were full of slow traffic. He wished he lived somewhere like Germany, where Bishin told him you could fly along their *Autobahns* as fast as you liked. *How cool would that be?* But it was a relief to be in motion with a simple purpose: *Find the stone, get home.*

However, now it was hooting and cursing and stop-start-stop, with camel carts and trucks jamming the left lane and tiny Marutis crawling on the right and barely a space to weave into. *I should have rented a motorbike.* 'Hey! Shift your carcass!' he roared out of the window as yet another bike cut him off. The girl sitting side-saddle behind the rider cast him a disdainful look and then they were gone, weaving through *his* gap. 'Bah!'

Nevertheless, he was getting there. A hundred and twenty

miles or so would be three to six hours, depending on whether the traffic was merely awful or near-impossible. His stomach was just starting to grumble about lunch by the time he made it to Ajmer, an ancient town set amongst hills where Vikram said they'd lived in a previous life, although Amanjit had no such memories. The roads were so jammed that he gave up trying to get into the city centre and instead squeezed into space beneath a tree and found a street stall for lunch.

Slurping on a Coke, digesting two samosas and three sticky-sweet swirls of jalebi still hot from the pan, he felt himself grow calmer by the moment. He'd wrapped a turban on his head that morning and had restored his dagger to his person, in an inside jacket pocket. He hadn't shaved for over a week now, and his sword was in the car, beneath the driver's seat. He felt like a Sikh warrior again.

On Vikram's advice, he'd swapped a few texts with Deepika, although he'd not told her what he was doing. Dee would only go and do something rash; she was safer in Mumbai at Uma's secret apartment. He was thinking they should all shift there when he returned with the stone.

He finished lunch and headed back through the crowded streets towards the car. There was no real sidewalk; the street vendors took up most of what paving there was and piled rubbish put paid to the rest. The press of people was thick, everyone fighting for space. The streets smelled of fresh spice and smoke underpinned with old dung, dust and petrol fumes. There was a coating of grime on everything. The men were wiry, whiskery and laconic, with a strut to them; the boys lazed in shops, smoking and calling out to shoppers. Rajasthani women swayed past in dark emerald and crimson, with veiled, sun-beaten faces. The old ones had dark skin and bad teeth; the young ones were demure and sassy all at once. Amanjit found himself grinning. It was good to be back in central Rajasthan, closer to home.

Then he felt a prickling of his skin and some instinct made him dart into a doorway. He glanced back and saw a big bird of prey – a kite – alight on the stained dome of a decorative cupola atop a dirty old housing row. He pressed himself against the door as it looked around and was chiding himself for jumping at nothing when suddenly the bird took off again – and as it crossed the golden disc of the sun it was silhouetted for an instant, and the image seared upon his eyes wasn't a kite at all, but something larger, with an antlered skull, beating huge wings. The after-image slowly faded, leaving him blinking, and when he could focus again, the kite-thing was gone.

*Time to move.* For a moment he debated whether he should go on at all, but he didn't think he'd been spotted, and he reasoned that if they were hunting him, they didn't know where he was, or where he was going. *So it was just a chance encounter, right? A scout maybe, one of Ravindra's minions – all bad guys had minions, didn't they?* So he thumbed a text to Vikram, warning him to keep his head down, then hurried back to his rental car. He pressed on, trying not to think that this was a wild goose chase, and all the important matters were happening somewhere else.

'Pushkar's one the holiest sites in Rajasthan,' Vikram had told Amanjit before he left, reading from the cheap guidebook he'd found in the hotel lobby. 'The small lake in the Rajasthani hills it's built around was, according to the legend, formed by Brahma himself from one of three drops of fluid from the sacred lotus. His followers believe that the God-Creator's role was then complete, and that he is sleeping until Shiva destroys the world, and Brahma awakens to create the next. So Brahma temples are rare, and the one in Pushkar is the most important in India.'

Life with Vikram was like having your very own historian lecturing you, Amanjit reckoned, but it was increasingly need-to-know stuff, so he was learning to listen.

All Amanjit knew of Pushkar was that every November camel-traders and tourists would flood in for the annual camel fair – Bishin always used to drive his taxi to Pushkar and make quadruple his normal rates, ferrying dumb Westerners between hotels and the fair sites, day and night.

But this was March and the town was drowsing in the heat of a spring afternoon as Amanjit wound his way through the traffic and found a place to park near the Sikh gurdwara west of the lake, its white and gold domes a homing beacon for him. From there it was an easy stroll through sleepy streets, his sword concealed in his sports bag. Old men dozed in the shade and shopkeepers performed chores desultorily, barely glancing at him.

He reached the lake – and flinched at the warm wet fug rising from the wide brown expanse that stretched the several hundred yards to the far shore. He wrinkled his nose as the smell hit him. Apart from a few dank puddles, there was no water in the lake at all. The monsoon was four months away, but this was surely worse than that. There were machines and trenches everywhere, and labourers trudging through the dirt. It looked more like a building site than a lake.

'Hoping for a swim, lad?' an old man cackled up at him from beneath the shade of a tree. He was wearing a Rajasthani turban of green and red, and a badly stained white kurta. He spat a wad of paan, revealing broken teeth stained red-brown. 'You'd be better off going to your gurdwara,' he said, eyeing Amanjit's Sikh attire.

'What's happened here?' Amanjit asked incredulously.

The old man gave him a calculating look. 'Got any smokes, young man?'

'One moment.' Amanjit hurried to a nearby stall and bought a packet of cigarettes, then squatted down by the old guy. 'Take 'em all, Uncle. They're bad for you.'

'I'm seventy-three, boy. I wouldn't be any older if I didn't smoke.' He lit up and dragged on the cigarette with relish. 'People doing pooja can go to the north side. They've got some pools there that they're filling up daily.'

'But what happened?'

'Well boy, it's like this: the government decided in their wisdom – and who'm I to say they were wrong? – that they needed to dredge the lake. They were worried it was getting too shallow. In recent years it's been only a few inches deep for most of the year. Mind, I remember it lapping right up to the ghats on every side when I was a boy.' He paused and puffed. 'Though I guess everything is bigger when you're young.' He mused on that for a moment, then continued, 'Anyway, so what happened is, they dredged away the silt and dug the whole lake twenty feet deeper, well and good.

But it must have been all that silt keeping the water from seeping through the rock. Result: one dried-out sacred lake.'

'And the monsoon wasn't enough to refill it?'

'Not the weak monsoons we've been having lately. It did almost fill at one point – but it all just drained away again.' He spat. 'Climate change, they say.'

'So what are they doing about it?'

The old man waved his cigarette at the mess before them. 'Digging holes. Filling them in. Running round talking on mobile phones. Shaking their heads a lot.' Smoke wreathed about his head. 'They've pissed the gods off, boy, good and proper. The gods are so angry they've sent the White Lady back to Pushkar.'

Amanjit stared. 'The *what*?'

'The White Lady. Haven't you heard of our White Lady? She goes walking on the water just before dawn.' Looking at Amanjit's incredulous face, he wagged a finger and said, 'Mark my words, boy, she's a bad luck omen, sent by the gods as a warning. She hadn't been seen for years, not since before I was born, but I saw her myself a few months back.'

*One of the dead queens? Or is it the final part of Padma's fractured soul?* Amanjit struggled to keep his voice calm. 'Where does she usually appear?'

The man pointed across the lake. 'Western side, boy, by the island-shrine.'

*Bingo!*

Amanjit grinned. 'Cheers, Uncle.'

'Thanks for the smokes, kid. Young folks like you don't usually have time to talk to an old man.'

'It's been a pleasure. Hey, is that island-shrine still there?'

'Still there, but you can walk to it now without getting your feet wet. They're digging around it. Far side boy, a few yards offshore – if you can still call it a shore when there's no water.'

'The water will come back, Uncle. Have faith.' Amanjit scanned the scene. *Maybe I can pretend to be a worker and get a closer look.* Then the shadow of something large swept across the dried lake and he glanced up. There was nothing there except a kite circling . . . but he remembered that strange silhouette in the sky over Ajmer.

He thanked the old boy again and hurried away towards the lee of a whitewashed building, thumbing his mobile. 'Vik? Vik, I think I'm rumbled . . . which means maybe you are too . . .'

Amanjit headed for the narrowest of the alleys on the north side, mingling with people shopping and running errands as he wound his way through the streets behind the northern ghats. Occasional glimpses showed the dried-up lake, and the roar of heavy machinery throbbed behind the din of the streets. His eyes swept the rooftops, peering up through the festival banners and the tangled power lines, seeking . . . *anything*. The sports bag was on his shoulder and partially unzipped, the sword hilt near to hand. Every eye that caught his felt laden with menace.

*If I go to the island, they'll see me . . . it's too open. I've got to get to a vantage point, narrow the approach, so if I really am being tailed I can spot the watcher and maybe take him down.*

He followed a sign that promised an upstairs bar, pausing

ostentatiously in front before walking towards it, and from the corner of his eye he saw a shape briefly silhouetted against a wall. Warily, in case his tail rushed him, he climbed a stone stairway. An arrow painted on the wall, surmounted by the word 'bar', pointed towards the next floor.

*Perfect*. He drew into the shadow of a doorway and waited where he could check out both directions, looking first up, then down. He gripped the hilt of his scimitar, still inside his sports bag, and waited.

*First it'll fly over the rooftop, then it'll wonder why I don't show . . . then it'll worry that my goal is somewhere inside . . . It'll face a dilemma: does it follow me, try and get close and risk blowing its cover? I guess we'll just have to wait and see. But if it comes looking for me, as it should, I'm going to turn it into mincemeat.*

A minute ticked past, sweat trickling from beneath his turban and down the back of his neck. Then came a bustle of noise and a family group came past, a prancing pair of children giggling as they leaped down the stairs, followed by a harassed-looking mother and an indifferent father, be-suited and arguing with someone on his mobile. They all eyed Amanjit a little nervously as they passed, but he ignored them. Another tense wait followed and he flexed awkwardly, trying to stop his limbs stiffening. He saw the shadow first, horned, and descending from the top floor, and pulled the sword half-out, ready to move. He could hear the oncoming *thing* breathing, feel its uncertainty.

Suddenly the door behind him opened inwards with a rattle and he spun, wrenching at the sword, while the shadow on the stairs around the corner hissed and went still.

A frightened young woman stared at him from within the doorway. She saw the sword and opened her mouth to scream, but Amanjit was already moving; in an instant he'd stepped in and wrapped his big hand across her mouth. Kicking the door shut, he swept her against him, whispering, '*Shhh!*' He wrapped his other arm around her. 'Don't make a sound,' he begged as she struggled, trying to get her hands free, trying to bite. 'Stop,' he hissed, 'I'm not going to hurt you, but you *must* be quiet – something's out there—'

She went stock-still as they both heard a *scratching* at the wooden door. He put his weight against the barrier to hold it shut; the girl fell to her knees, clinging to his thighs and staring wide-eyed.

The scratching stopped and everything fell silent, but Amanjit could hear it, waiting.

*If I wrenched open the door and thrust . . .* He nudged the girl away from him and she crawled backwards on her haunches, her eyes round as plates, nodding when he raised a finger to his lips and pressing herself into the opposite wall as if trying to flow through it. Her eyes were fixed on the sword, her limbs poised for flight.

With a sudden rush of air, he felt the presence outside leave; flowing away from the door with a rustle and a faint gust of wind. *Damn!* Then he heard more footsteps coming up the stairway and two Indian boys laughing over something.

He turned to the girl. 'Is there another way out of here?' he whispered.

'Please, don't hurt me—' she started.

'I won't. It's gone now. Thank you for not giving me

away.' He glanced about the hall and spotted a door on the right. 'Is that the other way out?'

Still speechless, she nodded again, and he grinned. 'Well, that was exciting.'

She looked at him oddly and then, realising the danger was over, her whole demeanour changed. She fixed him with an appraising eye and ran her hands down her kameez, straightening it – and somehow making it hug her curves provocatively.

'I could make you some chai?' she suggested, with a winsome look. 'My name's Sabina.'

*I'm so glad Dee isn't here . . .* 'Is anyone else home?'

'Just me – I'm the maid. No one's going to be home for hours,' she added, tilting her head. She'd clearly practised the move in mirrors.

*So danger's her aphrodisiac? I'm not on the market: and "Sabina" sounds a little too close to Surpanakha for my liking . . . And she's a bit too pretty.*

*It'd be a shame to have to cut her nose off . . .*

'Ah, no, thanks,' he said hurriedly, 'I've got to go—' With that, he hurried for the back stairs.

On the level below, he found another door, nudged it slightly open and peered out into a tiny courtyard facing another door, where a girl in black robes sat on her haunches, tracing rangoli around the threshold with a paintbrush dipped in a saucer of rice-water paste. He pulled it closed.

*Is the rangoli-painter what she seems?*

'What are you doing?' Sabina asked, slipping down the stairs behind him and striking a languid pose against the wall. 'Hey, are you hiding from the cops?'

It was as good a story as any. 'Yeah.'

'Cool! I won't tell. You can hide out here – my mistress won't be home for ages, and if she comes back early, you can climb out the window. There really is a pot of chai in the kitchen,' she added.

He gave an internal shrug. Until the girl outside was finished, he couldn't really go anywhere. 'Is there a room which overlooks the street?'

'Just one,' Sabina purred. 'My bedroom.'


Amanjit sipped his tea and examined the maid's room: just a narrow bed, a chest of drawers and a shelf on one wall, all painted a sterile blue and smelling of cleaners and incense. But the little curtained window did indeed overlook the street and he could not only watch the passers-by, but if he craned his neck, he could even peer at the opposite roofline. The maid kept looking in on him, but she'd not tried anything. He thought nobly of Deepika and resumed his vigil.

Was *anyone* out there who they seemed? He was beginning to doubt them all: the old man sitting opposite the steps – was his shadow natural? What about the monkey on the wires above the door? Or the raven perched on the corner of the house across the way?

Suddenly everyone turned and peered to the left as sirens blared, then a group of policemen jogged past, holding guns at the ready. The passers-by pushed themselves against the walls, and it felt like even the distant thrum of the lake machinery missed a beat.

Amanjit put down the chai and ran to the front door.

'Hey,' called Sabina, 'don't go – I've nearly done my chores and—'

He threw a grin over his shoulder, shaking his head, slipped down the back stairs and opened the door. The rangoli-painter was gone.

'Thanks, Sabina,' he called, as he sidled into the street and lost himself in the crowds peering after the policemen. *Phew, escaped that one alive . . .*

'What's going on?' he asked a plump shopkeeper, but the man didn't know.

Amanjit wavered for a second, and then decided to follow. Even though the crowd was growing by the minute, he managed to reach the cordon. He picked a nervous-looking young cop awkwardly brandishing a sub-machine gun and asked, 'Hey! What happened?

The cop looked at him stonily and turned away, but Amanjit persisted, 'Aw, c'mon, bhai. What's going on?'

The policeman eyed his superior, but as soon as the older man turned away, he leaned towards Amanjit and whispered conspiratorially, 'A gang hit the gun-dealer behind Varah Ghat. Three men are dead – the two armed guards looking after the shop, and the owner.'

'Shot?'

The policeman flinched a little and shook his head, suddenly looking anxious to get something off his chest. 'No, I saw them before they covered the bodies. They had their throats ripped out. And some kid who saw them reckoned one of the guards emptied a whole clip into one of the attackers – *and he didn't even fall down.*'

*Uh oh.* 'Did the kid see the attackers? What did they look like?'

'That's all I know, man.' The cop glanced at an officer approaching. 'Sorry, gotta go.'

As he turned away, Amanjit scanned the crowds. Were his enemies arming themselves with modern weapons now they knew where he was, or was it just coincidence? Suddenly feeling horribly exposed, he hurried away and started walking around the lake, hoping for a vantage point overlooking it. He ended up at a restaurant and found a spot with a good view.

The barman looked at him oddly when he pulled a small pair of binoculars from his pocket and trained them on the lake, but shrugged; as long as he kept ordering food and drink, that was all that mattered.

An hour passed, and it was nearly five o'clock when he caught sight of what he'd been dreading to see: a kite swooping down and landing on a balcony near the Jain Temple on the western shore. A tall man in a long leather jacket emerged and stood nearby, almost as if conversing with the bird. When Amanjit focused in closer, he caught his breath. *Majid Khan – or is it really Ravindra, like Vikram thinks?*

As he watched, the man strode down some steps from the balcony and walked blithely through the construction site, right past men who apparently didn't even sense his presence.

*He's going straight to the island*——Amanjit watched in horror as the man stepped on to the shrine, peered around then leaned nonchalantly against a wall, staring thoughtfully into space.

Amanjit thumbed his phone, and staring through the glass, whispered, 'Hey, Vik, Majid Khan's here – right here – and you know what he's looking at? The island where the heart-stone used to be . . . *He knows!*'

'Shit . . . Majid? You've actually seen him?'

'I'm looking at him right now. It can't be coincidence. You were right: he has to be Ravindra.'

At the very moment Amanjit spoke that name, the man in his binoculars turned . . . *and looked right at him.*

'*Chod!* Vik, he's seen me—' Amanjit thumbed the connection dead, threw money on the table, snatched up his belongings and ran for the door.

# CHAPTER TWENTY-SEVEN

## THE ANGUISH OF CHOICE

*Udaipur, Rajasthan, 4 March 2011*

The voice broke off and the connection went dead. The words echoed in his mind: '*Chod! Vik, he's seen me——*'

Vikram looked at Ras and Sue, a sickening feeling in his belly.

'What is it?' Ras demanded.

'It's Amanjit – he's in Pushkar, but Ravindra's there. I think . . .' He swallowed. 'I think Amanjit's in danger.'

Ras looked at Vikram, dread in her eyes. 'We should never have let him go . . .'

He was grateful she'd said 'we' instead of 'you', but the truth was, it had been his decision. 'We've got to think this through. Majid Khan – who's likely now Ravindra – is in Pushkar, so *somehow* he knows that's where we sent Amanjit. *How does he know that?*'

Ras glared at Sue, but the American flared indignantly. 'Jesus! I've been unconscious or under your eyes ever since you hypnotised me – you won't even let me pee alone!' She stood up and smacked the wall. 'I can't believe you people' – she rounded on Vikram – 'especially *you*, Vickers! How about standing up for me for once and not this vindictive bitch? You know I've done *nothing* to hurt you, even though I'm the one who's been kidnapped and mentally tortured—'

Vikram gripped Ras' arm. His face burning, he said urgently, 'She's right, Ras: it can't possibly be Sue. She's been totally isolated from the outside—'

Looking agonised, she whispered, 'Why are you taking her side?'

'I'm not, I'm taking the side of logic,' he shouted, cringing inside as she flinched. 'Dammit, Ras, we're all on the same team in here, don't you get that? The Enemy is *out there* somewhere.' He started to reach for her then stopped, trying to think. 'Maybe Amanjit was spotted en route – or maybe we were being watched and they tailed him. Or perhaps it's just sheer coincidence – we just don't know.'

Ras looked at him with hurt eyes, while Sue looked sullen and aggrieved. He turned away from them both, thinking hard: *If Amanjit's been tailed, they know we're here . . . but Ravindra's in Pushkar, so that must be where the action is . . . If he gets the heart-stone, he can get to Ras the way he did Deepika when he had her stone. He must believe it's in Pushkar . . .*

He tried to imagine how Ravindra might know this. *Could he have just happened upon the same information as us, at exactly the same time? After a hundred and fifty years? No, that's impossible . . . so he must be watching us somehow. But* how?

The only thing he could think of was that Ravindra's people had spotted Sue in Varanasi and linked her to him, perhaps that was why she was dangerous: not because she was Surpanakha, but because they'd recognised her as Kamla and let nature take its course.

*That fits ... They watched Amanjit leave and tailed him ... which means they're still watching here too ... They're all over us – but if I don't get to Pushkar, Amanjit will be alone against Ravindra and whoever he has with him ... he won't stand a chance.*

He turned back to the girls. 'I have to go to Pushkar.'

'You can't leave us here!' they gasped simultaneously, for once in agreement.

'If I don't go, Ravindra's going to kill Amanjit.'

'Then we should go together,' Ras insisted.

'It won't work,' he explained. 'I can't get all three of us there fast enough. He needs me as soon as possible and I can get there in an hour or two if I go alone. But I have to make you safe here ...'

'How? You can't be in two places at once.'

'There are things I can do, but you have to trust me: you'll be okay, as long as you *stay here.*' He glared at them until they both nodded reluctantly. 'Okay, here's what we'll do ...' He paced the room, casting his mind back over the three different lives when he had studied at the Gurukul. 'I can create protections and traps – they'll nail anyone who tries to come in. All you have to do is stay put. We'll be back by dawn, I'm sure.'

Within the hour, just as the sun went down, he was soaring through the air on a musafir-astra, heading northeast towards Pushkar, desperately praying he wasn't already too late.

# CHAPTER TWENTY-EIGHT

# RAKSHASA

*Mumbai, 4 March 2011*

Deepika perched on the bathroom stool in her underwear and admired her make-up in the mirror. Just enough rouge, just enough mascara, and a sexy green eyeliner. *Amanjit, you'd drool!* She winked at herself, then pouted a little, wishing her fiancé were here and coming with her. *He's with Ras and Vikram: I wonder what they're all doing right now?* Probably they were all stuck at home playing cards, like Uma and Tanvir were in the lounge.

She still felt a little irresponsible, but the chance to corner Lalit was irresistible. And she'd gone drinking with Meenakshi before, and nothing had gone wrong. Meenakshi was their lawyer: she had a vested interest in helping them. *Anyway, I'm not being entirely frank with her . . .* She'd told Tanvir about the clandestine meeting and he was going to tail her discreetly.

*She'll never know, and as long as I take things carefully, I'll be fine.*

At ten, the appointed hour, she emerged from her room wearing a slinky blue-green sequined mini-dress that looked like peacocks' feathers. Uma gave her admiring coo and Tanvir stared open-mouthed: just the sort of reaction she was after. She couldn't see how Uma would ever have fitted into the dress, but it wrapped about her own slender form perfectly.

'Girlfriend, you are rocking that look,' Uma exclaimed, then she sighed. 'I could never fit into that thing, but you're really working it, babe.'

'You look like a man-trap,' Tanvir commented, wiping his brow.

'Excellent,' she purred. 'Lalit won't know what's hit him.'

She let herself out of the apartment block, knowing Tanvir would be only a minute behind her. She'd arranged to meet Meenakshi at a nearby café, but no sooner had she got outside than a black Porsche sedan purred up the narrow street. The back door opened and Meenakshi got out. In a bright red dress with her hair loose about her shoulders, she looked like every man's fantasy date: a wicked, sexy thing.

'Hey Dee, fancy a ride?'

Deepika paused. *How does she know I live here?*

She hesitated, glancing back at the apartment. Tanvir was supposed to tail her, but he'd be on foot — they'd not expected a car to be involved. And the policeman hadn't appeared yet. If they were going to drive, he needed to accompany them openly, after all.

Then she realised there were two more people in the car: two men, young, and almost preternaturally gorgeous with flowing black hair, fiendish goatees and gleaming teeth. They were both clad in black sequinned silk shirts, unbuttoned almost to their belly buttons.

Meenakshi indicated them casually. 'These are my friends. They've been *dying* to meet you.'

The two men smiled, disturbing smiles, full of implied promises.

*No, this isn't what I signed up for* . . . Some girlie fun was one thing, but these two looked like they wanted something entirely different. *This was supposed to be about getting a line on Lalit.* 'Um . . . I thought it was just us?'

Meenakshi rolled her eyes. 'Come on, Dee. These guys are harmless,' she said in reassuring tones. 'They're gentlemen. And ladies' men too . . .' She giggled. 'And you'll have Tanvir with you, to protect your modesty.'

One of the men got out and smoothly opened the door facing her. 'Please, get in. Your friend will be down in a minute, I'm sure.' He met her eyes. 'I'm not really harmless, but you'll be as safe as you want to be.' He gave a lascivious grin and reached out his hand.

His words tugged at Deepika as if he had wrapped sticky webs about her and was now reeling her in. For a second she couldn't think at all – her hand came up and he gripped it. Something about his touch conveyed a warm, liquid feeling, an intimacy that went well beyond holding hands. She felt enticed and endangered at once.

'Deepika?'

She blinked, as if waking from a dream, and looked behind her. Tanvir was on the steps of the building, some twenty feet away, eyeing the car warily. He was holding a gun. 'What's a car doing here? Did you tell them where we live?'

'It's just me, Tanvir,' Meenakshi called in a sensuous voice. 'I've known where you live for a while now. I just wanted to save Dee the walk.' She tilted her head enticingly. 'Come on, get in.'

The man's grip on Deepika's hand tightened and she felt suddenly afraid.

A car came around the corner and for an instant they were all illuminated by the glare of the headlights. She was looking at Tanvir, then her eyes flashed to the glass doors behind him, where she could see her own reflection as clearly as if it were a mirror.

*And a massive hunched thing with ram's horns was holding her hand. A rakshasa, just like those from her past-life experiences — a very particular rakshasa.*

*Prahasta.*

She whirled, trying to wrench her hand free, but it wouldn't come. In that instant of knowing, the illusion was stripped away: the creature before her leered, its bestial face smirking beneath coiled horns, his eyes glowing amber. His red tongue slurped between thin hooked teeth. 'Trishala,' it hissed, 'remember me?' He wrenched at her arm and she staggered and fell to her knees, grazing her knees on the concrete as image after sickening image of what he would do to her tore at her mind. The sudden stench of him, a fecund, raw odour like wet bloodstained wool, overpowered her senses. She felt herself teetering on the edge of a precipice.

'Let her go!' Tanvir shouted, raising his gun and pointed it at the rakshasa — though all he was probably seeing was a party-boy. 'Step away from her, now!'

She clung to his voice as rage at her own stupidity sparked inside her. *They've been playing us for fools, the bastards . . .*

Meenakshi's heels clicked on the road as she walked around the car, her eyes flashing like emeralds in the streetlights. 'She's coming with us, Tanvir. The Master wants her.'

Now she knew, Deepika could see through her illusion: the svelte sex-kitten of a moment ago had been replaced by a hunched thing with snaggled teeth and thin, lank hair straggling over leathery skin. Her body was slope-shouldered and spindly, with a potbelly protruding, and her arms hung almost to the ground. Her fingernails were like daggers.

'You can let her go, or die getting in the way,' Tanvir said calmly. His face was a blank mask, except for the lines around his eyes tightening as he fired.

The gunshot shattered the silence, reverberating off the buildings, and Prahasta staggered as the first bullet struck his chest, then a second. His claws ripped Deepika's sleeve, tearing three gashes down her arm as she wrenched herself free, and she dropped her purse as she fell sprawling at the monster's feet.

The rakshasa lurched, then regained his balance and lunged at her, shouting, 'Trishala!' She felt herself falling into his eyes again and knew that if she did, she'd never escape them again.

*No, damn you!* The furnace inside her suddenly roared back to life and she slammed her right foot out, jamming her stiletto heel into his groin. She left the shoe there and staggered to her feet, wrenched off the other, threw it at him and ran. Above her on the stairs, Tanvir shouted, '*Get inside!*' and she ran past him and wrenched open the door. The rakshasa was on the lawn, convulsing, blood pumping through his hands, but Meenakshi was circling, hissing as Tanvir switched his aim to her.

'Watch out!' Deepika shouted as a spear flew out of the darkness, hurled by the other demon. Tanvir threw himself sideways just in time; the steel head struck the door, punching a hole through the wire-reinforced glass and sticking there. 'Tanvir! Come on!'

She stepped through the broken glass and a piece of glass sliced open the sole of her foot, but there was no pain, not yet. Tanvir backed inside, firing as he retreated. Meenakshi had vanished, but the other demon was storming towards them, snatching another spear from out of nothing and raising it high – but Deepika couldn't take her eyes off Prahasta, who was sitting up and snarling as the bullets in his chest popped sizzling from his wounds.

'*Tanvir, run!*' she shouted as she limped frantically for the elevator. Now she could feel the wounds on her feet. Tanvir reached her as the spearman was knocked backwards by a bullet, but he didn't go down. The policeman grabbed her arm and helped her to the lift well. He hammered on the button and a bell rang immediately: the lift was already there.

Prahasta had reached the glass door; his face, distorted by the fractured glass, was enough of a target for Tanvir, who fired again, but missed. Deepika hopped into the elevator and hit the top floor code, then grabbed Tanvir and pulled him in – just as something struck his left shoulder and he staggered and fell the rest of the way. She hammered the 'close' button, then turned to him. A carved knife-handle jutted from his shoulder. He reached up and wrenched out the blade; it clattered to the floor in a gush of red.

She clamped a hand on his wound, feeling her fury rise inside. *Idiot! How could I possibly have forgotten?* Meenakshi was Surpanakha's original name in the *Ramayana*. 'That bitch! I'm going to rip her apart,' she spat.

'Easy tiger,' Tanvir muttered through gritted teeth. 'Let's get through this first. There's a first-aid kit in the panic room: we've got to get to it and secure ourselves, then patch ourselves up and figure out how to kill those bastards.' He studied the dagger. 'I wonder how they'd like a taste of their own weapons?' He picked up the knife, wiped it on his jeans and handed it to Deepika.

The lift rattled to the top floor and stopped. Uma, looking frightened but determined, was standing in the lobby, clad in a sumptuous dressing gown of red silk and holding a huge kitchen knife two-handed in front of her. 'I heard shots below – oh my! *Tanvir*?' She dropped the knife on a table and rushed to help the policeman to his feet. 'I've called the police – and building security! Dee, are you okay?'

They staggered into the lobby as something hammered on the front door.

Uma yelped, but Tanvir panted, 'Get to the panic room – the doors won't hold them.'

'The doors are reinforced steel, honey,' Uma replied, though her voice was anxious.

'They still won't hold.' Tanvir stood up, cradling his gun. 'Dee, I've got another clip in my room. Uma, I need bandages, and—' He staggered, making Deepika and Uma cry out. 'Fuck! I think that damned blade was poisoned. I need . . .' He reeled, dazed.

Uma grabbed him and helped him stagger towards the main bedroom and the panic room, hidden beyond the bathroom. Deepika ran for Tanvir's room to get the ammunition – but she stopped dead when something hit the window with a crash and she whirled to see Prahasta there, his outline hammered into the reinforced glass. She could see his burning eyes through the fractured panes, leering at her.

*All right, you!* She snarled, gripped the knife and strode to the window as his fist slammed through the glass, spraying shards across the room. Deepika heard Uma squeal, but rage was driving her now. She slashed the demon's arm with the asura-dagger and Prahasta howled, black blood gushing – then the whole pane broke and he fell away into the darkness. 'Did you like that?' she shrieked after him.

Then Uma wailed as Tanvir's eyes rolled back and he fell to his knees, pulling her down with him, a dozen yards from safety. Deepika backed towards them, watching the windows – as the internal lift-bell sounded and they all turned in horror as something tried to rip the metal doors open. 'It can't get in without the passcode,' Uma gasped, but she couldn't tear her eyes away.

Two fingers, scaled and clawed, came through and began to prise the doors apart, and the voice of the other male demon called, '*Trishala!*' in a thirsty voice.

Uma gave a sob, snatched up Tanvir's gun and strode to the lift doors, which were now almost six inches apart. Deepika tried to shout a warning, but Uma raised the gun and holding it in both hands, screeched, 'Get out of my

house!' and fired at point-blank range into the face of the
rakshasa in the lift. The shot was deafening, but no louder
than the shriek of the rakshasa as its hands disappeared and
the lift doors slammed shut with a clang.

'And stay out!' Uma turned back towards Deepika with
an expression of fearless triumph.

The lift doors flew open again, a spear erupted and went
right through Uma's back. She fell face-down, the spear-
head scraping the marble floor, and rolled onto her side, her
face bulging. Deepika screamed in horror as a nightmare of
scales and spines emerged from the lift, its jaw broken and
bloodied, yet mending as it came. It gripped the spear and
with a sickening sound, wrenched it from Uma's torso. Her
corpse flopped to the floor, twitched and went still. Blood
gushed everywhere in a gory fountain as the thing turned on
Deepika.

She backed away, her bloody footprints on the marble
enveloped by the red tide pooling from Uma's body, brandishing the knife.

'Trishala, my Master wants you,' it snarled. 'Come to me.
Make it easy on yourself.'

Deepika went into a fighting crouch as the security system chimed and the front door clicked open. Meenakshi
stepped through and smiled. Deepika started backing away
towards the stricken Tanvir, trying to keep both the spearman and Meenakshi in sight.

'This is going to be so much fun,' Meenakshi leered, her
glass-like nails lengthening as she advanced into the room.

# CHAPTER TWENTY-NINE

# THE ONE AND ONLY

*Pushkar, Rajasthan, 4 March 2011*

'Amanjit Singh, come out with your hands up! We know you're in there – give yourself up!'

The words boomed and echoed through the streets from megaphone-wielding policemen tramping the streets in squads. Amanjit had glimpsed them through the gap in the curtains.

The maid stared at him. 'You're *Amanjit*? *The* Amanjit?'

Sabina's house had been the only place he could think to run to. Her mistress was home and ensconced in the living room, glued to some TV soap, the volume turned up to maximum to drown out the racket outside. Fortunately, Sabrina had answered the door and with a conspiratorial wink had snuck him inside. As soon as they were in her room, she'd thrown herself on him. It had taken several seconds to convince her that this wasn't an amorous tryst.

'Yeah, I'm *that* Amanjit: the one and only. Good to know my fame precedes me,' he added dryly.

'You killed Sunita,' Sabina said accusingly.

'No, I didn't, I promise you. The police did – it's all a cover-up.'

The girl looked at him with big eyes. 'Really?'

'Yeah. It happens all the time,' he exaggerated blithely. 'They framed Vikram and me to take the heat off themselves.'

'Wow! This is *sooo* exciting.' She sidled up to him again; clearly wanted men were another of her many fantasies. 'Are you sure you don't want to—?'

'No – not now – the cops might burst in any moment.'

'Cool!'

He rolled his eyes. *For goodness sake!*

Heavy fists hammered at the front door and the lady of the house bellowed from somewhere above, 'Sabina, get the door! Damned racket!'

'Okay,' Sabina called back, looking at Amanjit. 'What shall I say?'

'That I'm not here – that you've never seen me.'

'What's in it for me?'

He groaned as the hammering started again. 'I can pay you . . . *please*, just go!'

'Money's nice, but I had a little more in mind.' Sabina winked.

'Please!'

She ran for the door.

A minute later, booted feet tramped into the hallway.

*Uh-oh . . .*

'No, sahib, I've not seen anyone,' he heard Sabina babbling. 'There's only my mistress here. She's very grumpy, and she hates visitors. Oooo, I like your uniform! Do you—?'

'Shut up. What's in here?' A heavy hand rattled the door behind which Amanjit waited.

He tensed, readying his blade. The door would open inwards; with the hinges on the far side, it would give him an uninterrupted angle of attack. *I'll put the tip to his throat, whisk his gun away and use him as a shield if there's more than one.*

Someone gripped the door handle.

'That's just my bedroom,' Sabina said quickly. 'Would you like some chai? I've got a pot on and—'

'Open it,' the policeman growled. There was something about it, as if it were coming from a throat that had to contort to make intelligible sounds. 'I *smell* something . . .'

*That's no cop; it's one of Ravindra's demons* . . . Amanjit remembered the multi-armed nightmare he'd faced at Bakli's mansion and steeled himself. *You've taken one down before, Amanjit: you can take down another.*

Quickly he revised his plans as the door swung open.

For a second he saw something reflected in the mirror on the wall, a red-skinned pig-faced thing with tusks protruding from the corners of its mouth. It saw him too, and turned with preternatural speed.

But not fast enough.

He slammed the scimitar into the left side of its chest in a two-fisted blow, straight through the ribcage and into the heart. The beast-man choked and spat blood as it stared down at the top of the blade, the part that hadn't vanished into its body. Then its limbs gave way and it slid off the sword, falling to the ground with a metallic thump. Amanjit stepped through, blade at guard-position.

Sabina's hands flew to her mouth as the illusion of a

human policeman vanished, revealing the warty-skinned, bestial thing Amanjit had glimpsed in the mirror. Amanjit pulled her face to his chest and held her up until she seemed able to stand on her own feet again.

'Don't worry,' he whispered, 'I got him. He's dead.'

'Sabina? What was that?' the mistress of the house called.

They ignored her. Sabina prised his fingers from her mouth and whispered up at him, 'What *is* that thing? Where did it come from? Why is it chasing you?'

'I guess you'd call it an asura: a demon. It comes from wherever bad things come from. Its boss doesn't like me – and I don't like him.' He nudged the corpse and it started to cave in, as if it were a nothing more than a piece of fast-decomposing garbage. A foul smell erupted as it turned to ash and mud, disintegrating before their eyes.

Sabina clung to him. 'Are there more?'

'Yeah, probably. Sabina, I've got to move. They may be able to sense what's happened to their friend and I don't want to draw them here.'

'No,' she squeaked, 'don't leave me here alone—'

'You'll be in more danger if I stay. I've got to go.' He bent down and kissed her on the lips. She tasted of sweet chai. 'Thank you.' He held her for a moment, then eased away, bent to pick up the dead asura's gun and slung it over his shoulder, pocketed the spare clips, then gripped the lapels of the stolen uniform, which now encased nothing more than dried-out debris. He dragged it towards the upper door. 'I'll deal with this arsehole – I can dump him in one of the holes in the lakebed.'

Sabina followed him to the door and opened it for him.

Above them, the television was still blaring away while outside, loudspeakers loudly demanded his surrender, but they were moving away now.

'Good luck,' Sabina whispered. 'Come back if you can. I want to give you a special thank-you.'

'Sure,' he said, with a grin. 'I'll bring my fiancée to meet you.'

Sabina pouted, then winked at him. 'Sure, I'm cool with that.'

'I'm not sure she would be.' Amanjit could imagine Deepika's reaction to such a suggestion: *violent*. 'Keep your door locked,' he urged her. The door closed behind him and when he heard the click of the lock he hefted the dead asura, which stank of rotten eggs and was leaving a trail of decay and dust, and hurried down the alley towards the street. 'Come on, stinky. Let's find you a hole.'

He dumped the asura's remains behind a bulldozer, then began to sneak through the maze of muddy pools and machinery towards the island-shrine on the far side of the empty lake. Now that it was night, the site was devoid of life, just a graveyard of heavy machinery and mud. The town lights were ablaze, but here all was dark. The loudspeaker still blared, and he could see red and blue flashing lights on the southeast side of the lake where he'd left his rental car. He mentally abandoned it. All he really needed was his wallet and his weapons, and he had them here.

*I might as well have a look around – although if I was Ravindra, it's what I'd expect.*

He crept towards the tangle of machinery about the island-shrine, his eyes adjusting to the darkness. As they did he saw more than a dozen dark shapes also slinking into the empty lakebed, flitting from shadow to shadow.

*Looks like Ravindra and I had the same thought.*

He forced himself to crouch lower and move more slowly until he was nearly commando-crawling towards a large boulder. He was just wondering why it hadn't been cleared away when the boulder turned, red eyes flashed and a long-handled battle-axe swung down at him.

Amanjit rolled and the axe-head cleaved the mud. He drove upwards from a crouch and rammed his scimitar at a spot six inches below those blazing eyes, but the thing twisted away and all he did was scour its cheek. A massive fist slammed into his ribcage and he heard a rib crack as he left the ground – then he was ploughing into the mud on his back. The axe-wielder roared, and its cry was taken up from all about.

He scrambled to his feet just as the asura pulled the axe from the sucking ground. It swung a sweeping blow that would have cut him in half if he were upright, but right now was aimed at his neck. He ducked desperately, then rolled aside as the thing's massive cloven hoof, which probably outweighed a camel's, stomped down at his head.

*I guess they don't need me alive . . .*

He leaped up and sliced at the back of the asura's leg, aiming at the knee – but too late, he realised it was backwards-jointed and his blow gouged skin and bone instead of hamstring.

*Damn stupid demon anatomy!*

The thing roared and the axe whistled through the air. But instead of ducking again he stepped in and caught the handle of the axe just below the head, stopping it in its tracks, then slashed at the nearest forearm. It might have worked, if the asura had been human. But the power of the axe-blow ruined his aim and all he managed to do was cut the demon's arm before he was knocked sprawling again. Gasping for breath, he kicked wildly at the thing's groin, but it just grunted and raised the axe again.

Amanjit tried to move, but he was horribly winded. As the axe reached the peak of its arc he kicked out weakly, trying to get some purchase, even as his left hand found the false policeman's gun. He didn't wait to aim but brought it up and pulled the trigger. Fire spurted from the weapon as the recoil wrenched his wrist painfully, but the bullets struck home, making the asura stagger.

The gun fell from Amanjit's numbed hand as the demon snarled, then straightened again. Amanjit groaned and looked up at the raised axe-head glittering in the faraway lights.

'Bullets can't kill me,' the thing grunted thickly.

Over its shoulders, something like a skyrocket exploded, sending a dozen fiery white darts earthwards.

'Impressive,' Amanjit wheezed. 'What about astras?'

An instant later, a shining bolt struck the asura square in the back just as the axe began its downwards arc. It convulsed, its knees giving way, and the axe fell to one side as a white-hot explosion burst through its chest. It toppled forward on to its face, flopped about a bit, and went still. All about the lake cries echoed as another dozen white bolts found targets, while others sizzled into the mud and burst harmlessly.

Vikram, riding one of his traveller-arrows like a surfer, swooped to the ground. 'Aindra-astra,' he called. 'Lots of shots, but not always accurate.'

Amanjit clambered to his feet as Vikram landed, flicked the arrow up and caught it in his hand. 'Nice arrow-riding, brother. New style?'

'Thanks! Yeah – about halfway here it occurred to me that there just had to be a better way than clinging to an arrow until your fingers go numb. I don't know why I only just remembered that I'd actually done arrow-surfing in another life.'

'It should be an Olympic sport. So, did you kill them all?

'Not even close. He's got dozens of them here, bhai.'

'Are the girls okay?'

'They were when I left, and they've not phoned in the two hours it took me to get here. What's happening? The town's like a kicked-over beehive.'

Amanjit pulled Vikram low. 'Keep down – they've got loads of guns. Rav-boy spotted me – it was really weird: I was looking at him through the binos when we were talking and the moment I said his name, it was like he'd heard me – and the bastard set the cops on me, only not all of them were human . . . I've been hiding out.' At Vikram's quizzical look, he admitted, 'Well this maid took me in . . .'

'That was nice of her,' Vikram ventured. 'Very . . . um . . . public-spirited.'

'Yeah – look, nothing happened, right? Could we talk about something else, like the demons who want to kill us? They spotted me when I came out here.'

'Have you checked out the shrine?'

'No — couldn't get to it during the afternoon, and then things got toasty. But it's not far from here.'

Vikram peered into the darkness. Someone was shouting in a tongue they didn't recognise. 'Then let's go, before we have to fight our way to it.'

Amanjit flexed his left hand; his wrist and ribs were throbbing. Then he wrapped his fingers around the hilt of his sword and followed Vikram, darting between the machines towards the island, going fast and low, sliding in the damp mud as they slipped from cover to cover.

They were nearly there when three shapes darted in, hissing. There was no time to strategise: Amanjit caught the blade of a snake-headed swordsman with a high parry, riposted with a slash and leaped back. Vikram, standing beside him, fired an arrow that burst into flame in the chest of a shaggy goat-faced man, who screamed and collapsed, although the slug-skinned thing beside it lurched on, apparently oblivious. Another arrow flashed into Vikram's hand, but he didn't try to shoot, just jammed it into Slug-skin's eye, right through to the brain.

Snake-head leapt at Vikram's back; Amanjit's leg shot out and he tripped it, then buried his blade in the thing's back before it could rise. It slumped and quivered, and went still.

'How come guns won't kill them when swords do?'

'Don't they? I've no idea.'

'I thought you knew about all this stuff?'

'I've never seen more than hints of these creatures before in any life.' Vikram looked reflective. 'I remember some blurred photographs two lives ago . . . the occasional strange shadow, but that's it really—'

With a whoosh, something flew towards them from the north side.

Amanjit dived for cover, but Vikram turned, his hands blurring as he nocked and fired. A sizzling arrow roared from his bow and struck the incoming projectile, meeting it in a concussive explosion that throbbed over them, the blast resounding about the basin. Shrapnel fizzed around them amidst a wash of heat as they crouched, their heads under their arms.

'*Shit!* That was a fucking *rocket-launcher*!' Amanjit exclaimed in horror.

Vikram was scanning the place where it had been fired from. He pulled out another arrow, shouting a phrase to the heavens. Amanjit could have sworn the arrow coiled on the bow, its hood flaring, then it went rigid and flew. Vikram snapped off another, and they zipped off into the dark. After a moment, they heard a pair of strangled cries.

'Naga-astra,' Vikram said. 'Snake-arrows. The cool thing is, they never miss.'

'Then shoot Majid Khan with one, for God's sake!'

Vikram shook his head. 'A, I'd need to know more or less exactly where he is, and I don't. B, I think he'd just eat it up and spit it out.' He checked his quiver. 'I've only got nine arrows left. Come on!'

They scrambled up the slight rise from the lakebed and into the tiny island-shrine. It was clearly still in use, with offerings of food and fresh marigolds everywhere, and recently burned tapers of incense. A small, thin-branched tree of indeterminate species shrouded it. The shrine was tiny, only a yard wide and deep, with nothing more than four pillars a few feet high topped by a cupola. Beneath was an icon so old, repainted so many times that it could have been any god. Amanjit thought he discerned Ganesha, but he couldn't be sure.

Vikram touched a taper and it burst into light. He peered around the shrine, then extinguished it and slipped back into cover. 'I don't think it's here,' he whispered. 'Sue was right: it's gone.'

'Then we've wasted our time – and left the girls alone—'

'No.' Vikram was shaking his head. 'No, there must be something – why else would Ravindra come here? Especially if he knew we might follow? Why wouldn't he wait outside for me to leave, then attack the girls?'

'Vik, he might be doing that too. Just one asura would be enough to do it—'

'Not after what I did to the room . . . No, there must be something here.'

Amanjit suddenly remembered the old man and his White Lady. 'Actually, you might be right: I think they've been seeing Padma's ghost. An old fellow told me a White Lady's been spotted here.'

'Then the stone *has* to be near here. Remember what Ras said about the Rani of Jhansi's necklace being haunted? Some part of Padma must haunt the heart-stone—'

Suddenly floodlights blazed over the lake, turning the whole landscape a vivid white, so bright they had to shield their eyes. They felt exposed, naked. *If some sniper has a line on us, we're done . . .*

A megaphone blared. 'Vikram Khandavani – Amanjit Singh – this is the police – *surrender now!*'

The two friends shared an anxious look.

'Damn. Ravindra's using the police as a shield again,' Amanjit spat. 'He knows we'll hesitate to kill them. Gutless bastard. Now what do we do?'

# CHAPTER THIRTY

# COME WITH ME TO HELL

*Mumbai, 4 March 2011*

Deepika backed away from her attackers until her right heel struck the prone Tanvir and she swivelled, trying to keep both Meenakshi and the reptilian rakshasa in view. *But as soon as I step past Tanvir, they're going to kill him.* She tried to nudge him backwards with her heel, praying for him to recover, but he just groaned and rolled over. 'Please, Tanvir, get up,' she pleaded. '*Wake up——*'

'He's better off if he never wakes again,' Meenakshi jeered. She looked at the reptile-demon. 'Imtakh, take her alive.'

The policeman groaned as Imtakh raised his spear, his forked tongue flickering eagerly.

Then a mobile phone rang, playing a Hindi pop song, incongruous and surreal in the blood-spattered scene. The ringtone was her own, Deepika realised — as Meenakshi pulled the ringing phone from her own pocket. She must have taken it from the handbag she'd dropped downstairs.

Meenakshi winked at her. 'Oh, look, it's little Rasita calling . . .' The demon-woman backed away and Imtakh interposed himself between them, staring at Deepika as if daring her to move.

'Hello, this is Deepika,' Meenakshi answered, perfectly mimicking Deepika's voice.

Deepika opened her mouth to scream a warning, but the words froze in her mouth as Imtakh swept the butt of his spear at the side of her skull. She ducked instinctively, but the shaft glanced off her temple and she staggered backwards and tripped over Tanvir's prone body. She landed on her back in the doorway of the bedroom and rolled sideways – but Imtakh had stopped, probably awaiting Meenakshi's consent to press the attack. And somehow, Tanvir had roused himself: he rose to his knees and gripped Imtakh's spear-shaft. For a few seconds they wrestled as Deepika pulled herself to her feet, and tried again to shriek a warning to Rasita. To her despair, she heard the front door click shut. Meenakshi had left the apartment.

*I've got to get my phone back – I've got to call Ras and warn her.* She rose, raising the asura-dagger, a snarl on her lips. Tanvir was still battling for the spear, but Imtakh looked immensely strong. Old memories – *Trishala* memories – boiled through Deepika and she cried, 'Hold him, Tanvir!'

Imtakh raised a clawed foot and raked it across Tanvir's midriff, who jack-knifed at the waist, crying out as he fell backwards, then crawling toward the bedroom. Deepika leaped aside just in time to avoid being knocked over by his body, and slashed furiously. The rakshasa blocked her blow, the blade glancing down the shaft of his spear and gouging his hand. He hissed and stepped back, so she jabbed again. Her blood was up now, and she was moving more freely as if something were waking in her, from when she knew how to do this properly: *Abbakka* memories; *Trishala* memories.

*Don't get drawn into a contest of strength; just strike and move.*

She flashed a right-handed blow at his arm, slicing it open from elbow to wrist, and Imtakh staggered away. 'You'll pay for that,' he snarled.

She slammed the bedroom door in his face, stabbed a finger at the lock and heard it click.

*He'll have it down in ten seconds – we've got to get into the panic room.* She grabbed the still groggy Tanvir by his bloodied shirt. 'Get up, Tanvir – *come on!*'

The door shuddered at a thunderous blow.

*Where are the police? Where are the building's security officers?* She dragged the semi-conscious Tanvir towards the en suite bathroom, begging him, 'Please, *wake up.*'

But Tanvir was too dazed to react, even when the door splintered behind them.

*Make that five seconds—* Then the door flew apart, revealing Imtakh, snorting and spitting furiously.

'Give yourself up, Trishala – give yourself up,' he snarled. 'You know you want to. The Master has told us what a whore you were in his harem at Mandore . . .' He stalked towards her, dropped the spear and reached out with his huge hands. 'Let's see what you're made of—'

# CHAPTER THIRTY-ONE

# SLEIGHT OF HAND

*Udaipur, Rajasthan, 4 March 2011*

Ras waited impatiently as the mobile rang and rang. 'Come on, Dee . . . Oh, hello?'

'Hello, this is Deepika.' Dee sounded calm, controlled, reassuring.

It wasn't like Deepika to forget the codenames, but Ras was in too much of a hurry to worry about them either. 'Dee – we're in trouble. I'm stuck here with Sue Parker. Vik's had to go to Pushkar.'

'Pushkar? Why's he gone there?'

'They think the Padma heart-stone is there. Amanjit has seen Rav— Well, *you know who* – he is there. Vik was worried that meant he knows where the stone is, so he went to help.'

'So you're alone?' Deepika's voice sounded concerned. 'That's not good.'

'It's okay. Well, maybe – Vik's booby-trapped the room, so hopefully we'll be safe. What about you? No problems there?'

'I'm fine. Stay there, Rasita: stay there, where it's safe. All will be well. If anything happens and you need to run, then run to me.'

'Okay. Thanks. Good night, Dee, and good luck.'

They hung up and Ras sat back on the couch, glaring at Sue. *The sooner she's gone, the better I'm going to feel.* 'Go to sleep,' she ordered her, trading scowls with the American girl.

*Hurry, Vikram. And you, Amanjit: both of you, be safe.*


The lawyer known as Meenakshi scowled as the phone disconnected. *Useful information, but not everything I need. So they don't know where the heart-stone is either* . . . She'd gone to the lift-lobby to escape the sounds of Deepika's cries, but as she returned she heard Imtakh hammering on the bedroom door. She licked her lips in anticipation — but before she could join the fun, she had one more call to make — and it might as well be on Deepika's dime. 'Maricha? It's Surpanakha.'

'Where are you, Niece?' the rakshasa panted softly down the line.

'Mumbai. I've succeeded: we've broken into their secret location, the hijra's dead and Imtakh is finishing off Tanvir Allam and claiming the Darya as I speak. Prahasta will be joining us in a few moments. Are you in place?'

'Yes, I'm perched outside their hotel room in Udaipur. They're trapped: I'm about to break in.'

'Have a care,' Surpanakha warned him. 'I just spoke to Rasita — the stupid bint thought she was speaking to her friend. She and the American are still in the hotel you're watching, but it's been warded. Don't go in alone.'

'Warded? Noted. Thank you, Niece,' Maricha snickered. 'I have two lesser rakshasas with me, and more are coming. We'll strike within the hour.'

Her uncle wouldn't tell the lesser demons of the wards, she knew; he'd let them bear the brunt of whatever had been set. 'Remember, Rasita is for the Master and the Master alone,' she warned.

'You don't need to remind me, Niece. I know my role.'

'Then try not to die,' she shot back. 'Isn't that your "role" in the epic?' She smirked and hung up.

She went back into the room and smiled in satisfaction at the sight of the hijra's dead body. She could sense Prahasta outside, flapping heavily back up the side of the building on his leathery wings. Inside the main bedroom she heard the sounds of fighting: Imtakh had obviously seized the girl.

*I'd better remind him that she's Prahasta's: he'd better not get carried away.*

Then she felt something else: first a trembling, then a *tearing* sensation, as if this world was made of wallpaper and something behind that paper wall had *moved*. For a second, she felt a twitch of fear. Pocketing the phone, she drew a gun and ran towards the bedroom in time to see Imtakh stretching his hands towards Deepika.

'Let's see what you're made of,' he was saying in a leering voice.

'Back off!' Deepika growled.

*I am Darya. I am Abbakka. I am Trishala.*

Words sizzled into her mind from another life and

suddenly the dagger in her hand blazed with blue light, while her body started moving on muscle memory from another time. She moved the blade in elaborate patterns, and the rakshasa hesitated, doubt crawling across his ghastly visage as she advanced, feinting high then low and slashing grimly. Something was welling up inside her: the energy she had tasted so briefly, first as Abbakka and again as Trishala – something she had caught glimpses of at times, but had flinched from, afraid of herself.

*I should have embraced it . . .*

Imtakh must have sensed it too, because he began to back away – but she didn't let him. She stabbed viciously, with all her strength: an uppercut arcing towards his throat. But Imtakh blurred into motion as she struck, ducking and catching her wrist as she spun. He twisted it viciously as his other arm wrapped about her throat and he started pulling her to him. He grunted triumphantly, then stared at the hand he'd caught: an *empty* hand.

She'd switched the dagger to her left hand as she spun and even as he twisted her right hand, her left was plunging the asura-dagger into his torso and ripping upward. He shrieked and fell, pulling her onto him as he tumbled, black blood gushing over them both. His left hand sought hers as the right, claws flashing, went for her face. She twisted her head away, taking a rake across the cheek, and stabbed again, full into his chest, and again, and again, heavy thudding blows. Blood was spurting in gushes, black and hot on her skin.

Imtakh looked up at her with fading eyes. He coughed blood, his limbs convulsing, and went still beneath her. Panting, she sagged as a wave of euphoric relief flooded her.

Then Tanvir groaned, bringing her back to reality, and she crawled towards him as the reptilian rakshasa's body behind her began to disintegrate into ash. 'We've got to get that phone back, Tanvir,' she said urgently. 'We have to—'

Meenakshi stepped through the door, a gun in her hand. 'Too late, Deepika.' With business-like disdain, she fired the gun three times into Tanvir's chest. The policeman jerked at each impact, moaned softly, looked at Deepika with a stricken face . . . and his eyes emptied.

Meenakshi turned the gun on Deepika, her hideous face scowling, yellow teeth bared. She lined up the gun at Deepika's stomach. 'Move and I shoot. I only have to get you back alive. Intact is optional.'

Deepika froze, and in that fatal second Meenakshi stepped in and smashed the butt of the gun into her temple.

The world imploded.

Ras and Sue sat in oppressive silence for half an hour as the sky darkened towards sunset before the American finally found her tongue. 'If Amanjit was spotted in Pushkar, then he must have been followed there, right? They must be watching us – they must have seen him leave here and tailed him.'

Ras resented having to agree, but she did. 'There's no other explanation I can think of. And if we leave here, we leave Vikram's protections,' she added. 'Deepika said we should stay put.'

Sue indicated the three arrows spinning gently in mid-air: an impossible sight they were somehow starting to take for granted. 'If more than three come, we're dead anyway. Or captured, at least. They might want you alive, but they don't need me.' She peered through a crack in the curtains. 'They're probably watching us right now.'

A past-life memory made Ras sit up. 'Back in the days of the Raj, I met Vikram – his name was Doc Chand in that life. I was an English girl called Jane. It was a Gauran-life: I was kinda crazy.'

'Then too, huh?'

Ras ignored that. 'Doc told me all he knew of our past lives, and once he showed me some photographs he'd taken – cameras were a new invention then. He thought he was being watched, so he secretly took photographs of any possible watchers . . . He was convinced photographs would reveal truths that the eye couldn't see – the camera "sees" mechanically, you see, so it couldn't be fooled.'

'Did it work?' Sue asked, interested now.

'It was hard to say – the images were quite blurred. Mind you, cameras were pretty primitive back in those days.' She pointed to Sue's bag. 'Have you got a camera?'

Sue frowned, then drew an expensive-looking camera from her bag. She pursed her lips thoughtfully as she crept over to the front window and pointed it through the crack in the curtains.

'Take photos of everything you can,' Ras whispered. 'If they're there, maybe it'll reveal something.'

She moved to the other side, where rattling French windows opened onto the service balcony that ran the length of the building, and started shooting in a wide arc. Then they hunched together over the camera and leafed through the digital images.

Sue looked at Ras with widening eyes. 'Jeez, Rasita – look at 'em!'

There were at least three watchers, man-size smears of indeterminate shape that somehow warped the light around them. One was crouched on the roof opposite: they could make out branched antlers, which stirred a warning tremor in Ras' memories. The other two were on their haunches posing as crows, at the back of the building.

'That's amazing,' Rasita whispered. 'So Doc was right all along . . .'

'It means we're trapped,' Sue muttered. 'This crappy building is all concrete – walls, floor and roof. The door's thick wood. The balcony's overlooked by two of 'em so that's a dead end. There's no way in or out that they can't cover.' She sighed. 'I guess we've got no choice but to wait, and hope the guys make it back in time.'

Ras *tsked* in frustration. 'If we just wait here, we're sitting ducks. For all we know, they're just waiting for reinforcements, or maybe for full darkness. Or to jump the guys when they get back. But if we can somehow give them the slip, we can text the guys to meet us somewhere else and then we'll all be away clear. All we'd need is some transport.'

Sue tapped her pocket. 'Well, *that* I got covered; gotta Maruti parked around the corner. It's a red one with a Shiva sticker on the back window.'

'Vikram told us stay here,' Ras said doubtfully, 'but he didn't know how many of those things were out there. I think we have to go.'

'Me too.' Sue pointed at the hovering arrows. 'Three arrows

in here, three demons out there. If one misses, or there are more demons, we're screwed. This place is a death-trap.'

Ras was becoming more and more certain of impending disaster. 'Then somehow we've got to get out from under their noses.' Her eyes darted about the room, mentally listing their resources. Finally she snapped her fingers. 'You're right,' she said, 'we can't slip past them unseen – so we're going to have to do it right under their noses . . .'

Maricha hunched over and peered curiously at the young serving girl in a grey hotel uniform who was carrying two trays along the balcony opposite him. She knocked on the door where the Sita and the American were hiding and was ushered in by the American. The door closed, but she emerged a minute or two later.

*Just a meal as they await the return of their menfolk.*

He thought about the wards Surpanakha had mentioned, which had dampened his urge to attack immediately. He'd encountered the traps that Gurukul-trained warriors could leave in other eras and had no intention of being first – or even fourth – through that door. But two more of his kind were here and more were coming; he just had to be patient. By midnight, he should be ready to strike.

But thirty minutes later, a team of policemen swooped along the balcony, guns at the ready, and smashed in the door. He heard no squeals of surprise, no struggle, no cries, but within a few seconds the American girl was being shoved out of the door in handcuffs.

Her shrill voice carried to him. 'I'm an American citizen and I demand to see an embassy official, *immediately*!'

Maricha hissed, confused – especially as minutes later they led out the Sita, also cuffed and wrapped in a blanket. 'No, you're making a mistake,' she wailed.

Her voice sounded odd.

One of his fellow rakshasa flapped down to join him. 'What's happening?'

*What indeed . . . ?* Maricha sat back on his haunches and tried to think it through. *How would the police know where to find them?* 'Get down there,' he told the demon, 'get close, find out what's happening.'

*Damn them!* Using the police as a shield hadn't occurred to him. *We can still get to them,* he brooded. *Police custody will delay and complicate things on a night which should be our great triumph.* He muttered a curse under his breath and took to the air.

Twenty minutes later he was striding into the local police station in the shape of an officer he'd snatched from the street and slain. He'd memorised his temporary identity – one Constable Rajesh Bhagwan – and fitted himself into the uniform before breezing through the closed doors, making noncommittal noises as he headed to the cells. Outside was a media storm as word spread that the police had captured one of the infamous three wanted for the murder of Sunita Ashoka.

'Bhagwan,' someone shouted at him, 'you can't go in there.' It was an older, senior-looking man with resigned eyes: doubtless a cop whose career had disappointed him.

'Why not?' he asked truculently.

'They've got the maid in there.'

'What maid?' he asked, struggling to sound disinterested.

'Some serving girl from the hotel. She says the American and another woman mugged her, stripped her and took her uniform – Bhagwan——?' The man broke off, staring at his colleague's rapidly retreating back.

The drive out of town was slow, but no one had stopped Ras on her way out of the hotel and no one pulled Sue's car over as she drove away from Udaipur. Sue's words, when Ras outlined her plan, still resonated in her mind: 'Rasita, I think I'm getting to understand what Vickers sees in you.'

She found herself hoping that Sue would be okay.

She wasn't used to driving, although she'd passed her test – Bishin had insisted, even though she was always sick – and the traffic required her total attention. It wasn't until she reached the outskirts that she was able to pull over and use her phone.

*Should I call Vikram and Amanjit, or Deepika?*

She elected to try Deepika. The boys could be in the middle of something big, and going to them meant going towards danger. But Dee didn't answer and for a minute she sat, wavering. Then she gunned the engine again and headed south towards Mumbai and Deepika.

# CHAPTER THIRTY-TWO

# WAKING THE BEAST

*Mumbai, 4 March 2011*

Something stung Deepika's face, then icy water poured over the smarting skin, into her nose and mouth, and she spluttered awake. Her head was throbbing. She tried to move her hands, but found them bound behind her back, right to the elbows. Her arm and cheek throbbed from scabbed-over cuts.

Three horned heads loomed above her then resolved into one as her vision steadied. Prahasta sighed, dripping drool on to her face. 'Hello, Trishala,' the rakshasa leered, his heavy musk filling her nostrils. His clawed hand reached down and stroked her lacerated cheek.

She was on the bedroom floor, alone with the rakshasa. Out in the lounge, Meenakshi was speaking urgently on a phone. According to the clock beside Uma's bed she'd lost three hours. Where were the police? Or had they been met by a beautiful young lawyer who reassured them that all was well . . . ?

Then she remembered Uma and Tanvir. The policeman's body had already been dragged away, leaving a huge dark stain on the carpet. She closed her eyes and let out a sob – until a damp, heavy hand, shaggy with fur and tipped with claws, caressed her thigh. Her eyes flicked open unwillingly.

Prahasta pressed his face close to hers, his slitted eyes unblinking. 'Remember what I promised you, back in Jhansi, Trishala? Remember what I said I would do to you? You escaped me then – but you won't again, not in this life.' He grunted hungrily. 'The Master says we cannot despoil Rasita – but you are a different story entirely. I can have as much fun with you as I like, as long as you can still draw breath afterwards.' With brutal strength he twisted her on to her belly and pushed her face to the floor. Wedging a knee between her thighs, he grabbed the skirt of her already torn dress and wrenched it up. 'So, let's get acquainted, shall we?'

Meenakshi scowled at the phone in her hand. There had been no word from Maricha for too long. Should she risk the Master's wrath and call him? When would their transport arrive to take them home to Lanka with their prize?

For hours Prahasta had been dribbling over the unconscious Deepika Choudhary, waiting for her to wake so that he could claim her. 'Have her now,' Meenakshi had offered, but he wanted her to be *aware* of what he did to her, which was fair enough. She scowled again, brandishing the inert phone. *Maricha, where are you?*

She'd had to see off the stupid police and that idiot property manager, and there were even reporters outside – the last thing she needed was to be photographed. Eyes could be deceived; cameras and mirrors were harder to fool, and this night had already been far too messy. She needed guidance, so she steeled herself and called Ravindra.

'Brother, we have her. Where's my transport?'

Ravindra's voice purred in her ear. 'Well done – keep her drugged and disorientated. She's dangerous. A winged beast will come for you soon.'

'Where are you, Brother?'

'Pushkar still. The Rama is here, and the Lakshmana. They're trapped by a police cordon but refuse to surrender, so it's become a stand-off. They came here seeking the Padma-stone but it's obviously remained unfound, else they would have tried to leave by now. We've lost many of our kin.' He sounded frustrated.

'Involving the police is a two-edged sword,' she commented.

'I only resorted to them so that we could search door to door for the Lakshmana – I didn't realise Aram Dhoop had come until too late. I'm losing patience.'

'Do not,' she counselled. 'Patience will serve us well, Brother. Maricha has Rasita penned and I have Deepika. This day is ours.'

Ravindra was silent for a time and when he spoke at last, his voice was uncharacteristically full of doubt. It was strange to hear it, for she remembered distant times when uncertainty had had no place in his mind. 'I dislike how closely this life is following the tale. We have always destroyed them before, without so many parallels to that accursed story. I wish that—'

'Brother, your past lives achieved *nothing*. Only in this one have you come so close to your goal! Be patient: we'll triumph – we always do. But this time, victory will be total.'

He went silent, then finally he sighed. 'Very well. We'll do it your way, Sister.'

'Have we not been reunited, and after so many years? I won't let this opportunity for final victory slip past us.'

'Don't fail me in this, Surpanakha.'

'My Lord,' she responded, and hung up, then looked around. The smell of blood was intoxicating, reeking through the apartment, so sweet and fresh. And in the other room, Darya was awakening. She heard Prahasta's voice, the deep throaty sound he always made as he contemplated the ruin of a helpless woman. She licked her lips and felt a stirring in her own loins. *I think I'd like to watch this.*

*I am a queen. I will die before I let him do this.*

Deepika snarled, struggling as she plunged her whole being into the fires that welled through her soul. She had no idea what she was doing, except that finally surrendering to the rage that had been bubbling up inside her felt like a release. But it was also the *rejection* of surrender; *like hell* was she was going to let this rakshasa scum degrade her!

The shrinking, sane part of her fled. The rest of her burst into flame.

She *twisted*, and her hands came free of her bonds as the ropes turned to ash. Prahasta gasped, and she hurled him furiously from her; meaning to splatter him across the wall — too late she realised that the wall was a floor-to-ceiling window. He went through it in a cacophonous crash of breaking glass — and was gone. The night air surged in, dragging the curtains out, snatching away the falling demon's receding cry. She poised to leap after him, to rend him limb from limb and finish the job, when Meenakshi appeared at the door, her jaw dropping. '*You!*' she shrieked.

Deepika roared at the demon, then her hand jerked and she flung Meenakshi at the solid concrete wall without even touching her. The rakshasa woman smashed against the stone and slid down, leaving a smear, but she was still conscious.

*Good. I wouldn't have wanted it over so quickly.*

Deepika wished for a sword . . . and one appeared in her right hand.

*And a trident, for my Lord Shiva . . .*

A trident appeared in her left hand.

*And a bowl for Meenakshi's blood . . .*

So she grew another arm and gripped a copper bowl in it.

And then another, to wield the asura-dagger — and another to gesture with, and another, just because she could.

Her hair caught fire, for her skull was unable to contain the heat inside, and her skin blackened to the colour of coal. She strode through the door — which wasn't wide enough, so she made it wider. Meenakshi crawled backwards like an old spider, her wizened true-face filled with utter terror.

'*Holy Queen, mercy!*' she begged.

Deepika flung her against the wall again, then seized her by the throat. 'Meenakshi, you've been *Surpanakha* all along – you've been *laughing* at me! I'm going to rip you to pieces!'

'No – no – *please*, spare me!' the demon blubbered, dangling in Deepika's arms. 'Holy Mother, spare me – it was the Master – he made us do it all!'

'Like I care . . .' *Holy Mother? Why call me that?*

'Spare me, and we'll give you the girl back—'

'*WHAT?*' she thundered, and the demon-witch visibly *vibrated* to the sound.

*How am I towering over her? How is this happening?*

'We have her,' Meenakshi babbled, 'we have the Sita – yes we do! Spare me, and there can be an exchange. A ransom, yes! Spare me, I beg you—'

'*WHERE?*'

'Please, I don't know . . . *I don't*—'

'Don't you?' she sniffed the air, tasting scents old familiar scents, and new ones too, and . . . *yes* . . . 'Liar! You are *lying* to me – I *smell* your lies!' She shook the rakshasa until her bones cracked and Surpanakha's skull lolled dazedly. 'Tell me why I shouldn't bite your head off, bitch.'

*How am I doing this?*

'Please, please, Holy Mother—'

'Why are you calling me that?' She raised the sword. '*Answer me!*'

'Because it's who you are . . .' Surpanakha's eyes fluttered pleadingly. 'You don't know? Then I can teach you, Mistress, yes I can, please – if you only let me live.'

She squeezed the rakshasa's throat and demanded, 'What is going on? Who am I? Who's Ravindra? What does it have to do with the *Ramayana*? Speak – or die!'

'It goes back to the beginning, Mistress,' Surpanakha choked out. 'All the way to the beginning—'

'You mean Mandore?'

'You don't know?' Surpanakha gasped, despite her helplessness. '*None* of you know? Your ignorance will kill you all.'

'Then tell me—' Deepika bared her teeth. It would be so easy *to just bite . . .*

The demon blanched. 'Lanka – it all began in Lanka—'

*Lanka?* She roared and hurled the demon at the wall again. 'ARE YOU MOCKING ME?'

Surpanakha splattered against the wall, bounced and fell to the floor, her splintered bones reforming as she sat up slowly, in agony. 'Please, Great One,' she whimpered. '*Mercy.*'

Deepika abruptly tired of the hag's carping voice. She strode over, grabbed her by the throat and slashed with the asura-knife. Surpanakha screamed, writhing and clutching at her face as her nose was severed. It fell to the floor, dissolving to ash on impact. The demon howled in terror, gibbering for mercy. Deepika threw her down and raised her blade to cut again, deeper.

Then she caught a glimpse of herself in the mirror. Her skin had gone completely blue-black and her hair was all shifting reds, like flames. Six arms protruded from her torn dress and there was blood everywhere. She considered, and then laughed bitterly. It was obvious who she was.

*I have turned into Kali . . .*

It made no sense to her. *Everything is impossible.* She turned back to Surpanakha, then shrieked in frustrated fury as the demon, her face bloody and marred, somehow became transparent and began to vanish from sight. The ruined face flashed hatred as it faded. Her blade sliced the air, an instant too late. She slashed over and again in futility but the demon was gone, and all she was doing was carving rents in the wall.

Finally a measure of reason intruded. *I have to reach Sita . . .*

She straightened, smashed a hole in the roof then sprang through it, onto the top of the tower block. Pigeons scattered as rocks crumbled and fell. She stared about her at the night sky, at the stars, tasting them on her tongue. Beside her stood a massive decoration: the statue of a lion, perched at the corner of the building. She placed a hand on it and spoke a word.

The stone became flesh and roared. She sat astride it, whispered in its ear and it morphed, sprouting wings, taking another shape entirely. Together, they leapt into the night air.

# CHAPTER THIRTY-THREE

## FROM SHRINE TO TEMPLE

*Pushkar, Rajasthan, 4 March 2011*

A pompous policeman, clad in the sort of braided and medalled uniform South American dictators from the Seventies favoured, slopped through the mud under a flag of truce. He smoothed his moustache, straightened his cap fractionally, murmured to the man holding the flag, then came on ahead.

'That's far enough,' growled Amanjit, pointing the submachine gun he'd recovered. Vikram stayed in the shadows: either the man was a real cop, in which case they didn't want him to know they only had one gun and a bow; or he was an asura, and they didn't want him to know how few arrows remained.

'I am Chief Inspector Rajesh Konalipat of the Rajasthani Police,' the policeman announced. 'I demand that you surrender – otherwise we will take you by force, at the risk of loss of life.'

They'd already discussed their response: at some point,

they were going to have to cut and run, but they needed a
better look at the island-shrine, without having to worry
about possible snipers. Inadvertently, Chief Inspector Konalipat had provided them that opportunity.

'I'll talk to you,' Vikram called back, 'but only if I have
your personal guarantee of safety.'

The police chief was visibly conscious of all the cameras
trained on him at this moment. To be the officer who recap-
tured 'India's Most Wanted' would be an excellent addition
to his CV. 'You have my word of honour – provided I have
yours that I won't be taken hostage,' he said stiffly.

Vikram was reminded of any number of English officers
he'd met in his lives during the British Raj. 'I give you my
word also,' he replied, matching the chief inspector's for-
mality. 'May we sit beside the shrine over there?'

Chief Inspector Konalipat gave his assent and they met in
the shrine. Vikram pretended to listen to the man's lengthy
set of terms and conditions: it was clear that Konalipat had
no idea that the man directing his actions was Majid Khan –
who was doubtless using another false identity and other,
subtler powers to assume control. Vikram wished he could
just send the man away and go over the shrine inch by inch,
but as he listened, he did his best to examine it. It was newly
whitewashed and obviously cleaned regularly, but there was
nothing he could see that suggested any sort of clue.

Then a faint movement caught his eye on the small western ghat some fifty yards away. He caught his breath. The
ghost of a woman was lingering there, all cobwebs and
mists. His chest went hollow and his pulse quickened at the
sight of the White Lady: the ghost of Padma.

She met his eyes, and beside him, the chief inspector paused, sensing Vikram's attention was elsewhere. He followed Vikram's gaze blankly, apparently seeing nothing.

The ghost turned side on and raised a hand, pointing away from the lake, up some stairs.

Vikram turned back to the police officer, who'd resumed his discourse, and held up a finger to interrupt him. 'Excuse me, Chief Inspector, that all sounds very reasonable. Could you please return to your position so that we can consult?'

Konalipat blinked twice in surprise. 'But I've not finished outlining—'

'That's fine. It's all detail anyway, isn't it? We'll only be a few minutes.'

The policeman stood abruptly. 'Very well. You have five minutes.' He marched off irritably, muttering about the inherent rudeness of the modern criminal.

Vikram hurried back into cover. 'Did you see that?' he demanded of Amanjit.

'Western ghat steps – and she pointed west, inland.' Amanjit pursed his lips, then exclaimed, 'Oh, I think I've got it: that's where the Brahma temple is, the famous one you were blatting on about this morning.'

'Ahhh.' Vikram nocked an arrow.

'I guess we're not surrendering, then?' Amanjit noted, glancing at his watch. It was nearly eleven.

'Not this time.' Vikram noted the positions of the floodlights. 'Get ready to roll – and cover your eyes.'

One arrow split into eight as it streamed upwards and each newly formed blazing shaft veered away until they were all flying in different directions. A murmur rose from the banks and someone fired several shots; the bullets went well wide. Then the astras hit – and the floodlights, as one, exploded.

Amanjit grasped the musafir-astra hovering before him and it took him streaming out into the sudden darkness. Following Vikram's directions, he wrenched it first one way, and then the other, shaping its course, as behind him, Vikram rode his like a surfboard, firing as he went. Something big and ox-like rose from behind a bulldozer close by; an agneyastra transfixed its chest and ignited the demon, who fell away howling. Blinded by the sudden switch from glaring brilliance to almost total darkness, the police guns were largely silent; those few that did fire were well off-target.

The two friends swept over the buildings and soared up the street that climbed from the ghats to the Brahma temple. Something leaped at Amanjit but he jerked his legs away from its scything blade then kicked it squarely in the face and soared on, concentrating on keeping control of the musafir-astra. Behind him there was a sudden radiance as Vikram's bow sang again; another monster shrieked and fell.

He looked ahead and started pulling the arrow into a shallow dive towards a pale, diaphanous figure on the temple steps who vanished as they alighted before her. Her eyes disappeared last, an after-image seared on the air. Behind them, something bellowed with rage, making the narrow, empty streets reverberate. Amanjit whooped as he stormed into the temple, Vikram close behind him.

An old man stepped from the shadows to confront them, a withered sadhu in white and orange, his daubed face anointed with holy symbols, his dreadlocked hair reaching almost to the ground.

Amanjit looked at Vikram, whose face had widened in wonder and hope. 'Vishwamitra? *Guruji?*'

'Chand Bardai,' the old man wheezed, 'is that you?'

# CHAPTER THIRTY-FOUR

## MARICHA

*Udaipur, Rajasthan, 4 March 2011*

The duty sergeant at the police control-room desk didn't understand the order – but orders were not to be questioned, not when they came from so high up. He put down the phone, took a long breath and proceeded to carry it out.

Half an hour later, the American prisoner, still cuffed, was placed in the back of an unmarked van in the yard behind the station, away from prying eyes, with two police-women to ensure she didn't do anything to harm herself – and more importantly, couldn't bring any false charges of brutality against the Rajasthani police. She was sullen, and kept demanding to see an official in that irritating American drawl, and when she tried to speak Hindi, it was weirdly accented. He was grateful to slam the door on the van.

'This didn't occur,' the detective told him. 'She was questioned and released with a warning about wasting police time. You will forget this moment, understood?'

There was something disturbing about the detective, not

to mention the hulking driver, whose gaze hinted at barely restrained urges.

The duty sergeant didn't like it, not by any means, but the detective pushed notes into his hand and he realised he'd reached a point in life he'd long anticipated – one he supposed every policeman must eventually face: to be true to his oath, at some great personal cost, or to bend to a stronger power. He'd thought it would be more dramatic, somehow, but it happened so quickly he barely thought, just pocketed the money and stood there, momentarily sickened with himself. But he'd worked hard to get this far in life, and he had a young family and too many bills . . .

'Understood, sir. It's already forgotten.'

The detective smiled and turned away, but the driver stared at him, measuring.

The sergeant backed off, then fled inside, hating himself, yet mightily relieved to have been permitted to walk away.

The van doors slammed and they instantly turned on Sue. The first policewoman, a bulky East Indian with dead eyes, grabbed her head and slammed it against the side of the van. Sue screamed as the pain ricocheted through her skull, leaving her vision reeling.

'Where is the Sita?' the woman hissed. Sue blanched as the disguise fell from its face, revealing a toothy monstrosity with three eyes. 'Where is the Sita, you *farang slut*?'

'The Sita left you behind to die,' the other whispered in her ear. This one was smaller, with a furred body and doe-like ears – almost pretty, if you ignored her luminescent purple eyes and yellow hooked fangs. 'She betrayed you to us.'

'Actually, it was my call,' Sue told them as calmly as she could, which wasn't all that calmly at all.

The smaller demon cocked her head incredulously. 'And you thought you'd get away with that? Did you think we couldn't reach you?' She splayed her hand and caused three-inch claws to sprout. 'You'll regret that foolishness, girl. But not for long – the dead don't have regrets.'

The van drove out of the courtyard, unremarked, and vanished into the night.

Maricha rose into the air, leaving the police van in a secluded siding, and soared away towards the line of head and tail-lights in the distance: the southern highway to Mumbai. His two female rakshasa aides followed, struggling to match his speed and grace. His night sight pierced the gloom, seeking an old-model red Maruti with a large sticker of Shiva in the back window.

The American had spilled her guts – metaphorically speaking at least, although it had been tempting to spill them literally as well, for all the trouble she'd caused. But centuries of obfuscation and stealth had taught him lessons. In this day and age, crimes were harder to conceal, and those involving foreigners were investigated closely: the Indian Government hated anything that endangered tourism. But more than that, Maricha aspired to a higher code: one that didn't condone the murder of helpless women.

*Our people are not demons*, he told himself, *at least not in the sense these farang believe. Once, we weren't monsters, although most of us are now, inside and out.*

So he'd settled for intimidation: 'Tell no one what you've

seen and heard. *Ever.* Go straight to the airport and leave this country – but know this: we can reach you, wherever you go,' he'd snarled into the girl's face, reducing her to blubbing jelly, for all her bold front. 'Believe me, mercy doesn't come easy to my kind.'

His companions were disappointed – they'd wanted fresh meat. But he was of the high rakshasa and his deeds were not theirs to question.

'Come,' he told them, 'the hunt is on – we must find the Sita!'

Others had joined the search, smaller asuras, semi-intelligent, but capable of simple tasks like this. They babbled distantly in his mind as he stretched his vast leathery wings over the sky, soaring over the traffic, peering down intently. He didn't call his Master. Ravindra didn't forgive failure – he would find the Sita and deliver her alive, and admit to no difficulties or complications. The fact of his success would be all Ravindra needed to know.

But that success was still elusive. It was after midnight and he was deep into Gujarati skies now – when suddenly the amulet at his neck burned. He gripped it as he emptied his thoughts and allowed Surpanakha's voice to fill his mind.

*Maricha, where are you? Do you have the Sita?*

*No,* he hissed, *she slipped away. The mindless fools I was given to track her––*

*Don't try to shift blame for your own failings, Uncle,* Surpanakha chided. *But I too have been thwarted: the Darya invoked Kali somehow and I barely escaped into the Other Place. The Darya is travelling north now, and swiftly. I think we must work together, lest both escape us.*

Maricha trembled. If they failed, Ravindra's wrath would

know no bounds – and his mercy towards Sue Parker would seem an act of treachery if they now failed. *What can we do?* he asked, his mental voice coming out more plaintively than he would have liked.

*I've made contact with the Sita,* Surpanakha replied. *She's travelling south – she's just left Ahmedabad, making for Mumbai – find her!*

His heart lurched. Rasita was much further south than he'd guessed. *Where is the Darya-creature?*

*I don't know,* Surpanakha answered fearfully. *She escaped us – she was channelling the Dark Goddess herself. Imtakh is dead and Prahasta wounded. Uncle, this is spiralling out of control – what do we do?*

*We can't tell the Master; he'll burn us alive. We must solve this ourselves.*

*Then find the Sita: the Darya will come to her. Send all your resources south of Ahmedabad. We dare not fail.* Surpanakha broke the connection.

Maricha cursed his ill-luck, then flapped his black wings, calling his instructions into the minds of the lesser asuras and sending them winging their way south. All across Gujarat and south Rajasthan, dark shapes whirled away into the night air, streaming towards Ahmedabad and the Mumbai highway.

Rasita broke off the call. It'd been a strange conversation – Deepika had sounded stressed, but she'd agreed to meet Rasita on the road south. The traffic wasn't too bad and she was making reasonable time. She'd been unable to reach Vikram and Amanjit; their phones were apparently switched off, which made no sense. She prayed that Dee was okay, and that leaving Sue hadn't meant abandoning her to an ugly, painful death.

*She'll be safe with the police, surely*——? But there were many policemen like Majid Khan . . . *Dear Gods*, she prayed more fervently, *please: look after her.*

Her heart began to betray her as her stress levels rose, surging then slowing, making her dizzy, and each time it happened, she had to pull over until she could control her breathing again. It was so hard to stay calm when she felt like everything was falling apart. And this was the same route she'd come with her cousin Idli. All those months ago.

*Poor Idli: he helped me, and he died, too . . .*

It was three in the morning and she was in southern Gujarat, somewhere inland of Surat, but she was flagging badly. She pulled over into an empty siding, not far from a truck stop, and got out to stretch her legs. Shivering in the night air, she swallowed the dregs of the Coke she'd bought outside a village just before midnight, now warm and sticky in her mouth, then checked her phone, but she was in a reception blackspot. She cursed in frustration – and then something rattled behind her and she turned to see a large black crow on the roof of the car.

'Shoo, you ugly brute,' she snapped, stepping towards it and raising a hand, but another landed beside it and they both hissed derisively. It was night – surely crows shouldn't be flying at all? – and their manner felt wrong. She backed away while fishing out the make-up mirror she had stuffed into her pocket and used it to look at their reflection.

She sucked in her breath. Whatever they were, they

weren't crows. They looked more akin to little humanoid bats, with leathery skin and outsized teeth, and she realised she'd read about such beings at school: in folklore they were known as *baital*. She shuddered and thumbed her phone to Dee's number, trying not to show how afraid she was as another of the creatures landed behind her.

'Dee?' she blurted as someone replied. 'Dee, I'm frightened – there are crows here, but they aren't crows at all. What can I do?'

'Stay right where you are, Sita.' Dee's voice was edged with something alien.

*Sita?* 'What did you call me, Dee?'

The line went dead.

*That wasn't Dee . . . Someone else has got her phone . . .*

She felt like the sky was falling. And when she turned back to her car, there were a dozen baital perched on it, staring at her with mockery in their bead-like eyes.

She whirled, about to run for the trucks parked up the road and beg for help, not caring if she put herself into the hands of strangers, as long as they were merely human. But a dark shape with flapping wings and an antlered brow swept down and blocked her way and she recognised the outline of the largest of the beings that had been watching the hotel room. Two more half-human creatures landed behind it, smaller and clearly female but still too big for her. Their cloven feet crunched on the gravel.

'Sita,' the antlered one purred. 'I've found you at last.'

The air roared past as the huge eagle fought the coastal winds. Deepika named him Jatayu in her mind, not sure where the name had come from, but it felt right. Her flame-hair flew like a banner and her eyes penetrated even the gloom of night. She was seeing in patterns of light and heat, energies and auras, and some primitive part of her found this so normal that she didn't question it. Her face was a dark, implacable mask, but within she was seething. Her body had returned to something more like normal, her normal size and with only two arms, but the fury was there, right beneath the surface. It was *intoxicating*.

There were more than just night birds and bats in the skies; there were demon-creatures, malevolent half-beasts who also hunted the night. She had to find Ras before they did.

The eagle shrieked suddenly and she followed its gaze.

'Jatayu,' she snarled, feeling her anger begin to boil once more, '*dive*—'

Rasita backed towards the car, but there was nowhere to run: the baital yowled viciously at her, while the three huge demons closed, blocking escape. They were snickering at her as they closed in, clearly thinking her helpless – and they were right. *I have no weapons and my heart can't survive running. Is it better to die than be taken?* she wondered.

It would have to be dignity in defeat. She lifted her head proudly. 'Well, do with me as you will, if tormenting the helpless is the summit of your aspirations.' She took courage from the fact that her voice was not only steady, but managed to contain so much contempt. 'What wretched creatures you must be, to take pleasure in such things.'

The antlered rakshasa hissed. His face was tiger-like, furred and striped beneath his antlers. 'You have no idea what I take pleasure in, O Queen.' He held out a hand. 'Come. Your Lord awaits.'

His two lesser grinned evilly. 'Maricha, can we have some fun with her first?' one asked.

'She is the Master's,' the antlered one – *Maricha* – responded sternly. Ras knew that name: straight out of the *Ramayana*. Everything was completely surreal: they'd suspected they were living parallel lives to the great epic, and now it was reaching out to pull them in completely.

'Vikram and Amanjit are going to kill you, Maricha,' she said. 'Just like in the story.'

'I think not,' Maricha growled, stepping forward and seizing her forearm in his leathery fist. He smelled of damp fur and an overwhelming bestial odour, rank and musky. 'In this life, you go to the Master and submit to him willingly.' He fixed her with his uncanny stare. 'In this life you ascend to the throne of Darkness, at the Master's right hand . . .' Then he surprised her by dropping his voice and murmuring in her ear, 'and you show him the Light.'

She stared, not understanding, but reeling at the sudden realisation that even this moment wasn't black and white . . .

'I'll never do that—' she blurted, confused.

'Never is such a meaningless word when we know that life is about living and dying and living again, eternally, until Brahma wakes.' Maricha tightened his grip on her arm and turned to his two fellows. 'We must go: the Dark Goddess hunts.'

*The Dark Goddess hunts?* For some reason, that phrase gave Ras a modicum of hope, though the two lesser rakshasas dismissed the notion.

'The Goddess hasn't hunted in millennia,' one said, but Rasita heard fear in her voice, and saw them glance up at the night sky fearfully.

'She has woken,' Maricha said firmly. 'Come, let us open the ways.' He pulled at Ras, his grip hard and immensely strong, and she had no choice but to stumble along in his wake. They stepped over a broken stone fence and crossed a field, stopping near a copse of trees. Birds shrieked and fled into the night as they neared. The noise of the road faded into the distance.

Maricha's female companions drew their knives. Ras flinched, but Maricha held her fast as they began a weird chant. They started a primitive dance, the *baital* swirling about them, mirroring the dancers. A strange pungency filled the air, an odour that was positively enticing, somewhat to her surprise: clean, cool air filled with the scent of spices and the heady fragrance of frangipani.

'What are you doing?' she asked.

'We're going home,' Maricha murmured. 'We're taking you to Lanka.'

The word filled her with an uneasy mix of longing and terror. Lanka, the legendary island, the fortress of Ravana the Demon-King, filled with wonders and riches . . . and evil.

The rhythm of the female rakshasa's dance became more intense as their dagger blades took on a reddish-purple glow, leaving remaining traces in the air as they carved shapes that gradually became a tall, intricately patterned door: a portal in the air. It radiated cold and was as beautiful as any jewellery Ras had ever seen. She shivered in the rakshasa's grip and he turned to her suddenly, his expression for once containing neither contempt nor lust. Instead, he looked primaeval and powerful. With his free hand he reached out and pushed her hair from her face as if measuring her beauty.

'You feel it too, don't you?' he asked, in a gentler voice. 'You are the Sita, and I'm taking you home to Lanka.' Perhaps he was thinking that once she sat alongside Ravindra, she would remember her treatment at his hands? But weirdly, she no longer truly feared him – he seemed to think he was doing right, and that bewildered her.

The strange knife-dance ended and she was almost sad, because somewhere along the way it had acquired a primitive, trance-like beauty. But she fought that sentiment with anger. 'Sita's home was never Lanka,' she snapped tautly.

Maricha laid his hand on the spectral door, and its light coated him. There was a kind of pride and awe in his demeanour, like a man giving away his daughter in marriage, as he said formally, 'O Queen, will you come with me?'

She responded by lifting her head. *I won't give him the satisfaction of seeing me afraid*. 'It isn't my will to do so, but it appears that I have no choice.' She paused. *I mustn't forget what they've done to me, and those I care for*. She stopped and turned back to him. 'Where's Sue Parker?'

He stared back at her. 'We let her go.'

Rasita's eyes narrowed as she realised that as best as she could tell, he was sincere. She still didn't understand, but something in Maricha's demeanour gave her hope.

She tossed her head defiantly. 'Let's go, then, and play out this travesty.'

The two lesser rakshasas bowed low as Maricha pushed open the door in the air. As it opened, a rush of beautiful smells enveloped her as if she'd stepped into a flower shop. Surprised, she breathed in deeply, peering forward into a landscape as dark as the one she was about to leave.

She paused, wanting to bid farewell to her world – then her chest thudded as a huge mote of darkness fell from the sky with a roar of beating wings.

It was a massive eagle, and as it neared the ground, something huge vaulted from its back. The bird shrieked at the demons and the little baital scattered in terror – but Ras' eyes went straight to the woman who had stepped into the half-light of the portal door.

Her eyes burned, her hair glowed like coals, her skin was blacker than the night sky. She was clad in a torn dress the colour of peacock feathers – and she was caught up in a berserk rage, spittle collecting on her lips as heat poured from her, making the air about her steam.

Ras felt her knees go and she fell at Maricha's feet. 'Mother Kali,' she heard herself blurt.

It was also Deepika.

The Goddess stalked towards the rakshasa and his minions. Deepika knew the rakshasa holding the Sita, who was kneeling in the dirt, and she spat a gobbet of sizzling wetness as She conjured a blade into either hand. 'Maricha, give the Sita to me,' She growled.

The three rakshasas hissed fearfully, but Maricha pulled out a weapon and placed it against the Sita's throat. 'Begone, or I'll kill her.'

She laughed at that. 'Kill her and Ravindra will do things to you that even I can't begin to imagine.' She swished her blades, closing the gap. 'Give her to me, Maricha. You're outmatched.'

'Kill her,' Maricha told his companions, fearfully. 'She isn't fully formed – she's vulnerable.'

They looked at him and then Her, weighing their options.

'Come on then,' She invited, 'if you think you're good enough.'

The two female demons shrieked and leaped at Her.

Her blades burst into flame as She hefted them and parried the one on Her left. The rakshasa woman's blade broke against Hers and She struck back with the hilt, burying the iron in Her foe's skull. The female demon fell to the ground lifeless while the other lunged half-heartedly then tried to flee – but She sprouted another arm, seized her by her wing and hacked it off. The rakshasa howled as She kicked the blade from her hand, then Her burning blade went through the demon's torso as if she were made of smoke. She fell in two halves that disintegrated into burning ash in seconds.

The Goddess turned back to the rakshasa. 'Not so vulnerable,' She taunted, stalking closer.

Maricha whirled, grabbed the Sita in both hands and dived through the portal door. She screamed in fury and went after him, calling, '*Jatayu!*' The giant eagle came after Her and She leaped mightily, coming down on his back. Together, they rose into this alien night sky, following the rakshasa as he sped away over a rural landscape lit by a silver chariot crossing the sky.

'Jatayu, follow!' She howled again as Maricha surged

towards the north, carrying the Sita with him. The eagle responded and within seconds, they had the fleeing demon cut off and had forced him to turn. He banked and dived recklessly towards the east, as She laughed, caught in the thrill of the hunt. They tore after him above a darkened vista of forests and tiny specks of light beneath a clear carpet of stars: a primaeval landscape from another time.

# CHAPTER THIRTY-FIVE

# MEMORIES IN ANCIENT STONE

*Pushkar, Rajasthan, 5 March 2011*

'Guru Vishwamitra.' Vikram staggered forward and grasped the old man's hand in awe. 'How can you be here?' His mind reeled. 'It's been . . . by the gods, it's been six hundred years—'

'Has it been so long? Where have *you* been?' the old sage asked calmly.

'I've tried to find Gurukul in almost every life, but I couldn't find it; it wasn't there . . .'

'That's because Gurukul is where I choose it to be,' the old man said. He looked over Amanjit's shoulder at the way they'd come. 'Come inside. You appear to have stirred something up out there.'

The two young men looked back. The street was empty . . . and *wrong*. They could see right through to the lake, as if half the building had vanished, and the lake was full, its water glistening silver. Vikram couldn't see any electric lights, and the remaining buildings looked older in style, more primitive.

*No cars. No police. No digging machinery* . . . 'What's happened?' Vikram asked. 'Where are we?'

'The question is as much "when" as "where",' the sage replied. 'You're still in Pushkar, but not the one you know; this is the Pushkar of legend: the place where Brahma made a lake.'

Amanjit's eyes were round with shock, but he snorted, 'That's impossible.'

'Some old places retain memories of themselves – or perhaps it is that we can recreate them based on our own beliefs,' Vishwamitra told them. 'You must have noted this before, Chand?'

Vikram remembered that uncanny time in Mandore last year, when he'd been fleeing a thug and had suddenly found himself in an ancient temple, his skin turned blue and a bow in his hand. And there had been other similar events once or twice in his past lives. 'But the whole town . . . ?'

'Pushkar is an ancient and holy place,' the sage said. 'This phenomenon resonates further and deeper in such locations.' He hobbled to the doors of the temple and gestured them shut with a wave of a hand. 'There, that should keep out most things.'

'*Most things?*' Amanjit echoed. 'We've got Ravindra, a whole bunch of weird demon things and half the Rajasthani police force on our tail.'

The sage frowned. 'Ravindra is here? Rakshása too? Hmmm. That could be a problem.' He stroked the bars of the gate, then smiled. 'But I have worked my craft here a long time; this place has protections even a demon lord cannot break. We should be safe.' He looked back at Amanjit.

'And your modern police cannot come here – but why do they seek you?'

'They think we murdered Sunita Ashoka – er . . . she's a Hindi film actress,' Vikram said uncertainly. He wondered if he needed to explain the concept.

'Yes, I've seen some of her films,' the sage replied. He flashed a small smile. 'One can't just meditate all one's existence; one needs a few pleasures . . . And now you say she's dead? That is sad indeed. Especially sad, given her history, Chand. I saw her face on the big screen, pouring out her soul into the camera, and I knew her as the woman you sought.'

'We didn't actually kill her,' Amanjit clarified.

'It never crossed my mind that you did,' the sage replied.

Vikram bowed his head. 'How have we not met all these years, Master? How have we not found each other?'

'How could we, when I never know what identity you will take from life to life? And since Ravindra destroyed my ashram at Gurukul during the Mughal invasion, I've been a fugitive. You thought me gone, and had no idea you should look, let alone where. It's a miracle we've met here and now – although I expect I know why you're here.' He dipped his hand into a leather purse on his belt and pulled out a tarnished old necklace – which was so unexpected that Vikram and Amanjit stared at him, speechless.

Vishwamitra was holding the necklace that Rani Lakshmibai of Jhansi had once worn . . . and from it hung the beating heart-stone of Queen Padma of Mandore.

Vikram gaped. 'How——?' He pursed his lips and started slowly answering his own question. 'The stone is haunted.

After Emily Mutlow buried it here, the White Lady began to appear – and people were afraid and asked the priests at the temple of Brahma to intervene. You heard about it, found the stone and brought it into your safekeeping.'

'Correct,' Vishwamitra said, his voice approving. 'I had almost given up hope that you would come for it. As you say, it's been a very long time.' He held it out. 'Take it back, Chand, and treasure it. Find your Padma, love her, and never leave her again.'

Vikram took the necklace, blinking back tears. 'I will, Master. I'll give it to her as quickly as I can.'

Amanjit pulled out his mobile. 'Damn, there's no reception.'

'This isn't our world,' Vikram reminded him.

'Uh, well, hey, this is nice, and reunions are fun, but we should get to Ras and give her the heart-stone, you know,' Amanjit said awkwardly.

Vishwamitra's face lit up like a candle. 'You know where she is? *You've found her?* But I thought she was Sunita Ashoka – was I mistaken?'

'Yes . . . and no, Master – but it's more complicated than we imagined when I last talked to you, all those centuries ago. I knew so little then, compared to now.' Vikram described his theory of the fractured Padma-soul.

By the time he'd filled in the past centuries, Vishwamitra was beaming. 'Then in this life you've got the opportunity to set everything right at last.'

'Yeah – but only if we can escape from here and get the stone to Ras,' Amanjit put in anxiously. 'Maybe we could come back here for a chat later, okay?'

'Still just as impatient, aren't you, Prithvi?' the old sage murmured, to Amanjit's consternation.

'Prithvi? Do you mean . . . ?'

But Vishwamitra had turned away and was staring out into the night. 'Yes, you should go, but it isn't that easy. In *your* world, this temple is surrounded by police and hidden demons. And in *this* world . . .'

He pointed through the gates and they could see the walls of the streets outside were black – at first Amanjit thought it shadow or paint, and then some kind of moss – then he heard a chittering sound and when he looked closer, he shuddered. The walls of the buildings outside were coated with three-foot-tall black-furred men with bat faces and wings, clinging upside down and watching them. There were so many that they were clinging to each other in clumps. They hissed as they met his gaze.

'Baital,' the sage told him.

'Why are we suddenly surrounded by all these ghouls and creepy-crawlies?' Amanjit muttered.

The sage took his question seriously. 'I've seen one or two such creatures from time to time, but now they're roused. Perhaps as your lives come closer to mirroring the *Ramayana*, the epic itself is waking.' He pointed out a larger shape among the baital horde. It had a massive feline head and was leaning on a trident. 'See there . . . a rakshasa, an asura prince. There are more.' He closed his eyes and listened to something they couldn't hear. 'But Ravindra isn't here.'

Vikram blinked. 'He's not?'

'I can't sense him. I felt his presence earlier, but he's gone now.'

Vikram looked fearfully at Amanjit. 'What if this really is the lure we feared, and now Ravindra is after Ras? We've got to get back to her first—'

Amanjit turned back to the barred gates and drew his blade. 'Would you rather take on cops or demons? We appear to have a choice.'

# CHAPTER THIRTY-SIX

## PITILESS QUEEN

*Nashik, Maharashtra, 5 March 2011*

Maricha held Ras like a toy, clasping her waist in one hand as they soared above the dark landscape. She'd already thrown up, gobbets of vomit vanishing earthwards as they flew. She could scarcely move in his grasp; the demon was simply too powerful. Then her heart began to labour and she had to stop struggling lest she trigger another coronary episode.

But she had hope again: it was soaring after her on the back of a giant eagle. Deepika was coming in the form of Kali – how that could be, she had no idea, but it was undeniable.

Maricha fled so rapidly the air ripped past almost too fast to inhale. His wings were beating frantically, but Deepika was catching them, and Ras could *smell* the demon's terror. They were flying southeast now and the rakshasa was tiring, his gasping breath scented with despair. She heard him moan as he dropped lower and lower.

'Free me, and she'll let you live,' Ras shouted at her captor.

'Free you, and Ravindra will scourge my soul for eternity,' he panted. 'If this is fate, let it be so.'

Then he cried out as a black shadow, shockingly close, blocked out the moon. A giant eagle's claws raked Maricha's back, and with a sickening lurch, the world spun. Ras screamed in fright as the black earth spiralled up to meet her, then they levelled, just yards above the ground, racing in zigzag bursts towards a towering tree with squat buildings beneath, the first dwellings she had seen up close since they came to this *other* world.

A whistling blade parted the air above Maricha's head and he twisted, his wings bunching over him like a cloak, even as they ploughed into the ground. Despite his plight, Maricha still protected her from the impact, wrapping her in his wings as they rolled to a halt. He staggered to his feet and dragged her the remaining few yards to the cottage, a homely place no bigger than six yards square, while Deepika's eagle circled in to land. He conjured a halter about her neck and tethered her to a hitching post, then turned, inhaling sharply, and drew his blade.

Deepika leaped from the eagle's back as it landed and four more arms sprouted from her sides. She convulsed with pain at their emergence, her face a picture of ecstatic torment.

*How has she become such a thing?* Ras wondered, beginning to pity the rakshasa. He tossed his tigerish face defiantly though, shook his antlers and raised his sword.

'Pitiless Queen, I defy you.' There was a kind of nobility in Maricha's despair.

Dee hissed at him, spitting and snarling like a rabid beast

as she stalked forward, towering over him. There was no preamble, no offer to surrender or flee; she just shrieked in bloodlust and leaped into the attack. Maricha roared back and countered, moving with incredible speed, his blade a blur as he parried two blows in the same heartbeat.

As he jumped aside, his other hand was flinging sharpened disks of steel at Dee's eyes. His teeth protruded like stakes from his elongating skull.

But Deepika parried his blows almost contemptuously while her other blades swatted the discs from the air, each one clashing with a harsh clang. Her third set of hands reached out and grasped the rakshasa's shoulders and she pulled him towards her.

Maricha flailed in vain. Deepika pulled the blades from his hands and pinned him down. Her mouth stretched to match his and she roared back at him. He ripped at her belly with clawed feet, but the wounds only goaded her – then she dropped her face to his throat, bit into it and *tore*. Flesh parted from bone and blood spurted over her skin and steamed – then she clasped her hands around his neck, twisted and wrenched – and the antlered tiger-head came away in her hands.

She flung it away, and the headless torso fell twitching to the ground and went still.

Ras buried her face and fell to the earth, grateful she had nothing left in her stomach as she dry-retched, her vision seared with the horror of what she'd just seen.

Everything went silent, but for the heavy breathing of the thing before her, her mouth bloodied, her eyes still thirsty.

*The Pitiless Queen.*

\*

After the storm came the calm; after the eruption, the wreckage. This was the time when the survivors emerged, blinking, to assess the carnage, to count their losses and their blessings.

There is always an aftermath.

Deepika found herself on her knees. A few yards away was the body of some large animal, and not far from it, the head of a tiger with broken antlers. It was likely she'd had something to do with that – she was coated in blood and reeking of iron and seared meat. Her dress was a shredded rag that barely covered her. There was a sword on the ground, not an elegant thing, but a butcher's tool, wide and curved and dark with gore.

What she'd done felt like a dream, but she retained flashes of it, and she could feel that volcano within her still. She remembered a conversation, months ago with Tanvir – *poor, dear Tanvir* – when she'd said, 'I don't know if I'm the lava or the capstone. I don't know whether I am the fury, or that which holds the fury in.'

She knew now: she was both.

With an effort, she got to her feet, feeling exhausted, nauseated and haunted. Behind her, Jatayu had clambered onto the headless torso and was tearing meat from it with its beak.

'Ras?' she croaked to the girl tethered to the pole before her. 'Ras, it's okay. It's gone.'

By *it*, she didn't mean the rakshasa.

Ras gazed up at Deepika with dread, then held out her tethered hands. Deepika snapped the rope with a gesture and held her soul-sister until they both stopped shaking.

'Is it over?' Ras breathed.

'For now. We've got to go home—'

'They captured her: poor Sue – she called the police in, to shield herself from the demons. We thought that'd keep her safe . . .' Ras' voice was anguished. 'I think they must have killed her.'

Deepika felt tears well up. 'It's worse, Ras. Uma and Tanvir are dead too – they found the apartment and it was all my stupid fault. Surpanakha was Meenakshi the lawyer all along. She played me for an utter fool. *I* got Uma and Tanvir killed . . . *I hate myself*,' she whispered.

'But you've rescued me,' Ras whispered, stroking her back. 'We'll make it right. Somehow.'

They clung to each other until the pain became bearable again, but when they finally released each other, they still weren't really ready to face the world, though they needed to try: time was passing and they were far from safety.

'Jatayu,' Deepika called, 'time to go.'

'You shouldn't have called him that,' Ras warned. 'Jatayu is the name of an eagle in the *Ramayana* – he dies. Ravana kills him.'

'The name just popped into my head,' Deepika admitted. 'I wasn't rational.'

'Let's go before anything else happens – where are we, anyway?'

They looked around. The cottage was the only building there. One large tree towered into the sky, leaning askew, but still wide and strong. Neither knew much about farms, but there was no modern machinery and no electricity or vehicles.

'I can't imagine where we are,' Deepika said. 'It'll be dawn in a few hours – maybe that will help.'

'It's like another world,' Ras commented. 'Maricha told the baital to "open the ways". What if we can't get home? What if there's no way home?'

'Vikram will find us,' Deepika said, with a certainty she didn't feel. 'Come on, let's fly back and try to find that door they opened. I think it's towards the coast.' She sucked in a deep breath, looking about her. 'It's not so bad here, is it? Clean, sweet smells.' She walked to the well and tipped the bucket to her lips. It was the purest water she could ever remember tasting. She emptied the rest over her head and watched her normal soft brown skin reappear from beneath the gore and ash. She caught a strand of hair, which had returned to her normal glossy black hue, and sighed in relief. 'I wonder what this place is called.'

Rasita didn't answer, but another voice did: rich, melodious and arrogant, a voice that rolled sensually through the grove.

'Panchavati, it's called,' Ravindra said. 'Do you know the name? It's where Ravana met Sita.'

# CHAPTER THIRTY-SEVEN

# WAKING THE OLD THINGS

*Pushkar, Rajasthan, 5 March 2011*

'I don't even know how to use one of these things,' Amanjit said, peering at the bow Vishwamitra had given him. 'And I certainly can't shoot like Vik can.'

The sage had replenished their arrows and given Vikram a sword and Amanjit a bow, as well as producing helmets and breastplates from a storeroom. They all looked to date from many centuries earlier, though they shone like new. In the middle of the courtyard, at the head of the stairs, a two-horse chariot with lacquered exterior waited, the horses snorting viciously and pawing the paved floor impatiently.

Vishwamitra assured them they wouldn't need to drive; the horses would know where to go.

Amanjit *really* hoped they did.

'I think you may be a little surprised at what comes back to you in the heat of the moment,' the old sage told him. 'Remember, Prithvi, I've known you in other lives. I don't know what your friend has told you about your past—'

'As little as possible,' Vikram put in. 'His ego is big enough as it is.'

The sage grinned. 'Well then, I'll not elaborate. But let this suffice, young prince,' he said to Amanjit, 'the soul is a source of power. Call upon it, and it will respond to one such as you. It can empower arrows or sword at your command. Call *agni* for fire and your enemy will burn. *Bhumi* is for earth: you will have the endurance of a rock. *Vayu* is for the speed of the winds and *varuna* for the fluidity and quenching of water. Call on *chandra* for moon-silver to make your blade potent against the demons. And above all, trust in your body's instincts; let them guide your mind, not vice versa. You are a warrior, and you always have been.'

'Yeah, sure, whatever.' Amanjit rolled his eyes a little. 'Have we had this conversation before?'

'Every time we meet. I'm hoping one day it'll sink in.'

Amanjit eyed the horde of baital hissing outside the shrine. 'Today would be a good day for it all to come together, I'm thinking.'

'Indeed. I wish I could accompany you, but my warrior days are long gone. I will aid you as best I can, but once you leave here, you're on your own.' The old sage took Vikram's hand. 'When you have done what you need to do, look for me again here. We have much to discuss.'

'I will,' Vikram replied, 'and I'll bring you my Rasita, and Deepika too. They would love to meet you, Master.'

'You are kind, to still call me "Master", Chand. But you surpassed me long ago. I'm merely a guide now. It's time for you to assume mastery. I feel old things awakening because of you and who you are: doors are opening that have long been closed and it's all your doing.' He looked at the spitting crowds of demons outside the shrine. 'It's a mixed blessing.' He clapped his hands. 'Are you ready?'

Vikram nocked an arrow. Amanjit did the same. They'd agreed if they emerged into modern Pushkar they could end up killing innocents, and that was unacceptable. They would take the hard path and keep their consciences clean – although it meant facing a horde of asura, not mere men.

Amanjit had re-wrapped his turban so that it fit beneath his helmet, leaving a skirt of fabric over his shoulders. He took a deep breath. *Let my skin be rock and my blade moon-silver. Let my legs be swift as a tempest and my mind cold. Let us reap this harvest – and get out of it without having our arses kicked!*

Vishwamitra gestured and the gates flew open. The baital snarled and with a shrill roar, launched themselves forward – but the sage shouted, his voice like thunder, and a torrent of air poured from his hands, scattering the bat-men like wind-blown leaves. Then another volley of words washed fire over them and they crackled like tinder, shrieking as they died in droves – until the old man gave a cough, and his fires wavered.

'More I cannot give you,' the sage wheezed. 'The gods go with you, my friends.' He slapped the nearest horse on the flank and the chariot lurched forward. 'Godspeed!'

Vikram shouted a spell and fired his first arrow even as they rumbled across the threshold. A red bolt buried itself in the chest of a single-horned rakshasa leaping towards them; it burst into flame and reeled away. Another arrow followed; transforming into a torrent of shafts that scythed through the surviving baital as they tried to rise: a radiant storm, merciless and impersonal. Many of the shafts pierced two or three or more of the creatures before burning up.

Amanjit saw something move on the roof to the right and fired, shouting, '*Burn you scum!*' A trident-wielding rakshasa screamed and ignited.

*He was right: I can do it!* Amanjit punched the air.

They flowed through the shattered horde of baital, firing continuously at the asuras rising from the shadows, spitting and snarling as they came. It was nothing like Amanjit had imagined battle would be: there was no elegance to it, no dashing duels or contests of skill and courage between war-riors. There was no recognition of the lineage of the foe, no room for mercy, or final words. They hacked and shot and prayed that none of the burning arrows slamming into them from all sides would hit. Most did miss, because the chariot moved like a train and its sides were high, but one shaft glanced off his helm and exploded a few feet away, searing the side of his head and blinding him in one eye for a few seconds – then two rakshasas tried to climb aboard and he busied himself hacking off their hands with one sweeping slash.

They fell beneath the wheels, where hooves and the bladed wheels of the chariot did as much damage as he and Vik had managed.

'*Up!*' Vikram shouted, and the chariot climbed into the air as they hit the lake front. Searing arrows targeted them, but somehow Vikram was able to divert or disarm them with just a word. Amanjit remembered something in the *Ramayana* about shooting enemy arrows from the air, but surely that was impossible – arrows flew faster than sight.

But between Vikram's flowing tongue and the speed of the chariot, they emerged unscathed, carnage behind them, as they rose like an aeroplane, leaving the dark bulk of the town and the glittering silver lake beneath them. The demons fell behind as the wind whipped at their faces.

Once they were clear, Vikram spun an arrow on his finger. It stopped pointing south and the horses riding the air turned that way.

'You didn't tell me you could make things fly,' Amanjit shouted above the winds.

'I can't, usually,' Vikram shouted back. 'Not in our world – but the rules are different here, magical things are easier.' He sounded remarkably calm, even with so much at stake, but his expression was urgent.

'Where's Ravindra?' Amanjit asked.

Vikram's face took on a haunted look. 'I don't know.' He leaned forward and yelled, 'Faster – *faster!*' He held the heart-stone necklace aloft and shouted, 'We're coming, Rasita. We're coming.'

# CHAPTER THIRTY-EIGHT

# A WELL AT PANCHAVATI

*Panchavati, Maharashtra, 5 March 2011*

Ravindra stepped down from the back of his steed, a multi-headed, winged cobra – a legendary naga with translucent green and red mottled scales that glowed in the moonlight. 'Yes, this is Panchavati, where according to legend, Ravana abducted Sita. How strange you should end up here – and yet how predictable and convenient.'

He still looked like Detective Inspector Majid Khan of the Narcotics Bureau, though he wore a moustache now, and a rich, heavy sherwani in scarlet and gold hues, but as if reading Ras' mind, he said, 'I am no longer Majid Khan, and once I have claimed you, sweet Sita, I will no longer even be Ravindra: *I will be Ravana*. I have come for you, my Sita' – he inclined his head towards Deepika – 'and for you, fair Darya. I have come for you both. It'll be just like old days in Mandore.'

*No*, thought Ras. *Please, not that. Never that . . .*

Deepika gave a throaty growl. 'Keep away, you bastard.'

'I would counsel you not to take on the Goddess' mantle again so soon, Darya. There's only so much a human body and mind can withstand. Best you yield.'

Deepika drew in a smouldering breath. 'Let's see how much *you* can withstand, shall we?' Her eyes and nostrils flared and Ras felt heat begin to come off her in waves again. She conjured a sword once more, but Ravindra hissed, drew his own sword from the air and strode forward. It glittered like a crescent moon, opalescent and deadly.

With a scream, the giant eagle Jatayu leaped from the shadows — and with a bored sigh, Ravindra's arm swept around and the great bird fell on its side, blood spouting from the stump of his left wing. A second blow took the other wing and with the third he plunged the sword deep into the bird's chest. The eagle shuddered and collapsed at the demon-lord's feet. The three blows had been so swift neither Deepika nor Rasita had had time to move.

'And so another detail of the *Ramayana* is fulfilled,' Ravindra noted coolly. He turned to Deepika and made an elegant, arrogant salute with his blood-wet blade.

Ras backed towards the cottage, knowing no way of helping, but Deepika howled, a sound that shook the earth. The death of Jatayu had taken just a few seconds, but in those seconds she had become the Dark Goddess again. Her hair blazed out anew, her skin charred to black and her many arms flashed about her, each brandishing a blade.

But Ravindra also changed: with a shout that tore the air, new limbs exploded from his now-armoured body, each carrying a weapon. A banshee wail erupted from Deepika's mouth and drenched the clearing as she launched forward. They collided with an impact that shook the ground.

Ras backed away in dread until she met a wall of scaled flesh. The naga reared up and its tail traced a circle around her, not touching, but entrapping. Six heads bobbed menacingly above her and she froze, understanding the unspoken command: *Move, and you'll be bitten. Stay, and you may watch.*

She turned back to the titanic struggle before her. Deepika whirled like a dervish with blades and blazing hands, hacking and slashing, careless of counterblows. Ravindra could only stave her off, but from what Ras could see, his defence was impenetrable: each super-swift slash met a parry, every hacking blow struck his blade or silver armour and rebounded. The clearing rang with the rhythmic, deafening clash of tortured steel on steel, and sparks flew.

Deepika drove on, enraged beyond awareness of anything but the need to destroy her foe, and Ras saw Ravindra's face change from composed to alarmed as Deepika's attack redoubled in fury. Her face was livid: all glowing darkness, blazing eyes and hair; she looked more demonic than the demon-king himself, like a creature of nightmare. Deepika was spitting flames, her breath like bellows as her fiery swords set the bushes about the clearing alight, scoured the cottage walls and gouged the mighty tree. She was more terrifying than anything Ras had ever seen in any life.

But she was tiring.

It wasn't obvious at first, but then Ras could hear it as the rhythmic clash of metal gradually started faltering. 'Dee, *kill him!*' she shouted anxiously. 'Kill him — *kill him!*'

Deepika was trying with all her might, but she couldn't land a decisive blow.

Then Ravindra's left lower blade snaked out and slashed her thigh. She staggered. Bellowing, she kept on attacking, but now smoking blood was running down her leg. She hit out wildly at his head – and his middle right arm thrust out. Claws gouged her midriff; she howled again, and floundered.

Ravindra was on the offensive now, trying to chop Deepika apart, first slicing off her top right arm; slashing into her other thigh, then, with a roar, leaping into a wind-milling attack and hacking off the hand of her left bottom arm at the wrist.

Ras and Deepika shrieked together as Dee staggered backwards and crashed against the well where she'd washed so recently.

Their main blades locked together – but Ravindra con-jured a heavy dagger in another hand and savagely, with the full force of his body behind the blow, punched the blunt hilt into Deepika's belly.

'Dee—' Ras was sobbing as Deepika doubled over in agony, the vivid hue of her flaming hair fading.

Ravindra hit her again and again until her lower arms withered away – and when he dropped his sword and smashed a fist into her face, Ras realised he was trying to take her alive.

Deepika's head rocked back, her body arching as the force of the next blow lifted her and flipped her backwards – and Ravindra reached out and grasped her heart-stone as Deepika plunged into the well. For half an instant the cord held her in place – then it snapped, and she was gone.

Ravindra stared down the well-shaft in bemusement and cursed.

Rasita went to run to the well, but a massive naga-head lowered itself in front of her face and faced her, its eye fixed on hers. It bared its fangs, and she went rigid.

Ravindra held aloft the heart-stone and made a gesture, as if he were lifting something. 'Come back, my queen – come back to me now,' he called, and Ras sensed rather than saw him battling Deepika on a different level: a battle of wills. By the triumphant look on his strained face she could tell he was winning – until, with a roar, the well collapsed in on itself, stones falling inwards as dust billowed in a cloud. With a bellow of rage, Ravindra staggered away from the crumbling pit, glaring first at the newly formed crater and then at the pulsing red heart-stone in his fist.

It slowed and went grey.

Ravindra cursed, then announced, 'She's gone. She's dead . . .' He snorted heavily. 'No matter. I have her heart-stone: her ghost will come to me when I call for the final ritual.'

Ras stood like a statue, her eyes stinging, blind with tears. Numbness crept over her like snake venom. She was scarcely aware when the demon lord placed her before him on the back of the Naga and took to the air. She thought for a moment she heard Vikram calling, telling her that he was coming. She tried to call back, but didn't know how. There was only roaring air, a scaled serpent's back beneath her and Ravindra's arms about her waist like giant manacles.

# CHAPTER THIRTY-NINE

## LATE

*Panchavati, Maharashtra, 5 March 2011*

The chariot flew to earth as the sun began to rise and they landed in a field on the outskirts of some major city from an ancient time, the roads all dirt, the city walls surrounded by old cottages. Vikram shouldered his bow and Amanjit his sword. The seeker-arrow had lost Rasita an hour before and their hearts were full of dread, but they pressed on towards the place where she had last been.

They alighted beside a cottage beneath an ancient tree. The place looked like a battlefield, with destroyed bodies, the detritus of dead demons mounded up and a giant bird, wings hacked off and stabbed to death. The stench of violence made them both gag at the reek of opened bodies. There were scorch-marks on the tree and a crater in the middle of the clearing.

There was no sign of Rasita.

Amanjit sank to his knees in the dust and ash. *We're too late*, he thought bleakly.

Vikram pulled out an arrow and muttered the seeking spell, but all it did was spin slowly. 'She's not here – not in this place.' He rubbed his brow, unknowingly smearing it with ash. 'Perhaps she's back in the real world,' he added, before admitting, 'Actually, it's more likely Ravindra has her hidden. There are ways to do that.'

'Where are we?' Amanjit asked.

'Panchavati,' Vikram replied, as if this were a given. Amanjit didn't need to be told the significance: this was where Ravana had abducted Sita. There were no coincidences; the *Ramayana* had their number.

He looked up at Vikram from where he knelt in the dirt and said, 'We've got to find Dee.'

'As soon as we cross back I'll look.'

'No, check here first, before we leave, in case she's in this land . . . wherever it is.'

'I think I know what it is,' Vikram said thoughtfully. 'You know how we've been seeing ghosts and demons, the sort of things from fairy stories? I think this place is the legend they step out of. Like that other Pushkar that Vishwamitra showed us.'

'*Ramayana*-Land,' Amanjit intoned bleakly. 'Great. Just try to find Dee, bhai. *Please.*'

Vikram spun the arrow again, without hope – then he froze as the arrow stopped and pointed at the crater at his feet: down into it.

Amanjit leaped to his feet. 'DEEPIKA!' The shout came from his soul. He began clawing at the rocks, but Vikram pulled him away.

'Let me help. I invented an astra a few lives ago: I call it the *bhumi-astra*.' As Amanjit gave him space, Vikram nocked an arrow and took aim at the crater. When the glowing arrow struck, the rocks disintegrated in a cloud of dust.

'Where is she?' Amanjit called anxiously. 'I can't see—'

Suddenly the rubble in the crater exploded outwards, and the concussion threw them into the air like toys. One instant they were staring down at a filled hole in the ground and the next, Amanjit found himself spiralling through the air in slow motion – until the ground smacked him in the back. He lay there, stunned and winded. *What the—?*

Gasping for breath, he rolled over to see Vikram lying prone beside him, blood running from his nose. Then something moved, and he lifted his head and squinted.

Deepika emerged from the crater – but it wasn't Deepika at all. Fire came first: the fire that was her hair. Her face was ferocity sketched in black inks and limned in flames. Her eyes were volcanic, her ashen skin throbbing, searing the air as she came like a spider up the slope. There were too many limbs, somehow; she was some kind of arachnid horror with blades and hooks.

Her face turned towards Vikram and she scuttled towards him, shrieking as she came, rising onto her hind legs, taller than three men. There was murder in her eyes.

Amanjit threw himself into her path, with no more plan than to buy Vik a second or two.

Her heel landed on his neck – and she paused, halfway to crushing him. Her foot was hot, almost searing, but all her arms came up as she saw him for the first time. Her face contorted in fury. Her blades caught the dawn in painted scarlet, as if in anticipation of blood.

'Dee,' he wheezed beneath the mountainous weight of her foot, 'Dee, it's *me*.'

# EPILOGUE

Amanjit stared across the dining table at the young woman wrapped in a blanket. 'I love you,' he whispered again.

'Only because I didn't squish you both when I had the chance,' Deepika said, opening an eye. 'Is that breakfast coming any time soon?' she added in a loud voice, eyeing the kitchen door. They could hear the young family who owned the dhaba working frantically. '*We're hungry!*'

'Calm – stay calm,' Amanjit advised, rubbing the raw skin of his throat, which was still blistered and painful.

'Go bite yourself.'

Vikram looked like he'd done ten rounds with a heavyweight boxer. He pulled the poultice from his face and winced. 'Thanks for not squishing us,' he said. 'How do you feel?'

Deepika groaned. 'I feel like you look, only worse. AND I'M HUNGRY,' she shouted towards the kitchen, making Amanjit and Vikram wince painfully; their heads were already throbbing from the concussive blast they'd endured earlier.

The owner emerged from the dhaba kitchen, followed by his wife, bearing trays of steaming food. 'Are you sure you aren't that Vikram Khandavani, the fugitive?' he asked timidly, as they served the food. 'You look a lot like him, and they do say he's been seen locally.'

Amanjit laughed. 'Not likely — the real Vikram is much taller than him, and far better looking. And clearly I'm not the other one — what's his name? — oh yeah, Amanjit Singh, because I'm not wearing a turban. Now give us some peace, yeah?'

Once the family had scampered away, reduced to peering at them round the door, they tucked into their food in brooding silence. Finally Vikram leaned forward and muttered, 'Okay, status report: Ravindra has Dee's heart-stone, but not Dee.'

'And he thinks I'm dead,' Deepika put in. 'Somehow She — *the Goddess* — tricked him by stopping my heart, then restarting it . . . I felt it happen, and it was *freaky*. But if I do *anything* to attract his notice he'll realise I'm alive, and then I'll be in deep trouble. He's got the heart-stone and we already know what he can do to me with that. He might have already sensed me when you released me.'

Vikram shook his head. 'I think we'd know by now — and anyway, I've got a hiding spell on you. You'll be fine — well, unless you try and take on the Goddess aspect again, or they actually see you. We'll have to keep you hidden.' He looked perplexed. 'This whole Kali-thing really complicates matters. Kali doesn't even feature in the *Ramayana*, so I have no clue what to make of it.'

Deepika and Amanjit looked at each other. They had no idea either.

'Plus, Ravindra's got Rasita, but we've got *her* heart-stone,' Vikram went on. 'And we don't know where he's taken her. I can't trace her; the seeker-arrows aren't working in either world.'

'Lanka,' grunted Amanjit. 'They're obviously in Lanka. We're living the *Ramayana* now, like it or not. So that means he's got them in *Sri* Lanka. So here's my plan: we rock on down to Colombo, kick his butt and rescue Ras. She walks through the fire or whatever she has to do to fulfil the story, then you guys marry, have lots of kids and live happily ever after.'

'That simple?' Dee said sceptically.

'Simple plans work the best. And it fits the story.'

They contemplated that. It sounded a little *too* simple, even to Amanjit's ears.

'You know what's puzzling me?' Deepika asked suddenly.

'Apart from demons popping up out of Never-Never Land and you going psycho?' Amanjit asked. 'No – what?'

'It was something Meenakshi – I mean, *Surpanakha* – told me. She said that Mandore wasn't our first life, the one where all this started – but it's the earliest one you and Ras remember, right?' she asked Vikram. As Vikram nodded slowly, she went on, 'She said "it all comes back to Lanka" – so what happened in Lanka? And *when*?'

Amanjit scooped up some dal on a piece of naan and wolfed it down. 'Let's go there and find out.' Then he looked at Deepika. 'But first, we're all going to see that old guru-sage-pandit guy in Pushkar and he's going to marry us.'

Deepika's eyes flew open. 'But – Mum and Dad – I thought we'd agreed to wait – and—'

'I'm *over* waiting. If we're going to war, we're going to do it as husband and wife.' He looked at her expectantly. Deepika glanced at Vikram meaningfully and Amanjit blushed, realising her concern. 'Hey Vikram-bhai, sorry if that's a bad idea – I know you're missing Ras and everything. If you want us to wait, of course we will.'

'What I want pales to insignificance besides wanting you two to be happy,' Vikram replied. 'I've laboured many lives to see Darya and Shastri united as one.'

Amanjit seized his hand and squeezed it, grinning madly, then turned back to Deepika again. 'Well?'

Her face went through a dozen emotions until she erupted into a girlish squeal and flung her arms around him, upending the table in the process. 'Yes! Yes, let's marry,' she shouted as their meals crashed to the floor. 'I love you—'

'Only because I want to marry your sorry little butt.'

'There's nothing sorry about my butt,' she told him.

'That's one of the reasons why I'm marrying you.'

Vikram's eyes stung with happiness and pain, so much he had to look away.

Rasita felt the heat of a fire on her face and the touch of silk on her skin. Her eyes flew open.

A young girl sat in attendance on her in a room of antique luxury, all gilt, marble, silk, woven rugs and elaborate hookahs, vying for her attention. There were eight oil paintings of a young woman – the same woman, differently attired: eight paintings with her own eyes staring out of them. It wasn't *every* life she'd lived – but she'd not realised Ravindra knew of some of those Gauran-lives depicted. The last was a photograph of Sunita Ashoka, the still from *The Actor's Wife* that hung on millions of Indian bedroom walls.

'Greetings, Holy Queen,' the girl said. She had a delicate, perky face and a bright smile; the light shift she wore was more lingerie than dress. She also had goat-like slitted pupils and deer horns protruding from her temples, clawed fingers and hoofed feet. The girl handed her a sheaf of photographs. 'My Lord asked me to give you these,' she said.

Ras knitted her brow and looked down and let out a slow, sickened breath. The photographs – there were several – showed Vikram with his arms around Sue Parker. He was kissing her on the mouth.

She buried her head in her hands.

'Welcome to Lanka,' the girl-demon said cheerily.

# Glossary

| | |
|---|---|
| Astra | A magic arrow. |
| Asura | A demon of Hindu mythology, usually portrayed as being a blend of man and beast, often with some magical power. |
| Ayah | A maid. |
| Baksheesh | A backhander; bribe money. |
| Bhai, bhaiya | Brother, used between male siblings, and sometimes by friends. |
| Bhoot | A ghost. |
| Bowri | A step-well: an old underground well with stairs descending to the water surface, often used for bathing by the well-to-do in summer, in times gone by. |
| Burkha | The coverall used by Muslim women when they go out in public. |
| Chai | Indian tea (the drink). |
| Chapatti | Indian flatbread. |
| Dhaba | A small family restaurant or road-house. |

| | |
|---|---|
| Dupatta | A woman's long scarf traditionally used to cover the face for modesty and protection from the sun. |
| Ghat | A stepped bathing area on the banks of a lake or river. |
| Gurdwara | A Sikh temple. |
| Haveli | A guest house. |
| Henna | The henna tree, or the dye that it produces, commonly used for decorative skin patterns and hair dye. |
| Jalebi | An Indian sweet (*the author's favourite*). |
| Kameez | A smock garment, primarily worn by women with salwar, pantaloons or trousers. |
| Kurta | A long overshirt, typically knee-length. |
| Lungi | A sarong worn in many areas of India by both men and women. |
| Maruti | A brand of Indian car. |
| Masjid | A mosque: an Islamic place of worship. |
| Mullah | A man educated in Islamic theology and sacred law, generally applied to clergy. |
| Paan | A concoction of betel nuts, betel leaves and spices, chewed as a mild stimulant by many Indians. |
| Pooja | Prayer. |
| Raita | A yoghurt dish, often a side-dish with Indian food as it counteracts hot spices. |
| Rangoli | Decorative floor patterns with religious or cultural meaning, painted on floors within and on the threshold of houses. |

| Sadhu | An itinerant holy man who typically wanders the country accepting charity and living (usually) at temples. |
|---|---|
| Sahib | A Hindi form of address, equivalent to sir. |
| Sati | The now-illegal practice of burning the widow of a man on his funeral pyre. It comes from the legends of the god Shiva, and was prevalent in parts of India until the nineteenth century, when it was banned. |
| Swayamvara | A bridal competition. |
| Thali | An Indian dish featuring small tasting-size dishes of different types. |
| Wadi | An Arabic term for either a valley or a dry riverbed. |
| Zenana | The women's quarters of a Muslim household. |

# Author's Note

Abbakka-Rani may have been one person, or several merged by traditional stories. The records are somewhat contradictory: she fought the Portuguese and in folklore is known as the last person to use an agneyastra – the fire-arrow – which made her an obvious candidate for inclusion in this tale. Her strained relations with her husband contributed to her eventual defeat, and she died either in battle or attempting a prison break; I opted for the latter in this story. She remains a little-known figure outside her native Karnataka. Pietro Delavale, an Italian who met her and reported on that meeting, provides the best documented physical description and temperament, and I have used this as my basis for her character.

By contrast, Rani Lakshmibai of Jhansi is a renowned figure: India's Joan of Arc. Like many famous figures, there is some ambiguity around her true motives and nature. Some (primarily British) sources have her as manipulative and double-dealing, pretending subservience to the British while plotting against them, and coldly sending the refugees trapped in Jhansi Fort to be massacred. Others (generally Indian) have her a reluctant rebel, forced into action when others massacred the refugees. Both sides agree on her martial abilities, her courage under fire, and her intelligence and boldness in strategy.

She did indeed maintain an all-woman guard, the Palaka-Rani or Durga Dal, who fought at her side and died with her in battle. Mrs Mutlow and the other British named in that section of the tale were also real people, and Emily Mutlow did indeed escape the massacre with the help of her ayah. The necklace Trishala takes from the Rani of Jhansi is my own fabrication, of course. And there is (at least to my knowledge) no White Lady legend of Pushkar Lake.

I am a New Zealander, and my wife and I had the privilege of living in India between 2007 and 2010. A day doesn't go by that I don't fondly recall our time there, and the wonderful people we met (and are still in touch with, thanks to modern technology). These books are my link to our time in Delhi. I hope you enjoy them for what they are: entertainment, and a little insight into the things that I found most striking about this rich and intoxicating country.

David Hair
Bangkok, 2017

# A Brief Introduction to the Ramayana

## The Story of the Ramayana

The Indian epic known as the *Ramayana* forms the core mythic background for the four books of The Return of Ravana series. For readers unfamiliar with the *Ramayana*, here is a very basic summary of the story.

In ancient India, Dasaratha, King of the northern Indian kingdom of Ayodhya, is childless. He makes an offering to the gods and is rewarded with a bowl of magical food called kheer. His three wives each eat a portion and become pregnant, and they give birth to four sons: Rama and Bharata and the twins Lakshmana and Shatrughna.

The children grow up under the tutelage of the sage Vishwamitra, and learn all the skills of the warrior-prince. Rama is the most-gifted, and the heir apparent to the throne. He kills demons plaguing the land and, like all the brothers, is loved by all the people. When a neighbouring king announces a swayamvara, a bridal challenge, for the hand of Sita, the loveliest maiden in the land, Rama competes, and by breaking the supposedly undrawable bow of Shiva, wins Sita's hand in marriage.

He returns to Ayodhya with his bride – but Queen Kaikeyi, mother of Bharata, his brother, is goaded by her maid (who in some versions of the tale is really a rakshasa in disguise). The maid plays on the queen's jealousies and insecurities, convincing her that if Rama ascends the throne, he will ill-treat her son. The king had granted Kaikeyi a boon, years before, for saving his life, and she uses it to prevent this perceived threat. She demands that Rama is banished for fourteen years, and her own son Bharata made heir. The king, honour-bound to grant her the wish, reluctantly banishes Rama.

Rama goes into exile in the forest with his wife Sita and his devoted brother Lakshmana, settling in a cottage there. King Dasaratha dies of sorrow, making Bharata king, but in defiance of his conniving mother, Bharata goes to Rama and begs for his return. When Rama refuses – for this would compromise his father's honour – Bharata takes Rama's sandals and places them on the throne, in token that one day Rama will return and take his rightful place as king. Kaikeyi and her conniving maid are ostracised, and eventually the queen pines away and dies.

In the forest, Rama, Sita and Lakshmana lead an idyllic lifestyle for twelve years, troubled only by the occasional demon, which the two princes destroy. In one such encounter, they dismiss the advances of a female demon, Surpanakha, who has taken a fancy to the two brothers. Rama spurns her attempts at seduction, as does Lakshmana, who mocks her. When she attacks Lakshmana, he wounds her, cutting off her nose and driving her away — but Surpanakha is actually the sister of Ravana, the demon king. In a fury, she goes to her brother and tells him of these men who so insulted her, and of the beautiful Sita. Ravana, who is not just mighty in war and magic, but very proud, resolves to have revenge for his sister's injury. He sends a shapeshifter demon, his uncle, Maricha, who takes the form of a deer and succeeds in luring Rama and Lakshmana away, although he is hunted down and killed for his trouble. While the princes are distracted, Ravana kidnaps Sita, killing Jatayu, the giant eagle sworn to protect her. He takes her to his island kingdom of Lanka and sets about trying to seduce her, but Sita resists his advances.

Increasingly frustrated and obsessed, Ravana ignores all his wives, even his chief wife Mandodari, daughter of a celestial sage and, before Sita arrived in Lanka, accounted the world's most desirable woman.

Meanwhile, Rama and Lakshmana are hunting for the missing Sita, following clues and encountering numerous perils. They fall in with Hanuman, the monkey god; he is the son of the wind god and can fly, and is able to locate Sita in Lanka. Hanuman is advisor to the Monkey King Sugriva, who agrees to help Rama. He assembles a monkey army to invade Lanka — normally the monkeys would have little chance against the asuras, but with Rama and Lakshmana both masters of archery and using astras, arrows with magical powers, the odds are tilted. In the battles that follow, despite various setbacks and crises, the princes and their allies gain the upper hand, killing many of the rakshasa, the demon-lords, who surround Ravana.

Finally Ravana has no choice but to come out and fight in

person. In an epic duel, he is slain by Rama, the demons flee or surrender and Sita is recovered. However, knowing that his people will suspect Sita of infidelity during her captivity, Rama asks that Sita undergo a test of fidelity. Though insulted to be doubted, Sita is determined to prove her loyalty to him and invokes the fire-god, asking that she be consumed, should she have been unfaithful. She is surrounded by flames but isn't burned: having proved her fidelity and chastity, the couple are reunited.

With this accomplished, they are free to return home triumphantly, reclaim the throne of Ayodhya and live happy lives. At his eventual death Rama learns that all along he has been Vishnu, the Protector God, in human form, sent to save the world from Ravana.

## Holy Book, History or Myth? Or all three?

There is considerable debate on how much of the *Ramayana* is history and how much is mythology. It is also a religious text as the hero Rama is seen as an incarnation of the god Vishnu, who in Hindu mythology is the Protector of Mankind.

Some Indians have described the text to me as a sacred holy book and therefore one hundred per cent fact; others as a history and others as a fairy tale for kids. By and large, consensus tends to place the *Ramayana* on a similar level to the *Iliad* or *Odyssey* and other mythic epics: it contains divine characters whose actions can be studied to provide a moral example, but primarily it is seen as a heroic myth with some possible basis in history.

Putting aside this issue (because everyone will have their

own opinion and I'm sure no mere fantasy writer is going to change yours), the next question is: if some of it relates to real events, when did these take place? The *Ramayana* was composed around 400 BC (Valmiki, its composer, is believed to have taught poetry to Rama's sons). How far it looks back is the question.

Discounting many extravagant claims and seeking a historical period, one possibility is that it looks back to the first great civilisation of the Indian subcontinent, now known as the Indus Valley Civilisation, which, at its time possibly the most advanced in the world, flourished between 3000–1200 BC in and around the Indus River valleys, the modern India/Pakistan borderlands. The people of that time had sophisticated mathematics, science, trade and art, and predated Hinduism. The civilisation failed when climatic and tectonic changes caused the rivers to dry up and the land to become arid, leaving the major cities without water. The people largely abandoned the region as it turned to desert and migrated south and west across the Indian subcontinent in what is known as the Vedic period. So perhaps the *Ramayana* a fanciful reimagining of the fall of India's first great civilisation, written with a religious slant.

A second possibility is that the *Ramayana* looks back on the battles and rivalries of the north Indian kingdoms during the Vedic period (1500–500 BC), during which Hinduism was codified. This option isn't entirely satisfactory, as the historical tie-ins to known events are tenuous. I don't pretend to know which is right, but I have taken a stance in the story, as you'll find in book four.

It is probably fair to say that the *Ramayana* is regarded by educated Indians today more as a legend and quasi-historical tract than a purely religious document, but the religious aspects cannot be ignored. The reign of Rama was seen as an exemplary model for all rulers, and his role as Protector mirrors that of Vishnu in Indian cosmology. Gandhi invoked Rama during the creation of the Indian Republic. The tale remains as much a part of the fabric of Indian culture, society and religion as Old Testament tales do in Christian countries.

As the origins and meaning of the *Ramayana* are hugely contentious, and I don't claim any expertise, I've incorporated conventional truths if they suited the story and ignored others that don't. The Return of Ravana is an adventure series written to entertain, first and last. If this all sounds like a plea to not be hounded by historians and scholars – it is.

## Hinduism at a Glance

Hinduism is arguably the oldest living religious tradition in the world, and the third largest, after Christianity and Islam. However, almost all of its adherents live in one country, India, with the remainder primarily in Southeast Asia. It has a plethora of holy texts, including the Vedas, Upanishads, Puranas and the epics *Ramayana* and *Mahabharata*.

Hinduism was not even seen as one religion until the nineteenth century; it still has huge regional diversity. It is often seen by outsiders as having many gods, but this isn't entirely the case: each of the gods (and there are millions of Hindu gods if you take into account local deities and ancestor worship) are seen as part of one supreme being, so taking one set of rules and saying *this is Hinduism* is never entirely correct. Nevertheless, taking a broad consensus approach:

The supreme being (known as Ishvara, Om, Bhagavan and many other names) created and maintains life. The goal of existence is to merge in eternal bliss with the supreme being. Attaining this state requires purifying oneself spiritually by the pathway of dharma (righteousness), artha (livelihood/wealth), kama (sensual pleasure) and moksha (release). A person must experience what the world has to offer and learn from it before setting life aside in favour of the spiritual and divine. Hindus believe that a person reincarnates, living many lives, until they attain moksha.

To guide mankind, the supreme being manifests in many different forms, which enables different people to find moksha in their own way, which is why there are many gods and goddesses in Hinduism.

Nowadays, the three primary male gods are known collectively as the Trimurti: Brahma, the creator who made the universe, is usually seen as having done his work, so he is seldom actively worshipped. He is portrayed as resting, until he is needed again. Hindus believe the universe has been created and destroyed several times already.

Vishnu the Preserver protects and champions mankind, especially against forces of evil like asuras and rakshasas. Vishnu as a deity embodies the manly virtues, and is said to have become an avatar, or a god embodied in flesh, in many forms, including the god-heroes Rama and Krishna, always to guide and protect mankind.

Shiva represents destruction and rebirth. Unlike Vishnu, Shiva teaches the putting-aside of worldly concerns and the seeking of moksha, and he is said to have invented yoga to facilitate this. He is normally portrayed in furs and a loincloth, dancing or practising yoga. He is also, with his consort Parvati, the prime fertility deity.

Each of these gods has a female consort. Saraswati, Brahma's lover, is the goddess of music and learning, and a favourite of schoolchildren. Laxmi is the goddess of wealth, Vishnu's consort. Her image is to be found in most business premises. Parvati, Shiva's wife, is the example of the good wife and beautiful woman, the most sensuous and loving of the female deities. She is also the most dangerous: when roused she is warlike, becoming Durga, who embodies the female warrior spirit, and when pushed to the limits, she becomes Kali, a bloodthirsty force of destruction.

Other important Hindu deities include Hanuman, the monkey god, who is a spirit of fidelity, cleverness and courage devoted to Vishnu. Ganesh, the elephant god, is lucky and provides good fortune.

There are also beings akin to angels and demons, called devas and asuras respectively. Asuras are not always evil: both sets of beings co-operated with Brahma in the creation of the world, but devas are celestial and asuras are baser and more malicious. Rakshasa are also demons, but more powerful than asuras.

In the Hindu cosmology we live over and again, seeking release and the divine. The gods help with their wisdom and interventions as we make our way in the world, become wiser until we eventually turn to the divine.

## A Quick Note on Sikhism

Some characters in this series are Sikhs. Sikhism was founded in the fifteenth century in the Punjab in northern

India, and teaches of a universal god without form, and that salvation comes from merging with that god. The Five Evils – ego, lust, greed, attachment and anger – are seen as the main obstacles to oneness with God.

There are a number of behavioural tenets (wearing turbans, bearing knives, etc.) by which traditional Sikhs may be recognised. The religion is guided by teachers called gurus, and worship is carried out at a gurdwara, where the holy texts are read and there is traditionally a bathing pool and a kitchen dispensing free food. Sikhism, the fifth largest organised religion in the world, has most of its followers in the Punjab.

# Acknowledgements

With thanks once more to:

Jo Fletcher, for her faith in this series.

Also thanks to Mike Bryan and Heather Adams for their role in its creation: never let it be said that nothing creative has ever come out of a hospitality tent at the polo in New Delhi!

And to my rakhi-sister Tanuva for her contributions to this series, and deepening my understanding of Indian culture.

And of course, thank you to my wonderful wife Kerry for the adventure that is being married to her. This revision was penned in our new (temporary) home of Bangkok, Thailand, as we begin another posting in foreign climes. But no matter where we go, the best part of the trip is being with you.

David Hair
Bangkok, May 2017

The Return of Ravana

concludes in

THE KING